WHITE HOUSE
HORRORS

EDITED BY
Martin H. Greenberg

DAW BOOKS, INC.
DONALD A. WOLLHEIM, FOUNDER
375 Hudson Street, New York, NY 10014

ELIZABETH R. WOLLHEIM
SHEILA E. GILBERT
PUBLISHERS

ELECTED AS
TERROR'S NEXT VICTIM . . .

Every four years voters go to the polls to determine who the next tenant will be in that most famous of American residences, the White House. But in a building which has seen so much of importance occur, there are bound to be the ghosts of memories and events both good and ill. And when the time is right, the ghosts can come back to haunt not just the presidential family but the entire nation. So before you step into the booth to pull those fateful levers again, do yourself a favor and read the all-original stories included here, tales of life-and-death decisions, of fateful turning points, such cautionary recountings of both past and future candidates for the highest office in the land as:

"Homesick"—Maybe his father was ready for the White House, but Timmy had other plans . . .

"Assassination Days"—With the country torn apart by a new civil war, time was running out to find a way to restore peace—and only his long-dead predecessors could help the President now . . .

"Scandal"—A reporter who'd been handed the hottest story of her career, would she live long enough for it to see print?

WHITE HOUSE
HORRORS

Washingtoniana

ACKNOWLEDGMENTS

Introduction © 1996 by Ed Gorman.
Healing the Body Politic © 1996 by Brian Hodge.
Homesick © 1996 by Richard T. Chizmar.
The Ghost and Mr. Truman © 1996 by Bill Crider.
Assassination Days © 1996 by Billie Sue Mosiman.
But Somewhere I Shall Wake © 1996 by Gary A. Braunbeck.
Scandal © 1996 by Jill M. Morgan.
Night of the Vegetables © 1996 by Edward Lee.
The President's Mind © 1996 by Robert J. Randisi.
Future's Empty Pages © 1996 by Stewart von Allmen.
Creature Congress © 1996 by Terry Beatty and Wendi Lee.
The Cabinet of William Henry Harrison © 1996 by Barbara Collins and Max Allan Collins.
Hildekin and the Big Diehl © 1996 by J. N. Williamson.
Release © 1996 by Kevin Stein and Robert Weinberg.
Broken 'Neath the Weight of Wraiths © 1996 by Tom Piccirilli.
A Worse Place than Hell © 1996 by Peter Crowther.
Jack Be Quick © 1996 by Graham Masterton.

CONTENTS

CONTENTS

INTRODUCTION

Mark Twain once noted that the only thing Americans can agree on is that they hate politicians.

Nobody knows this better than the men (and soon to be women) who have occupied the White House.

American Presidents, from George Washington on, have been reviled by press and public alike.

We've used this book to turn horror writers loose on the subject of both the White House and the presidency. As you're about to find out, the writers have chosen to approach the subject in a variety of ways, from humor to scorn to pathos.

We feel that this anthology is particularly appropriate in an election year.

We hope you'll vote—and we hope you'll enjoy these sardonic looks at 1600 Pennsylvania Avenue.

—THE EDITORS

HEALING THE BODY POLITIC
by Brian Hodge

Brian Hodge's sixth novel, *Prototype,* was released in early 1996. He's since broadened his interests into crime fiction with *Miles to Go Before I Weep,* an expansion of the *Thrillers 2* novelette. Several of his sixty-some stories have been corraled into his first collection, *The Convulsion Factory,* themed around urban decay and offering no answers save that cities should brush after every meal. Spare time is devoted to tribal ritual music, movies with astronomical body counts, and, cash permitting, wanderlust.

The sun, he thinks, is too bright, too golden, for a day of transatlantic mourning. Spring is a time for life.

Some other year, maybe.

The crowd is everything he used to dread, thronging around the steps of the Cathedral of St. Peter and St. Paul. Washington Cathedral, it's called sometimes, too. A crowd is an animal unto itself, steeped in primal emotion. Like any nervous animal, it needs little to spook it. He's spent years studying such things. Studying the faces that make up the crowds, like cells to a body.

The Mass is over. Mourners they may be, but how quickly they forget themselves. Starstruck. It's not every day the First Family is so close, ringed by security as they're first to leave, rushing from the cathedral's nave and through the south transept to the black stretch limousine waiting at the bottom of the steps. A stampede of clicking shoe leather.

President Joseph Flannery is five feet away from him.

He feels the cold weight of the Sig Sauer pistol beneath his jacket—its power to change lives, to change worlds—and in this citadel of faith prays that he's doing the right thing.

Yates was stepping off day shift, the evening agents coming on, when he'd gotten word down in W-16. He kept his cool on the way out to the parking lot, killing impulses to run, attracting no attention; on the White House grounds you never knew who might be taking notes. Yates clung harder to the stone-faced visage that years and training had tattooed into second nature.

He broke sweat in his car, fought traffic from Pennsylvania Avenue halfway through Arlington, until he got to a neighborhood he'd last seen a month ago, at a lazy Labor Day barbecue. Agents and wives and spares had filled the back yard, drinking beer and wine as hickory smoke billowed from the grill.

Karl Heindel's house was now the focus of the entire block's attention, half a dozen police cars converged out front, plus drab government issues. Officers in tactical vests aimed assault rifles at the windows, and a few men in gray suits like Yates' own fumed behind shades used more to keep emotion in than sunlight out. He found the officer in charge, learned that Karl had been holed up for the last one hundred and twelve minutes after firing on a UPS delivery man, then threatening to kill his wife.

"But nobody's been hit yet, right?" Yates said. Hoping that the best friend he had on the Potomac hadn't demolished his entire life along with his career.

"Got a shit-stained UPS van, but that's the worst of it," the cop said. "He let the wife go five, six minutes after we found out he was one of yours."

With casualties it might've been a different story, but Yates caught a smug glimmer of satisfaction in the lieutenant's voice, eyes. Gloating as if Karl's crack-up were a jurisdictional victory over the Secret Service itself. But observing anyone higher and mightier plummet from his firmament was the Washington equivalent of bird-watching.

They'd gotten Karl to answer his phone, but the first agents on the scene had shut down the police cellular link to thwart media eavesdropping, then reestablished contact with a wired phone in the house across the street. Yates stood in the kitchen and placed the call.

"Karl? It's Timothy," Yates said. "You going to let me walk through your front door without giving me a third eye?"

"Hey, hey, a friendly voice." Karl's own scraped across the connection like rust on high tension wires."Pass, friend."

Yates crossed the street, felt the rifles at his back as he covered the no-man's-land of the front lawn. Bullet holes—exits all—pocked Karl's door like splintered blossoms.

He found Karl back in the kitchen, smelled the reek of Scotch and vomit before seeing the man himself, sad and paunchy, stripped to his underwear, his body hair gone gray, jittering on the floor against the cabinets while playing with his blue-steel Sig Sauer. Excruciating to find him this way—thirty-seven years old and looking a rough fifty. The White House protection detail aged a man two years for every one in real time, according to NIMH; here was proof.

"What's up?" Yates said, as offhand as in a bar, asking, "Is that seat free?" Same way he talked to nut-jobs in a surging crowd, when their demons had them sweating in twenty-degree weather.

"Take off those aviators." Karl motioned with the gun. "This is me you're looking at, who do you think you're fooling?"

It felt like removing the faceplate from a helmet, leaving himself naked, open to attack. Behind the shades no one could tell where you were looking, what you might be thinking; if you were distracted, frightened of dying. Or worse, of disgrace.

Yates dropped the shades onto the kitchen table; pulled out the nearest chair and sat, casual, still coiled and ready to pounce.

"Do you have some beef with delivery men these days?"

Karl's eyes were red and his hair as disheveled as a field of half-mown stubble. "When they're bringing listening devices to my door, I do. I damn well fucking do."

"Listening devices." Jesus. "Who's been sending those?"

"For, for starters? In this town? Anyone with three letters in their name. And then? After that? Then? People *you* never heard of, bright boy. Very *old* people, got roots like, like those trees. Sequoias."

Yates tried to get him to clarify, but Karl would no sooner do that than surrender his gun. He hopped from topic to topic like a restless kid who couldn't find the seat he wanted on a merry-go-round. Sometimes paranoid, sometimes nostalgic, none of it seemed connected, everything freeform, as if his whole life were trying to squeeze loose on a deadline. Yates decided not to tell Karl just yet that he'd seen the suspect UPS package himself; that it was nothing but his wife's latest order from L.L. Bean.

"Remember when you first came up out of Treasury?" Karl said. "Started classes? Remember? What made the biggest impression on you, Tim? Of everything they taught us, everything they showed us, drilled into our heads . . . what sticks with you like nothing else?"

"I'd have to say the Zapruder film. You?"

"That's it. That's the one."

They'd watched lots of assassination footage, analyzing what had happened, where security collapsed. But the film from Dealey Plaza occupied a special grim place in everyone's heart. Over and over the instructors played it, the gruesome unexpurgated version that the public didn't generally get to see. Every snap of JFK's head, every gout of blood, every splatter of brain onto Jackie. Over and over. *Watch. Learn. Remember.* Over and over. *Imagine you were there.* Over and over. *Imagine it was in your power to prevent this.* There had never been a point at which it no longer seemed real. Never a day when it had ceased to be painful to watch.

"I'd see it in my sleep. Every frame," Karl said. "I used to wonder why they showed it so much. You think you get the point the first few times. But you don't, do you? Not the *real* one."

"No," Yates said. "That comes later."

The real point came when you realized you could scarcely watch it one more time without screaming; that you'd do anything to change the outcome. Hurl yourself through the screen, if you could, and your flesh and bone in the line of fire.

The real point came when you realized your life wasn't worth the nation's grief if it lost another one like this, reliving the moment on every newscast for weeks to come.

Karl squirmed, soiled and near-naked on the floor, rubbing his pistol for security. He looked at a window starred with another of his bullet holes and began to laugh, began to cry.

"Send me to Saint E's for this one, won't they?" he said. St. Elizabeth's was the D.C. area's federal mental hospital.

"Forty-eight-hour observation, maybe? Nobody's hurt, Karl. We can salvage this situation, you and I. If you'd feel better about it, I'll drive you myself. I'll just need that gun first."

But Karl was fast slipping past the bargaining stage—Yates could see it happen, with an instinct for psychosis honed by years of interviewing and confronting presidential threats. He tensed as Karl began waving the pistol—

"I'm supposed to be the hole," he said in a cracked

whisper. "In the net around Archer. *They want me to be the hole.*"

Ready to jump, Yates caught himself at the sound of the word. *Archer.* Wished his shades were in place.

Karl suddenly grinned. "Special Agent! *What* is the official response to an assassination attempt?"

Yates relaxed a notch. A joke. Been running for years in the Service. Demand the official response, and everyone around flails their hands like wide-eyed, flustered nitwits, shrieking, "Hooooly shit!" Yates went through the old predictable drill with him.

One last time.

"Exactly," Karl said, then brought the Sig Sauer's muzzle up beneath his chin.

Yates leaped, almost got there in time. The closest thing to the moment he'd trained for but had never been tested on for real, and with no room to throw himself in front of the bullet.

Karl's head snapped and the air misted red, and later, Yates would think of Jackie Kennedy and wonder if, when the brains hit, she, too, dismissed it as a trick of perception, something beyond contemplating, at least until seeing how thick the evidence was, and how defiant the stain.

The Cathedral of St. Peter and St. Paul resounds with organ music, but he hardly hears it. Yates rarely notices the ordinary while on a protective detail. He'd take notice if it stopped.

Around him and the rest of the agents, around the President and his wife and daughter, the cathedral is grandeur on a massive scale. English Gothic, built on a cruciform floor plan, flying buttresses all around, with a 300-foot bell tower rising from its center. The stones are pale gray, and look almost white, blending well into the city of alabaster-hued monuments to Presidents past.

All in all, a great place to be a martyr.

* * *

He was debriefed for hours—Secret Service brass, FBI, a few from President Flannery's staff. They tried not to show it, but Karl Heindel's suicide pitched the entire White House detail into a grim and stubborn funk. It rippled across the country, clouding one field office after another, from D.C. to L.A.

One agent's disgrace belonged to all, like shares of stock. Each seeing in it their worst possible future, and no matter how improbable, it could never be dismissed outright . . . because it *happened* sometimes, and to the unlikeliest people. They'd get lost in crowds; wander away from the cordon around the President and keep on going. Or find that they couldn't get out of bed one day. Worse, on occasion. During the Carter administration a uniformed guard vanished from his post directly outside the Oval Office; was later found up a tree in the Rose Garden, watching the air traffic from Washington National and murmuring about Russian spies.

Yates grimaced over the expected spin doctoring and damage control applied to the suicide, everything routed through the office of Public Affairs, Karl's legacy thrown directly atop the grenade of potential embarrassment. The official statement was distancing and succinct. Four-star Pentagon generals had looser lips than Public Affairs.

It was newsworthy for barely a day—dull footage, no peril, no blood, just a stress casualty toted from his house in a bag. Neither public nor media would remember after a week.

Neither public nor media were privy to any of Karl Heindel's last words—*I'm supposed to be the hole. In the net around Archer*—yet even if they had, this would've meant little.

Presidential code names were zealously guarded secrets.

Yates passed on the information, knowing it would be relayed to Intelligence, where analysts fit together, like puzzle pieces, scraps of threat and rumor. Reassuring himself that, in the end, Karl had gone out high on

paranoia the same way Joe McCarthy had been high
on phantom Communists.

From the south transept of the Cathedral of St. Peter
and St. Paul, the Presidential party emerges into the
dazzling light of day. The small plug in Yates' ear continually crackles with scene updates, an all-clear signal
to move for the limousine.

Five feet away, Flannery looks gaunt today. At his
side, his wife, Genevieve, appears more the stoic
mourner, their presence making it a bit easier, perhaps,
to bear the loss that everyone here is feeling. A death
mourned in Rome, and across the whole of Italy and
throughout the Catholic world. Their daughter, Caitlin,
would clearly rather be somewhere else. The wisest
of them all, maybe. Popes come, Popes go. And life
goes on.

Yates realizes he's always liked her best.

Autumn deepened, and then winter, white snows
drifting over a city of whiter monuments and crack cocaine. Randomly distributed homeless began to cluster
toward warmth, and fought over the prime sleeping turf
of steam grates. A few of the more enterprising made
token attempts at scaling the White House fence, de-
void of intent, just goading the palace guard, who
obliged by sending them to St. E's for a warm night's
watch and hot food. On a city bus, a frightened rider
capped two teenage would-be extortionists armed with
a nail file, and was applauded by the other passengers.
The same day, a Congressional majority triumphed
over opponents of a $5.2 billion allocation for a new
McDonnell-Douglas fighter plane that the Pentagon
claimed was not needed.

Yates served as part of the advance team for Flannery's trips to London, Stockholm, and Krakow, fighting jet lag alongside lengthened shifts. Relishing,
finally, a seasonal wind-down as the holidays approached and the man kept himself generally confined

to Fort President, with the days as routine as they ever got.

Yates found himself standing vigil outside the breakfast room one Saturday morning, trying his best to look alert while kitchen stewards catered to Flannery and five of the more sanctimonious guests he'd entertained. This prayer breakfast with leaders of the Christian Caucus had been weeks in coming, but this was the first time Yates had seen the President looking happy about it.

Most of the talk was coming from Garret Osborn, spiritual and executive head of the Caucus—an Orthodox Presbyterian minister gone national, and in nine years from a Minnesota school board to the front ranks of religious right activism.

Lulled by the steady clink of silver on china, Yates tuned in whenever the conversation picked up interest, tuned out whenever it dulled or crosstalk sounded in his earphone.

"I'm wondering if you recall something we discussed last year in Atlanta," Osborn was saying. "Now, correct me if I'm wrong, but I'm unaware of any action being taken on it since. Reestablishment of the Hays Office in Hollywood?"

"Will Hays is still dead, Garret," said the President.

"A lily by any other name . . ." Osborn spread his hands. "We may not be able to resurrect the man, but the time has come to resurrect the ideals, don't you think?"

"There's one thing you appear to keep overlooking." Flannery was wearing a blue-and-white ski sweater and corduroys, by far the most casual at the table. His ruddy face was composed, his sandy brown hair silvering at the temples. "The Hays Office was no more a government outlet than the MPAA."

"Nonetheless, certain pressures *can* be brought to bear." A pink jowl waggled beneath Osborn's chin. "Previous tenants of this house have negotiated peace accords between countries on the other side of the globe. Do you *really* mean to give the impression that you have no interest in championing simple cultural accountability on your own land?"

Yates saw the President cock his head with a deflecting grin that had made it into more than one cartoon caricature.

"Where did your ordination come from again?" Flannery asked. "*60 Minutes,* wasn't it?"

Footsteps at his side; Yates turned his head.

"I can save you from all this, if you want," she said. "Say the word, and you're on top of my short list."

Caitlin Flannery had just turned eighteen; would be starting her freshman year at Dartmouth the end of next summer, and taking a detail of agents along with her.

"The way I see it," she went on, her voice that of a bemused conspirator, "a few more months of listening to coffee klatches like this, and you'll be screaming for four years of academe duty."

"Have to get your father reelected first, don't you?"

"I'm not worried, as long as the polls just stay where they are." Then she sighed. "But they never do, do they? They're like nervous little dogs."

Caitlin had gotten her lanky frame from her dad, a china doll complexion from her mother; the auburn hair apparently came from an earlier ripple in the gene pool. Easily the loveliest First Daughter in several administrations. Of the family's transition to national scrutiny, it was Caitlin's adjustment that Yates found most impressive, by virtue of inexperience. What she didn't ignore completely, she was usually able to laugh at until it withered.

She flicked her gaze toward Garret Osborn and the rest of the Christian Caucus. "Those godless liberal media heathens, you know what they're calling this group now, don't you?"

"The Osborn-Agains, isn't it?"

"So you heard that one." She leaned closer, Yates wondering how much was discretion and how much flirtation. "I heard Mum and Dad talking last night. He thinks Osborn's going to declare himself a candidate before the New Hampshire Primary. Republican side of the board, of course."

"So what are he and the Lollipop Guild doing here, then?"

"Grandstanding, what else. Duh." Caitlin hushed while one of the White House staffers whizzed by. Most of them Yates hated on general principles, some half a decade younger and snotty with power, treating him like a valet they could send to fetch their low-fat decaf cappuccinos.

"Well," Osborn was saying now, "nobody can accuse you of not knowing which side your manna is buttered on."

"He's been pushing for this meeting for months," Caitlin told Yates. "A win-win situation. If he gets his sit-down, he goes back to his people looking like he's carried his agenda straight into the enemy camp, whatever the results. And if he's turned down—"

"Your dad looks antagonistic to millions of evangelicals," he finished for her. "You pay more than passing attention to this side of things, don't you?"

She appeared pleased. "And you don't, I've noticed. Or is that just part of 'the Face' all you clean-cut samurais wear?"

"No . . . you're right. Politics just gets in the way of doing the job. You can't protect a man as well once you start asking yourself whether or not you agree with him."

"But suppose you did agree. Then wouldn't you work just that much harder?"

Yates shook his head. "Then you get distracted. That's how Bobby Kennedy got shot. Even though he was surrounded by guys who could've broken Sirhan Sirhan in half. But they never noticed him, and you know why? Bobby'd just won the California Primary, and they couldn't've been happier for him. They were too busy celebrating to pay attention."

"So it didn't even matter to you when Dad got elected?" She looked at the floor, gloomier now, showing her teen years more freely than usual. "You didn't think he could make a difference?"

"A few years ago, I ran interference for too many candidates who'd muddle through as many primaries as possible before their till ran dry." He kept his voice as gentle as he could. "As long as I was watching the crowd, it could've been the same guy behind me all along. The rhetoric was all the same. Nothing against your father, Caitlin. I'd just quit listening before he ever got here."

She nodded. "That's okay. I understand." Turning to go.

"Caitlin?" he said, and she turned back again. "Um. Listen." He dropped his voice to a whisper. "I wanted to believe. I really did. But don't tell anyone."

Her departing smile of tiny victory stayed with him through the rest of this farce of a breakfast, subtle hostilities held at bay over Eggs Benedict, while Garret Osborn professed crocodile fears for the soul of the nation.

At the top of the steps outside the Cathedral of St. Peter and St. Paul, Yates nearly stumbles, catches himself just in time. He jostles another agent, the one who always carries the attaché case. Most civilians assume it's filled with papers, documents the President or the country can't live without.

An Uzi, actually.

Down below, at the bottom of the steps, where guards do their best to hold the crowd back, the limo door is opened. Ahead of the limo the press van sits idling; inside it rolls what the reporters call the "death-watch camera." It's a TV network contingency—they never want to be forced to rely on a home movie again.

Professionalism counts for a lot.

Shifts were juggled on Christmas day, and with neither wife nor children, Yates went temporarily back on night shift, standing post at the residence quarters.

Flannery's parents and in-laws had flown in the day before, as safe this day as they'd ever been in their lives, while two miles away, a young woman who'd spent hours serving dinners in a shelter was assaulted on the way to her car, left lying beside it with snowflakes clinging to eyelashes that blinked a few last times, then fell still, half-open and unseeing.

In its extremes, the White House detail wasn't much different from being in a war—interminable stretches of boredom, punctuated by flurries of action and stark terror, never knowing if a bullet was coming. Mostly, it meant just standing in a hallway somewhere.

The rest of the First Family was asleep when Flannery sought Yates out, handing him a cup of eggnog, keeping one for himself.

Yates sniffed it, reluctant. "This has bourbon in it."

"Your boss isn't here. You are," Flannery reminded. "Play the odds. No one's coming to kill us tonight, Tim, so drink up."

He'd long since gotten over the awe of standing in proximity to the most powerful leader in the world. Guard him twenty-four and seven, and you saw him as few were able, certainly the press, but even other Washington power brokers, who waited their turn for an open slot like everyone else. Guard him and you saw the man at his most mortal, in his worst moments of defeat and temper, doubt and sorrow. You heard the noises he made in the bathroom.

Yet for all that, Yates could never quite get over the small acts of kindness. Because they were superfluous to the man's job description, and not always practiced by former officeholders, who might be at best condescending, at worst downright cruel.

A cup of eggnog on Christmas night—Yates knew he'd remember the moment for the rest of his life.

Gerald Ford had been like this, he'd heard. Making sandwiches for guys on duty at Camp David, sneaking them coffee. His daughter had married an agent, too.

Just idle thoughts.

Flannery said he felt like some fresh air, so they got

coats and gloves, carried their cups out to the Truman Balcony, into the gentle cold bite of the night. In the far distance rose the spire of the Washington Monument, like a sharpened bone.

"Caitlin tells me you two had a few laughs the other morning over the Osborn-Agains," the President said.

"Well . . . yes, sir. Not too loudly, I hope."

Flannery brushed it off. "Tell me something. If Garret Osborn declared candidacy, what do you think his chances would be?"

"Mr. President . . ." Yates began, finally, to feel flustered. "You have advisers that eat, breathe, and sleep this sort of thing. I'm not even especially well-informed."

"I know very well your professional detachment. But you're at least as informed as the average voter. And as far as advisers are concerned?" Flannery shrugged. "Thirty years ago, one of you guys belted Lyndon Johnson in the eye. Believe me, I couldn't *buy* autonomy like that out of my staff. So your opinion interests me."

Yates shuffled his feet, stared into the drifting snow, the fog of their breath. Saw Flannery watching him with a patient eye, genuinely wanting to hear him out.

Last election, the man had parlayed a two-term northeastern governorship into a successful run at the White House, appealing to a constituency hungry for change, reform—the usual mantras. His dynamism and relative youth meant JFK comparisons were likely; his Catholic upbringing made them inevitable. He'd spent the bulk of his first term learning to negotiate Washington's treacherous waters, largely swamped by partisan gridlocks, but scoring enough victories, foreign and domestic, to keep him generally buoyant in the polls. Anymore, Yates thought, a President was doing well just to survive his term free of ethics probes, and with no one other than his wife who could describe his penis.

"Garret Osborn," Yates said, "doesn't stand a chance

in hell of winning the nomination, much less the election."

"Why not?"

"Too far right of that average voter you were talking about?"

"For now. But would you agree that a fundamentalist minister stands a better chance today of a winning a national election than two campaigns ago?"

Yates gave it some thought. "Yeah. I would."

"Which means they're getting closer. That they're learning how to package themselves as friendlier to the mainstream with every election that goes by." Flannery shook his head. "Sometimes I think that the Japanese and the religious right are the only ones who consistently plan twenty, thirty years into the future.

"Osborn isn't politically suicidal. He's never made any claim to have raised someone from the dead, like Robertson. He doesn't preach economic isolationism, like Buchanan. Oh, he'll yelp about Hollywood, because that's the easiest way to score family values points. But whatever extremism he represents, Osborn and his handlers and the ones just like him running for local and regional office . . . they're getting better all the time at concealing it. And they're winning seats. It may be a small start—school boards and state legislatures—but they're gaining ground every election, and one day they're going to start counting heads and realize they're in a position, finally, to be as intolerant as they want to be."

"You don't think the American people would see that coming and put a stop to it?"

"It's the last thing I'd go on record as saying," Flannery grinned bitterly into his eggnog, "but a huge cross-section of the American people is sick to its very core. Heartsick, soulsick, and apathetic about it." He studied Yates' face. "It surprises you to hear me say that?"

"It's . . . about as blunt a thing as I've ever heard you say."

"You'll notice it's to an audience of one. To whom secrecy is second-nature. But can you deny ever having felt the same?"

"No, sir. I can't."

"I'd be surprised if you could. You're a trained observer of human behavior." Flannery emptied his cup, absently stuck it into his coat pocket. "There's a very stubborn puritan strain that runs back to the earliest days of this country's settlement. They've always meant to have their way with the place, but I don't believe that, since before the signing of the Declaration of Independence, they've been any closer to getting it than they are today."

Yates imagined the fallout should the man go public with such misgivings. Have half the country screaming for his head.

"This sounds a bit beyond the usual party line-drawing."

Flannery nodded. "They'll wrap it up inside partisan labels, but it has almost nothing to do with conservative versus liberal policies. The religious right is embracing a lot of ideals that aren't truly conservative at all. That are actually alien to Jeffersonian democracy. Can you imagine Thomas Jefferson approving of branding homosexuality a crime at all, much less a crime punishable by death? Can you imagine Thomas Jefferson sanctioning church takeover of public schools and their curricula?"

Yates frowned. "Rhetorical questions, right?"

"Between reasonable heads like ours? Sure. But these goals are part of their long-term agenda, and I don't mind telling you, Tim, that scares me. Their theocracy is *not* the regime I want my daughter living under one day. Even if they only achieve half of what they'd like to do to this country in the name of God."

Flannery rubbed his hands as though they were growing cold, then began to laugh. "You don't know how good it feels to be able to say some of those things aloud."

"I'd imagine in the wrong company they could be problematic."

"Nixon had his secret war in Cambodia. Now you know mine." He brushed snow from the balcony railing. "Since it's expected that you leave your politics at home, what compelled you to take this job? That intrigues me. Because I can't think of anything *less* democratic than accepting as a given that your life is worth less than mine, and dedicating yourself to acting accordingly. So why?"

Yates shrugged. "I try not to look at it as coming down to individuals—me and you and the guy with the gun. I try to look at it as protecting the office. The morale of the country. Trying to keep those things safe, even when they're—" He stopped, fearing he was about to go too far.

"Worthier than the people who embody them?"

"You said that, I didn't."

"And you have the nerve to deny that you're an idealist." But Flannery laughed when he said this, clapping Yates on the back.

They stood a while longer at the balcony railing, in the hush of falling snow, listening to the distant keen of sirens, and for a moment Yates thought the President looked as though he could hear every drop of blood that might somewhere even now be slipping to the cold, hard pavement.

Halfway down the cathedral steps, Yates thinks for the first time that he's spotted the quarterly, up on the right. Anything but just another face in the crowd. Probably the first time the guy's worn a suit and tie in fifteen years. He looks astonishingly benign when compared to the FBI file photos, which never show a man at his best.

The quarterly has learned to blend.

Clearly, his thoughts are no longer his own.

On the second Tuesday of March, Garret Osborn pulled twenty-nine percent of the vote for a close second in the New Hampshire Primary, far higher than anyone outside the Christian Caucus had predicted. Yates watched the coverage on CNN that night, turning off the sound when the camera lingered on the man and his jubilant supporters at their campaign HQ. Studying him free of distraction by his voice, searching his eyes for any mania of inquisitions to come, seeing only the self-assurance of a man who could never conceive of people in their right mind seeing anything differently than he did. But this was hardly unique to the evangelicals.

Perhaps it was this facade of sameness, though, that should be the most worrisome thing of all. The mask of righteousness and concern advocating concessions to begin healing a nation drunk on its own liberty.

Before he shut off the TV, Yates spotted in the background a couple of the agents assigned to guard candidate Osborn. Wondered if any agent had ever been so appalled at the things he was privy to that he felt a passing impulse to draw his pistol and stop the menace on his own. Living proof that the system had broken down, and could no longer be trusted to weed out candidates a healthier nation wouldn't even allow to chase after its vagrant dogs.

It was times like this that he missed Karl Heindel the most. Seven years older, with five years' seniority in the Service, Karl had been like a big brother in an environment too competitive to reveal fears to anyone who might use them as leverage.

Talk me through this, Karl, he'd say. *A man with my access shouldn't even fantasize about doing the voters' job for them.*

You're a cog, Karl might once have said. *Cogs do one job and one job only.*

He wondered what Karl would say now, were he alive and still in last fall's frame of mind. If, having been let down by devotion to duty, he might now admit that even cogs could develop ambitions to wield control over the entire machine.

It was, after all, the substance of all things political.

And this swiftly became a moot point.

A scant ten days after his triumph in New Hampshire, Garret Osborn's world shattered during a fundraiser in Oklahoma City. After he and his entourage had returned to their hotel, Osborn slipped away from his protective detail, and was eventually found after barricading himself in a deserted second-floor conference room. Beneath him was a crying eight-year-old girl he'd snatched upstairs on a trip to the vending machines.

Hours later, in tears himself, Osborn told police and lawyers that he had been possessed by a demon. The demon, some of the cops were quick to point out, declined to make a statement.

By the next day the spine of the Christian Caucus was clearly broken, its sponsored local and regional candidates disassociating themselves like rats fleeing a sinking ship. But the taint was not so easily dispelled, press and public and opposing candidates alike loath to forgive and forget where children were concerned.

Pariahs, these candidates with Bibles clutched over their hearts and family values on their lips. They retreated, if only to regroup. Yates knew they would rise again as soon as they could. The convulsions in the body politic demanded nothing less.

The next month, Yates happened to meet up with one of the fallen Osborn's erstwhile agents, now in Washington with the next candidate he'd been assigned to. Yates and Ben Marlowe had come up out of Treasury at the same time, gone through training together; had crossed paths again for a year while working out of the same field office in Illinois. They'd done a lot of threat evaluation, interviewing the senders of semi-literate poison pen letters, or crayon drawings of the President-as-voodoo-pincushion. Little of it had ever amounted to anything.

Then, too, they'd been responsible for keeping close tabs on the area's high-risk group, chronic threatmakers who'd long passed muster as legitimate dangers. "Quarterlies," they were called, for the Service's policy of interviewing them four times per year, be they in jail or a mental ward, or loose on the street. It was the quarterlies who could send you seeking the bottle after work, the cold ambitious fixation in their eyes.

"You know the way some of them, they'd be like part of them was missing, or dead," Ben Marlowe said in the bar that evening, after the first of too many Scotches, "and they were sort of like puppets? And somebody else was jerking their strings?"

"Oh, yeah," said Yates. "They were the worst."

"Well, that's exactly the way Osborn looked when we heard the girl crying and came through that door. And him crouched over her on that table? When he looked up at us? The man whose sweat I'd been smelling for weeks was *gone*." Marlowe hunched over his drink, a black man with heavy stubble now, shaking his head. "I shouldn't even be telling you this. You pass it along, I'll deny every word. But I felt something else in that room. I'm not saying it was any devil Osborn blamed it on. But something . . .

"Remember when we got fitted for earphones, got our wrist mikes, started working as a team in crowd situations? And how pretty soon we almost didn't need the earphones anymore?"

Yates nodded. It'd been a peculiar phenomenon, if not unheard of—a mental oneness that seemed to link the agents. A heightened sensitivity that verged on the telepathic.

"Don't ask me why," said Marlowe, "but I've always been real cued in like that. Feeling when a crowd's about to spook. Picking out that one guy in three thousand who's about to blow, he doesn't get defused. I home in on that, so I'm telling you: I felt someone else hanging around the room where Osborn had that girl."

"Do yourself a favor," Yates told him. "Hold onto that one for your memoirs, after you've already got your pension locked."

"Oh, yeah." Marlowe nodded. "I may be psychic, but I'm not crazy."

* * *

Near the bottom of the cathedral steps, the quarterly drifts along at an oblique angle, making the most of Yates' position to keep him shielded from the closest other agents. Their eyes meet for the first time, and for the last, sparking with a peculiar recognition.

Instinctively, Yates' hand dips beneath his jacket for his gun, because old habits die hard.

The Christian Caucus was electoral history by mid-spring, when Flannery stopped along the campaign trail to deliver a eulogy of sorts in a Texas town where, days before, a jobless man had shot to death fourteen people in the bank that was foreclosing on his house. Yates thought the President looked ready to keel over, needing makeup to conceal strain and an ashen pallor.

Genevieve at his side, Flannery spoke of the need for putting aside petty differences and getting on with the rooting out of the true cancer eating away at the country. He asked how low a nation had sunk when mass murder no longer surprised. Asked what it would take to get people respecting themselves and each other again. Said that government was the last place they should look to for answers. He spoke with a passion and eloquence that prickled hair on the backs of necks.

And when he could no longer continue, and turned from the podium, the crowd remained as silent as tongue-lashed children, while executive staffers reached for antacid tablets. Even Yates recognized that it was probably the riskiest speech any President had given in generations.

"If I'm remembered for any of them," he said later in the limo, "then let that be the one."

Within two days, the approval ratings of a fickle public had soared. Opponents, naturally, cried foul and cheap sentimentality. But nobody much listened.

That weekend, Marine One choppered Flannery to Camp David. To Yates, seclusion in the Maryland wilderness was a welcome respite from the rigors of travel, the paranoia of crowds. And nearly a vacation, even, during the two hours he rode horseback alongside Caitlin, watching her show off, talking philosophers and film with her, and wondering how bad duty at Dartmouth could be.

The guests arrived on Saturday, throughout the afternoon; came in on the beating of helicopter blades, in clouds of dust and pollen. Some Yates recognized from Washington: the Vice President, generals, congressional bigwigs—from both parties, oddly enough—even a pair of Supreme Court justices. Others were private sector, faces he might've seen on the business pages. Others he failed to recognize at all, knowing only that some of the accents he heard were not American. British, in one instance; what could've been Italian in another. As quickly as they arrived, they vanished into the main lodge with their attendants, and no more was seen of them, nor of Flannery for the rest of the day.

While evening came and went, and shadows stretched across the grounds to become indivisible, one shadow over all, Yates knew the moment had come to be honest with himself. It was time to transfer off the White House detail. He'd allowed his objectivity to become eroded to the point he might no longer do his job as effectively.

Why the man had chosen him to confide so much in over recent months, Yates didn't know. Discretion, maybe? For all the staffers and hangers-on, the Presidency had to be horrendously isolating.

Flannery sought him out that night, asking Yates to accompany him on a walk. The moon was full and bright as it shone on paths trod by Presidents past, these same woods where Anwar Sadat and Menachim Begin had once chanced across each other, then walked together before making peace between their countries.

"I saw an editorial this morning," Flannery said, "suggesting that my outburst in Texas was the single crassest exploitation of tragedy for political gain that the writer had ever seen."

Yates grunted. "There's that liberal media bias for you."

"I've told Ginny more than once that anybody who'd actually want this job should automatically be disqualified as mentally incompetent." Moonlight clearly shadowed the bags under Flannery's eyes. "Your presence has meant a great deal to me the past months, Timothy. I want you to know that. Anyone can hire advisers. In you I like to think I found a friend. I hope it hasn't caused you any trouble with your superiors."

"No. No, sir. I—" He didn't know what to say. "No."

"You're a good man. Not just a good agent, but a good man. I was quite touched last autumn by how you cried at Karl Heindel's burial."

"You . . . were there?"

"I watched a surveillance tape. Karl was important to me as well." A long, pacing silence. "I have something to ask of you. It will go against every instinct you hold dear. But first there are some things you need to know.

"Undoubtedly you're wondering who my guests are this weekend, what we all could have in common. Quite simply, Tim, we're part of a tradition that dates back long before there ever was a United States, and played no small part in its creation."

Yates flashed on something Karl had said in the end. About old people, with roots like sequoias.

"You were a Treasury agent first, so you know the back of a dollar bill as well as the back of your hand. What they may not have taught you was the symbolism behind the Great Seal of the U.S. And how most of it drew from the occult traditions prominent at the time— Masonic, Rosicrucian, Illuminist. The all-seeing eye symbolized what Masons called the Grand Architect of the Universe. The truncated pyramid? Loss of wisdom incurred by Christianity's eradication of much older religions. All but six of the signers of the Declaration of Independence belonged to the Freemasons. Some, to other esoteric societies as well. Hardly something the history books teach. The puritans wouldn't stand for it.

"One such society was called the Illuminati. It was founded in 1776 in Germany by a man named Adam Weishaupt. There's even one school of thought that says he and George Washington were the same man. *I* don't believe it, but that goes to show you how prominent a hand the secret societies had in this country's origins."

Yates felt his head swimming, in too deep. "And you're saying they still do?"

"Our influence fluctuates depending on our numbers, and who's where . . . not only here, but Europe as well. Sometimes we've failed miserably, failed ourselves and our forebears. But we've always been committed to safeguarding the ideals of the founding fathers: maximum freedom, and belief in a Creator who doesn't meddle in mortal affairs. This automatically puts us in conflict with those who would impose their will on everyone else, and call it God's."

"Mr. President," Yates said, "you know I don't disagree with these principles, but I'm not seeing how I fit into this. You're talking about people with power. I don't have any."

"You have far more than you realize," Flannery said. "You have the power to let me die for my country."

Near the bottom of the cathedral steps, while the quarterly makes his move, Yates' hand freezes on his gun, as does the breath within his lungs, and his heart inside his chest. His feet carry him forward as though without his consent. The President five feet away, Yates wonders if the symbiosis of dread that he feels with the man is authentic, or a trick of nerves left raw by the burden of their shared knowledge.

Hand on his gun, as the limo awaits the First Family, and the death-watch camera rolls, Yates understands why Karl Heindel chose to blow his brains out rather than endure the obscene tragedy of this moment.

* * *

They were waiting in the lodge, milling about the conference table when Yates and the President walked in. The floor wasn't steady enough underfoot when he saw all heads turn, evaluating with eyes that hid behind masks of power, justice, avarice. Puppeteers all. He wished for his sunglasses.

"You're the only one present," Flannery told him, "who didn't already know that I'm dying. Not even the doctors at Bethesda know yet. But the cancer's in my lymphatic system now. I doubt I'd even make it until the end of my term next January. And even if there was a point to campaigning for the party nomination this summer, through the general election, by then I couldn't handle the pace."

"This is insane," Yates whispered.

"Why? Because it spares my family and me a lingering death? Because it'll make my death count for something rather than hiding it away until it's over, like something shameful?"

"No," Yates said. "Because it'll break this country's heart."

"This country's heart is almost past the point of beating."

Flannery settled into his chair at the head of the table; had one beside it reserved for Yates.

"Let me recount some distinctly American prophecy," Flannery said. "Last century, the grandsons of John Quincy Adams took a long look at where they saw this country heading. They predicted that by 1920 we'd've begun a slide into barbarity and materialism that would last throughout the twentieth century. They foresaw us as leaders in worldwide warfare, with a military-based government ruling over a society bankrupt of the humanistic and spiritual values of its founders." His eyebrows arched. "Sound familiar?"

"This is insane . . ."

"Any more so than a random sampling of daily news from across the country?" The President laid a hand upon his trembling arm. "Whatever the forces behind it, JFK's assassination sounded the death knell for whatever innocence this nation still possessed. Of course there'd been assassinations before. But none brought right into the country's living rooms. When his head came apart, so did something in the American psyche. The malaise has not only been with us ever since—it's deepened."

"But another assassination, my God . . ."

"How better to shock the American people than reflecting the bloody face of their own apathy? That is, if they're not too far gone already. Rhetoric alone won't do it. But death always brings people together. So as long as my life is forfeit anyway, I'll gladly play the role of the sacrificial lamb. The American people are prepared to grasp the mythic at least as far as they can watch it clearly played out on their televisions. If it makes for good TV, they'll get it."

Yates slumped onto the table, felt the pressure of all those eyes, all those agendas. Smelled the smoke of pipes and cigars; heard their murmuring voices, like ghosts of decades gone by.

And they all sat there wanting him to let a killer slip in, right up to the most powerful man in the room. Wanted him to live with the disgrace of that for the rest of his life.

Wanted him to be the hole in the net around Archer.

"You had this planned once before," he said. "Didn't you?"

"It was four days from execution last fall," Flannery said. "Karl Heindel was a seventh-generation grandson of Adam Weishaupt. Members of his family have played key positions in our Society for two hundred years. But Karl cracked under the pressure of what he saw as conflicting duties."

"And what makes you think I wouldn't?"

"We're not giving you as much time to feel the strain."

Was he to feel grateful for this?

"In three days, the current Pope will die in his bed in the Apostolic Palace. He's quite frail anyway, by now. It will look entirely like natural causes."

"The Pope," Yates whispered. "This involves the Vatican, too?"

"The world's about to change. About time, wouldn't you say?" Flannery rubbed bleary eyes. "After a week's conclave, a successor pontiff will be elected by the College of Cardinals. He'll take the name John XXIV, and assume the mantle of reform left by John XXIII at his death in 1963. The same mantle that John-Paul I tried to pick up when he was poisoned in 1978, after little more than a month on the throne. John XXIII instituted the first reforms the Church had seen since the Middle Ages. His first genuine successor will be the one to continue the reformation that John-Paul I never had a chance to: Relax the hardline on birth control. Abortion. Homosexuality. Divorce. Celibacy for priests. He'll acknowledge the androgynous nature of God. It'll take years, of course, but he'll revitalize American Catholics hungry for reform. And they'll provide the biggest challenge that the Puritan Fundamentalists of this country have ever faced."

"Since when," said Yates, "has Rome been anything other than fundamentalist itself?"

"Oh, they've quietly been mending their ways. In March of '94, the Pontifical Biblical Commission issued a document equating fundamentalism with intellectual suicide. So, our groundwork, you see," Flannery smiled, "has already been laid. My only regret is . . . I won't even live long enough to see the election of Pope John XXIV."

Back to this again. Always this. This abominable theater.

"Where do you envision it . . . happening?" Yates asked.

"On the steps of the Cathedral of St. Peter and St. Paul," he said. "While Vice President Bancroft is in Rome representing the U.S. at the papal funeral, my family and I will attend a special Mass at the cathedral. To share our grief with fellow Catholics. It'll happen as we leave. But only with your cooperation."

"But your family," Yates said. "Do they even *know?*"

"Ginny knows of the cancer. We haven't told Caitlin yet, but I think she's starting to suspect something's wrong. I've chosen not to tell them about . . . this side of things."

"And who's doing the shooting?" Yates not believing he was asking these questions with such . . . resignation.

"His name's Lee Edson. He's from Missoula, Montana. You never encountered him personally, but he's what you call a 'quarterly.' " A sheaf of papers was passed forward around the table as Flannery continued. "He's twice been institutionalized. Dishonorable army discharge, an excellent pistol shot. And his antipathy toward the Presidency is well-documented. The FBI has a nine-year collection of hate mail. He'll arouse no suspicions of conspiracy."

Only incompetence. Yates looked at the photo clipped to the file. Saw those eyes shimmering with single-minded purpose.

"I've met dozens of guys like this," he said. "You can't be sure of anything with them. Attention spans like gnats, sometimes. And do you really expect him to keep his mouth shut about being put up to this? He *will* be taken alive, you know. The Secret Service hasn't returned fire since Truman's day. They want these guys alive, in case there're more of them."

"It won't be a problem."

Yates couldn't fathom such confidence in a madman. Then:

"You want me," he whispered, "to kill him on the spot?"

But the President was shaking his head. "Don't worry about Edson, or his performance. Or anything he'll have to say later.

"Mind control, Timothy. One person dictating the actions of another? It's a reality. We've had infrequent success at it since this country's infancy, but now we have one among our ranks who's really quite extraordinary. So even if Lee Edson spends the rest of his life talking, all he can blame is . . . voices in his head."

"This can't work," Yates was murmuring, "this *can't* work."

"It's worked already. It worked well enough to bring down Garret Osborn."

Yates stared, then shoved back from the table. "He molested a child. *You caused him to molest a child?*"

"We regret that. Terribly. Our agent is able to push someone into giving vent to his deepest impulses, but we weren't sure with Osborn what that would be. With Lee Edson we know, and can work with that accordingly." Flannery tried to usher him back to the table. "Tim. Osborn's desire was there already. He'd've acted on it eventually. Repeatedly, probably, once he got started. And he might never have been caught. This way . . . he was."

Yates held his head in both hands. Felt the terrible weight of his Sig Sauer pistol in its holster. Its power to change lives, to change worlds.

"From Popes to eight-year-old girls," he said. "What kind of monsters are you?"

"The kind with ambitions tempered by all-too-human failings. A wise public servant once wrote, 'A man who wishes to make a profession of goodness in everything must necessarily come to grief among so many who are not good. Therefore, it is necessary to learn how not to be good.' "

Yates lifted his head. "Who said that?"

"Machiavelli. He dealt with people as they were . . . not as they should be," the President said. "Great pragmatists, the Italians."

Gun right!, he should yell, but doesn't say a word, and so, with the popping of shots nearly lost to the day, all hell breaks loose. Real live gunshots never have the same drama as those heard in the movies. They do no honor to their situation.

Yates has already angled his body sideways, to present a smaller target—the exact opposite of his training, the theory and practice of catching an assassin's bullet. They'll never know the willpower it has taken.

He feels the bullets whizzing past, as the day plunges from order to chaos. Any transition is too minute for human awareness. The steps outside the Cathedral of St. Peter and St. Paul explode with panic and uproar, a whiplash of surging bodies and a frantic buzz of voices in his earphone. And the blood, and the brains.

Unable to move, he's left behind as the Flannerys are swept toward the limousine like scarecrows, as agents jam the President and his wife through the door, then fling themselves on top, even while Genevieve fights as only a mother can for the scrap of skull that went whirling from her daughter's head.

Caitlin is last, then the limo is gone in a streak of black lacquer and a scream of tires. Yates wonders what the ride to the hospital can possibly feel like to a mother cradling a shattered skull in her lap, as she brushes sodden hair from her daughter's face and tells herself there's still hope.

The limo is gone, and still Yates can see that look of final surprise on Flannery's face. Saying no. No. It's not supposed to happen this way.

The limo is gone, and Lee Edson is nowhere to be seen, still buried beneath a pile of gray-suited agents. They'll cry later.

The cameras, meanwhile, keep on rolling.

Yates wanders away from the carnage, post abandoned. Digs his earphone free and casts it to the mercy of feet behind him. He loses himself in the crowd, and wonders who besides himself is to blame. If Lee Edson did exactly what he'd wanted, an unpredictable quarterly to the end. Or if Flannery had been lied to, and Caitlin was the target all along. For Presidents come, and Presidents go, and take their chances, but murdered children live forever young.

Surely he hasn't sacrificed her himself, like a chieftain's virgin daughter to a tribal god in some barbaric hell.

Surely not that.

Regardless, the object lesson is ever so clear.

And the dialogue is officially opened.

Yates loses himself in the crowd, deep in the fibrillating heart of the body politic, living and listening now only for the autopsies to come.

HOMESICK

by *Richard T. Chizmar*

Richard T. Chizmar is the author of over forty published short stories, and the World Fantasy Award-winning editor of *Cemetery Dance* magazine and numerous anthologies, including *Cold Blood, Thrillers, The Earth Strikes Back,* and *Screamplays.* His first book, *Midnight Promises,* was published in hardcover earlier this year.

Timmy Bradley hates his new house.

He hates the slippery, shiny floors and the long, winding hallways and the big fancy rugs. He hates the stupid, ugly paintings on the walls and all the weird looking statues that sit on the furniture. He hates just about everything.

Including the strange way that his father and mother have been acting ever since they moved here. To this house.

He sits alone in his bedroom—lights off, door closed—looking out the window at the darkened city. Crying.

Timmy misses his old house and the way things used to be when they lived there. He misses his friends and Sarah and he even misses his school. But he *especially* misses the way that his father—even though he'd been busy back then, too; after all, his father had been the Governor of Massachusetts for goodness sake—used to take time out to play with him each and every day. That's what they had called it back in those days— "time out." No matter what was going on, his father always found a few minutes to go out for a walk with Timmy or play a card game or watch some television.

Sometimes he would even take Timmy along on a short trip when it didn't interfere with school and his mother said it was okay.

None of this happens anymore.

His father is always surrounded by people now. And on those few occasions when he *is* alone or just with the family, his father is always so quiet and serious. And distant. Nothing at all like the goofball who once danced around Timmy's bedroom with a pair of Jockey shorts on his head or the father who once bounced on his bed so hard that the frame broke and they lay there giggling for what had to be fifteen minutes.

This house has changed him, Timmy thinks.

He moves away from the window. He sits on the edge of his bed and stares at the back of the bedroom door. He is no longer crying.

Timmy knows that his mother is trying to make things better for him. She, too, is much busier now, but *still* she plays with him a lot more often than before and seems intent on kissing him on the cheek at least a hundred times each day. Or at least it feels like a hundred times.

And, of course, once or twice a week she gives him her little speech: "You have to understand, Timmy. Daddy's job was important before, but now he's the President. For the next few years he's going to be very, very busy with real important things. But you'll get used to it here; it's such a beautiful house. It really is . . . "

That is part one of the speech; some days he gets part two; other days, he gets both: " . . . And soon you'll meet new friends and find fun and exciting things to do. You just have to be more patient and remember, we *all* have to make sacrifices. Especially your father. Don't you think he'd rather spend time with us than go to all those stuffy meetings? Of course he would. Just remember, sweetheart, he's the President now, and that's a very big deal . . . "

Timmy almost always comes away from these talks feeling sad and lonely and a little guilty. Jeez. What

can you say to all that talk when you're only twelve
years old?

Some days—usually on those days when his father
smiles at him the way he used to or spends a few extra
minutes with him after dinner—Timmy thinks that his
mother might be right. That things might turn out okay
after all. He thinks this because sometimes if he con-
centrates long and hard enough, he can remember not
being so happy in their old house for those first few
weeks after they'd moved in.

Back then, like now, there were so many adjustments
to make. All the fancy stuff he wasn't allowed to touch.
All the secret service men and the stupid security rules
he had to memorize. The stiff, new clothes he had to
wear and all the dumb pictures he had to dress up for.
And, worst of all, he remembers, all those boring parties he had to go to.

When Timmy thinks back to all those things and
how, over time, he'd learned to live with them, he
sometimes thinks he is just being a baby. A big, fat cry-
baby, just like he'd heard his father whisper one night
last week when he thought Timmy wasn't listening:
"I've *got* to get going now, dear. I'll talk to him later.
Besides, he's just being a baby again."

Timmy sits back on his bed and listens to his father
call him a baby. *(He's just being a baby again. Being a
baby.)* Just thinking about that night hurts his feelings
all over again, makes his face red and hot and sweaty.
And it also makes him angry.

Who is he to call me a baby, Timmy thinks. *He's* the
one who messed everything up. *He's* the one who made
us come here in the first place.

Timmy looks up at the picture frame on his dresser
at the pretty, smiling blonde girl in the photo. His stare
locks on the wrinkled pink envelope sitting next to it.

Dear Timmy,
*I got your letter and the package. Thanks so much; it's
sooo beautiful. This letter is so short because I have to
eat dinner in a couple of minutes. My mom says I have*

*to stop mooning over you, can you believe that she ac-
tually said that, that I was mooning over you. Anyway,
she said that I was wrong to promise you that we'd still
go steady and she made me go to the dance with Henry
Livingston this past weekend. I ended up having a lot
of fun. Henry sure can fast dance. Not as much fun as I
would have had with you, but what can we do?—you
being there and me being stuck back here. Henry asked
me to go to the movies with him on Friday and I told
him yes. He's a bunch of fun, not like you, but what can
we do? So, I guess we're not going steady or anything
any more. My mother's making me show her this letter
before I mail it, so she'll know I "broke it off." Sorry.
Those are her words, not mine. I miss you, Timmy, and
I'll write again soon if my mom lets me. She said she
had to think about it. Please write back as soon as you
can and don't be mad, okay?
Love, Sarah.
P.S. Henry said to say hi and don't be mad at him.*

Timmy feels the tears coming and looks away from
the picture. But it's too late. He's already crying.
Again. Jeez, maybe he is a baby. Maybe his father is
right about him after all.

But that doesn't matter now. Timmy no longer cares
what his father thinks. Besides, he knows this is different than last time. Last time they moved he didn't get
sick, he didn't cry, he didn't have nightmares. This
time is different, he thinks.

He looks at the bedroom door and wonders what is
happening downstairs. He figures it is just a matter of
time now. If all goes according to his plan, he'll be
back in Massachusetts in time for soccer season. Back
holding hands and walking home from school with
Sarah. Back playing video games and tag-team and
roller-ball with all his friends (except for that back-
stabber Henry Livingston).

Timmy looks at the clock on the wall. It is after
seven o'clock—Sarah and Henry are probably inside
the movie theater by now—and he wonders again why
it is still so quiet outside his bedroom.

Just be patient, he thinks. Just like his mother always says, *you have to be more patient, Timmy*. To pass the time, he tries to imagine everything as it happened. Inside his head, he watches himself as he . . .

. . . pours the poison directly into their coffee, careful not to get any on the edge of the cups or on the tray. Then he swirls it around real good with his finger until all the white powder disappears. Finally, he pretends to stretch out on the sofa and read a comic book but he really waits and watches them take their first sips, then tip-toes upstairs to his room.

He looks at the clock again. He can't imagine what's taking so long?

He walks to the window and sits down with his back to the door. He wonders what movie Sarah is watching. He thinks of her there in the dark, eating popcorn and sipping soda, Henry's fingers touching her hand. Closing his eyes, he whispers a quick prayer. He asks only that everything goes according to his plan. That soon it will all be over and they will send him home again. Back to Sarah. Back to his friends. Back to his old house.

A few minutes past eight, when he hears the loud, angry voices and the heavy footsteps outside his door, he knows that his prayer has been answered. He is going home.

THE GHOST AND MR. TRUMAN

by Bill Crider

Bill Crider won the Anthony award for his first novel in the Sheriff Dan Rhodes series. His first novel in the Truman Smith series was nominated for a Shamus Award, and a third series features college English professor Carl Burns. His short stories have appeared in numerous anthologies, including those in the *Cat Crimes* series, *Celebrity Vampires,* and *Werewolves.*

(For John Duke)

I
AUGUST 24, 1814

The wind tore ragged clouds to shreds and found every hole in John Simmons' jacket as he watched the British seamen from the cover of a darkened doorway. Led by their commanders, the seamen marched two by two toward the White House.

"Dolley Madison locked the doors when she left; you can count on that," Gage Barrow whispered at Simmons' side.

Simmons dug a sharp elbow into Barrow's ribs to shut him up. The blathering fool would give them away if he weren't careful. One of the British commanders had already grabbed someone from shadows that thickened along the street and forced him to accompany the naval brigade on its march.

"Are ye sure there's treasure in there?" Barrow whispered, seeming not at all discouraged by Simmons' rude poke. "Are ye sure Dolley didn't carry it all away? The richies always takes it with 'em if they can."

There was a roll of thunder, followed by a flash of lightning. Simmons clapped his left hand over Barrow's mouth and dragged him deeper into the doorway. Putting his own mouth next to Barrow's ear, Simmons whispered, "Shut yer hole, or I'll shut it for ye," and to prove his sincerity, he pulled his dagger from his belt and stuck the point into the soft flesh of Barrow's stubbled chin.

A thin line of blood trickled down Barrow's throat. Barrow ignored the pain and breathed heavily through his nose. He didn't struggle, and after a few minutes Simmons relaxed his grip. The seamen were past them now, and above the whistle and whine of the wind Simmons could hear them breaking in the front door of the White House.

"Locked it behind her, Dolley did, just like I told ye," Barrow said.

Simmons didn't bother to try to silence him now that the danger was past.

"Locked the British bastards out in the rain," Barrow continued with satisfaction, as if locked doors would stop the British, and as if it were already raining, which it was not, in spite of the wind and thunder and lightning.

Simmons leaned out of the doorway and watched as the seamen entered the White House. When they were all inside, Simmons heard the splintering of glass as they began to smash out the windows.

"Getting ready to burn it down, they are," Barrow said. "If we're to take anything of our own, 'tis time for us to be going in ourselves."

For once Simmons agreed with him. Holding his hat to his head, he slipped out of the doorway and along the street, a tall, skinny shadow lost in the other shadows of the cloud-dark night. Behind him came Barrow, a shorter, fatter shadow but equally silent.

A sudden lightning flash froze them to the wall as it illuminated them briefly, showing Simmons' beaky nose and his glittering, greedy eyes. Barrow's mouth was fixed in its eternal crooked grin. Then the night was dark once more, and they continued on their way.

Simmons' plan was quite simple: get inside the White House and carry away all he could. Earlier he had seen several carts of goods leaving, but he knew that they could not have carried away half the treasures stored inside. He knew, too, that the British bastards would not take anything for themselves, or at least not anything of great value. They would not want to be accused of looting.

Simmons, on the other hand, didn't mind in the least being called a looter. He'd made a living for most of his life as a killer and a thief, so what was the difference? Skirting the White House grounds, he and Barrow made their way to the back. It was very dark, and the wind was blowing even harder.

"They're leaving already," Barrow said as he and Simmons neared the building. "You wouldn't think they could work so fast."

"And so had we better work," Simmons said. "Else they'll find our charred bones inside the rubble come tomorrow."

Barrow giggled at that, and Simmons had to restrain the urge to hit him. He did so, however, and the two men found a broken window out of sight of the seamen. Simmons made a stirrup of his hands to help Barrow climb up and held him while he cleared away the shards of glass that still remained. When that was done, Barrow slithered through the window, then turned to give Simmons a hand.

When they got into the White House, the darkness was so thick that they could see hardly at all. Their way was lighted only by the occasional lightning flashes, and even inside they could not escape the blustering wind that howled through the shattered windows.

Most of the furniture had been heaped into piles in the middle of the rooms, but Simmons wasn't interested in furniture. He was interested in silver: silver knives and forks and spoons. He gathered in all he could see and feel, sticking everything into a bag that he had carried under his coat. He was reaching for a silver candlestick when something heavy and hard smashed into the back of his head, sending him quickly into unconsciousness.

After a time he came back to himself. He found that he was tied to a heavy wooden chair on a stack of other furniture and that struggle as he might, he could not move at all. He tried to speak, but his mouth was stuffed with a filthy rag.

"Ah," George Barrow said, "so you're back with us, are ye? Take a good look around, John Simmons, as it's likely to be your last."

Simmons strained against his bonds, but Barrow had tied them well.

"Tell me to shut my hole, will ye? Stick your nasty knife under my chin and hold your grubby hand over my mouth, eh? Always telling me to do this and to do that, hitting me with your horny fists. Well, there'll be no more of that, John Simmons." Barrow held up a bag heavy with loot in each hand. "I'm sure you won't care at all that I'm taking your share, and if you do care, you won't for long. Good-bye to ye now." Grinning his crooked grin, Barrow made a mock bow and left Simmons there, writhing uselessly. Barrow went to a back window, tossed the bags out, and followed them. Then he was gone across the grounds, disappearing into the night.

Shortly afterward, fifty of the British seamen carrying long poles tipped with oil-soaked rags ringed the house. A torch went around to light the rags, and the poles were then thrown through the open windows.

The fires began slowly, but, helped along by the wind, they spread quickly, flashing wildly through the building. Soon the White House was ablaze, the bottoms of the bloated, low-lying clouds reddened by the leaping flames.

Overhead the thunder boomed and the lightning sparked. John Simmons started screaming when the rag in his mouth had burned away, crying revenge on

"Yes," Truman said. "I've seen them."

"Then you know that I'm telling you the truth. I recommend that you move into Blair House as soon as possible. You should be safe there."

"What does your blasted spirit have against *me?*" Truman asked.

"Oh, it's not you, not especially. It's anyone and everyone. He's been gathering his power for a century and a half, nursing his revenge. Since he can't reach the one who murdered him, he's striking out at whoever happens to be handy. He doesn't have anything against you, unlike all the Republicans and not a few of the Democrats."

Truman chuckled at the joke, but he wasn't sure that Winslow had the straight of it. It almost seemed that there was some message the spirit had for him, personally.

"Mostly, he just wants to be set free," Winslow said.

"And how are we supposed to do that?" Truman asked.

"Ah," Winslow said, puffing at his pipe, "that's the part he hasn't told me yet."

III
NOVEMBER 5, 1950

Truman stood on the catwalk and looked down into the hollow shell of the White House. The paneled walls, the floors, the chandeliers, the doors, the ornaments—all were gone. The interior space was filled with steel girders, and far below the president a front-end loader excavating the subbasement clanked and groaned and finally dropped a load of dirt into a waiting dump truck.

The renovation, which was what they called it even though it had become much more than that, was continuing at a rapid pace, and there was almost nothing of the White House left now except the bare stone of the outside walls. Truman and Winslow had hoped to save some of the paneling and flooring at least, but a great deal of it could not be salvaged. Much of the old, historic material could not be reused and was to be packaged and sold as relics, even down to the nails and original bricks.

The selling of relics did not bother Truman. He was naturally frugal, and he liked the idea of making the rebuilding project at least partially self-supporting. What bothered the president was that even now, with almost nothing remaining of the original structure except the husk, the noises continued. The night watchmen had complained about them, and the complaints had reached Truman's ears.

And then there were the accidents. Little things, most of them, though the workmen likely didn't think of them that way. Losing a finger or breaking a leg wasn't a little thing to the man to whom it happened, but at least no one had died. Yet.

Truman turned to Winslow who was standing beside him. The ever-present Secret Service men were a discreet distance away.

"I don't understand why we haven't found anything," Truman said. "We've torn out the walls, we've torn up the floors, we've completely destroyed the place from the ground up, and it's still haunted. You said—"

Winslow took his corncob pipe from his mouth, inverted it, and knocked it against the heel of his hand. Black and gray ashes filtered down and were blown aside by the breeze coming in through the windows. Winslow put the pipe into the side pocket of his jacket.

"I said that I believed we would find some evidence of the murder, not that we would find a body. In any case, I was obviously incorrect, and John hasn't made much of an effort to clarify things."

Truman looked at Winslow. "John?"

"Yes. That's the name he gave me. Apparently he is somehow more an ingrained part of this place than I realized."

Below them, the front-end loader backed away from

the dump truck and clanked over to scoop up another pile of dirt.

"We haven't found any bones," Truman said, the light from a nearby window flashing off his round glasses. "Or any sign of foul play."

"There were plenty of skeletons in the closets," Winslow said with a grin, but Truman didn't laugh.

"I've been thinking about calling a priest," Truman said. "Having him perform an exorcism."

Winslow nodded. "It might work. But it would be impossible to keep secret. What would the voters think?"

Truman didn't give much of a damn what the voters thought. He wouldn't be running for office again. Still, he wouldn't want to do anything that might reflect badly on the party.

"Do you have any suggestions?" he asked.

Winslow didn't answer for a while. He reached into his pocket and fingered his pipe, but he didn't bring it out. Finally he said, "I might have one. But I'm not sure I should even make it."

Truman was ready to try anything. "Why shouldn't you?"

"Because there's more to the story than I've told you."

Truman wasn't surprised. He was the President, after all. People didn't like to give him bad news; he was accustomed to being told half-truths and even outright lies. But that didn't mean he liked it.

"Tell me now," he said.

"The man who died here," Winslow said. "His name was Simmons."

"So what? It's a common enough name."

"It's my name, too," Winslow said. "Lorenzo Simmons Winslow."

"Family name?" Truman asked.

Winslow nodded.

"And you think this ha'nt we've got in here is kin to you?"

"I know he is," Winslow said. "That's why he's become so agitated now, I believe. Because I'm a distant relative, and because he can communicate with me after a fashion, he expects me to set him free. And I know something else. Until he's set free, he's going to be very dangerous."

Something about the remarks didn't ring true to the President. He didn't think that Winslow was holding anything back, not this time, but he still believed that the spirit had a message for him and that whatever it was had nothing to do with the fact the spirit might be some long-lost relative of the architect.

"You don't have to tell me he's dangerous," Truman said, watching as the front-end loader finished dumping another load of soil into the truck.

A workman carrying a shovel was walking across the open space behind the loader when its driver, without looking around, began to back up.

"Oh, hell," Truman said. He began shouting, jumping up and down on the catwalk as he did, "Look out down there! Get out of the way! Get out of the way!"

The workman stopped walking, but instead of looking in the direction of the danger, he looked up at the gesticulating President.

"Move, you idiot!" Truman yelled.

The workman seemed to hear the front-end loader for the first time and turned to run, but something that Truman couldn't see tangled his feet together and he fell sprawling. The treads of the loader passed over his legs, crushing them into the soil. His screams echoed off the sandstone walls.

Truman and Winslow got to him long after the Secret Service men and the other workers, and by then he was unconscious. Truman looked at Winslow.

"Tonight," the architect said. "We have to come back tonight."

Truman didn't like it at all, sneaking away from Blair House without the Secret Service men. Normally he didn't think of himself as needing a bodyguard, but now he wasn't so sure. Bess had been particularly vehement on the subject, but he had silenced her objections. He'd had some trouble with the watchman, too, but he'd managed to convince him that the President had a perfect right to take a late-night tour of the White House, even if no one else did.

So now here he was, skulking through the shell of the White House at nearly midnight, with nothing but a flashlight containing a couple of weak Ray-O-Vac batteries. It was very dark, and even though he could hear the traffic on Pennsylvania Avenue, he felt isolated and alone.

"I'm not so sure I get the point of this," he told Winslow, who didn't even have a flashlight.

"I think he died at night," Winslow said. "In a fire."

Truman took a deep breath, smelling the freshly-dug earth. It should have smelled like a newly-turned Missouri field, but it reminded him much more of open graves.

"There's never been a fire that serious in the White House," he said.

"There was one," Winslow reminded him, "though maybe you couldn't say it was *in* the house. Remember the War of 1812, which, of course, was fought in 1814?"

Truman was familiar enough with history. "There was no one in the White House when the British torched it," he said. "It was deserted when they got here, and they didn't leave anyone behind."

"That's what history tells us," Winslow agreed. "But then when were history and the truth ever synonymous?"

Truman had occasionally wondered the same thing. "All right, then, I'll grant you the possibility. That might explain why we haven't found any trace of him, assuming that he exists at all. Maybe he was burned to ashes."

"Maybe," Winslow said. "And he exists, all right. You saw what happened today."

"An accident," Truman said without conviction. "Things like that happen on construction sites."

"Too many things like that have happened here, and the man's spirit has been talking to me. He's here. There's no question of it."

Truman knew that Winslow was right. He shined the weak flashlight beam along the base of one of the walls. "You keep saying that he's talking to you, but you're never very specific about what he says."

Winslow was examining the stones in the light's wavery shine. Some of them had odd markings on them, Masonic markings Truman called them, and at first Winslow had agreed. But of course they could be something else.

"You don't understand," Winslow said. "It's not *talking* exactly. It's more that he's in my mind somehow. We don't have normal conversations."

Truman could believe that. How could you have normal conversations with a ghost? They continued to walk along the wall, stopping every now and then for Winslow to examine something or other. Several minutes passed without either man speaking. Then Truman heard something.

Winslow heard it, too. The men stood silently, looking up into the darkness overhead, listening to what sounded to Truman like a long, low scream.

"He's in pain," Winslow said. "That's what he wants to be freed from. Somehow his spirit was trapped here, and part of his physical self is still here as well."

"His ashes," Truman said. "If he burned to death, his ashes might be in cracks and crevices in the walls. We could never locate them all."

The screaming seemed to rise and fall, like the wind on a winter day. But there was no wind that night. Truman felt something cold touch the back of his neck like the finger of a dead man.

He whipped around, but there was no one there.

"Shine the light over here," Winslow said. He was crouched by the wall, brushing at one of the stones with his open hand.

"What is it?" Truman asked. The back of his neck still felt as chill as a grave.

"These markings," Winslow said. "They're different from the others."

Maybe they were, but Truman couldn't tell it. They looked the same to him.

"What if," Winslow said, and paused.

"What if *what?*"

"Remember when these stones were laid," Winslow said. "The eighteenth century, not a hundred years after the Salem witch trials. Magic was still abroad in the land at that time. Suppose someone, one of the stoneworkers, knew a bit of that magic, enough at any rate to carve it into the stones."

"And that's keeping your long-lost uncle around?" Truman didn't believe it for a minute.

"It's as good a possibility as any other."

Truman wasn't a man who agonized about decisions that had to be made. "We'll get rid of the stones, then," he said.

"All of them?" Winslow asked. He stood up and brushed his hands on his pants.

"Why not? We have to be sure." Truman had already thought of a way to make political capital out of the move. "We'll start tomorrow. Tell your uncle. See if that's what he wants."

The screaming behind them rose incredibly in volume, and Truman dropped the flashlight, pressing his hand over his ears and wondering for the first time if the sound really existed anywhere other than inside his own head.

And inside Winslow's. The architect had fallen to his knees, his eyes shut tightly and his head jerking from side to side.

Truman put out a hand to help him, but as he did, something began to materialize in the middle of the vast empty framework of the White House, seeming to rise up from the very dirt that was now serving as the floor.

At first Truman couldn't tell what it was, but after a few moments he could see it clearly. It was the figure of a man all afire, his ragged clothing flapping around him as the flames licked through it, his skin as brittle and brown as bacon, grease popping on its surface, his eyes seething in their sockets, his blazing hair fluttering around what must have been his face, though it was so swollen and distended that it resembled nothing human at all.

And then something happened to Truman that surpassed even that marvel. The image of the burning man was joined by others, not so many at first, but then more and more—hundreds of them, thousands, large and small, women and men and children, all of them screaming.

"Jesus Christ," he said aloud, his head about to burst from the sounds that filled it. "Where did *they* come from?"

He blinked and they were gone, vanished into some kind of cloud that disappeared at once, but the spirit of John Simmons remained, raging and screaming, consumed by the fire yet not consumed by it at all.

Winslow was staggering to his feet, and Truman could see his mouth moving though he couldn't make out the words. Winslow moved a hand appeasingly and stepped toward the burning figure, and the flames seemed to lessen slightly. Winslow took another step, and the flames burned lower still, continuing to fade as Winslow talked.

But the burning man wasn't looking at Winslow. His bubbling, admonitory eyes were looking straight at the President.

Truman didn't know how long the three of them stood there, the two men and the spirit, but after a while there were only two of them, the President and the architect.

Neither of them spoke for quite some time. Finally Truman said, "Will he be back?"

Winslow shook his head. "I don't think so."

"It was the stones, then. Wasn't it?"

"I . . . I'm not sure. Maybe. But there was more to it

than that. I . . . well, never mind. At any rate, I get the impression that we've seen what we were meant to see."

"You saw them, then?" Truman asked.

"Them? I saw a burning man. That was all. Was there something more?"

Truman started to tell Winslow about all the others, the thousands of others, then changed his mind and said, "No. No, there wasn't anything more."

He knew in that moment that Winslow was right. They had seen what they had been meant to see. Or rather Truman had. The message of John Simmons had been for the President all along.

IV
NOVEMBER 15, 1950

The package had arrived at the grand lodge that morning, and the Masons were eager to have it opened. It wasn't every day that they got a package from the White House.

"It's a rock," said Lawrence Kelley when the wrapping was off and the box was opened. "There's a letter with it."

He started reading, but a chorus of voices interrupted him. "Tell us what it says!"

"It says this is a stone from the wall of the White House and that these markings on it show that Freemasonry was intimately connected with the founding of our government."

"Hey," someone said, "that's great. A stone from the White House wall."

"He's sending one to the grand lodge of every state in the union," Kelley said. "What a great guy."

"He's not such a great guy," someone said. "Let's see how he handles this Korea mess."

"He can always drop the bomb."

"He wouldn't do that, would he?"

"He did it before."

"I'm glad I didn't have to make a decision like that."

"Yeah. You think it bothers him?"

Kelley looked down at the stone. "Who knows?" he said.

ASSASSINATION DAYS
by Billie Sue Mosiman

Billie Sue Mosiman is the author of the Edgar-nominated novel *Night Cruise*. She has published more than ninety short stories in various magazines, including *Realms of Fantasy* and in various anthologies such as *Tales From the Great Turtle* and *Tapestries: Magic the Gathering*. Her latest novel is *Stiletto*, from Berkley.

> "Those who make peaceful revolution impossible will make violent revolution inevitable."
> —John F. Kennedy
> Speech, 13 March 1962,
> the White House.

President Myers woke sweat-drenched and chilled, his pajamas stuck to his barrel chest, his eyes rolling like those of a frightened horse. He came into a sitting position in the bed, throwing back the covers as he did so.

In the twin bed next to him his wife hadn't moved, so he must not have made a sound when he turned in the dream and saw the assassin in the crowd. At least that was some blessing, that Betty didn't wake. She had been urging him for weeks to talk to the doctor about the night terrors plaguing him. If she didn't know about them, if he didn't tell her they continued—aye, were increasing in occurrence and intensity—maybe she'd believe he was all right again.

He slipped from the sheets and padded to the bath to wash his face with cool water. And to take a pill prescribed for sleeping. He had to sleep. The nation was in momentous turmoil, more than at any time since the War Between the States, and it was on his shoulders to save it. Why wouldn't he suffer nightmares, given such a weighty dilemma?

After splashing his face and drying it, downing two sleeping tablets chased by water from the tap, he wandered from the bedroom to the hall where a Secret Service man, a mechanical, sat at attention.

"Yes, sir!" the man said, standing to face the President. "How may I help you, sir?"

"Would you mind reading to me until I grow sleepy again?" This was a good man, specially picked to guard the sleeping President, but most important of all, considering the many sleepless nights Myers endured, the guard possessed a good speaking voice and a flair for recitation. He was remarkably good with the poems and essays of Emerson.

"No, sir, I don't mind."

Myers handed over the leather-bound volume and strode down the carpeted hall to the living area of their quarters in the White House. The guard, Jim, followed. When seated, Jim opened the book to read from the essay on self-reliance.

Myers shut his eyes and laid his head back on the chair to let the words tumble through his mind and dispel the awful nightmare.

"To be great is to be misunderstood," Jim read. And later: "An institution is the lengthened shadow of one man."

Perhaps Emerson was not a soothing author, but he put meat into his words, making of them a hearty stew that stuck to the ribs and sustained a weak man. Myers had a great many favorite old classic authors that he read or had read to him when his mind would not be still. None of them, he now admitted as he listened to Jim's sonorous voice, could be called joyous Pollyannas.

He smiled to himself and drifted a bit on the rich rhythm of Jim's delivery. The sleeping medicine was about to whisk him over the brink of sleep again, and he would not fight it. If he slept, Jim would eventually notice and close the book, and sit quietly, watching, until the President awoke of his own accord or morning came, whichever happened first.

Myers imagined the brink separating sleep and wakefulness as a ledge along a chasm of darkness. He willingly stepped into space, falling through deep blackness that eerily cushioned him as on a cloud so that he floated far and deep away through nothingness, returning to nothingness, embracing the death time that sleep brings.

And then it was as if his mind snapped open, a trapdoor knocked up and out to let the light in, to admit life, but a life of the dream.

He could not hear Jim reading to him and didn't know if he still read or had stopped now. He knew he was in dream and it would be best if he pulled down that trapdoor against it. It would even be better to wake again, spoiling his slumber. But will could never assure event in the dreamworld, and there was nothing Myers could do but go forth.

There he was, the assassin, garbed in the tattered rags of the Have Nots. He raised a weapon and bulky blurred shapes flung themselves in front of Myers to save him, but just as in all the dreams before this one, they were too late. The bullet came zinging, aimed directly for his heart. He held his breath, stunned, frozen in space, while a hole blossomed blood in his wide chest and he was knocked back a step, stumbled, fell.

Dead.

He shuddered in death, knowing he was dead, it was over, all his work for naught, the Union split forever. If he died, there was no one to hold the ranks together, to inspire the Union Haves army to fight against the Western Have Nots until they defeated them, just as the army had fought the Confederates and healed the rift so many hundreds of years ago. If a real assassin ever killed him, the United States hadn't a prayer to be united ever again.

Then he woke. Or thought he did. But Jim wasn't in

the chair opposite where he had been. Myers sat alone in the room so he must still be caught in the web of dream, he realized.

Lincoln and Kennedy sat on the sofa together, watching him. He sucked in his breath in surprise, though it was obvious to him why these particular dead Presidents had come. He said, "At least enough of your work was done before the assassin got you. What about me? Will I have time?"

"Would we tell you that if we could?" John Kennedy asked in his distinctive accent.

Lincoln stood, craggy face hanging like folds of old dusty theater curtains from his prominent skull bones. He went to the cold hearth and put his long veined hand on the mantel. With his back to them he said, "It's the same one."

"Same one what?" Myers asked, perplexed.

"Booth. Oswald. Your assassin. They are all one and the same. He comes from the deep, from the fiery deep, sent by powers no one has ever understood, trying to ensure the nation falls. We are and have always been a nation of God, an affront to the Old Fallen One."

"What about Leon Czolgosz who killed McKinley?" Myers asked. "Was he the same assassin, too?"

Kennedy said, "No, not him. McKinley's assassin was of a different stripe. Not connected to the determined one who came for us and will come for you."

Myers tried to imagine it. A supernatural being clothed in new skin, coming back again and again to take down the President right when there was a chance to destroy the Union. It had not worked with the presidencies of Lincoln and Kennedy, but the assassin kept coming back, kept trying.

Myers had never believed in the fables of religion and therefore found it nearly impossible to entertain the idea of a being from "fiery depths" who returned to earth over and over to stalk Presidents in crisis.

Nevertheless, he should listen closely to these august ghosts. So he asked, "How can I avoid him? You wouldn't appear to me and not give advice, would you?"

"We're constrained," Lincoln said, "not to interfere. It took great heated debates to get here now, to tell you anything. You can find my advice in a letter I wrote to Horace Greeley dated August 22, 1862."

Myers watched him fade from the room, a faint white mist that scattered before an errant breeze.

He turned to Kennedy and said, "And what of you? What can I do to save the Union before someone guns me down?"

"When written in Chinese, the word crisis is composed of two characters. One represents danger and the other represents opportunity."

"But what opportunity . . . ?"

The room stood empty then grew dark as a pit and Myers struggled to wake. He had to . . . had to . . . find something, a quote, the one Lincoln mentioned . . . And he had to remember that a crisis presents both danger and opportunity . . .

His head lurched from the back of the chair and once he had his eyes open, he was startled to find Jim still sitting with him, the book of Emerson held in both hands on his lap. He had not blinked or moved for however many minutes or hours his President dozed.

"Yes, sir! How may I help you, sir?"

If anything grated on the President about having the new prototype mechanicals as staff and guards in the White House, it was the preprogrammed response: *Yes, sir. How may I help you, sir?*

"Could you go to the library and find me a book of letters written by Abraham Lincoln, the sixteenth President?"

"Certainly, sir." Jim put the Emerson on the side table and left the room. As he passed out the door, another mechanical entered to keep the President company. And guarded. She had been made in the image of a Hollywood sex goddess—very possibly the same movie star that had so captured the affections of Kennedy for all Myers knew—so that she would be pleasing to the eye, but she distracted him now as he paced, hands behind his back.

"Would you like some warm milk, sir? How may I help you, sir?"

"No, thanks. Just stand by until Jim returns. I'm thinking."

She turned her back to him and remained perfectly still, a statue that waits and watches to intercept danger. He glanced at her voluptuous hips rounded in the clinging cloth of her short dark blue suit skirt and looked away again. Distraction! He had a wife, he had his affairs, he had any man, woman, child, or roboticized female he wanted. There wasn't time tonight to ponder an assignation with the mechanical guard despite those alluring hip lines.

He put her from his mind, turned his gaze away, and paced.

Maybe the Have Nots, those pitiful poor, had raised the battle cry and seceded from the States because Myers' predecessor had not deemed it necessary to give every American his own mechanical. It would have bankrupted the country, perhaps, and they would have had to raise taxes on the rich, the Haves, but in the end could that have prevented the war? He, Myers, would give any number of his mechanicals away if it could stop this insanity raging across half the land.

Jim returned and the female departed. Jim said, "Is there a particular letter you wish me to read to you, sir?"

"Yes. It was written to Horace Greeley, August 22, 1862."

Jim checked the contents page and turned to the letter. He read it all, but what struck Myers as being salient was the passage that said, "My paramount object in this struggle is to save the Union, and is not either to save or destroy slavery. If I could save the Union without freeing any slave, I would do it; and if I could do it by freeing all slaves, I would do it; and if I could save it by freeing some and leaving others alone, I would also do that."

Myers asked for the book and sat in his chair to read the letter again to himself. Lincoln's appearance in his dream was telling him, as was Kennedy's, that the only way to save the nation was to put aside any thoughts of equality if that equality would not stave off dissolution. His problem was not slavery, but something quite close to it. If he could take from the rich and give to the poor to save the nation, he would do it. Or if he could institute real socialism and discard the republic, and that saved them, he would do it. Or if he must systematically dispose of all the Have Nots, as that old bugaboo Hitler disposed of races he found distasteful and disruptive, and *that* solution saved the country, he would even do that.

He must do whatever it took. How long did he have? When would the evil reincarnated assassin come from out of a crowd and take him down in blood?

He must hurry and try every solution, try them one by one if the Congress agreed. He was determined not to be the President who went down in history as having lost the country for good. No, never.

He put the book of letters aside and rose. Jim stood too. "How may I help you, sir?"

"Call for a special joint session of Congress. I want to address them at eight o'clock this morning." He consulted his wrist and saw that was but two hours away. He might as well dress and have his breakfast. He had to be firm and persuasive, at his tiptop best; everything depended on him.

He had been without sleep for three days. He and Congress wrangled like dominant male bears mad and penned together with no way out except through engagement. There were terrible clashes when he suggested all wealth be equally divided, doing away with the two-class system. They called him names no President should be called and he stood before them shaking with rage, his fist raised against them, threatening a veto on any bill passed to him unless they listened and compromised and tried to help him.

Then he put before them the next idea. They didn't have to redistribute the wealth overnight. What if they brought in a new form of government beneath the notice of the people? What if they did away with the Constitution, voted it out! Voted it null and void, and the Bill of Rights with it? Then they would sneak the new economy in on cat's feet and that way assure the Have Nots of a rising standard of living. Why, they had been sneaking away the rights of the people for generations, who would notice?

He asked them: How would you like to live in a cardboard box? How would you like to be underqualified and undereducated so that you could find no work?

Oh, but again the Majority Leader banged the gavel trying to restore order because the joint session growled and screamed and shouted such pandemonium that Myers thought they would mob the podium and string him up from the nearest railing.

On the third day, Myers called for order and brought forth the third possibility for saving the Union. His ace card.

"If you will not share what you have with the unfortunates, if you will not dispose of the government as we know it and institute new socialism, then I beg you, give me the funds to create crematoriums and let us proceed to rid the land of the revolutionaries, their families, their friends. All of them. All of the starving, raving, fighting Have Nots."

A silence as ringing as the lack of sound after thunder fell over the rotunda.

Myers slumped against the podium and Jim stepped forward to hold his arm so that he would not slip right to his knees. He was so tired his vision was doubling and his heart fluttered like a trapped butterfly. He had not wanted it to come to this. But he must remember Lincoln's words. That great President, that revered man, had been willing to keep the slaves if it resolved the conflict. Or let some go free and not others.

Myers was ready to go to any lengths, just as

Lincoln had been, and if the Congress did not approve of this one last plan, he had no other. They were lost.

Perhaps because they knew they were lost if they did not decide, first a murmuring and then a rising clamor arose from the Representatives and Senators. They came to their feet as a wave rushes into shore, and their hands came together in scattered applause that broke into unanimous clapping. Myers' ears hurt from the noise and he saw spots before his eyes.

He waved his arm for them to cease. It took ten minutes, but finally with the Majority Leader's help, the audience sat down like school children before a principal, their eyes glittering and happy. He had finally come up with a strategy they could live with and he was again their hero, their strong and capable leader.

"Then it is settled? This is what you want? That we destroy our dissenters? That we wipe them from the face of the earth in order to save ourselves and our country?"

He looked around and saw that this was so. This is what they wanted.

"We'll take a vote, then."

He turned wearily and let Jim help him leave the spot he had held onto by sheer stamina and willfulness for three days. His heart was heavy and yet content. Already the army was taking the lives of thousands in the skirmishes and battles being waged against the Have Nots. Half the cities in the interior of the country were shell-shocked into rubble.

This dedicated eradication would simply usher in the end by commanding more men in the field to take the captives to be burned to ashes.

He had saved the Union.

Hadn't he?

That night Myers sailed forth into sleep on a sturdy ship of complacency. It was not until after the midnight hour that the ghosts came to see him in his black vacuum of death sleep.

The sad-faced Lincoln took him by the arm and

walked him into a cold communal shower room. The water jets overhead spewed poison that made Myers cough until his guts felt as if they would come up his throat. "Let me out of here!" he screamed.

"This is what you've done?" Lincoln asked. "You would have it come down to the wholesale murder of your own people?"

"I thought . . . I thought . . . "

"You are not only a wicked man, but you are an ignorant wicked man, Mr. President."

Kennedy appeared and took hold of him. The concrete showers disappeared and Myers sat in a jet flying low over his beloved Washington, D. C.

"Do you see what you have done? How could you have thought this is what we meant to advise you?"

Down below the wing span Myers saw potholed streets, burning buildings, emptiness everywhere, no man or woman or mechanical anywhere to be seen. The city had been abandoned to the rats.

"This is the future? But how . . . ?"

Kennedy sighed and put a hand to his back as if it hurt him. "You turned what started out as a peaceful revolution against injustice into a violent revolution that took down innocent and guilty alike. This will be your reward. You must turn back. You must go again to the lawmakers and convince them not to go ahead with this ungodly idea."

Myers grieved as he saw the broken windows of the White House, curtains fluttering through the jagged glass. "This must be a lie," he said. "Cleaning out the dissenters is all we can do!"

The jet vanished, the presidential ghosts faded away, and Myers woke from the nightmare, the trailing fear causing his heart to pound hard and fast. He sat up in bed and tried to return to the world. As his eyes adjusted in the dark bedroom he saw someone poised at the foot of his bed. The person stood in shadow, a block of impenetrable black.

He whispered, "Who's there?"

"Yes, sir. How may I help you, sir?"

"Jim?"

Betty woke and said sleepily, "Donny? What is it?"

"Go back to sleep, Betty. It's just the guard." Myers swung his legs to the floor and put on his slippers. He took up his robe from where it lay over the end of the bed and moved toward Jim. As he did so, Jim turned and walked to the door and into the hall. Myers followed.

"What's wrong?" he asked. "You're not to wake me up. You know I don't get enough sleep as it is."

"You woke on your own, sir. I was just waiting, that's all."

"But why were you in our room, standing at the foot of my bed? Has there been a threat?"

"No sir. None that I know of, sir. That is the problem."

That's when Myers saw the weapon and the dream returned full force, the usual dream, the one where the assassin dove from out of the crowd to murder him. But there was no crowd, he was giving no speech, he was standing just outside his bedroom in the hall of the White House with his specially hand-picked and trained mechanical guard. Yet the gun was real and this was no dream, he knew that.

The truth dawned slowly and gave Myers such a start that he actually shivered as if he'd been dunked in a vat of iced water. "You're the assassin."

"Yes, sir. I'm sorry to have to be the one, but this was ordained before my time, before my memory was ever created. I am under orders, sir."

"Why now? You could have done away with me at any time."

"You've finally posed a threat the Have Nots cannot overcome, sir. We can have no President in the White House who would follow in the steps of the ancient madman it took this country to defeat. Until you happened upon this final solution, you were safe. Now you must be exterminated."

"Assassinated."

"Yes, sir."

"But the Congress ... they agree with me. They passed the vote."

"Without your leadership, it won't stand a chance. It will be overturned by your successor. No one but another madman would consider genocide a fair judgment, sir." Jim paused. "I suppose I should tell you that it would have worked. The Union might have been saved. Even madmen are brilliant in their madness. Unfortunately for you. We can't chance that, sir."

The gun was fitted with a long silencer and it did its job with little pfft-pffting sounds. Myers looked down at the burning in his chest, his eyes widening even as his heart stuttered and stalled and leaped again, trying to recover. He fell to his knees and crumpled over onto his side, hands to his wounds.

Jim stooped and watched him curiously, the gun hanging between his knees.

"Jim . . . "

"Yes, sir. How can I help you, sir?"

"Where did you come from? From the fiery deep, from hell, is that where you came from? Tell me."

"Yes, sir. The mind that programmed this event was transplanted from that place, sir. At least that is what I understand to be so."

"Then am I an evil man or are you an evil man? Tell me, which is it?"

"Does it matter, sir?" The mechanical reached out with the gun to squeeze off one shot into the President's forehead. He pulled down the lids on the dead man, rose, and left the White House.

Division was assured. Destruction was at hand. The people would now murder one another and a once great civilization would fall to plunder by invaders. If the government had followed President Myers' sanctions, only a portion of the people would have succumbed. This way, they all would. In the end.

It took three assassinations over a span of four hundred years to do it, but now, finally, it had been accomplished. Jim, the mechanical, moved through the quiet Washington neighborhoods tingling in all his electronic nerve ends, exploding with the mini-connections that continued to set off pleasure hits in his sophisticated chipset brain. He was doing something rare for a mechanical. He was smiling.

His Master would be so tremendously pleased with him, yes, sir. Hell would be a lively place tonight.

BUT SOMEWHERE I
SHALL WAKE

by Gary A. Braunbeck

Gary A. Braunbeck has sold over sixty short stories to
various mystery, suspense, science fiction, fantasy, and
horror markets. His first collection, *Things Left Behind*,
is scheduled for hardcover release this year. He has
been a full-time writer since 1992. He lives in Colum-
bus, Ohio, with his wife Leslie, and their two cats—
Tasha and "the Winnie"—to whom he is severely
allergic (the cats, not his wife) and must take tons of
drugs in order to be around, but loves them anyway.

> "That which is most unendurable in war, the awful,
> ordinary daily routine of war, is relegated to those
> dim regions of the mind where men hide all bad
> memories. But those memories survive, no matter
> how deeply buried, and sometimes they emerge."
> —Jean Larteguy

I

*The soldier standing in the entrance of the East
Room of the White house removed his helmet, ran a
trembling hand through his long-unwashed hair, then
set aside the rusted M2 Carbine rifle and pulled open
his battle-ruined coat. A wave of unspeakable foulness
filled the air.*

*A few feet away President James Albert Ryan, eyes
wide and unblinking, blanched as he covered the lower
half of his face with his right hand, clamping closed his
nostrils and breathing through his mouth.*

Beneath his coat the soldier's flesh had rotted off his

lower ribs and belly, and the clotted skin that still clung to the ribs and hipbones bordering the chasm was in a state of gelatinous putrescence. The President could easily see the soldier's spine through the hole, as well as shadowy clusters of internal organs. There were sutures on the soldier's intestines, and jagged paths of hasty, field-hospital stitching that almost, but not quite, drew your attention away from the groups of burned and discolored organic vessels bound together with translucent plastic strips in order to keep them from spilling out. Whenever the soldier drew in a breath, the black-tipped strips of flesh hanging from his rib cage fluttered like the ends of hair ribbons caught on a summer's breeze.

Wordlessly, the soldier reached into one of the pockets of his coat and removed a folded newspaper, brown and brittle with age, and tossed it at the President's feet. The paper fell open as it hit the floor, revealing the banner:

71st Infantry Division
RED CIRCLE NEWS

Augsburg, Germany

Volume 1, Number 6   September 2, 1945

"Does that mean anything to you, Mr. President?" asked the soldier, his voice grating, full of dirt.

"My father was part of the 71st in WWII."

"What about the date, sir? Do you recognize the date?"

*"... yes ..." choked Jim Ryan, slowly kneeling down to pick up the paper, which nearly came apart in his hand. "It was the day my father died in a hospital in Munich. I w–was ... I was three years old. I only knew the man through pictures my mother had and the stories she'd tell me." Pulling in a deep breath and holding it, he removed his other hand from his face and gently opened the front page of the paper to full size, his mind barely registering some of the headlines—**Division May Lose Four to Eight Thousand Low Point***

Men Shortly; Move of 14th Infantry Canceled; 5th Choir Set to Sing at Salzburg Fest; Polish DPs Leave Dilligen Lagers—before a small, badly focused photograph in the lower right-hand corner caught his attention.

Behind him, lining every wall, sprawled across every rug and stretch of grandiose carpeting, rammed into every corner, sitting or lying upon each step on each flight of stairs, were others as forever dead and lost as the soldier before him; wretched and worn people who had never known any of the good things in life, who'd ended their days in fear and desperate discomfort as war fell on their heads like a curse from heaven; bundled-up, patched-up, used-up people with lined faces too full of pain and minds too full of dim memories of a lifetime that had been too bleak; many of them were children, bleeding and starving, trembling hands reaching out from emaciated bodies as from outside came the cry of shells chasing each other across the sky, making sounds like cold wind through leaves on a winter's night; and, of course, there were the soldiers themselves—spirit-dead, grenade-blown, strafing-riddled, some with cigarette stubs hanging from the corners of their ruined mouths as they sat, arms crossed over knees, sightless eyes staring futilely at the hopeless night as they waited for the radio to squawk with new orders to take the next hill, push back the next line, hold the next position: from Manassas and Bull Run to Ypres and Messines Ridge, from the fall of Pusan to the Quang Tri Offensive, and from the delusional glory of Desert Storm to the tragedy of Bosnia, all of the dead—military and civilian—were represented.

They had come to speak to the President about matters of conscience.

They had come to speak of personal responsibility.

And they had come to talk about war. . . .

II

It started with the smell in the Oval Office.

Even someone who has never been close to a decomposing body can recognize the stench of a rotting animal without actually having to see the thing, and Jim Ryan was no exception; he'd come across enough dead mice in his time to know what they smelled like, and it was obvious to him that at least one—and possibly several—of the things had had the poor taste to expire inside the walls of the Oval Office near his desk. He urgently requested the General Services Administration to do something, but his request was declined because the GSA's responsibility (he was told) ended at the inside wall. Contacting the Park Service, the President was informed by a *very* nervous office clerk that the PS's responsibility ended at the *outside* wall.

"It's the same wall," shouted the President into the phone.

"Well, sir, no—it's actually not. When the Executive Wing was rebuilt in 1952, the wooden frame of the Oval Office was replaced by concrete and steel, and the overall circumference increased by something like fifteen or twenty yards. They made it bigger, but no one ever bothered to, uh . . . to rezone the boundaries that both the GSA and the Park Service are responsible for."

"So you're telling me that I've got about, oh, four or five feet of hollow space in parts of the wall that no one's responsible for maintaining, is that it?"

"Yes, sir."

"So if I want these dead mice removed from the wall, I'm either going to have to hire a private exterminator or go at it myself with a sledgehammer?"

"I don't know what to tell you, sir." The kid sounded almost in tears.

"It's all right, Carl, it's not your fault. You've been very helpful, not to mention informative, and I'll write a letter telling your supervisor just that."

"Th–thank you, Mr. President. It'll mean a lot."

"Well, it should; I *am* the boss, after all." *Or I used to think so,* he silently added.

Hanging up, he leaned back in his chair, looked at the pile of paperwork on the desk, then took a deep breath and immediately felt like dry-heaving; *Christ*, it smelled like a slaughterhouse in here!

At times like this, Jim Ryan remembered something Nietzsche was purported to have said: That there were times in life when things got so bad you either had to laugh or go crazy. And here he was, the President of the United States, faced with a country whose post-World War II utopian vision of endlessly rising incomes, stable jobs, declining racism, vanishing poverty, unlimited personal freedom, and a generously compassionate government had been mocked, compromised, then beaten and thrashed until all that remained was a perpetual, shapeless anxiety. At times it seemed as if each and every last person in the country felt overwhelmed by a roving discontent about threatened living standards, embattled social programs, selfish special interest groups, and race relations which were, at best, turbulent. If that weren't enough the third Election Year of the new century was just beginning, the polls showed that his popularity was slipping, and—as the icing on the cake—American troops were now engaged in a "military action" in east-central Africa. With all of this waiting to greet him upon waking every morning (when he was able to sleep through the night, that is), he'd just pissed away an hour of his time arguing with nine different people over a dead mouse.

So you either laugh or go crazy.

Jim Ryan opted for the former.

He buzzed his secretary, and she came through the doors a moment later. "Any luck, sir?"

"No," he said, rising to his feet and putting on his jacket. "I thought if I made the calls myself, *someone* would spring into action—if for no other reason than to win brownie points."

"And you were wrong?"

"I was wrong."

She made a note on her pad. "I'll have the Press Secretary alert the media."

"Are we through with the witty banter now?"

"I didn't realize that we'd started."

"This is not respect," said the President, straightening his tie, then taking a few folders from his desk. "I am going to my study. Please have my lunch sent there."

"What about the wall?"

Jim Ryan rubbed his eyes and exhaled. "Have someone go to a hardware store and buy a sledgehammer—no, make that three sticks of dynamite."

Gina laughed (but not all *that* much, he couldn't help but notice), then offered a sealed folder to him. "I hate to ruin your lunch before you've even had it, but this arrived from William MacIntyre's office a few moments before you buzzed me."

The President's face grew noticeably more solemn. William MacIntyre was the Assistant Secretary of Defense, and a sealed folder from his office these days meant only one thing: Casualty updates from Zahirain.

As soon as Jim reached for it, Gina's grip on the folder tightened slightly so that, for a few seconds, both of them were holding it. "I've got some friends over at Belinda Robertson's office; so don't worry about . . . you know."

"You're going to get someone from the Secretary of the Interior's Office to come over here and pull rodent corpses out of the wall?"

"Uh-huh. Promise."

Jim Ryan nodded, then gently but firmly pulled the file from her hand. "I'd appreciate it, Gina. That smell is making me sick." He looked down at the sealed file, then—without looking at her, asked: "Just between you and me, Gina, what do you think about this Zahirain situation?"

"I basically agree with the steps you've taken, Mr. President. The rebel forces over there have killed almost half-a-million people, and there're something like—what?—four million others who're starving to death in migrant camps because they can't get help."

Jim Ryan nodded. "Eighty million dollars' worth of food and medical supplies were either stolen or destroyed by the Rebels in the last two months. The UN Peacekeepers couldn't keep them at bay, and every goddamned main port is in their hands." He looked at her then. "Do you think I was right to send in ground troops?"

"Yes, sir, I do. And I really hate that you had to practically *beg* for Congress' support, and now they're pressuring you to withdraw the troops. No wonder you haven't been sleeping well—oops, I'm sorry, sir. That was out of line."

"No, it wasn't. You understand, don't you, Gina? This hasn't got a thing to do with politics or a show of muscle at the start of an election year. It's simple human decency."

"Yes, Mr. President, I understand. And I think it took a lot of guts to push for military intervention."

"It's easy to be courageous when you're not the one who's going to have to do the fighting." Then, putting on his best Chief Executive Yes-I've-Got-A-Lot-On-My-Mind-But-Can-Still-Be-Courteous smile, made his way through the offices.

III

The stench was in his study, as well.

If anything, it was even *stronger* here than in the Oval Office.

Still, at least it was spring and he could crack open a few of the windows and let in some fresher air.

His lunch tray was brought in, along with the day's newspapers, and for the next fifteen minutes, alone in his private study, Jim Ryan allowed himself to feel more like an Average Joe. He glanced around the room, savoring the moment. When he and Karen had moved in after the election, they agreed that it was vital to have some sense of normalcy to their lives, some way to escape the hectic Washington lifestyle of excess and pretense, and so they'd gone to some expense (at least a third of it out of their own pockets, to keep Congress happy) to remodel the second floor so it was more homey, the type of place where an Average Joe would feel comfortable; no Empire furniture, no Georgian ceilings, no gold damask draperies, no ornate chandeliers.

He wondered where Karen was, then realized that she'd said something about a speaking engagement at Georgetown University this afternoon—the Psychology Department, no less.

He smiled. One of the nice things about being married to a First Lady who also happened to be a licensed (but currently nonpracticing) psychiatrist was that no one dared play any head games when she was around, which was why Jim made it a point to have her present at all Cabinet meetings: her bullshit detector was flawless.

Pouring himself a cup of coffee, he shuffled through the newspapers, making it a point to ignore the headlines and op-ed pages. Today, he felt like the comics, or maybe a crossword puzzle, perhaps even—if he could muster the courage—an anagram or—

—he paused, staring at the newspaper at the bottom of the pile.

That it was old was easy enough to see; brown and brittle, many of the edges ripped and discolored, dark stains (*water or coffee,* he wondered) obliterating a column in the lower left of the first page—yes, old, no doubt, but the smell . . . *God*!

The thing reeked of death and decay, as if it had been pulled from a pile of rotting, burned bodies.

The President held his breath as he unfolded the paper—*The Red Circle News,* the official newspaper of the 71st Infantry Division.

He suddenly felt very cold.

With Veteran's Day less than two weeks away, it wasn't unusual for people to start hauling out their military memorabilia, but items from World Wars One and Two weren't so common anymore, seeing as how everyone who'd participated in both wars were long dead and gone, his own father included.

Frank Henry Ryan, who'd been part of the 71st.

The entire country knew that Jim Ryan had never met his father, that the man had been killed in Germany when the President was only three. Frank Ryan's death had emotionally crippled Jim's mother, who spent the rest of her life going in and out of various hospitals for treatment for severe depression. She had finally committed suicide three days short of Jim's twenty-first birthday. By then, Post Traumatic Stress Disorder was moving into the limelight, largely because of problems suffered by Vietnam vets, but almost no one had thought to address the problems being suffered by veterans of WWII and Korea, let alone the trauma inflicted on their families.

Jim had won the last election (according to analysts) largely on the basis of his proposed programs to aid "both financially and spiritually" the families of vets diagnosed with PTSD. Karen had been central to shaping his proposals, and his campaign had, in a backhanded way, been aided by the fact that the last five Presidents, either by choice or compromise, had steadily been cutting veteran's benefits.

Vets turned out in record numbers to support Jim Ryan, a man who had never been in the military, let alone endured the horror of combat.

"He understands what it's like for our families," one Vietnam vet had said. "That should count for something."

The words of that vet had been the catalyst for one of Ryan's strongest campaign slogans:

JIM RYAN FOR PRESIDENT
Understanding Should Count

He caught a glimpse of something in the middle of the far right column, gasped, then turned to one of the middle sections, coughing as bits and pieces of the aged paper flecked apart in his hands.

And there, halfway down page 5, just where the brief highlight box on the first page said it would be, was an article by none other than Ernie Pyle, the most widely-read correspondent of WWII and the first war correspondent to win the Pulitzer Prize, entitled:

FRANKLIN RYAN: A Tribute
71st Division, Darmstadt, Germany
Dec. 1945

Sometimes it's too easy in war to become numbed to the sight of cold dead men scattered on hillsides and lying in ditches; it's too easy to look at a soldier who has seen his closest friend destroyed by a grenade or land mine or machine-gun fire and say, "You'll get past this, son." We have seen too many dead men the world over, dead men in winter, dead men in summer, dead men by mass production, dead men in such familiar abundance they become monotonous.

At a special ceremony held outside Darmstadt Castle this past Sunday, members of the 71st Infantry Division paid tribute to their fallen soldiers, and as I stood there listening to the chaplain read off the names I was struck by the expressions on the faces of the soldiers present there; to many of them, the names were just that—names; but the chaplain had gone to the trouble of finding out something about each of the dead men, some little, insignificant, even forgetable detail about the man that might burn itself into the memories of those attending the ceremony so that a part of the dead men might live on. This is understandable, because a man dies twice when people forget he was here.

Of all the names read this day, only one stood out for me; not because the names of the others were less important, but because, unlike the others, this name was only a name: Franklin Ryan. No little anecdote about him, no insignificant bit of trivia, no forgettable detail: only his name.

No one seemed to notice; no one seemed to care.

And for the first time since this war began, I wept openly for a fallen GI.

And while I wept, I saw in my memory the faces of all the dead men I had encountered, saw them parade before me in such monstrous infinity I could almost hate them.

You at home can't hope to understand this, but of all the cold dead men of this war, I think I will mourn most the loss of Franklin Ryan, for no one knew him.

I was allowed a glimpse of his record. Before he died, Franklin Ryan had fought in Regensburg, Straubing, Reid, Lambach, Weis, and Steyer; he had crossed the Rhine, Danube, Isar, Inn, and Enns Rivers; and he had helped to liberate the concentration camps of Strubing and Gunskirken Lager. He was a loyal soldier. He was born and raised in Ohio. He never made it past the eighth grade because he had to go to work in the mills to help support his ailing mother and three younger siblings after his father abandoned them during the Great Depression. He worked at a dozen different factories before he married Mary Virginia Hards in 1936. The two of them lived in the same three-room apartment over a neighborhood grocery store until Frank was called to duty in '42. The only information of an intimate nature in Franklin's record was a brief, two-sentence notation made by the chaplain at Fort Bragg a few days before this man no one knew shipped out to war: "He wants to raise chickens for a living after he returns home. He feels bad that he can't leave more behind for his wife and mother."

I imagine he was a man accustomed to making sacrifices. I imagine he wasn't a saint (who among us is?), that he probably drank with his fellow infantrymen whenever liquor was around to be shared, that he smoked, and could easily curse a blue streak when his temper got the better of him. I imagine that he wrote to his wife when he got the chance and paper and pen were available. I imagine I can hear his voice as he talks with dreamy pride about the chicken farm he wants to start when he gets back home.

I imagine all of this, but I will never be sure, nor will anyone who didn't know the man. And it seems that no one really did, except for the wife and mother he left behind in Ohio.

The details of how he died are unclear. What is known is that a small detachment from his unit disappeared in the mountains of Eberstadt five months ago, and that Franklin—barely recognizable as human, but alive—was discovered by a group of Darmstadt children who were hiking up to Eberstadt to visit the famous Castle Frankenstein. If it had not been for his dog tags and fingerprints, Franklin Ryan might very well never have been identified.

He spent the last months of his life in a Munich hospital in a coma. He died without regaining consciousness. What happened to him and to the other men in his detachment will never be known.

When I get back to the States, I will go to Ohio and see if I can't find Mary Ryan. I hope she'll understand why. And I hope if there is a son or daughter that I will be able to look them in the eye and say, truthfully, "I knew your father about as well as anyone. He was a good man and you should be proud."

The war is over. In the joyousness of high spirits it is easy for us to forget the dead. Those who are gone would not wish to be a millstone of gloom and sorrow around our necks. Franklin Ryan probably wouldn't want that, either; he would want to be remembered with warmth and affection. I am reminded of part of a poem by WWI soldier Rupert Brooke; I like to think Franklin Ryan would have enjoyed it, would have understood what Brooke was getting at, would even perhaps want it to be read over his grave as his widow's tender hands placed roses at the base of his headstone:

*—Oh, never doubt but, somewhere, I shall wake,
And give what's left of love again, and make
New friends, new strangers . . . But the best I've known
Stays here . . .*

Jim Ryan slowly and calmly placed the paper on top of his tray, then sat back and stared at the words.

He felt so very, very cold.

He blinked, wiped his eyes, and reached for the sealed envelope.

The stench of death was heavy in the room.

IV

The afternoon briefing (held in the Cabinet Room because of the stink in the Oval Office) did little to ease the President's anxiety.

Not only had the U.S. ground forces lost another twenty-seven soldiers to Rebel attacks, but sources inside the Zahirain capital were reporting that a large shipment of arms intended for government forces had been intercepted by the Rebels and that U.S. soldiers were facing the very real prospect of being fired upon by American-made weapons as well as Kalashnikov rifles of Russian, Eastern European, and Chinese manufacture, Soviet RPG-7 rocket-propelled grenades, AT-3 "Sagger" antitank missiles, Chinese "Red Arrow" antitank missiles, and mortars ranging from 82-millimeter to 102-millimeter. Though possessing far less manpower than the combined U.S. and NATO forces, the Rebels were now nearly as heavily armed, and had blown up no fewer than three ports, making supply drops even more dangerous than they had been in the first place. Outbreaks of cholera and other diseases in the migrant camps had wiped out nearly all the medical supplies; even basics such as bandages and peroxide were scarce. Another supply drop was scheduled for Thursday, but whether or not U.S. military vehicles would be able to get safely through the blockades Rebels had placed on the road which linked Zahirain to the Uganda-Kenya railroad system—the only viable option, since the port of Mombasa had fallen—was still to be seen. It didn't look very promising—unless, of course, U.S. soldiers staged a full-scale offensive to take back the main supply road—an action that would leave, conservatively, at least two hundred American soldiers dead.

Jim Ryan's advisers made it clear to him that there were now only two choices; he must either withdraw ground forces from Zahirain or "escalate considerably" U.S. military presence.

When the briefing was finished, the President buzzed Gina and asked if Larry Seagrove had gotten back yet.

"Yes, sir; he's waiting out here."

"Send him in."

There was a knock on the door, and a moment later there entered a lanky man in his mid-30s whose steady, quiet control, red hair, freckles, and boyish grin might cause one to dismiss him as a computer geek or CPA, an office gofer, meek as lamb, harmless as fly. You couldn't be more wrong. Larry Seagrove, friend and White House Secret Service agent, was easily one of the deadliest men ever to be allowed near the President. Rumor had it that he knew over sixty ways to kill a person without leaving a mark on their body; he was an expert marksman, first-rate bodyguard (who on many occasions seemed to possess eyes in the back of his head), electronics expert, computer hacker (read: former geek), avid Buster Keaton fan, and had no qualms whatsoever about performing any task the President asked—including those other agents would consider "flunky" work.

"Mr. President," said Seagrove, closing the doors behind him and standing there as if someone had just stuck a gun in his back and told him to act natural.

"Anything on that damned paper?" asked the President.

"Yes, sir." He made no move to either open or present the folder he was holding.

Jim gestured for Seagrove to take a seat. "I gather from the pallbearer expression on your face that the news is going to upset me?"

Clearing his throat as he sat down, Seagrove blinked and said, "I think it's safe to say that, yes."

Jim rubbed his eyes, took a deep breath *(Jesus—was he going crazy or was the smell spreading over here, as well?),* poured himself a glass of water, and said, "Let's have it."

Seagrove opened the folder and began. "The paper itself is authentic, sir. The lab results confirm that it's at least seventy-five years old, but they won't speculate as to why it hasn't deteriorated worse than it has. That particular stock of paper was highly acidic and almost none of it is still in existence."

"Fine, so they've established that it's a newspaper. What else?"

"The 71st Infantry Division *did* have an official newspaper, and it *was The Red Circle News,* produced in Ausburg, Germany. We cross-checked all of the information contained in the various articles with everything in the Pentagon's computer, as well as the FBI's and other—"

"—yeah, yeah, yeah," said the President, his impatience growing. "I know about the paper, all right? My father used to send his old copies to my mom when he was overseas before he was . . . was killed."

Seagrove nodded his head. "There's a lot of information in here, sir. Maybe it would be easier if you told me what you specifically want to know."

"The stains on the first page."

"Blood. O negative. At least seventy-five years old."

"How did the paper get onto the tray?"

"We don't know. We've questioned all the staff members twice and will be questioning them again in the—"

"—absolutely not. I won't allow it. Twice is enough. If no one knows how it got there, no one knows."

"We examined videotape from all security cameras, Mr. President. As far as I was able to see, there were only the usual four newspapers placed on your lunch tray."

"What else?"

Seagrove stretched his neck as he slightly loosened his collar. "It's about the article."

"The basic information in it is the truth. That's all Mom or I ever knew about how Dad died. You know what's been bugging the shit out of me, though? She never showed me that article. She showed me all the other old editions of the paper that she had, but she never—"

"—she *couldn't* have shown you that article, sir."

"Why not?"

"We contacted the Weil Journalism Library at Indiana University in Bloomington. All of Pyle's wire copy, every last dispatch, is housed there in its complete and uncensored form. The article about your father is not part of that collection. It couldn't have been. Ernie Pyle was killed at Ie Shima, Okinawa on April 18, 1945. He'd been dead eight months when the 71st held that memorial service in Darmstadt."

Jim Ryan made a fist and pulled in a deep breath, his eyes watering at the ever-strengthening stench. "So it's a phony?"

"I don't know."

The President glared across the table at Seagrove. "Why don't you unclench, Larry, and just tell me what's on your mind?"

"I don't understand how it could be possible for someone to fabricate a piece like this. The paper, the ink, the style of typeset used, all of it's authentic, and all of it's as old as it should be if it was published during WWII—except there's no *if* to factor in here. This is from 1945, there's no doubt. But Pyle's death was major news that year; it would have been impossible for another correspondent to fabricate an article by him." He closed the folder, then leaned forward.

"Not only that, sir, but I personally scanned the 71st's CD files for a complete set of *The Red Circle News* editions, then located Volume 7, issue 3."

"And . . . ?"

"The article about your father never appeared, not in that edition or any other *Red Circle News* published in 1945. It would seem that the only copy of that article in existence is the one you read this afternoon."

"Do you . . . do you know where it is?"

"Yes, sir," said Seagrove, reaching to the back of the folder and removing the article, which had been carefully cut out of the paper, then laminated. "I thought perhaps you'd like to keep it."

"I would, even if it isn't supposed to exist," whispered Jim Ryan, taking the article and reading it once again.

"It sounds as if he was a good guy, your father."

"Does, doesn't it?" Jim placed the article on the table and stared at it. "He never saw me. I always used to wonder what he'd think of me now. Still do, sometimes."

"I think it'd make any man proud, to see his son grow up to become President."

"I can hope. Maybe he'd have some opinions about what I should do." He looked at Seagrove. "What about you, Larry? This has been my day for soliciting opinions about Zahirain. Do you have one?"

"It's not my place to—"

"—oh, for chrissakes, I'm not going to have you reassigned or fired if you don't agree with me. I just want some opinions that're free of PolitiSpeak. I'd like to hear what you have to say."

Seagrove thought for a moment, then said, "It seems to me, sir, that the same people who're screaming for your head, who say that we've got no business being over there, are the same ones who go to dinner parties and in order to show that they're deep thinkers ask questions like, 'How in the world could people back in WWII allow something like the slaughter of six million Jews to happen?' That's all I care to say about it, if you don't mind."

"You're not a political person, are you, Larry?"

"I share your views, sir. Do you remember a speech you made back in 1998 when you were running for Governor in Ohio?"

"Good God, Larry—I can barely remember what I said to the First Lady at breakfast this morning, let alone a speech I made—"

"You said, 'All problems confronting the human race are and always shall be at their core *moral ones,* matters of conscience, human decency, and compassion; they only become *political issues* when someone or a large group of someones can gain wealth, power, fame,

or real estate—preferably all four—by exploiting them.'
I never forgot that one."

"I said that?"

"Yes, you did, sir."

"Karen must've written that speech."

"That's what the First Lady claims, sir."

"Thanks, Larry. For everything."

"You're welcome, Mr. President."

V

In the haze he thought he heard the screaming.

He knew he felt the tingling; the soft, almost pleasant tingling sensation right between his eyes that quickly spread, becoming painful: a box of needles thrown into his face.

That's when he knew it was coming.

The corkscrew, as he'd come to think of it.

It was 3:47 in the morning and for the fifth night in a row Jim Ryan was afraid he was going to die in his sleep.

Wake up, come on! some part of his mind cried, but like all the other nights the rest of his brain failed to heed the command.

Not this, God, please, not again, not—

Corkscrew.

Twisting, turning, drilling through his forehead until it broke through the bone and hit the gray matter, eating away at every nerve in its path, cramping his body into a tight ball, knees against his chest as the pain gripped and squeezed until he could feel something seeping from his ears, running down his cheeks, staining the pillows, always constant, hungry, insatiable, and he tried to move, tried to open his eyes and force it away—but he couldn't make it stop as it snarled and chewed and ravaged its way to the back of his skull where it paused, teasing him, before probing like a dentist's tool against the exposed pulp of a tooth, scraping, clawing, snagging against a nerve-ending and locking him rigid as it rammed forward to explode out the back of his head, vomiting out bits of skull and clumps of his brain, leaving him—

—*on that damned snow-covered mountain road in Eberstadt, crammed in the back of the transport truck with the other GIs in the unit, a few of them passing around bottles of some cheap wine, and as the tarpaulin flap snapped against the wind, he caught sight of that decrepit castle looming in the distance, then he looked toward the front and saw through the grimy windshield that there was a dog sitting in the middle of the road staring at the truck as it approached and he shouted something at the driver, Lou, who was too busy chugging on a bottle of his own to notice the animal, so the President rose to his feet and made his way through the men, stuck his head out one of the side flaps, and banged a gloved fists against the driver's door, trying to get Lou's attention—*

—tingling, hot, hard to breathe—

—*but Lou just laughed and told the President to sit his ass down, then looked out and saw the dog and laid on the horn like it would do any good—*

—another blast of pain, another box of needles tossed into his face with the force of a storm wind—

—*and the truck skidded, then fishtailed and lurched sideways, hit a patch of ice, flipped three times and soared over the edge of the cliff, everyone screaming at once, helmets and gear and mussette bags and stray cans of C-rations flying all over the damned place as the truck plummeted downward, slicing through the air upside-down, wind howling through the flaps before the whole tarpaulin was ripped away by the force, bodies slamming against one another and glass shattering—*

—"Jim? Jim, c'mon, honey, wake up."

He rolled over, shuddered, and opened his eyes.

Karen was there, sitting on the edge of the bed, a glass of water in one hand, two small white pills in the other.

Jim Ryan smiled at her. "How did you know?"

The First Lady sighed, smiled, then handed him the water and aspirin. "For the last four nights—five, now—you've woke at the same time from the same nightmare with the same headache. Will the aspirin be enough? I could call for some Tylenol 3—codeine, your favorite."

"Oh, right; kill the headache and leave me looking hungover. I can see the headlines now: 'Your President, The Morning After: Is This Leadership?' "

"You can't be feeling *too* bad if you can come up with a pithy reply like that."

"*Pitiful* would be more accurate."

Karen leaned in and kissed his cheek. "How far did it go this time?"

"The truck had just gone over the cliff."

"Thank God!" She saw the look he gave her, then added: "At least they hadn't started in on the bodies yet."

Jim shrugged. "I suppose."

They looked at each other. A silent parade of memories passed between them, warm and comforting, momentarily making the President forget the bitter taste of terror coating the inside of his mouth.

Karen waited while he took the aspirin, then she reached over and squeezed his hand. "Tell me the whole thing again. Start wherever you want."

"You've heard about it enough already."

"No, I haven't. You just *think* I have. Whether you've noticed it or not, every time you've talked about the nightmare you've brought up something you didn't remember before. So tell me about it."

The President said nothing, only sat on the edge of the bed staring at the doors which led to the second-floor terrace of the South Portico; it might be nice to slip on his robe and slippers and go out there for some cold fresh air, to stand in winter silence and see the Jefferson Memorial and the Potomac in diffuse 4 a.m. light. Harry Truman had had the right idea when he added the balcony in 1948; the President needed a place that was both open and private where he could collect his thoughts and be reminded that there was more to the world than violence and duplicity and a Congress that wanted your head on a platter and a nation that didn't much like you at the moment and starving children trapped in disease-ridden camps and newspaper articles that shouldn't exist written by a famous war correspondent eight months after he was killed . . .

He was still lost along these lines of free-floating anxiety when Karen put a hand on his shoulder and said, "I take it from the silence that we're having a Marcel Marceau moment?"

"Working on my Boo Radley imitation, actually." He turned and kissed her, then lay back, his head cradled in her lap. "All right, here goes: I'm crammed in the back of this truck with a bunch of other soldiers and we're driving along a mountain road somewhere in Germany—"

"—Eberstadt," prompted the First Lady.

"Right, Eberstadt. We've got these bottles of some godawful wine that we're drinking, passing around, and I look over and see that this dog's sitting in the middle of the road up ahead. I get up and move toward the front and try to get Lou's attention but he tells me to sit my ass down—only it's both me and not me he's talking to; I'm there in someone else's body but everyone still thinks I'm this guy, whoever he is."

"I think we both know who it is."

Jim sighed, shaking his head. "I know you went through the textbook explanation for it, but I still find it hard to believe that I've invented this scenario to explain what happened to my dad."

"Do *you* have any guesses?"

"Yeah, but they all sound like ideas Rod Serling would've used on *The Twilight Zone*."

"Go back to the dream. I don't want you to lose anything because I sidetracked you."

"Fine. Lou looks over and sees the dog and lays on the horn and slams down on the brakes, we skid, the truck flips and goes over the side, and the next thing I know I wake up pressed between all these bodies. It takes a few minutes for full lucidity to return to me, but when it does I realize that most of the bones in my body are broken, and that all the guys on top of me and beside me and underneath me are dead. It's cold outside the wreckage of the truck—ten, fifteen below zero—and the only thing that's keeping me from freezing to death is all the dead bodies. And as I'm lying there the thing that keeps going through my mind is: *What were we doing here in the first place?*

"Then the dog comes down the side of a hill formed by a secondary mountain road—more of a foot-trail, really—and I manage to move my head enough to see that there are men following the dog, and that they're dressed in black uniforms, and then I remember we'd been tracking a band of renegade SS officers through part of the Black Forest along the Rhine for I don't know how long—a week, ten days, maybe longer—and they'd led us right into the mountains outside Darmstadt. But that doesn't much matter now because I can see that not only are these guys bughouse crazy but they're drunk as hell and screaming for Ally blood.

"They start dragging bodies out of the wreckage and mutilating them, cutting off hands, slicing up faces, plucking eyes out of their sockets and ripping flaps of skin away from bone, then throwing everything into this . . . *pile*. I've got my eyes open and I can't blink, I don't dare to because if they knew I was alive they'd rip me to pieces, torture me to death, cut me up into bite-sized chunks and feed me to that dog. The worst part, though, is my breathing; I have to breathe slow and quietly, so they don't notice any movement in my chest area. I'm okay for a little while because they've still got a few layers of bodies to go, but then two of them grab onto me and toss my body out into the snow, and while they're looking away I blink and take in a deep breath and have just enough time to figure out they're piling everything up for a human bonfire because the rest of the bodies and body-parts are drenched in gasoline . . .

"A few other bodies are tossed on top of me, and I can hear the SS officers laughing. It gets really quiet—it's not just the absence of sound, it's the absence of *spirit*, as well; like my soul has decided to abandon ship before the thing goes down in flames. Then I feel the heat and smell the burning uniforms, the searing flesh and guts—God, it's awful! I can't hear anything because of the crackling of the flames and some of the smoke is starting to snake downward between the bodies, so now I'm trying like hell not to cough or choke or throw up because a few of the more mutilated bodies start falling apart and I can see through the spaces that the SS officers are still there, but that's *not* the thing that tells me in no uncertain terms that I'm dead because in the distance behind them I see Lou scrambling up the side of the hill and then throwing himself face-down onto the foot-trail, and I know that he's all right, that he's been hiding, waiting for his chance to escape and for a second I feel happy for him because it was a miracle he wasn't killed, let alone badly hurt, but then . . . then I get angry because *he's* going to be safe and I'm not, I want to live, too, and by then I figure there's nothing to lose, so I scream, I scream for all I'm worth for him to come back and get me, to take out that pistol he always carries and shoot these murdering Nazi bastards and put out the flames before they get . . . get to me, and it's so loud, my screaming, I know it's loud because the SS officers are pulling me out of the pile and throwing me aside and I can hear my skin *hissing* as the flames are snuffed out by the ice and snow and pretty soon all I can see are black uniforms and rotted teeth, and all I can feel is something cold and sharp slicing slowly along my jaw, and all I can hear is the sound of someone screaming *No! No!* over and over, but I don't know if it's me or not . . .

" . . . and then I wake up."

"Jesus." Karen brushed some hair back from his forehead, leaned down, and kissed him.

"Yeah." Jim sat up, put on his slippers, then crossed

over to the antique Victorian wardrobe and removed his evening robe. "It doesn't take a Jungian scholar to figure this one out."

"I think you're oversimplifying it a bit," said Karen.

The President shot his wife an irritated glance. "Really? In a little under twelve hours I have to go on television and tell the country that we need to either withdraw our troops or escalate our military efforts in Zahirain. Christ, honey! Sixty-seven percent of the people don't think we should be over there, anyway, and now I have to tell them this less than a day after the latest casualty figures have been released. I'll be surprised if someone doesn't try to shoot me before the week's over!"

"Don't say things like that," whispered Karen, her eyes unblinking.

Jim realized that he'd just crossed the Line with her.

Karen Ryan was an outstanding First Lady, graceful, courteous, and—if the polls were to be believed—much more popular at the moment with the American people than her husband. The role of First Lady had been greatly expanded over the last several decades; whereas the President's wife was once little more than stage dressing, the position now held a great deal of unspoken power; she not only served as an adviser to her husband, but served as the White House's #1 PR person, pushing not only its agenda but her own personal one, as well. The fact that Karen Ryan was a psychiatrist made her even more imposing in the eyes of the people, as well as nearly every member of the government. Jim was well aware that he sometimes used her as a shield when things got too hot for him, and she was always willing to stand in front of him in order to give him a chance to catch his breath—on the understanding that, when they were alone, he never make jokes about their personal safety.

Karen Ryan, at age four, had been with her parents in Dallas the day John Kennedy was shot, had, in fact, been standing along the parade route; she'd been less than fifteen yards away when part of Kennedy's skull blew backward. She'd never forgotten the sight, and her one "rule" was that Jim never make cracks about assassination.

"I'm sorry, honey," said Jim. "That was uncalled for."

"Goddamn right it was," she said, leaning back against the headboard. "All right, if you're having problems with the 'textbook' explanation, then let's go back to Psych 101 and try the sixth-grade Readers' Digest version: You don't know what to do about Zahirain, fine; you also don't know what happened to your father in Germany; the casualty reports from Zahirain have been pretty specific about how the soldiers were killed: ergo, you have taken some of those graphic details, unconsciously projected them onto your father's missing history, and have created a scenario that's manifesting itself in your dreams. Don't look at me like that—I know it's a shitty theory, but you look like you need a straw to grasp at."

He came over to the bed and kissed her. "You're right, it's pretty lame."

"It's also a quarter after four in the morning and you're not being charged, so you'd damned well better take what you can get."

He looked into her eyes and almost told her about the newspaper article but decided not to; despite his more pragmatic instincts, Jim had a sense that something more was going on here than anyone could easily explain.

"I think I'm going to go to the study for a while, putter around for a bit, and see if I can't relax."

"I think that sounds like a good idea. Want some company? Puttering's more fun with two."

He kissed her again. "No. Some things a man has to do alone."

"That's a lousy John Wayne."

"I was trying to do Gary Cooper."

"Oh. Thank God you never wanted to be an actor."

VI

The first thing that hit him upon entering his study was the smell of cigarette smoke.

The second thing was the harsh clacking of someone pounding away at the keys of a manual typewriter.

Then a soft hand was placed on his shoulder and Jim Ryan spun around to see his mother standing next to him.

" . . . oh god . . . "

"Shh," said Mary Ryan, smiling. "You don't need to be afraid, hon. Now you just go over there and have a sit-down and I'll fix you some tea."

He couldn't speak. Everything within him knew that this was his mom, but not the worn-out, beaten-down, used-up emotional zombie he'd known through his adolescence; this was Mom the way she looked in all the old photos, the way she'd been when he was three: Demure, almost girlish, vibrant and alive.

He moved to embrace her, but she stopped him with a hand against his chest. "I'm sorry, hon, but you can't touch me. I can touch you and you'll feel it, but if you try to touch me, you'll just get yourself a bunch of air."

"The word you're looking for," said a voice from the other side of the study, "is 'ghost.' You're a ghost, Mrs. Ryan, so why not just say it?"

" 'Cause it sounds silly, that's why," she snapped at the unseen typist. "Not everybody has your way with words, Mr. Pyle."

"You can say that again." The feverish typing began anew.

Jim felt tears in his eyes and forced himself to not cry; if he allowed anything to obscure his vision right now, she might vanish and he didn't want that; there were so many things he had to say to her, so many things he wanted to know.

"You comin' or do I have to send a written invitation?" said Ernie Pyle, crushing out his cigarette and lighting a fresh one.

Jim stood rigid until his mother pressed a hand

against his back and started to gently push him in the direction of his desk. "Don't you worry," she said. "I'm not going anywhere. You can blink, you can cry if you want, you can even take a nap and I'll still be here when you wake up."

She pushed him down into a chair opposite his desk where Ernie Pyle sat pounding out a story on an ancient black typewriter, using the two-finger method of the self-taught.

"So you liked my piece about your dad, did you?"

"Y–yes, I did. Very much." He rubbed his eyes, then said, "So you *did* write it?"

"Hell, yes. Damn good thing your buddy had it laminated for you. Stories don't come any more exclusive than that."

"What are you . . . what are writing now?"

"The speech you're gonna give on TV tomorrow night. Looks pretty good so far—ah, who'm I kidding? It's gonna be great. Hell, you'll be right popular again." He stopped typing for a moment, read a few passages to himself, then smiled. "Y'know, if they'd had TV when I was around, I could've been a star. Shoulda kept my head down in the foxhole. Ten seconds. I'd waited another ten seconds before poking my mug up, I'd've lived to be an old man."

Jim looked from Pyle to his mother. "Why . . . why are you here? What's going on?"

"Well, hon," said Mary Ryan, handing him a cup of tea and two Fig Newtons (his favorite late-night snack), "you're having some trouble making an important decision. We just decided to give you a little help."

"I got two versions of your speech here," said Pyle, pulling the sheet from the roller and laying it on the desk. "In the first one, you tell everybody that you're pulling the troops out. In the second one, you announce escalation. Trust me on this: whichever way you go, I'll be damned surprised if 90% of the country don't rally to your support."

Jim said, "But I—"

"Don't say anything," said Pyle. "You're not on the

same plane as us, and we can do things you can't. Give you an example—I got three thousand dispatches I wrote about Vietnam that're being read in a world just to the side of this one. Over there, just to the side, your dad made it out of Germany alive and your mom is livin' a long and happy life by his side. Move a little to the side in *that* world, and you'll be in one where I *did* live to write that piece about your father when he *didn't* make it out of the war. Good thing you recognized the value of that piece, Mr. President; it traveled a helluva long way to get into your hands."

"And in the world where your dad lived, you *still* became President," said Mary. "I think that's nice."

"We're getting off the point here," said Pyle. "We've got to deal with what's going in *this* world, right now. You know full well, Mr. President, that whatever you decide, a lot of people are going to die. Can't be helped. It's the way of war, goddammit."

"People're going to die," said Mary Ryan from behind Jim's chair as she put her hands on his shoulders. "That doesn't make you their killer."

"Then why does it feel that way?" whispered Jim.

" 'Cause you're the President, that's why," said Pyle. "When you took this office, you agreed to shoulder all the responsibility that comes with it, and this Zahirain business is part and parcel of that responsibility. You don't create the evil of war, but it's on your shoulders to deal with it. You just have to go back to your core, son, and see what beliefs have survived the last fifty years. Forget all the doubletalk and hot air that's getting blown up your—"

Mary Ryan cleared her throat.

"Sorry," said Pyle. "Forget all the hot air that's being blown in your face; you once said that all problems are a matter of conscience, and that's not changed one whit. What you have to do is look into your conscience without dragging Jim Ryan, the politician along with you."

"I don't know if I can still do that."

Mary patted his cheek. "We kind've figured that, so it was decided that there's something you need to see."

"Go out the door and just follow along. We'll still be here when you're done."

"We'll be around until whatever in Zahirain is over," said Mary, pulling Jim to his feet and kissing his cheek. "But don't tell anyone. They'll say you're nuts. And you're not. I know all about being nuts."

"You were so sad."

"I loved your dad very much, Jimmy. I always will. Now, get on your way, there's a lot to do before everyone else wakes up."

"By the way, Mr. President," said Pyle, rising to his feet and extending his hand. "I want you to know that it's a great honor to meet you. You're doing a fine job, in my opinion."

"Ernie," said Mary. "He can't take your hand."

"Oh, right." So Pyle took hold of the President's hand and shook it vigorously.

Jim Ryan smiled.

Pyle had a good, strong, trustworthy grip.

VII

Beyond the study doors, the White House was clogged with bodies; Jews with flayed flesh hanging by their ankles from small gallows, Japanese citizens with nuclear-blast tumors covering every inch of their bodies, Vietnamese children with skin seared by napalm, Bosnian refugees wasted away by disease and starvation, Union soldiers whose torsos had been ripped open by 6-pounder cannon charges.

And the smell of death was everywhere.

One by one, the bodies of war's victims became animate, pointing the President along his way, guiding him through a White House he barely recognized any longer.

The dead guided him through hundreds of years of war as he walked along, and as he passed each one, they whispered to him their names, names that had been recorded in no books, names lost to history under the dirt of graves or piles of rubble.

And Jim Ryan found that he was able to remember each one.

At last he found himself standing before the entrance to the East Room, facing a gutted soldier who tossed a copy of *The Red Circle News* at his feet.

"Do you recognize the date?" asked the soldier.

" . . . yes . . . " choked Jim. "It was the day my father died in a hospital in Munich. I w–was . . . I was three years old. I only knew the man through pictures my mother had, and the stories she'd tell me."

"Then it's time you two met," whispered the soldier, gesturing for the President to follow him into the East Room.

At the far end of the room stood an opened doorway, one that hadn't been there before.

The soldier handed the President a flashlight. "You'll need this, sir." Then he stood back and gave the President a salute. Jim Ryan returned it, then fired up the flashlight and stepped through the doorway and began his descent down the winding stone stairway.

Without having to look behind him, he knew the dead were following him.

He reached the bottom of the stairway and stepped into a massive stone chamber. There was light down here, but he couldn't see the source.

He couldn't see anything except his father, who stood next to a large podium upon which lay a massive ledger, opened to a blank page.

Jim walked very slowly toward the man he had never known, his heart triphammering against his chest.

"Hello, Jimmy," said Franklin Ryan. "It's nice to finally meet you."

Jim couldn't help it, he didn't care what Mom and Ernie Pyle had told him, he *had* to touch the man, had to know he was real, so he threw aside the flashlight and ran across the room and threw his arms around his father—

—and felt nothing but emptiness.

And for a moment it all came forward, the aching loneliness of all the years without a father there to guide him, to scold him, to take him to movies or baseball games or parking-lot carnivals in summer, and the sadness was joined by rage at the loss, selfish rage, that they should have been born into a world where people were more than willing to slaughter one another for land or power or increasingly abstract ideologies, and as Jim Ryan pulled away from the ghost of his father, the only thing that mattered to him was that he hated the idea of condemning children and families all over this country to the same legacy of grief that he and his mother had known, and maybe it would be easier if something called the American Spirit still existed. But it didn't, it probably never really did, was just a colorful phrase written down a few hundred years ago by legislators so they'd feel better about sending men off to die, but, goddammit, if not them, then someone else would have to do the dying, and why in hell was he thinking about this when his father was standing right here in front of him and—

"Get a hold of yourself, Jimmy," said Franklin Ryan, putting his arms around his son, and this time Jim did feel his father's embrace, and drew strength from it.

"Hi, Dad."

"Hi, yourself." Pulling back, Franklin said, "I'm sorry about the dreams, son. But I know you've been wondering for years what exactly happened to me. It was time you knew."

"It must've been . . . horrible for you."

Franklin shrugged. "Actually, once that first bastard cut my throat, I didn't feel much of anything. I was unconscious for most of it. All things considered, I'm kind of glad I didn't wake up. I guess they dragged me along for a few miles before they got bored and just dumped me. By the time them kids found me, there'd been another snow that caused an avalanche back by the truck. All them other guys was buried pretty deep. Funny thing is, they still ain't been found. Lou, the fellah upstairs that gave you the paper?—I thought for the longest time that he got away, but he didn't. Dumb-ass got to feeling all guilty about running away and come back about an hour later, just in time to run right smack into those SS soldiers. They got him with a grenade, then went at him with their knives. Poor guy was awake for most of it. Terrible thing."

"Dad, what's—no, please, don't—don't let go of my arm. Sorry, I like the feel of your hand."

"Don't apologize. Don't make you any less a man in my eyes. In fact, I kind of like it."

"What's going on here? What is this place? That book?"

"This place, son, is where War sleeps in times of peace. That book is the Ledger of the Forgotten Ones. C'mere, take a look." Franklin led Jim over to the ledger and flipped back several of the pages; each page was easily three feet wide and four feet long, and contained thousands of handwritten names.

As he read down the columns, Jim noticed that the handwriting changed every so often.

Then, on the last few pages, he recognized the handwriting.

The flowery script was that of Edward Lee Montgomery, his predecessor.

"Getting the idea, are you, son?"

"I'm . . . I'm not sure."

The dead were surrounding them now, lifeless eyes gaining light.

"Every President who's held office since the White House was built has been guided down here eventually," said Franklin Ryan. "It is the President's very private, very secret responsibility to catalog the names of the forgotten dead of war. Not just the American soldiers, but the names of those soldiers they were fighting, as well, and those of war's innocent victims; the children, the old folks, the families, all of them. For every name of a dead one that's been written down, there's another one that no one's ever known about. That has to be corrected, son."

"Why?"

Franklin Ryan's face grew still and serious. "Because on the day that the number of names in this book equals the number of names of war's *recorded* dead, the War will return to this chamber, lay down its head, and sleep for the rest of time. Pick up that pen, son, and do your duty to the dead.

"Not just *these* forgotten dead, but those that *have* to follow them in order to achieve the balance. Do you understand what I'm telling you?"

"Yes, Dad, I do."

Franklin sadly shook his head. "I feel for you, son, I really do."

"There never *was* a choice about what to do, was there?"

"You don't really need me to answer that, do you?"

"No," said the President, taking pen in hand. "No, I don't." Then he laughed. "The country's going to want to hang me out by my short and curlies."

"Not after you give that speech Ernie wrote for you. You're gonna make history with that thing, son. *Damn,* son, I'm proud of you. You made my dying count for something."

The first of the Forgotten Dead, a Japanese girl no older than four, stepped up to the President and gave her name: Matoko. He wrote it down.

Just as she was turning away, Jim said, "Matoko?"

"Yes, sir?"

"Would you mind ... telling me something about yourself? Something you want people to remember?"

She thought about it for a moment, then said, "I made very good bamboo dolls. They were pretty like my mother."

Jim smiled, and wrote down those words next to her name.

"Why'd you do that?" asked his father.

"Because something like that needs to be here, Mr. Chicken Farmer."

His father smiled, clapping Jim on the shoulder. "It won't be long, son. You may not live to see it in your lifetime, but it won't be long. I'm just sorry that you'll have to keep it to yourself . . . and that so many people are still gonna have to die."

"I understand," said the President, turning to the next person and asking him his name.

"All of us understand," said the soldier named Lou.

"That's good," said Jim, his throat clogging with a strangely liberating sorrow. "Understanding should count."

It was a prayer.

> *(Dedicated to the members of the*
> *71st Infantry Division)*

SCANDAL
by Jill M. Morgan

Jill M. Morgan is the author of twenty-one novels and numerous short stories in the genres of horror, suspense, and mystery. She has written for adults, young adults and ages 8–12. In addition to her fiction, she co-edited the horror anthology *Great Writers & Kids Write Spooky Stories*. Her novel, *Blood Brothers,* is the first in a vampire trilogy. She resides in Southern California.

Sovereign James aimed the glass eye of the camera lens into the street scene, panning the area of South Brownwood Avenue in a slow sweep of steady clicks. Through the viewfinder she saw a long row of idling cars seeming to hover over the dark road, their tires hidden beneath breathy clouds of exhaust vapor. Cold this time of year in the nation's Capital.

Prostitutes in short-shorts and high-waisted midi tops leaned against the doors of cars, offering pleasures of the night to men waiting behind the wheels.

A reporter for D.C.'s most disreputable rag sheet, *The Washington Spy,* Sovereign was like the hookers; she was prowling for johns. A string of recent murders in D.C., four prostitutes in four months, inspired the city's most street smart reporter to attempt capturing the serial killer in the act of choosing his next victim—not capturing him with guns or handcuffs, but in a photograph she could sell to *The Washington Spy.*

If she captured him her way, not waiting for the cops to do their job, the photo could be sold to every newspaper and news program in the nation. The money would be unbelievable. For this reason, she ignored the assignment given to her by her editor.

These were her rules. It was play the game her own way, or lose. She was a woman willing to risk losing, but determined to win. When the stakes were high enough, the risk was worth it.

Sovereign blew on her fingers, rubbing them to force heat back into the stiff joints and icy muscles. She was thin, not enough fat on her fingers and toes to insulate them from the early November cold. Hidden in a two-trash-can-width narrow alley, she hadn't been noticed by the slowly cruising parade of men looking for their own kind of warmth.

The girls on the street knew she was there. It was okay by them. A redhead called Flame even brought her a steaming cup of coffee in a Styrofoam cup.

"Thanks, let me pay you for it."

"No, baby. You're our insurance. I'll carry the tab on this one."

Flame swung her wares out onto the street without looking back, doing nothing to give away Sovereign's hiding place. Hookers ducked into alleys all the time. If anyone had seen her, they would probably assume she was doing business. Admiring the tall black woman, Sovereign aimed at the retreating figure and took her picture. The bulb shattered, creating a bright light and a loud pop. Heads turned at the unexpected sound.

Someone said loudly, "What the hell?"

Another man's voice said, as if in reply, "It's a woman with a camera—there, in the alley. Get her. And get her camera!"

"Run, baby," said Flame.

Sovereign hadn't waited to be told. As a reporter for a news rag fondly referred to by its critics as the *parrot's paper*, Sovereign had learned how and when to run from a story. This wasn't the first time people she was photographing hadn't wanted their pictures taken. She'd been knocked down, kicked by a six-foot football player, and had her camera broken—but she'd been a rookie reporter then. After getting caught and having the breath knocked out of her enough times, she'd learned how to get away fast.

Long before settling into her place in the alley that night, she'd practiced an escape route, just in case. She'd had broken ribs, and didn't want more. She liked her smile with teeth in it.

She didn't run along the dark alley the way anyone would think she would, but up a fire escape ladder and over the flat roofs of buildings. *Just like New York.* Childhood was a long time ago, a circle of memories that chained in her mind like a string of kids leaping from rooftop to rooftop. The little girl she'd once been had raced over the roofs and disappeared down the sides of buildings before anyone could spot her.

"Where is she?" someone yelled. "I told you we shouldn't have done this. I told you!"

"Shut up and keep looking."

"If she gets away . . . if she gets away—"

"Keep quiet or I'll shoot you myself."

Sovereign slipped off the last rung of the fire ladder and onto the sidewalk. She removed her shoes and ran on bare feet for half a block, ending where she'd parked her car behind the grocery store. She didn't shut the car door. The only noise was the click of her seat belt, then the roar of the car's engine *thrumming* to life. Not waiting for the promised gunshots, she shifted into drive and peeled straight down the parking lane between the row of buildings.

The car door swung wide as she took the corner, turning a sharp left, then swerving on two wheels for a right at the next street. The seat belt held her in place. The camera hung on its strap around her neck. No bullets, broken ribs, or balled fists.

Safe. So long. See ya.

At the stoplight before the Washington Bridge Parkway, she paused long enough to grab the door and slam it shut. Once on the expressway, she made good time out of the city, past the suburbs, and into the exclusive and expensive Crestline community of Searl's Wood. She didn't live here, couldn't afford it. The man she slept with did.

Joel would be there. Once in his house, her car hidden in the garage, she'd be okay. No one would find her. No one knew about Joel, and no one had followed her here. Tomorrow, when rested, she'd develop the film and see what she had.

Her blue Accord pulled into Joel Seton's driveway. A motion light triggered and brightness flooded the scene. A man in his early thirties stepped out of the house and onto the front porch, his hand shading his eyes from the motion light's glare.

"Reigna, is that you?"

"Turn out the light," she said.

He did.

In the sweet secret dark she came to him, pressing her cold body into his arms. "Warm me," she said, "please."

He did.

The house—Joel called it a cabin—was large, built with generous, comfortable rooms, high ceilings, and loft windows that let in both light and dark. From bed, Sovereign looked straight up and saw a world of ink-black sky and stars. *Like camping in a forest, Joel's kind of camping, surrounded by sturdy walls, a fire on the grate, and a glass of Bordeaux in his hand.*

"What happened tonight?" he asked, his voice tight with concern for her. He worried, she knew. He'd seen her hurt, not badly, but more than any other woman he'd known. He loved her. He'd never said it, but she knew. Lots of men had said the words, but hadn't cared. Joel did.

"Look at me. I'm all right." What she did for a living scared him. He was afraid for her, so she kept it simple, telling him only what he needed to know. He didn't say he loved her; she didn't say she'd been chased by men with guns. It was better that way for both of them.

"Are you in some kind of danger?" She watched how he stared at the wine, swirling it slightly in the thin glass.

"I had a little trouble. Some people chased me. It seemed like a good idea to get out of the city for a while."

She didn't lie to him—didn't always tell the whole truth, but didn't lie.

"Do you need my help?" The question was an offer, sweet, without accusations, Joel-like.

"I'm just glad you're here," she said, setting down the wine and moving into the cove of his arm. "That's the only help I need."

They made love again. This time, she let herself believe the look in his eyes, the words she never heard but always felt in his embrace. If she wasn't sure she belonged as a wife in his world, at least she was sure of one thing; she belonged in his bed.

Light shone through the loft window, crowning a glow of morning in the high ceiling of the room. Sovereign reached for Joel, but he was gone. *When had he left?* His was an early rising world, on the road by eight, at work by nine, leave the office by five.

She didn't fit into his schedule. Or rather, he didn't fit into hers. She got up to make coffee. A pot was already brewed, ready for her on the stove. A note from Joel read, MAKE YOURSELF A DECENT BREAKFAST, NOT JUST COFFEE. He'd signed it simply Joel, but she thought it should read, *Mom.* He mothered her, more than she needed, not more than she wanted.

She turned on the morning news, showered, put on one of Joel's flannel shirts, and padded around barefoot, making toast. She took the roll of film out of the camera for developing. Joel had a dark room in the cabin, built solely for her. He didn't know a thing about photography, but knew if he gave her a dark room, she'd use it. If she used it, she'd be there for him.

The smell of reheated coffee made her hungry. She'd just taken a big bite of hot buttered toast lathered high with strawberry jam when she heard the anchorman say, "Another murdered prostitute's dismembered body was found by an early morning commuter today. The latest victim makes the fifth similar homicide in the D.C. area during the past four months. Detectives are calling this possibly the work of the serial murderer known as the Capital Killer. This photograph of the victim was released to the press just hours ago. The young woman's name is being withheld until notification of family."

Sovereign stared at the screen. The face of the latest murder victim was startlingly familiar, someone she'd seen. Scrutinizing the photo, she leaned forward to set her mug of coffee on the low glass table before the sofa, but concentrated so much on the television—what she saw, what was being said—that the mug only touched the lip of the table, and tumbled to the floor. Scalding coffee flew from the mug as it bounced on the hardwood floor, droplets splashing against Sovereign's bare legs.

"Damn!" she yelled, doing a quick toe dance away from the mess. At least there was no carpet, but the sofa was stained, and she'd have a couple of burns on her legs that might blister. She put a cold wet cloth on the burns, then sat in a chair across the room, thinking.

I know that face.

It took a couple of minutes . . . then she was sure. Bolting upright, she dropped the washcloth and rushed to the bedroom and her purse. Rummaging brought forth the roll of undeveloped film. Hands shaking, she went inside and shut the darkroom door.

"Who are you?" she asked the strip of film, preparing it for developing solution. "You're not one of the regulars, I'd know your name. You were there last night, weren't you?"

In one frame, an unknown young woman leaned

against a car. It had to be her. Most of the regular girls, Sovereign knew by name. This was a kid, not more than sixteen or seventeen, she guessed.

In D.C., the regulars worked specific territory. Woe to any seasoned hooker who crashed the boundaries of that reach. The only exception to this rule was runaways and kids too new at the business to know better. Prostitutes didn't have hearts of gold—at least, not the ones Sovereign had met—but they sometimes turned a blind eye to a kid who had, by ignorance, invaded their reach. She guessed this is what had happened last night, a runaway or first-timer had wandered into the area and hadn't been hassled by the regular girls. Yet.

Now, if memory was right, this kid was dead.

Nervously, she transferred the film from the developing solution to the stabilizing bath. There were many photos, thirty-six on the roll, with only four left unexposed. As she hung each print by its corner to dry, she studied it, wondering—*Are you there?*

And then, as if she had called the image forth, there it was. The photo had captured the girl perfectly, dark hair falling in a straight line to mid-back, young sweet face, no smile, eyes seeming a little scared.

With good cause. Sovereign waited impatiently for the stop bath to end development, then rinsed the print in clear water and hung it to dry. The girl leaned provocatively against the car, caught in the instant of soliciting a man whose face was becoming clear in the photo.

Something about the man's profile . . .

It was safe to open the door now that all the prints were developed. She stepped from the darkroom and headed toward the kitchen to pour a second cup of coffee. She never made it that far.

Another press announcement on the unfolding American-Russian-Chinese Alliance taking place this week at the White House. Stainless-steel microphone-headed forests lining the speaker's podium, and a bevy of reporters waiting hungrily for any information.

Sovereign stopped, turned slowly to face the TV, and felt the realization wash over her like icy water. *It's him, the face in the photo . . . the reason I was chased . . . good God, it's the President.*

Her knees buckled. She sat on the floor, then started shaking. Uncontrollable. Unstoppable.

"He killed that poor girl. The President, it was him."

She sat in total stillness, too stunned to move. Even her quick mind, always racing ahead with options to problems, found no alternatives now. If the President had been in a car solicited by the prostitute the night she was murdered, there was no other answer: he did it.

Slowly, present reality surfaced. She had the photo. She'd been there. The President's profile was clearly identifiable in the picture. The murdered girl was last seen with him. This was the scoop of a lifetime. She had it in her possession.

And nobody would believe her.

No, that was wrong. Somebody believed her, the Secret Service. They knew she'd seen the President and taken a photograph. If they were willing to protect him while he murdered prostitutes, would they be willing to silence Sovereign and bury her and the evidence?

It was a question she didn't want answered.

She went back to the darkroom and released the print from its drying clamp. She pocketed the strip of negatives, and moved back into the light of the kitchen. Morning brightness streamed through the window. She stood within it, the photo held in her hand. There was no doubt. President Quinlan's features were unmistakable.

Now what? The first thought was to present it to her editor. No other story would hold a candle to this.

"If only it weren't the *Washington Spy*." She thought with envy of being a credible reporter from the *Post,* or another newspaper. The envy lasted only long enough for her to dial her editor. The *Washington Spy* was her scandal sheet. She worked for it. She was damn good at what she did, and nobody edited her articles.

The *Spy*'s Editor in Chief answered her call. "Dan Peroff," he snapped. He always sounded like that. For a newspaper man, Peroff was about as sociable as a hungry gator with a toothache. He'd chew you up for lunch, then complain about the bite.

Sovereign was used to him, and not in the least put off by his manners, or lack of them. "Dan, it's me. I've got something so big, you won't know whether to put it on the front page or go into hiding."

"Where the hell have you been? I've been trying to reach you all night. Some stiff shirt from the Office of the White House has been busting my ass to find you."

"You didn't tell them?"

"I don't know where you are," he boomed back at her.

"Dan, I'm trying to tell you, I have a *major* story, that's why they're after me."

"Wha'ja do, kid?" His tone became conspiratorial.

"I robbed a bank. Are you going listen to me?"

"Sure. Spill."

"It's about the D.C. Killer, the one who's been killing all the prostitutes."

"I told you not to go after that story. You're gonna get yourself hurt around those people. Besides, nobody gives a damn about dead prostitutes. They don't sell papers, kid."

"Will you shut up and listen to me!" She'd never yelled at him. This was unprecedented. Because of that, she knew she had his attention. "I was on the street last night with the hookers. I took a roll of pictures, hoping I might spot one of the guys with . . ."

"The next murder victim?"

It sounded so cold and calculated. It hadn't seemed so awful last night, but today, in light of what had happened, it seemed nearly as sordid as the murders. She had been lying in wait for the killer to come by and choose the next girl, and she'd had no more thought to the safety or life of that girl than the killer had. In fact, she'd been hoping it would happen so she could get the photo and the story.

"God, I *am* working for the right paper," she muttered.

"So, what are you telling me?" asked Dan. "You got the picture?"

"Yeah," she said, "I got it."

"No lie? You got the guy and the dead girl?"

"She wasn't dead at the time."

"Yeah, yeah. But can you see her face? I mean, there's no doubt it's her?"

"It's her."

"Straight up, Sovereign. You're the best reporter I've got. Hell, you're the best reporter Washington's got!"

She didn't *feel* like the best anything. The realization that she hadn't given one spare thought to the dead woman was really starting to bother her.

"When do I get it? You got the negative with you?"

"Dan, there's something else."

"There's always a problem. Fill in the details later. I want that picture and I want it now. This isn't the kind of thing to sit on for a day or two. Get the picture on the streets by tonight, tomorrow tops. A week from now, it'll be old news."

She wished she could believe the Secret Service guys wouldn't care a week from now, but knew better. They'd already figured out who she was, contacted her editor, and were probably waiting for her to show up at her apartment. And then what? A little accident with an eighteen wheeler?

"How did they link this to me?" She went over every detail of the night, trying to remember if she'd left any evidence for them to find, something that would tie it to her. She got away clean, they hadn't seen the car, so how had they found her name? One of the girls might have given her up, but she didn't think so. She'd never given any of them her name, not even the one who'd brought her coffee.

"Damn," she said, "the coffee."

"Huh?"

"They got my prints from the coffee cup. I left it in the alley. Of all the stupid, amateur moves . . . What a rookie thing to do."

"If you're through beating yourself up," said Dan, "you might start writing the feature. You can open your wrists later. Right now, we don't have time. Get moving on this. Bring me the picture. I want it in my hands."

"Can't."

"I've got ulcers, you know."

"Look," Sovereign tried to explain, "I've got myself into a little situation here. If I show up at the office, I'll be picked up, probably arrested on some bogus charge, and spirited away along with the negatives. You'll never see me again, and you sure as hell won't see the pictures."

"Okay." He sounded docile, so gentle-voiced it was scary. "This is what you do."

For the next few minutes, Dan gave Sovereign pointers on avoiding people tailing her, on disappearing from the law and any other resourceful types, and on leaving evidence to be found by others in case all her escape routes failed.

"I thought Brooklyn was tough," Sovereign said, after hearing his life lessons on the school of evading trouble. "Where did you grow up?"

"A little suburb, just outside of Hell."

She believed it.

"One last thing," said Dan.

"Yeah?"

"I want the story and the picture, negative included, by tonight."

"You don't ask much, do you?"

"I'm a newspaper editor, not a father confessor. I get it by tonight, we'll go to print tomorrow. When it's news, they'll quit chasing you."

"Maybe, but I don't think these guys give up so easily. I have to go," she said, feeling sick. "This place isn't safe anymore."

She hung up and raced around the cabin, throwing

on clothes. She was struggling with one shoe when she heard a sound that made her grab the shoe, snatch her purse from the bed—holding the negatives and one developed photo—and run. She didn't take the car, but headed for the break of trees bordering the highway. Only when she was hidden deep enough behind the treeline did she pause to put on the second shoe and take a good look around.

The cars she had heard coming up the long foothill drive now hugged the winding road like a black centipede. They were coming for her. There was only one way down. Taking the car would have led her right to them.

She ran along the forest track, keeping the cars in sight until they turned and climbed Starlight Crest Drive, the road leading to Joel's cabin.

Sovereign ran in the same heart-stopping way she'd run as a girl, when kids from a gang chased her and she'd known she'd wind up dead if they caught her. She ran until she saw a road with a low drop, then slid down the hill and sprinted along the sidewalk to the small town boulevard with its folksy shops. A free, community shoppers' bus gave her a lift to the other side of town, where she paid a sulky-eyed teenage boy to drive her out of town in his dented-door Honda.

It was two o'clock before she settled on a place to stop running. She'd taken a bus from where the boy had dropped her off, to a town about fifty miles north. If the Secret Service agents were following a trail, she didn't want to be on it.

If only I could talk to Joel. The idea was so tempting. He'd listen and care about what would happen. Dan didn't. He only wanted the story. Joel loved her. Sometimes, she believed that.

Calling Joel was dangerous. Coming to his house that morning meant they knew about him. They'd probably tapped the phones at work and home by now.

But maybe not the car phone. If he was in the car, maybe she could take a chance and tell him what was going on. God knows what they'd told him. Right now, she was too alone, too vulnerable. She needed to hear Joel's voice. Maybe this once, she'd ask him what to do. And maybe she'd do it. *Maybe.*

The pay phone was in an old brick building off Main Street. In a coffee shop, she sat in one of the dimly-lit phone booths against the back wall, its accordion door closed. She listened as the mechanical sound of the rotary-dialed numbers connected her to Joel.

"Be there. C'mon, Joel. Be in your car."

"H'lo?"

"You have no idea how glad I am to hear your voice."

"Reigna? Do you know how many people are looking for you? The White House, for God's sake! You're a witness to something or other, they say."

"They're lying to you, Joel. They want to kill me."

"Where are you?"

"I saw something I shouldn't have, and they want to make sure I don't tell anyone about it. I'm scared."

"Reigna, these were Secret Service men."

"I know."

There was a long pause, where she was afraid she'd lost him, but then he asked, "What the hell did you see?"

"It's better if you don't know. Safer."

"So, you're just going to hide?"

"For now, until I can figure out how to expose them and what they've done. I can do it. I know I can."

"At the risk of your life?"

It was a hard question. She'd asked herself the same thing a dozen times since morning. Was it worth it? So what if the President was a killer? So what if the Secret Service protected him, enabled him, and kept his dirty little secret? What was it to her?

"Nobody gives a damn about those dead girls, Joel. That's not right. And besides, this is the biggest story of my life. If I let it go, I'll never forgive myself."

"What dead girls? Reigna, where are you?"

She'd forgotten he didn't know about the murdered prostitutes. At least, he didn't know how or why she was connected with it. "Tell me one thing. If somebody does something really wrong, even if that person is powerful and rich, the press can't let him get away with it, can they?"

"Why do I feel you're making me put your life on the line? Nothing's worth that."

"I know. But answer me."

He sighed. "Okay, it stinks if the guy gets away with it. The press should expose him. But your paper is hardly—"

"I know, it's the scandal sheet of Washington," she finished for him. "I've heard."

"Come home," he said.

She tried to think of something, anything that would tell him how serious this was without endangering him with the information. It came to her in an instant, and she said it without hesitation. "Joel, I love you."

She hung up, ready to open the door and leave the phone booth, when she saw the man in a dark gray suit talking to the coffee shop waitress. She couldn't hear the conversation well enough, so she opened the door slightly. The booth's light went out, and she scrunched down, hoping he wouldn't look in her direction.

"Yes sir, some woman who looked like that was here earlier, about twenty–thirty minutes ago. I noticed her because she wasn't from around here. I have a good eye for newcomers."

"Did she say where she was going?"

"No, she sure didn't. I expect she couldn't have got too far. Must be around somewhere."

"Call this number if you see her again."

"Secret Service? What's she done?"

"I'm not at liberty to tell you that, but you'd be helping your country by finding her."

Sovereign waited until the man left the coffee shop, and then waited longer, until she was sure the waitress was busy in the back room. When her chance came, she bolted from the booth and dashed across the shop to the front door.

Outside, she ran from the building, ducking into an alley beside a hardware store. Two blocks down was the post office. By now, Secret Service men had probably warned all shopkeepers to be on the lookout for a woman matching her description. If they were still in the area, they might even spot her themselves. She *had* to get the negative to Dan. But first, she had to write the best feature article of her life.

What she desperately needed was a . . .

Presto Printers, Fax, and Computer Rentals. It was a ratty-looking little storefront, the front window shaded by closed mini blinds. Not the kind of place the guys after her would bother with, she hoped. Right or wrong, she had to take a chance.

She might risk going to the print shop, but not the post office. At the street corner, she saw a young man of about sixteen crossing when the light turned green. He headed her way. She stepped from the alley and into his path.

"I wonder if I could ask a big favor of you?"

"What kind of favor?"

She hoped he hadn't spoken to or seen the men who'd been asking about her. He reacted to her as though she were a stranger, not a criminal.

"I need to mail something but I don't have time to get to the post office. I have to be somewhere else right away, so I can't do it myself. It's kind of important. If I paid you for your time, I wonder if you could take a letter to the post office for me and put it in the mail? I'd pay for the postage, of course, and give you twenty dollars for your trouble."

She was tempted to throw money at him, but didn't make the offer higher, fearing he'd get suspicious of what he might be mailing. This way, she just seemed like some tourist with more money than sense.

She pulled a small white envelope from her purse. It held the negative strip she'd brought from Joel's darkroom. She held it up to let the kid see how innocent it looked. "I'll write the address on a slip of paper for you," she offered, "and you fill out an Express Mail envelope at the post office, then slip this inside. Write the address on the hard envelope, seal it, then give it to the postal clerk. Would you do that?"

The boy shrugged. "Sure, why not. I could use twenty bucks."

"Great."

She wanted to warn him not to say anything about her to the clerk, but didn't dare. The last thing she wanted was for him to become so wary that he might not put the letter in the mail.

She wrote a fake return address for her old apartment in Brooklyn, using a quickly invented name. She couldn't use her own name, and didn't want the clerk asking the boy why there wasn't a return address. The less conversation, the better.

The kid stood impatiently as she stepped back into the alley and hurriedly scribbled the name, Cathy Wong. On the inside of the envelope, where the boy couldn't see, she wrote the words: FOR DAN.

Cathy Wong was Dan Peroff's longtime mistress, the woman he'd managed to keep secret from his wife and family, but not from Sovereign. She wrote Cathy's address on the scrap of paper and gave it to the boy.

"I appreciate the favor."

"No big deal," he replied, proving chivalry was not dead in America. "I won't say a word about seeing you either. It's nobody's business."

"Thanks." She could have kissed him, or ruffled his thick hair, or offered to come back in a few years, when he was over eighteen . . . but she did none of these things. Time was running out, and she still had the story to write. "I won't forget you," she said, and let it go at that.

She waited until he had disappeared into the post office before she ran across the street to *Presto Printers*. There, she picked an IBM clone at the rear of the shop, put her money in the change slot, and started typing.

The words came at the speed of her pulse, which was fast and jumpy.

Every time the door opened, she crouched low, but it was never one of the men chasing her. The words flowed from her mind to her fingers at the keyboard, in logical, clear sentences and paragraphs. She told everything, how she had been watching the street that night in hopes of spotting a Congressman or Senator, or of identifying the D.C. Killer. Never, she explained, had she imagined anything like this.

I am in hiding, she wrote, *afraid for my life. If something happens to me in the next few days, the actions of this administration, and the Secret Service agents who protect and shield the President, should be held directly responsible.*

Have we sunk this low? she asked, in the feature's last words. *Does anyone care about the murder of these women?*

The final page was a note she wrote directly to Dan. *Get this in the paper tomorrow,* she told him. *This article may be my only safety net.* She told him the photo was on its way. Before she could change her mind, she faxed the pages to Cathy Wong's machine, hoping Cathy would have the good sense not to call Dan at the office—which she almost never did—but to tell him about it in person that night.

Sovereign had done Cathy a sizable favor once, and now hoped this would be a chance for her to pay it back. "Come on, Cathy," she prayed as she faxed the pages. "Be smart, figure it out."

"Find everything you needed?" asked the clerk.

"Do you have a paper shredder?" She handed over the pages and watched as they turned into confetti. "I'm a little obsessive about privacy."

Outside, it was growing dark. The sky was marled blue-gray, showing a threat of storm. Sovereign wished she could hide herself in the massing cloud cover, find safe passage back to her life, and pretend she hadn't seen what she had. Like clouds, wishes were nothing more than hot air. She was a reporter who could no more give up an incredible story like this one than she could give up her personal freedom. It was why she hadn't married Joel, why she hadn't married anyone. She wouldn't let anybody tell her how to live. Ever.

Thinking of Joel triggered emotions she hadn't allowed herself to feel in a very long time. Living the way she had could be lonely. She remembered the long spell of emptiness before Joel had come along, Joel and his love that simply accepted her and never demanded anything. She cared more about him than she wanted to, and thought about him now, when she was tired and scared. Wished she were with him. Safe.

She couldn't hang around this town, too many people had heard of her and been shown a picture. The nearest airport was fifty miles away. The bus depot was certain to be a place the agents would be waiting for her. Hitchhiking was an option, but included the very real danger of being spotted on the road, not to mention the possibility of getting into a car with some pervert. Not all serial killers were Presidents.

She couldn't stay and couldn't run.

"Lady," a man's voice behind her called.

She turned, saw nothing but the press of darkness that had sealed over the town. Leaves blowing in the trees along the boulevard hissed a warning.

"Lady, are you lost?"

Is that what people in small towns asked a stranger?

"I'm fine," she yelled back, hoping whoever had called to her would go away.

"There's nothing out there, lady. Not even houses. You're going the wrong way. Do you hear me?"

Go away! she wanted to scream at him. *Shut up and go away.* All hope of leaving town unnoticed vanished with the shouts back and forth. Now, who *didn't* know where she was?

A car started from somewhere far down the block, and a twin track of headlights aimed into the road and headed right for her. The accelerating speed of it told her this wasn't a local. Rumbling evil bearing down on her at over eighty miles an hour.

She ran into the empty space . . . *nothing out there, lady.* Ran, though the car's headlights caught her in their glaring eyes. Ran like the wild creature she was, heart pounding, breath shuddering, legs trembling but carrying her.

Heavy footfalls behind her, three or four runners, told Sovereign she had lost. A hand snaked out and grabbed her ankle. She fell hard against the ground, scraping her face on the gritty shale. All breath left her body, knocked from her lungs by the force of the fall. A knee bent into her spine, and another one on the back of her left leg. Her arms were wrenched behind her and twisted cruelly as handcuffs locked onto her wrists.

Air. All I want is air.

There was none. A boot on her neck ground her face harder into the dirt. Someone's finger caught and twisted in her hair, pressing the back of her head, pressing . . . until the clouds of night covered everything, even sound, and she heard and saw no more.

She came to in the back seat of the car, one man on either side of her, and two in front. The wide sedan hurtled along the highway, its beams cutting an eerie swath through the surrounding dark.

"Am I being arrested?" She tried not to wince from the pain of what felt like a broken rib when she breathed—a reminder of the knee on her back.

"No need for that," said the man to her right. He didn't look in her direction.

They plan to kill me. If I don't do something to save myself, I'm dead. The thought inked through her, a spreading dark. Wherever they were going would be isolated, secure, and she wouldn't leave. She tried a few more questions, but they ignored her. It hurt to talk, anyway. Soon, there was nothing but the constant road, the pain from her broken rib, the handcuffs twisted at her wrists to make her know she was still alive, and fear.

She didn't see the building until the car turned off the road. Even then, it wasn't visible until the headlights touched it—a large, square, concrete box set in the middle of nowhere. It looked like a jail cell, or a tomb.

She didn't go easily. This was an invitation to a house party she worked hard to refuse. They insisted. She screamed as soon as they took her out of the car. *Maybe someone would hear.* The man to her right punched her in the stomach, hard. The screaming stopped. No air.

The concrete block house was divided into two rooms. The first had a table and four chairs. A television was propped on a metal cabinet. One of the men switched on the set.

"Turn it up loud," said the one who'd punched her. "I don't want to hear."

Turn it up loud so you can't hear? What does that—

They dragged her into the second room. It was bigger than the first, and completely empty. A single light bulb, without any glass globe, burned from a dangling wire at the ceiling. There were no windows to jump out of, no closet to hide in, no escape.

Sovereign made up her mind she wasn't staying here and rushed for the open doorway. A dark-haired man shoved her back into the windowless room and slammed the door.

She would have beat on the door with her fists, but the handcuffs were still on. Instead, she kicked the wood, over and over, kicked until her foot went numb. From the other side of the door she heard the loud voice of the television, blaring a commercial.

Stark, unrelenting fear made her step away from the door, stumbling until her back was pressed flat against the far wall. *Nowhere else to go.*

Time passed, five minutes, an hour—she didn't know—and then the door opened.

The man who stepped into the room was clean-shaven and dressed in a blue-gray business suit. She didn't recognize his face, but saw he was a political animal by the look of him. A heavyset body, thick lips, and a broad beefy face showed him to be a man of power and brute strength.

"I need to know a few things about you, Miss James. You've been very unwise, snooping into matters that didn't concern you. Only a fool does that in Washington."

"I'm a newspaper reporter. Unless you want a lot of bad publicity, I suggest you let me go immediately." It was a lame bluff, and he didn't bother to discuss the point. That told her one thing for certain; she wasn't leaving this place alive.

"Where are the photos you took?"

"In a safe place. Let me go, and I'll drop the story," she bargained. It wasn't much of an offer. In his position, she wouldn't have believed it.

He didn't. He advanced on her. "I'm not a patient man."

"Why'd you let him do it? He killed all those women, and you let him. Why?"

"The ARC Alliance will be completed this week, the most powerful agreement ever negotiated. Far too important to our country to allow scandal to destroy it. President Quinlan is the undisputed voice of that agreement. Without him, the Alliance would never be happening."

"He's a psychotic killer."

"Yes, that is a slight flaw in his character."

"You're going to let him keep doing this? Someone will find out, I promise you. Washington's not a town for secrets."

"When the Alliance is negotiated to our satisfaction and signed, the President will suffer a massive stroke. He'll linger for a week or two, but Vice President Bennett will step into power immediately and take over the Office. Quinlan will die a few days later. The country will mourn a national hero, and no one will ever suspect a thing—I *promise* you."

Sovereign saw contempt for her, and a passion for cruelty in his eyes. This was a man who enjoyed his work. He had the kind of behind-the-scenes political power that Senators and Congressmen never acknowledged, but knew was part of the system. They feared men like him, and so did she.

"Now," he said, moving so close she could feel his breath on her face, "you were going to tell me about those pictures you took."

Sovereign *was* going to tell him. Anything, because as long as she talked, he might let her live. She would have ... but the door opened again. This time, there was no doubt about what was going to happen. President Andrew Quinlan stepped into the room.

He was completely naked. Sovereign felt her legs give way when she saw the knife. It was a scalpel, the kind used in the serial killings. She slid to the floor, her back rasping against the wall. Her mind flashed on the autopsy photos she'd seen of the murdered girls ... dismembered, horribly mutilated, deep slashes on their faces, and always, their eyes stabbed into final blindness. *So they couldn't see him.*

"Don't," she said.

She needed no words from him to tell her he was mad. The fixed stare was enough. The stress factor of the Presidency was high. This was the leader of the nation, a brilliant negotiator, and a monster who butchered women to relieve his tension.

"I'm a reporter, President Quinlan—" if she could break through the barrier of his insanity, "not a prostitute. I work for the *Washington Spy.*"

"Bitch!" He came at her.

She found the strength to scramble to her feet and run. Her shoulders and back hit the wall again and again, moving faster than his shuffling gait, turning to see how close he was, turning to see the knife raised in his hand and the lifelessness of his eyes. They seemed dead, but he was terrifyingly alive.

She made it to the locked door and screamed, "Let me out!"

From the other room, she heard only the sound of the television, and someone's voice saying, "Turn it up, God damn it. I don't want to hear her scream."

"Help me!" she cried, kicking the door with her heels. *I'll make the bastards hear me.*

The volume rose on the television, drowning even the thoughts from Sovereign's mind. The sound was so loud, it pulsed through the concrete floor, pulsed right into her, and thudded into her heart.

Paralyzed with fear, she stood unwilling to leave the door, the only possibility of escape. Quinlan grabbed her hair and yanked her to the floor. The knife slashed, its blade descending to her face.

"No!" She fought for her life, twisting hard to the right.

The scalpel missed her face and stabbed through her right shoulder, just under the collarbone. It went clear through, the point scraping the concrete floor when it hit. She felt *nothing*. No pain. Not yet.

Her hands were locked behind her back, but her legs were free. With instinct nurtured in her childhood's rough streets of Brooklyn, Sovereign landed a well-aimed knee. Quinlan fell back and curled protectively over his injured groin. She kicked him again, hard as she could. It was only buying time.

"Now I'll hurt you," Quinlan said, when he caught his breath.

What was he going to do before, kill her nicely?

He was on his knees, then standing. She scooted away, desperately trying to push against the wall and stand. But she couldn't. The floor was slippery with blood. Hers. She felt pain now, tearing through her with every movement.

Quinlan's knee sank heavily into her chest, pinning

her. "Don't look at me!" he screamed. "All of you look. I told you not to, I told you!"

He stabbed for Sovereign's face, aiming for her eyes. His fingers gripped her hair so tightly, she felt the roots rip when she jerked forward. The blade cut into her scalp, instead of her eyes, scraping bone.

I'm going to die.

Quinlan smashed her head against the floor. The lightbulb hanging from the ceiling swung back and forth. Back and forth. She was losing consciousness. With that, would come certain death.

Quinlan worked the scalpel along her rib. Cutting. Now, he would mutilate her as he had the others. This time, she felt the searing pain. Brought back to full consciousness by it, she screamed.

The door burst open. It hit the wall with a crash so loud, it startled even crazed Andrew Quinlan from his bloody task. He glared at the four men rushing for him.

"No," he cried, like a child about to lose his favorite toy, "not yet."

They grabbed him, the same men who had grabbed Sovereign, tearing the bloody knife from his hand and kicking it across the room, where it clattered against the wall. In the background, over President Quinlan's childlike wails, Sovereign heard the television, still blaring, and the voice of the news anchorwoman.

"This photo from one of Washington's scandal sheets is being printed in nearly every newspaper in the country. The resemblance of the man in the photo, seen here soliciting a prostitute, is startlingly similar to the profile of President Quinlan.

"The reporter, Sovereign James of the *Washington Spy,* is reputed to be missing. Her story indicates that if any harm befalls her, police should investigate the Office of the President.

"White House Press Spokesman Carmichael reports that President Quinlan is unaware of this incredible story. He says, 'I don't read the *Washington Spy.* No one with any sense does. This article is slanderous to the dignity of the White House and to the President,' said Carmichael. 'It alarms me that such an obvious newspaper-selling ploy should be attempted on this regrettable subject at precisely the time when President Quinlan is working so hard for the all-important ARC Alliance.'

"The *Washington Spy*'s dismal reputation in professional journalism has been of the UFO-abducted-my-husband variety," said the news anchorwoman. "If nothing else, the photo will surely give the members of the impending ARC Alliance something of a less serious nature to discuss at the end of the day."

The last thing Sovereign saw before she passed out was the naked light bulb dangling on its wire, still swinging from the ceiling.

Before Sovereign was released by her captors, her wounds had been treated by someone with surgical skill. She had no need to go to a doctor. The stitches under her rib were tiny, but numerous. She would carry a scar under her breast for the rest of her life. The deep wound along her scalp was neatly hidden under Sovereign's hairline. Nothing showed. To the casual observer, she looked unharmed.

In the time following the events, she did not write another article about her experience with the four Secret Service men, or the unnamed man who decided the nation's fate, or the stark madness of President Quinlan.

The nation quickly forgot the seedy article and photograph from the *Washington Spy*. There were other matters of much more importance happening. Two weeks after the ARC Alliance was signed by the leaders from America, Russia, and China— creating a union that held the potential power to rule the world—President Quinlan suffered a massive stroke.

"President Quinlan's condition is reported to be very grave," said Press Spokesman Carmichael.

"Tremendous efforts recently given in the service of his country may have precipitated this health problem. Vice President Bennett has immediately taken over the duties of the Office until further medical tests can be done on President Quinlan."

A week after the initial report of his illness, President Quinlan died.

Sovereign kept her silence.

There is a price to silence. Sovereign paid it in the loss of her editor's respect at the *Washington Spy*. Dan Peroff didn't care whether the story was true or untrue—that wasn't the nature of his business—he cared that she had dropped it when it was hot. "Makes the paper look bad." Thereafter, he assigned her the kind of stories other reporters shied away from: *Rare Two-Headed Snake Has Entire Book of Genesis Inscribed On Its Belly;* and *Alien Skeleton Found In La Brea Tar Pits.* Such articles sold copies.

Sovereign didn't care about her credibility. That had ceased to matter.

Losing Joel had been harder. He hadn't been able to handle the publicity and disgrace that settled on her after President Quinlan's illness and death. For a time, she was possibly the most hated woman in the country, and definitely the most hated reporter in Washington. People condemned her for such a vicious written assault on a true American hero.

Joel left during that time. She missed him, but thought it was probably better for him to be away from the scandal. He'd found someone else, she'd heard. And so that tie was cut.

All her ties were cut . . . except one.

Each night of her life, in the stillness of her room, Sovereign wondered if there really *was* a body in President Quinlan's grave. Or had the announcement of his death been another lie?

Will he come back?

The house settled in the cold, its aged timbers groaning, its floors creaking. A scrape of metal rasped across a pane of glass, and Sovereign waited.

"Are you there?" she said into the trembling dark.

Silence.

For her, fear remained. Always.

Wide-eyed, she watched each night, and asked, "Are you there?"

NIGHT OF THE VEGETABLES
by Edward Lee

Former cop, tank gunner, and pump jockey, Edward Lee
has had nine horror novels published by Berkley and
Zebra, *Ghouls, Incubi,* and *Creekers* among them. In
addition, he has had dozens of short stories, reviews
and commentaries published in genre magazines and
major anthologies. His *Hot Blood 4* story "Mr. Torso"
was nominated for the Horror Writers' Association's
Bram Stoker Award. Lee lives in Crofton, Maryland.

He could see it in the tabloids. *Christ,* he thought.
THE PRESIDENT CHECKS INTO WALTER
REED ARMY MEDICAL CENTER . . . WITH CRABS!

"Crabs, Mr. President?" asked Dr. Greene. A real
smug smartass, this one. A light colonel, Chief of Dermatology. Short, muscular, a fucking human fireplug.
The pursed lips struggled not to smile. *Probably a goddamn Democrat,* the President thought. *If he blabs,
he'll be taking temperatures in fucking Alaska. . . .*

It was so humiliating, but what else could he do?
He'd told his assistant press secretary it was just a routine check-up. You couldn't keep anything from anyone
these days. *The minute you become President, they pry
into your life with a fucking proctoscope, the fuckers.*
And—Christ!—if the First Lady ever found out. . . .

"You're right, Mr. President," Greene agreed. What
an image this must be: an Army doctor on his knees, a
magnifying glass in hand, while the Chief Executive of
the most powerful country on earth stood before him
with his pants down, having his crotch examined.

"Yes sir, they're crabs, all right. Or, technically, sebaceous pubic mites. Looks like you gotta whole metropolis of 'em down here, Mr. President."

Funny guy. We'll see how hard he laughs in Alaska. "It's not like I can walk into Peoples Drug Store and buy a can of CROTCH KILL. So how about spraying some heavy-duty crab-killer down there and let me be on my way? I gotta country to run."

"I'll need to take a species sample, Mr. President." Now Greene wielded tweezers. "There are over five hundred different types of sebaceous mites; in order to prescribe the most effective medication, I'll need to identify the genus."

Maybe I'll prescribe my foot to your ass, Doctor. See if you can identify that. "Yeah, yeah, fine. Just hurry it up, huh? I have to propose a new tax bill to the Senate Finance Committee in about twenty minutes."

What a day—what a *year* for that matter. Ethnic cleansing in Macedonia, new revolutions in three more African countries, the goddamn Democrats threatening to filibuster again, and now this. *I got a smartass Army doctor plucking at my dick hair with tweezers.* Could things get any worse?

Quick raps on the door, then a barking voice. "Mr. President. We just got a P4 priority call on the flyline."

It was Clegg, the Transport Team Captain, SS. The President's penis jiggled when he barked back, "I'm busy!"

A pause from beyond the door. "It's a P4 call, sir. Chief of Staff Ketchum's on the line. You better take it."

"Aw, for God's sake, hang on!" The president, seething, pulled his pants back up, leaving Greene poised with tweezers the goddamn Pentagon had probably purchased for five hundred bucks. *How can things get any worse? Just watch.* Ketchum wouldn't be calling unless it was a true emergency.

He bolted out into the hall, where his team of Secret Service agents stood waiting, sunglasses, earphones on their heads, SIG P226's under their jackets. Clegg stood stiff as a wood post, cradling the opened briefcase which contained the transport phone. Another suit stood in the background holding the odd, circular briefcase known as "the football," which housed a mobile transponder relay full of coded permissive-action links, the means by which the President could launch ICBMs. *Christ,* he thought, *I hope I don't have to use that thing today. I was looking forward to dinner at Peking Gourmet.*

The President touched the phone. "Is this thing secure?" he asked, irritated. "I mean, I don't want my conversation to be in *People* magazine next week."

"It's a single-channel discriminator phone, Mr. President," Clegg replied, his voice as stiff as his posture. "Fifteen different discrimination prefixes are processed through the White House commo computer. The codes are changed three times daily, after which they're transmitted through five revolving hopper frequencies. In other words, Mr. President, this is a secure line."

You're going to Alaska too, smartass, you and that fireplug doctor in there. "Ketchum, huh?"

"That's correct, Mr. President."

He pulled the phone out of its mount, then inadvertently scratched his pubis. "What is it?" he demanded of the phone. "I'm busy. I'm here at Walter Reed for a check-up."

"A check-up?" Chief of Staff Dallas Ketchum inquired over the line. "That's funny, I heard it was crabs."

GodDAMN!

But the Chief of Staff did not banter. "Forget about your crabs, Mr. President. We've got a *big* problem. P'Tang, North Korea? Remember that liquid-metal nuclear reactor they built a couple years ago?"

How could he forget? "Yeah. That new design, the one that the NRC said could never melt down?"

Chief of Staff Ketchum paused, cleared his throat. "Well, it melted down, about a week ago, our sources are telling us."

"Fuck! Shit! Piss!" bellowed the President of the United States. "And let me guess, you asshole! The

wind is blowing all that radioactive shit over here, and
everybody's gonna die of cancer!"

"Nothing like ... that, Mr. President." Another
pause, another clear of the throat, "Keep your fingers
crossed. So far the outbreak seems to be limited to the
West Coast."

"Outbreak?" the President questioned. "Outbreak of
what?"

* * *

Like ... carrots, Robby thought.

Weird. He could devise no other simile. "I don't
know what's wrong with my skin," Karen Ann said.
"I've been trying to get a suntan."

Robby frowned at the wheel. *A suntan, huh? Suntans
aren't orange.* Maybe she was on some weird medication; after all, he didn't know her that well yet. He
turned down Martin Luther King Boulevard. *Her skin
is the color of ... carrots!* he kept exclaiming to himself. No wonder she wanted to go to the drive-in
tonight. Karen Ann *hated* drive-ins—("Tacky," she'd
told him when he'd first suggested it. "Low class.)—
but now she was begging to go, and that made sense,
didn't it? At Palmer's Drive-In, no one would be able to
see her ridiculous orange skin.

This would be his third date with her, and the other
guys at Taco Bell, where they'd met, assured him that
three would be his lucky number. So far no genuine action, just a little grabbie-feelie, a little of the old Kissy
Face. But, Christ, she was good-looking. A true blue
California blonde—or, for the moment, true *orange.*
Every so often Robby steered in order to, deliberately
catch a pothole, to throw a side glance at those big
36Cs jiggling. Robby's right hand had had many a vigorous workout thinking about them. And tonight, with
any luck—

I'll be seeing them, he ventured. But then the anticipation dwindled.

I just hope they're not orange, like the rest of her.

He knew she was self-conscious about it, too. Karen Ann was a motormouth, always chattering away. But not tonight—she'd barely spoken at all, except to complain about the odd, orange tint to her skin.

"I just don't understand," she lamented, appraising her forearm. It was tan three days ago. Now it was orange.

Dusk bled into the sky ahead of them. "Wait a minute," Robby considered. Of course! "Did you use any of that funky suntan lotion?"

She squinted at him, orange-faced. "What—"

"You know, that Quick Tan stuff. You put it on your skin and it gives you a tan without having to be in the sun."

"Of course not!" she replied, her vanity assaulted. "I have a *real* tan."

Uh-huh. A real tan? You look like a goddamn carrot. But Robby let it rest; girls never liked to admit they used that sort of stuff, just like they never liked to admit they dyed their hair. That was it, though—he'd figured it out! *She probably put too much of that stuff on her skin, and it turned her orange.*

"So what are the movies tonight?" she asked, quickly changing the subject.

Robby rode over a pothole. Bingo! "Uh, *Three on a Meat Hook, Barn of the Naked Dead,* and *Chopper Chicks in Zombie Town.*"

"Not *horror* movies!" Karen Ann griped. When she did, she crossed her arms beneath her bosom, which further accentuated the obvious attributes. "I *hate* horror movies, Robbie!"

"Look, you're the one who wanted to go to the drive-in. Palmer's is the only drive-in the county—the rest closed years ago." But now he was being cruel. "No biggie. We'll go someplace else. You want to go hang out at Hilltop? Or how about the Multiplex?"

Sheer terror flooded her ocean-blue eyes. Hilltop Mall? Or a multiplex theater? No way she'd want to go there. *Not with that Quick Tan gunk turning her skin the color of carrots!* he surmised.

She faltered, stifled a pout. "Well, I guess horror movies are okay."

Yeah.

Robby parked the Mustang near the back corner; he remembered back when he was a kid—all of five years ago—they'd sneaked in here in the trunk of Cage George's Hemi 'Cuda, with six-packs of Schlitz tall boys that he'd ripped off from Dad. *Those were the days.* But this was a *new* day, wasn't it? And hot stuff sit-ting right next to him. Before the first flick, James Woods came on, warning America's youth about the evils of cocaine. It took a while—like maybe five min-utes—to break the ice of Karen Ann's disconsolation. But in the dark she eventually reverted back to her old, luscious self.

Because, in the dark, you couldn't tell that her skin was the color of carrots!

They slid into a clinch. Just the shampoo-scent of her hair caused a familiar turgidity south of Robby's belt. And those big, buoyant, wonderful 36C's pressed against him when his lips met hers . . .

Robby flinched. His movements locked up.

Just one post-high-school kiss was all it took.

"Robby, what's wrong?"

But what could he say? The inside of her mouth tasted like—*Carrots.* . . .

* * *

"Mom!" Jeannie Straker cried out. "Horace isn't eat-ing! I'm worried!" She held the rabbit, like a careful prize, up in both arms as she strode to the kitchen with this dire emergency. "I don't think he likes that new rabbit food you got at Giant."

"Rabbit food is all the same, dear," her mother said, loading dishes into the Kenmore. Dad was in the family room watching baseball; "Goddamn Yankees!" he shouted. "Get that garbageman off the mound! If goddamn Ripken hits another home run, I'm gonna fly to Camden Yards and shove the bat up his—"

"Phil!" Mrs. Straker berated. "That's enough!"

But Jeannie wilted—nobody cared about Horace. "He hasn't eaten in a whole day, Mom! He doesn't like that food!" But then—*Wait a minute,* she thought. *Lettuce!* Horace loved to eat lettuce! "Mom, do we have any lettuce? Horace'll eat that."

"I'll get some, honey." Her mother smiled tolerantly and opened the fridge. At least Horace would have something to eat now. Her mother's face, however, lost its smile when she reclosed the fridge. "Oh, I'm sorry, Jeannie. There's no more lettuce in the crisper."

Tears welled in Jeannie's twelve-year-old eyes.

"But we'll get some tomorrow, and a different brand of the dry food." Her mother patted her on the head. "Don't be upset. Horace'll be up to his big ears in food tomorrow."

"I bet goddamn Chizmar a case of beer on this game!" her father railed from the other room. "I'm gonna lose *again!* And goddamn Ben McDonald—the Yankees oughta buy him! Then at least they'd have someone who can pitch! Christ Almighty, I could pitch better than Keyes with my goddamn *feet!*"

"Phil!" Mrs. Straker raged back. "Would you *please stop yelling* about *baseball!* You're upsetting Jeannie!"

"*God*damn Yankees . . ."

Jeannie moped off to her room, cradling Horace. *They don't care,* she thought. *Poor Horace* . . . She sat down on the bed with her lethargic pet, scratching his head, rubbing behind his ears. "Don't worry, Horace," the little girl avowed. "We'll get you lots of lettuce tomorrow."

Suddenly tired and without forethought, she lay back on the bed, then she drifted off to sleep.

Ever dutifully, Horace the white rabbit sat beside her, his pink nose twitching . . .

But when little Jeannie woke up, her screams nearly shattered her bedroom windows. What had happened? She'd taken a nap, and—

Her eyes bugged. She held up her hand, but there really wasn't much of a hand remaining, just bones. All the skin, it seemed, had been stripped off her little fingers!

And, worse, on the bed lay a patch of dampness, a stain, but it wasn't blood. Jeannie knew it *couldn't be* blood because blood was red, yet this odd stain was the thinnest shade of green, akin, of course, to the color of lettuce.

Horace looked up at his screaming master, nose still twitching, and his tiny white mouth similarly stained. . . .

* * *

"You've gotta be fucking shitting me!" bellowed the President of the United States. A closed session, now, in the Oval Office. Chief of Staff Ketchum was there, as was Secretary Sallee from HUD, Nutman from the Nuclear Regulatory Commission, and NSC Field Deputy Hodge.

"The contagion seems to have cessated, Mr. President," Sallee began. "We've received no reports of infection east of the Rocky Mountains. That's good news."

"Good news!" wailed the President. "Everybody west of the Rockies has turned into a vegetable, and that's good news!"

"First of all, Mr. President," continued Sallee, "the infection is selective—not everyone is affected, maybe only ten percent of those in the exclusion perimeter. And they're not turning *into* vegetables, sir, they're merely acquiring certain genetic *traits* of, well, of vegetable matter."

"You guys are all a bunch of assholes!" the President yelled. "Shit, I oughta fire ya all! How am I gonna get reelected if a bunch of West Coast twerps have turned into vegetables while I was in office? Christ, California? That's a fuck-load of electoral votes! And how the hell did this happen, anyway?"

Nutman, the NRC Chairman, was possessed of a

suspiciously British accent. The President didn't like Brits; they reminded him of all those limeys on the infomercials, selling miracle car wax and dripless paint brushes. "It seems, Mr. President," Nutman began, "that the P'Tang reactor suffered what we would call a Status 4 Meltdown, which is quite serious, like Chernobyl. Standard first-response protocol is to smother the core. Generally this is done by pouring in wet cement from helicopters. But the Koreans, evidently, had no wet cement on hand, so they dumped in dirt."

"Dirt?"

"Yes, Mr. President. Soil from a nearby field." Nutman paused to light a Marlboro. "Regrettably, though, said soil was taken from a collective *vegetable* field . . ."

Now Hodge, from the National Security Council, spoke up, adding the minutia of speculative detail. "What we think happened, Mr. President, is that some very obscure mode of genetic transfection occurred in the reactor core. Live-Vegetable Fallout is what our experts have dubbed it. Then a peculiar occluded weather front broke into a high-pressure center, quickly feeding the Live-Vegetable Fallout into a massive formation of altostratus cloud banks. The high-pressure center carried it all over here, whereupon the altostrati released a short but heavy amount of 'trough' precipitation."

"And that's why Secretary Sallee referred to this as good news, Mr. President," Chief of Staff Ketchum jumped in. "It means the worst is over. More than likely, the transmission of this new disease has stopped. So there's nothing to worry about."

Spittle flew off the President's lips when he eloquently shouted, "Get the fuck out of here, all of you no-dick busted humps! You're all fucking fired! Jesus Christ in a fucking hotdog stand! U.S. citizens are turning into fucking vegetables, and you assholes are telling me there's nothing to worry about!"

* * *

And so ensued what would, in the realms of modern history, come to be known as The P'Tang-Reactor Vegetable Epidemic. The National Guard was helpless, panic erupted in the streets. Maternity wards soon became dispossessed of familiar, squalling babies, replaced instead by roughly nine-pound satchels of queer, human-shaped vegetables. Street gangs looted grocery stores en mass, routing produce sections only. Emergency room floors were once slicked in blood; now, though, they were slicked in stewed tomatoes, creamed corn, and something suspiciously reminiscent of V-8.

Chaos ran rampant.

The government passed bill after bill: The Omnibus Plant Matter Survivor Package, Seedling Care Reform, The 1996 Vegetable Security Act, and, of course, the famous Civil Vegetable Rights Bill.

And, eventually, and by the grace of God, things got back to normal.

The United States Census Bureau, via crucial calculations made by the National Institute of Health in Bethesda, Maryland, would in time estimate that no fewer than 26.7 million people were infected with TIVS—Transfected Irradiated Vegetable Syndrome.

But at least, as Secretary Sallee had guaranteed, no new case of contagion ever spread past the Rocky Mountains. . . .

* * *

But, unfortunately, Secretary Sallee was wrong. A barometric anomaly known as an "altostratus high-pressure funnel" bloomed from the heavens during the contagion period. And, unfortunately, several hundred thousand more became infected with the dreaded TIVS.

* * *

"You motherfucking hunka walking shit!" shouted the President into his Oval Office phone shortly thereafter. "You gotta be motherfucking *shitting* me!"

It was Dr. Greene on the other end of the line, Chief of Dermatology at Walter Reed Army Medical Center.

"I'm sorry to have to tell you this, Mr. President," Greene apologized.

"I'll dig your eyeball out and piss in your head!" the President bellowed at the grim news. "I'll pop your balls off and hang them in my limo like sponge dice!"

Greene went on to explain, "Those crabs we thought you had, Mr. President? Those sebaceous pubic mites? Well, we analyzed them, sir, and they aren't sebaceous pubic mites after all. They're aphids."

THE PRESIDENT'S MIND
by *Robert J. Randisi*

Robert J. Randisi has had over 275 books published since 1982. He has written in the mystery, western, men's adventure, fantasy, historical, and spy genres. He is the author of the Nick Delvecchio series, the Miles Jacoby series; and is the creator and writer of *The Gunsmith* series, which he writes as J.R. Roberts and which presently numbers 185 books. His newest novel, *Alone with the Dead* (St. Martin's, 1995) received a starred review from *Publishers Weekly,* and is currently in its second printing. He is the founder and executive director of the Private Eye Writers of America.

I
APRIL 4, 1865

The pounding on his door woke James Eastman from a deep sleep. When Eastman was roused this way, he woke badly. One of the pleasures he took from no longer being in the service was waking at his own leisure. He checked his watch and saw that it was only four a.m. The pounding continued on his door. He was in a particularly foul mood when he finally opened it.

"What the hell—"

"Major Eastman, sir?" The speaker was a tall man in his late twenties, wearing a Union Army uniform and the insignia of a lieutenant. Behind him were three more soldiers, one of them a corporal and the others privates.

"I'm not a Major anymore, Lieutenant," Eastman said. "Haven't been for two years."

"Yessir," the lieutenant said. "I'm Lieutenant Winston. We'd like you to come with us, sir."

"Now?"

"Yessir."

"For what reason?"

"I can't tell you that, sir."

"Can't, or won't, Lieutenant?" Eastman asked, and then added, "And stop calling me 'sir'."

"Yess—I mean, I can't, Major."

"I'm just plain *Mister* Eastman, Lieutenant," Eastman said, "and why can't you?"

"Because I don't know, si—Mister Eastman."

"You want me to come with you, but you don't know why?"

"That's right . . . Mr. Eastman."

"Can you at least tell me *where* you're supposed to be taking me?"

"Yes, I can," the lieutenant said. "To the White House."

"Just give me a chance to get dressed, Lieutenant," he said. "I'll be right with you."

Eastman followed the lieutenant down the hall, flanked by the other three soldiers. At this time of night the halls of the White House were empty, and their footsteps echoed loudly.

Eastman had not been to the White House in over two years. There was a period of time when he actually worked there, but that seemed a lifetime away.

They stopped at the door to what Eastman knew was the Oval Office. Being summoned to the White House did not necessarily mean one was going to see the President, but at this time of night who else would be in the Oval Office?

"Come," a voice called.

Lieutenant Winston opened the door, stepped inside, saluted and said, "Major Eastman, Mr. President."

"He's not a Major anymore, Lieutenant," the voice said.

Eastman stepped into the office. "That's what I've been trying to tell him, Mr. President."

"James," President Abraham Lincoln said, "thank you for coming."

Lincoln stood and extended his hand. Eastman had to walk across the office to accept it, and the two men shook warmly. He was surprised to see that the cadaverously tall Lincoln was wearing his night clothes.

"If it had been anyone else, sir," he said, "I'd have slammed the door in the young lieutenant's face."

The mention of the lieutenant seemed to remind Lincoln that the young officer was there.

"That will be all, Lieutenant," he said, "and thank you."

"Thank you, sir," Winston said, and withdrew, closing the door behind him. Eastman knew the lieutenant and the three soldiers would wait right outside the door.

"Sit down, James," Lincoln said, seating himself at his desk. The curtains covering the window behind him were pulled open, and if it had been daytime, Eastman would have been able to see the White House lawn.

On the walls of the office were portraits of past Presidents, such as Washington, Madison, Jefferson, and others. Lincoln's immediate predecessor, James Buchanan, was not in evidence. Eastman imagined that after his term of office was over a painting of Lincoln would also hang somewhere in the White House.

Eastman crossed his legs and waited for the President to speak. Lincoln was six foot four with dark skin, dark hair and gray eyes, the right one of which was weak and sometimes tended to wander. He had a great beak of a nose, and his lower lip hung down. His cheeks were hollowed out, and he had a massive jaw. He had been described as homely, but Eastman had always found Lincoln's countenance stately and dignified—even now, when his hair was mussed and he was probably fresh from his bedroom. Eastman knew that Lincoln was 52 when he was elected to office in 1861.

Eastman noticed that the President was very pale, more so than he'd ever seen him before.

The ex-Army major himself was in his late thirties, not quite six feet, slender but strongly built. No one could ever have called him homely. He had dark, wavy hair, blue eyes, a firm jaw, and a strong profile. He was late of the Union Army until he was asked to leave under a cloud. One of his only supporters had been Lincoln himself, but Eastman had decided not to put the President in a bad situation. He resigned.

"You're probably wondering why I had you brought here in this manner."

"I'm wondering why I'm here at all, sir," Eastman said. "The time of the day, and the manner, just make me even more curious."

"I need your help, James."

"I'm always at your disposal, sir."

"To be frank," Lincoln said, "I wasn't sure."

"Why?"

"Because of what happened to your career."

"What happened to my career had nothing to do with you."

"Yes, well . . . I still think if I had been more supportive—"

"Mr. President," Eastman said, interrupting the Commander in Chief, "no one could have been more supportive. You never believed the charges that were leveled against me. I could have fought them, but it was my choice to resign."

Lincoln smiled, which seemed to change his face entirely. He looked tired, but when he was smiling, he looked anything but homely.

"I know you resigned to keep me from supporting you publicly, James."

"My choice, sir."

"Yes, of course," Lincoln said. "Well, it will be your choice now, as well, whether you help me or not."

"Just tell me what you want me to do, sir."

Lincoln hesitated, then said, "I want you to prove that the President has not lost his mind."

II

James Eastman wasn't sure he had heard the President correctly.

"Sir? I think you'll have to explain that."

"First of all," Lincoln said, "I cannot stress strongly enough that what is said here can go no further."

"Of course, sir."

"If this ever got out, if my detractors ever heard this, it would be fatal for the Presidency."

"You have my word, Mr. President."

"Thank you, James."

The President ran his hand through his unruly hair, then tugged at his prominent lower lip.

"Several times over the past few weeks," he said, slowly, "I have awakened to find myself standing on the White House lawn."

Eastman remained silent, knowing the President hadn't finished.

"Now, each time I have been closer to the wall, or to a gate," Lincoln said. "I believe that if this situation goes unchecked, I will eventually leave the grounds without being conscious of it."

"Mr. President," Eastman said, "have you ever sleep-walked before?"

"No, I have not," Lincoln said, "and I do not believe I am sleepwalking now, James. No, I believe it is something more insidious than that."

"Such as, sir?"

Lincoln hesitated, then said, "I believe that someone, some outside force, may have control over my mind."

Eastman didn't know what to say. He was aware, of course, of all the rumors concerning the mental stability of Mary Todd Lincoln, the President's wife. This sounded more like something she would have said.

"Mr. Lincoln, why would you say such a thing?"

"I know it sounds crazy, but I'm dimly aware, James, of having heard voices each time," Lincoln said, "and drums . . ."

"Drums?" Eastman asked, but the President didn't seem to hear him.

"Sometimes the drums are so loud I can't hear, and the voices . . . the voices are imploring me to leave the White House, leave the grounds and go . . ."

"Go where, sir?"

For one of the few times he could remember Eastman saw Abraham Lincoln at a loss for words.

Finally, the President simply stammered, "I—I don't know. I suppose that's what I want you to find out, James—that, and whether or not I . . . I actually may be losing my mind."

"I doubt that, sir."

"Why?"

Eastman leaned forward, as if the movement gave his words more credence.

"Because, sir, you have one of the strongest minds I've ever encountered. Even if we were talking about some sort of . . . of hypnotic spell, I don't think your mind would be susceptible to such a thing. From everything I've heard of such things, weak minds are susceptible, not minds like yours."

Now Abraham Lincoln sat forward in his chair, looking excited.

"Perhaps that's it, then."

"What is?"

"What if I'm resisting whatever force is trying to compel me," he said, warming to his subject. "What if I'm . . . snapping out of a spell each time, finding myself on the lawn."

"That's . . . possible, I suppose," Eastman said, although he still thought it more likely the President was sleepwalking. At least, that made more sense.

"You must find out, James."

"I will be happy to help in any way I can, Mr. President," Eastman said, "but if I may, I have to ask . . . why me?"

"Because, James," the President said simply, "I trust you."

"I'm honored by your trust, sir," Eastman said, "and I won't betray it."

"I know you won't, my boy."

"I'll have to ask some questions, Mr. President."

Lincoln sat back, put his hands in his lap and said, "Go ahead, then."

III

Eastman was unsure how to begin, so he simply worked through the questions in a logical manner:

Had this ever occurred during the daytime?

No, only at night.

Had anyone else ever seen him?

No, no one.

Was Mrs. Lincoln aware of what was happening?

No.

Had it ever happened to Mrs. Lincoln?

No.

These voices and drums that he'd been hearing, did anyone else ever hear them?

No. He always heard them at night and no one else was present, except for Mrs. Lincoln, and she had never commented on them.

Had anything unusual occurred within the last month or so, leading up to these incidents?

Lincoln did not answer immediately.

"Sir?"

"The answer to your question is yes, James," Lincoln said slowly, frowning heavily, "and I don't know why I didn't think of it before."

"What is it, sir?"

"Do you know what a seance is, James?"

"Yes, sir," Eastman said. "It's a group of people gathering together to try to contact the dead."

"Exactly," Lincoln said. "A month ago Mrs. Lincoln and I attended such a seance. It was conducted by a rather odd man who called himself Count Manzipore."

"Count . . . who?"

Lincoln repeated the name.

"I believe I'm getting it correct, James."

"And what did this Count Manzipore do?"

"Well," Lincoln said, "he was supposed to have contacted one of my . . . my sons."

"And did he?"

"I'm afraid something, uh, happened before he could."

"And what was that?"

"I, uh . . ." Lincoln said, looking embarrassed.

"Sir?"

"Fainted." The word was almost a whisper.

"What?"

"I fainted," Lincoln said, more forcefully.

"That is . . . odd, sir."

"I've never fainted before in my life, James. It was most upsetting."

"Describe it to me."

"Well, one moment we were sitting there, Mother and I, holding hands, and the next thing I . . . there was this odd odor, I thought I . . . yes, I heard voices, faraway voices, and then . . . then I was being picked up off the floor, told that I had fainted."

"Hmm," was all Eastman said.

"What does that mean, James?"

"Well, sir, it doesn't sound to me like you fainted, it sounds more like you were drugged."

"Drugged." Lincoln clung to the word like it was his salvation. "That would explain certain things, wouldn't it . . . but what about my . . . my walking about . . ."

"I don't know, sir," Eastman said. "Can you tell me where this seance took place? I would like to meet this Count Manzipore."

"Yes, yes," Lincoln said, "I can give you the address."

"Very good, sir."

Lincoln wrote it down on a piece of paper and handed it across his desk.

"Sir, I'm going to have to bring someone else in on this."

"Why?"

"Well, while I'm checking this out, I'm going to need someone to watch you."

Lincoln tugged at his earlobe, and then his lower lip again.

"Would this someone have to know the whole story?"

"Not necessarily."

"Do you have someone in mind?"

"Yes, sir," Eastman said. "Someone I've worked with before, a man with a brilliant mind."

"Trustworthy?"

"Utterly."

"I'll have to accede to your judgment, then, James."

"I'll not let you down, sir."

"My God, James, do you think it's possible that someone could have tried to harm me while I was there?"

"That's what I'm going to find out, sir."

IV

Eastman was returned to his home on North K Street by the lieutenant and his men. They dropped him in front of his building and left without a word. Loyal to the President, but there were too many of them for word of his visit not to reach other ears. He'd have to deal with that when the time came.

It was almost seven a.m. when he reentered his home. He washed up and dressed, leaving again at eight. He knew that the man he was going to see would be awake—probably still awake after working all night.

Martin Gordon was perhaps the most brilliant man Eastman knew—and probably the most misunderstood. He was in his forties and had worked, briefly, for the Government before they released him as being unstable. In actuality, they were afraid of some of the things he invented, and chose to brand Gordon a crackpot rather than admit he was a genius.

Most people feared genius, Eastman decided.

Gordon lived in a small apartment on Virginia Street, overlooking the Potomac. He often claimed that his view of the river inspired him. When Eastman knocked on his door at eight-thirty, he had no doubt that he'd find the man awake.

He did, however, have to pound on the door for a full five minutes before it was finally opened.

"Wha—James, is that you?" Gordon squinted at the sunlight. He had unruly dark hair, peppered with gray, and rings beneath sad brown eyes because he routinely slept so little. Eastman assumed he'd just come from a dimly lit room, rather than from his bed.

"Good morning, Marty. I brought breakfast."

Eastman held up a bag.

"Doughnuts?" Gordon asked hopefully.

"Yep."

"Come in, dear boy, come in."

Eastman entered and followed Gordon to the kitchen, where there was an ever present pot of coffee. Gordon poured two cups and they sat at the table and opened the bag.

"What brings you out this early?" Gordon asked.

"A summons from the President."

"Lincoln himself?"

"Yes," Eastman said, "at four a.m."

"Yikes. I know how you detest being woken at such an ungodly hour."

"Not for Lincoln."

"No," Gordon said, knowing the high regard in which Eastman held Lincoln, "I would think not. What's the problem?"

"Why does there have to be a problem?"

Gordon bit into a doughnut and said, "It's usually a problem that brings you to me for advice."

"Well," Eastman said, "I need a little more than advice this time. Are you busy?"

"I'm working on something for the Smithsonian," Gordon said, "but that can wait."

Eastman knew his friend was not exaggerating.

"Tell me."

Eastman told Gordon as much as he dared, not as much as he would have liked, and more than the President would have liked. The part he left out regarded Lincoln hearing voices and drums in the White House.

"I think you're right," Gordon said, when Eastman was finished. "It sounds more like an induced swoon than a faint."

"What would do that?"

"Any number of powders that could be carried in the air," Gordon said. "Did he drink anything that night?"

"I don't know," Eastman said. "I don't think so. He didn't mention it."

"That would be easier," Gordon said. "There's always a chance that something transmitted on the air would also have an adverse effect on bystanders as well as the intended victim."

"This only affected him."

"Well," the other man said around the last bite of doughnut, "there are ways to direct these things ... What is it you want me to do, James? Analyze something? Meet this Count whatsisname?"

"I'm going to see the Count today," Eastman said. "Marty, I need you to watch the President for me."

"Surveillance?" Gordon said, looking surprised. "That's a little out of my bailiwick."

"I know," Eastman said, "but I can't trust anyone else."

"You honor me," Gordon put his hand to his heart.

"Will you do it?"

"I will, on one condition."

"What's that?"

"When you find whatever it is this Count used, I want a chance to analyze it."

"Done."

Gordon smiled.

"I'm your man, then. How do I get into the White House?"

"They'll be waiting to admit you."

"What's my . . . what do you call it . . . cover?"

"You'll be there to advise the President."

"Regarding what?"

"Fake it."

"I can do that very well. Are you off to the Count's now?"

"Shortly," Eastman said. "I don't want to show up there too early. I'm not sure what tack I'm going to take."

"When you have time, will you take a look at a few things?" Gordon asked. He loved showing off. "I've got some new toys that will amuse you . . ."

V

The location of Count Manzipore's "shop"—for want of a better word—was on the east side, near the intersection of Massachusetts Avenue and 115th Street. The building was a four-story stone structure, but there was a stairway leading down from the street, and a sign that read: COUNT MANZIPORE, PAST, PRESENT & FUTURE.

Eastman checked his pocket watch. By now Gordon should be in the White House, "advising" the President. He put the watch away in his vest pocket and went down the stairs. When he reached the door he looked around for a bell ring, but there was none. Before he could knock, however, the door opened.

"Excuse me—" he started, but he quickly noticed that no one was there. Had the door opened on its own?

The floor seemed to be hardpacked dirt, but the interior was dark, and he could not see past a few feet. He narrowed his eyes, but it did no good. There was nothing for it but to enter and see what happened.

He stepped inside; as soon as he cleared the open

closed with a slam. His first instinct
…un, but he quelled it and waited.

… wish?" a voice finally asked. It was a
…med to echo.

…eak with Count Manzipore."

…usiness."

…t?"

…quickly, recalling the sign outside, he
…future."

…s a moment of silence and then the voice
…are a nonbeliever."

…ing to change that."

…forward."

…still pitch-black in the room, even though his
…plenty of time to adjust.

…re?"

…ard the light."

…was about to ask what light when he saw it,
…ght ahead of him. It didn't light his way, but it
…d him where to go. He moved forward gingerly,
keeping his eyes on the light, hoping he would not
bump into or trip over something. He wondered where
the voice had come from, and how it had been so . . .
amplified. It seemed that Count Manzipore might have
had some toys of his own, the way his friend Marty
Gordon did.

The light drew closer and closer, or he to it, or so it
seemed. When he figured he should have reached it, it
seemed to move away from him. He decided that this
must have been some sort of illusion. He breathed
through his mouth, as advised by Gordon. If there were
some drug in powder form, being transmitted on the
air, Gordon said that this might keep it from affecting
him completely.

"Mouth breathing might save you from the odor,
but not the effects," Gordon had told him, "not totally,

anyway. If I had time I could probably rig up son
of filtering plugs for your nose . . ."

But they didn't have time, so Eastman had to r
the method of breathing he was now using. So
felt no ill effects.

Finally the light seemed to be just ahead of him
a doorway came into view. When he reached the c
way, the light brightened and illuminated the room
had to shield his eyes for a moment until they starte
readjust. Eventually, he realized there was someon
the room, sitting in a chair against the wall to his ri

"Come in, Mr. Eastman," the voice, less ampli
now, said.

"Count Manzipone?"

The Count inclined his head.

Eastman entered and asked, "How do you know
name?"

The man in the chair spread his hands, which we
thick and covered with rings. In fact, the man himse
was thick from head to toe, except for his beard, whic
seemed to be clinging forlornly to the man's broad jav
Thick, however, did not translate into fat, for the mar
was not fat at all. Eastman judged that if he were st
ing, the man would easily be taller than even the President's six-four.

"I know many things, Mr. Eastman," the man said.
With its normal timber the voice was slightly wheez-
ing, as if the man had a cold in his chest.

"Such as?"

"I know why you are here."

"How do you know that?"

The man laughed, and Eastman waited for the cough
which never came.

"I've been expecting you, my friend—or someone
like you."

"Maybe you'll enlighten me?"

The man's eyes widened and he said, "That is what I
do, my friend. I enlighten people."

Eastman's gaze swept the room. As far as he could
see, they were alone. There were shelves on the walls,

and on the shelves were numerous items Eastman found strange. One in particular appeared to be a bulbous-looking squash with a long handle. On another shelf he saw what looked like bottles of rum with some kind of sticks in them.

"We're quite alone, Mr. Eastman," Manzipone said, as if reading his mind. "There are no other living creatures here."

Eastman frowned, wondering why Manzipone would choose to put it that way.

"Suppose you enlighten me, then," he said to the big man. "Why am I here?"

"Why, to save your President."

Eastman was starting to perspire. Was it warm in here?

"Save him from what?"

"Why, from me, of course."

"What does he have to fear from you?"

"I'm calling him," Manzipone said, "and he has no choice but to come."

"Calling him? How?"

"At night, in his sleep, he hears me, and he comes."

"He hasn't come yet."

"He has a strong mind," Manzipone said, "a strong will, but he will succumb—much as you will."

"Me?"

Eastman felt his heart pounding.

"Yes. You see, I'm surprised you've been on your feet this long. Another man would have collapsed when you first entered, but . . . ahh, I see you feel it now."

Eastman felt *something*. Perspiration was flowing freely now, and his heart was pounding so hard that the sound in his ears was deafening . . . like drums . . .

Hadn't Lincoln mentioned something about drums?

"Don't fight it, Mr. Eastman," he heard Manzipone's voice from far away, "don't fight it. You'll only make it worse . . ."

VI

The first thing Eastman saw when he woke up was the altar.

"That is my 'pe,' " Manzipone said, "or altar."

Eastman found he was lying on a straw pallet. He sat up and swung his feet to the floor. The altar was made of stone and was covered with candles, money, amulets, ceremonial rattles, flags, beads, small stones, and bits of food. What particularly caught his eye was an odd looking drum.

Next Eastman looked around the room and saw that they were in a different place.

"We're a little deeper underground." Manzipone said.

The big man was seated in a chair similar to the one upstairs, which seemed constructed to carry his weight.

Eastman looked down at himself. He was fully dressed, but his gun and gunbelt were gone, as was his hat.

"I had to disarm you, Mr. Eastman," the other man said. "And then I brought you down here."

"Do you think you can keep me here?" Eastman asked.

"Oh, but of course," Manzipone said. "The powder you ingested was mild, Mr. Eastman. There are other, stronger powders that I could have used—and still may use."

"Like the one you used on the President?"

"Alas," Manzipone said, "there I may have misjudged. I thought that a man who catered to his wife the way Abraham Lincoln does would be more easily controlled. I was wrong."

"Yes, you were."

"But I'll have him," Manzipone said. "Very soon I will have him."

"And what will you do with him?"

In reply, Manzipone clapped his hands together twice. Suddenly two men entered the room, but they were moving oddly, very stiffly. Also, they were pale and drawn and their eyes seemed . . . dead.

"I will make him like this," Manzipone said.

"How?"

"I am a *Houngan*, Mr. Eastman. Do you know what that is?"

"No."

"It's a Voodoo sorcerer. Do you know what Voodoo is?"

"I've heard of it. It's some kind of magic, or religion."

"Exactly, and I am well versed in its uses, just as I am well versed in other forms of black magic. I am a sorcerer of many cultures, Mr. Eastman."

"And what are these?" Eastman indicated the two men.

"Some call them Zombies," Manzipone said. "I call them . . . slaves." The big man laughed, thinking this funny. "Do you see the humor? Lincoln is seeking to free the slaves in the south, and soon he will be *my* slave."

"And then what?"

"And then I will control the single most powerful man in the world," Manzipone said. "We will be able to forget all about this silly fight to free the slaves and concentrate on more pressing matters."

"Such as?"

Manzipone smiled and said, "World domination."

Eastman stared at the man for a moment, open-mouthed.

"You're mad."

"Why? Men have tried to control the world before. Alexander the Great. Attila the Hun, if he'd been smarter about it and more ambitious, might have eventually done it. Why not me? Once I control the President, I control the armed forces of this country, as well."

"They were all mad," Eastman said, "and so are you. You don't think I'd let you do that to the President." He pointed to the two Zombies.

"You won't be able to stop me."

Eastman stood up.

"You can't fight them, Mr. Eastman," he said. "You see, when I told you there were no other living creatures here, this is what I meant. They are not alive. They are Zombies. You can't hurt them."

"I guess I'll have to try."

Manzipone frowned.

"That's too bad," he said. "I had hoped to persuade you to join me."

"As one of your Zombies?"

"No, as an associate. You see, I am aware of your background, your reputation. I am even aware of your recent difficulties, which led to the end of your army career."

"What do you know about that?"

"I understand that you were being considered to head up the newly formed Secret Service—you and another man?"

"Vincent Cooper."

"Yes, Mr. Cooper," Manzipone said. "I believe he was a little more devious than you were in securing the job."

"What do you mean?"

"He framed you, dear boy," Manzipone said. "The plans you were accused of stealing? He had them stolen, and framed you. You played into his hands when you resigned. That left the job open for him. You know, if Lincoln had supported you, you might have the job now. You worked for him in Springfield, and then again in the White House, and he didn't lift a finger to help you. Why should you care what happens to him?"

"You know a lot of things," Eastman said, "but you understand very little. I resigned to *keep* Lincoln from supporting me."

Eastman had figured that Cooper had framed him, but to try and prove it might also cause trouble for the President, who had been forced by circumstance into appointing Cooper to his position as head of the Secret Service.

"Ah. I see," Manzipone said, nodding, "a noble

gesture." His nod turned into a headshake. "You're right, there are things I don't understand, like acts of nobility."

"Why doesn't that surprise me."

"You are now planning to overcome my two friends here, and then apprehend me."

Again, it was as if the man was reading his mind.

"Well, I'll leave you to it, then." He looked at his two Zombies. "Kill him," he said, and then sat back to watch.

VII

The Zombies started toward Eastman who moved quickly to meet them. He threw himself at them in a cross body block, striking them both chest high and taking them down. Once on the floor he began to strike with his hands and feet, but his blows seemed ineffective. He rolled away and got to his feet to regroup.

Unhurt, the Zombies rose slowly to their feet. They started for him, and Eastman quickly realized that while they were much slower than he was, that was his only advantage. They seemed impervious to pain, as Manzipone had said.

He had two surprises for them, though. He had one of Marty Gordon's toys in each of his boots. Both were springloaded. He reached down to one boot and a small knife leaped into his hand. As the creature reached him, he stabbed one of them in the heart—or where the heart would have been, had the man been alive. He tried to withdraw the knife for another strike, but it was stuck. He pushed the two Zombies back, but after two steps they began to come forward again. The one with the knife in his chest didn't seem to feel it, and there was no blood.

Eastman reached into his other boot and a small gun appeared in his hand. While the gun was a derringer and tiny, the bullet inside was more high powered than any bullet ever fired before by a gun that size. Eastman pointed it at the Zombie who was not sporting the knife and fired. The bullet made a neat hole in the Zombie's forehead, but it kept coming.

Eastman had no time to be horrified by what he was seeing. Apparently, what Manzipone had said about the two was true. They were dead, and could not feel pain.

He turned quickly, preparing to fire the second bullet at Manzipone, but the man anticipated the move. Very suddenly the wall he was sitting against moved. It turned, so that there was now an empty chair on the outside, and Manzipone was somewhere on the other side.

"Good-bye, Mr. Eastman," his amplified voice said. "And good luck."

Eastman turned to face the two Zombies, who were advancing on him. He fired again, striking the second one in the heart, but to no avail. It had as much effect as the bullet in the head.

Eastman ran to the wall behind which Manzipone had disappeared. He pushed on it, but it refused to move. He started to search the chair for some sort of lever or button, but just as he thought he'd found it, two pairs of hands grabbed him and pulled him away.

He was in the grasp of the Zombies now and they were incredibly strong. He struggled, striking at them, kicking out, but he couldn't break their grip. Slowly, they started to pull in opposite directions and he soon realized that they were literally trying to tear him apart!

He could feel his flesh stretching and the pain was starting to become unbearable when suddenly he heard his name.

"James! Close your eyes!"

He obeyed without question. He felt something strike his face and suddenly he felt the Zombies release him. He fell to the floor and another set of hands grabbed him. He opened his eyes and saw Martin Gordon.

"Marty."

"You're all right."

"Yeah," Eastman said, even though it hadn't been a question.

He looked over at the two Zombies, who were now lying on their backs, bleeding from their wounds.

"They're dead," Gordon said, "really dead."

"Wha—what happened to them?"

"I changed them back."

"What?"

"I changed them back into real men, and their wounds killed them."

"Changed them . . . how?"

"I'll explain later. Where's the Count?"

"Behind that wall," Eastman said. "I found a lever . . ."

Gordon helped him to his feet, and they walked to the chair. Eastman tripped the lever and suddenly the floor beneath them moved and they were behind the wall. They found themselves in a cavern, from which there were four tunnels leading away.

"He could have gone down any one of these tunnels, James," Gordon said. "He's gone."

"The President," Eastman said. "He's done something to the President."

"Lincoln's fine," Gordon said.

"You're suppose to be with him."

"Now if I was with him, I wouldn't have been able to save you, would I?"

"But—"

"He's fine," Gordon said again, "and he's waiting for us."

"We'd better go, then," Eastman said.

Gordon tripped the lever and they were back in the room.

"Wait," Gordon said.

He walked to the altar and began to sweep it clean of its paraphernalia.

"We'll send someone back to dismantle it," he said, then. "Let's get to the President, and I'll explain everything to him, and to you."

VIII

Without telling them why, Martin Gordon had left the President in the care of Lieutenant Winston and his men. Now Eastman, Gordon, and Lincoln were assembled in the Oval Office.

"I'm pleased that you're all right, James," Lincoln said. "I was worried."

"And I was worried about you, sir. Marty, how did you know what was going on?"

"About the Voodoo, you mean? When I got here, I questioned the President more about his symptoms, how he felt when he fainted, and how he felt when he was . . . walking on the lawn. The more he talked, the more I realized that the symptoms were the result of certain powders and drugs that were used in Voodoo, to create Zombies."

"Zombies," Lincoln said. "Certainly you don't actually believe in such things?"

Eastman thought back to the Zombies he'd faced in Manzipone's basement. Knives and guns had no effect until Gordon sprayed them with another powdered drug designed to . . . well, bring them back.

"There are things that can't be explained logically, Mr. President."

"Perhaps," Lincoln said, "but I have a country to run and a war to finish. Can I safely do that, gentlemen?"

Eastman looked at Gordon, who nodded.

"Yes, sir."

"Then I am forever in both your debts," Lincoln said, "and I must ask you to leave."

"Yes, sir.

Lincoln shook hands with both men, who then left the Oval Office, and the White House.

"Tell me some more, Marty. Manzipone said he was a . . . a Hogan?"

"*Houngan,*" Gordon corrected. "They have the power to create Zombies. When I realized what Lincoln's symptoms might mean, I went to a friend of mine who is an authority on Voodoo. He gave me some of the powder that *Houngans* use to revive victims of Zombification. That's what I threw in their faces when I got there. I told you to close your eyes because I didn't know what effect it would have on a living man."

"Lucky for me when I closed my eyes, I also held my breath. How did you know where I was?"

"Well, Lincoln told me about Manzipone. I found his place and let myself in. I found the room with all the shelves and saw what was on them. He even had some rum bottles with his *Ju-ju* in them."

"I saw those, and something that looked like a squash. What are *Ju-ju?*"

"The *Ju-ju* sticks are—well, like a magician's magic wands, and the squash is a ritual rattle called an *asson*, which is sort of the symbol of the *Houngan's* office."

"It all sounds so fantastic, so unbelievable, and yet . . ."

"And yet you saw it with your own eyes, didn't you?"

"What if I was hypnotized, Marty?"

"Could you accept that more than you can accept Voodoo and Zombies?"

"Yes," Eastman said, without hesitation.

"Sorry, pal," Gordon said, "but I saw them, too, and I wasn't hypnotized."

"Should we go back there, do you think? Get some of that stuff?"

"I thought so before, but now it's probably not necessary. Manzipone's gone."

"What about the President, though?" Eastman said. "Will he still walk and hear drums and . . . you know."

"No," Gordon said, as they reached the White House gates and stepped out onto Pennsylvania Avenue, "I gave him some of the same powder I tossed in the faces of those Zombies, only I put it in a drink. He's cured. Lucky for him he has such a strong will."

"Lucky for this country, I think," Eastman said. "Thanks to us, it still has its President. We can be proud of that."

"You know," Gordon said, as they started down the

street, "we made a pretty good team on this. Maybe we should go into business together. . . ."

Author's note: Nine days later President Abraham Lincoln was assassinated, shot and killed by John Wilkes Booth while attending a play at Ford's Theater in Washington.

FUTURE'S EMPTY PAGES
by Stewart von Allmen

Stewart von Allmen is the author of one 70,000 word novel, *Conspicuous Consumption* (June 1995) which he wrote in three weeks, and a second book project published for a Bosnian relief charity in June 1996, *Saint Vitus Dances Eternity: A Sarajevo Ghost Story*, which is a 15,000 word novelette that consumed a year of his time. He's now working on a science fiction project he hopes will combine the length of the former and the quality of the latter.

> "The letters of a person form the only full and genuine journal of his life."
> —Thomas Jefferson to Robert Walsh, 1823

Charles Wilson Peale shouldered his bag and was admitted into the President's House at once. He didn't comprehend the necessity of the President's instructions that led him now to be slipping into the house under the cover of darkness, but he strictly obeyed the request.

As Mr. Jefferson had asked, Peale arrived at the southern door. He would therefore enter through the superbly furnished oval drawing room, which meant the room would reprise its role as a vestibule for perhaps the first time since the departure of John and Abagail Adams. This honestly suited Peale much better anyway, as he'd noted earlier that the supposedly more dignified northern entrance was still outfitted with a wooden platform and similar steps.

However, the secrecy worried him. He wondered what news Jefferson could possibly have that would lead the man to request such a clandestine entrance from such an old, in fact pre-Revolutionary, friend.

There had been a disturbing tone to the letter he'd received from Jefferson. It was an insight that caused Peale to almost overlook the fact that it was an original letter he'd received from the President. Because of the continuing correspondence between the two concerning the failings and benefits (mostly the latter) of the wondrous polygraph machine, which Jefferson now used almost exclusively to create the copies that formed his voluminous collection of letters, the President always sent Peale the copy created by the device. The recent letter, though, was fresh from Jefferson's hand, a fact that would be clear only to the eye of one trained in the polygraph's operation.

Of course, the President's polygraph could be broken, and hence the request to bring the new one that Peale carried in the carefully packed sack draped over his shoulder. The President's letter, though, said nothing of the current device not working. There was only the request to bring this new one. And, again, why the need for Peale to come himself when the package could have been delivered? And why the secrecy?

Regardless of these questions that raced through his mind, Peale relaxed. He'd arrived, and there would undoubtedly be answers soon.

The need for surreptitiousness immediately lapsed upon entering the "barnyard" mansion. Peale knew that Jefferson lived here with only a handful of servants and his two sons-in-law for company. Peale wondered if Jefferson was often lonely here, and he felt a pang of regret for not visiting more often. This was, in fact, only his second visit to the President's House.

The servant led Peale through the oval drawing room and out toward the Great Hall. When the servant turned left, Peale asked, "Is the President in the library, then?"

"No, sir," the young man responded. Peale did not

recognize the young man, but assumed he was Jefferson's current secretary. "Mr. Jefferson is upstairs in his sitting room. He awaits you there."

When Peale hesitated, the young man looked troubled for a moment, but then divined the problem. He said, "The main stairway is over here now, sir. It was completed some time ago, but perhaps not before your last visit here."

Peale nodded, repositioned the bag, and proceeded again.

The servant showed the way up to Jefferson's sitting room. He opened the door for Peale, but did not follow the man inside.

Peale entered the modest room and immediately met the gaze of his longtime friend, Thomas Jefferson. The President was seated in a tall-backed reading chair and was surrounded by at least a dozen open books that circled him on the floor. Three books were piled in the President's lap. The two underneath were open, but the one on top was closed and the spine was clutched tightly by the President's hand in such a way as to make Peale suspect that Jefferson had long sat with such uneasiness and lack of attention to the volumes around him.

Despite his friend's obvious distress, Peale barely managed to suppress a smile. Jefferson looked less Presidential and more the rural Virginia farmer in his threadbare blue overcoat, scarlet vest, ruffled white shirt, brown corduroy breeches, and yarn stockings. And, of course, his well-worn heeled slippers. But this was how he always dressed when not entertaining, and sometimes even when he entertained. Comfort was key for this President, Peale knew.

"My friend," stammered Peale, who now had to steel himself to keep tears from his eyes when Jefferson's distress melted away and the President smiled at his guest.

Jefferson stood quickly; he was still athletic and fit though his sixtieth birthday had been a few years ago during his first term.

Jefferson grinned broadly and said, "I am so relieved you've arrived, Charles. The past weeks have been most trying. For a number of reasons certainly, but for one in particular."

He paused a moment and then said, "Please, have a seat."

Peale was relieved already. He set his package beside another chair and took a seat. He knew he was here to lend strength to his friend (though the reason remained unknown), but it was Jefferson's stature and composure that in turn lent Peale some confidence now. Jefferson might dress the part of the bumpkin, though only his numerous political enemies would phrase it so, and seem a mite awkward at first, but Peale had personally witnessed many people put at ease by the President's courtly manners. Besides, his smile was contagious and seemed to reveal Jefferson as a most frank and guileless man.

Jefferson sat as well and smoothed his tousled gray hair. Doubt clouded his features again.

Peale felt his confidence ebb. "What ails you, my friend? Are you unwell?"

"No, no, not that. My physical health finds me most robust, though I could perhaps do with better sleep."

"Is it Congress, then?" Peale ventured timidly. "Some political maleficence? A conspiracy you've uncovered which perhaps you cannot reveal to anyone in Washington, hence you have summoned me?"

"You're imagination is, as ever, most vigorous, Charles. You made all these guesses in the letter announcing your imminent arrival. But no, it is nothing at all political. In fact, I'd prefer if we could heed our usual rules and put talk of politics aside for the evening."

"Most certainly," agreed Peale. "That agrees with me considerably, as it did upon my last stay when I brought Baron von Humboldt to visit. Has that been two years now?"

Jefferson's articulate voice seemed to swim in melancholy. "Two years to the month. Nearly the day."

"Yes," admitted Peale, knowing full well the can of worms he had opened. "About two months after the death of your dear daughter in '04."

"Yes," Jefferson sighed wearily. And then he turned to look directly at Peale and said mournfully, though evenly, "Though death is indeed closer to the matter."

A shiver ran through Peale and he jumped to feet, exclaiming, "Oh, dear, not your little Martha, too!" Peale's face was pale and his cheeks quivered fretfully.

"Goodness, no!" Jefferson said. His keen, intelligent eyes lit up and within their hazel depths Peale caught a hint of the eccentric twinkle he had seen there many times before.

"No," Jefferson said again.

The room fell silent then, and Peale composed himself by straightening his clothing that had knotted into a tangle at his surprise a moment before.

Peale regained his seat before breaking the silence. "Then it must be this awful affair concerning your mentor, George Wythe. I am terribly sorry for it, Thomas. I have read the news reports from Richmond and must say I have found it very shocking. The kindly old lawyer and three of his servants all poisoned. Quite purposefully it seems by the nefarious nephew. What's his name?"

"George Wythe Sweeney," Jefferson supplied. "He's Wythe's grandnephew."

"I am, of course, terribly sorry for this awful affair, and I understand how dear Mr. Wythe was to you, but he must have been eighty, Thomas. Surely you couldn't have expected Wythe to have been with us much longer in any event, with or without this mysterious affair with the grandnephew."

"Mystery indeed," Jefferson muttered.

"It seems like an obvious case, though, Thomas. Wasn't this Sweeney the benefactor of Wythe's will?"

"Yes."

"Then that settles it, though again, I'm sorry. I am most obliging to be of service to you now and nurse you through this traumatic event, Thomas. Here, perhaps I should ring for some tea. Or wine, perhaps?"

"No, no thank you, Charles. You don't understand. The mystery of the poisoning is not the mystery of which I speak. Or, at least, it's not nearly half the mystery that consumes me now." Jefferson trembled as if from a chill, though there was no draft in the room.

Peale was dejected. He had expected the matter solved. Perhaps not mended, but at least he had hoped it revealed. Then he saw the scrolled parchment on a nearby end table.

"Well, here's mystery, then," Peale stood with some excitement and also with the anticipation of drawing the President's mind from the troubling matter of the murder of his mentor. He stepped over to the table and picked up the parchment. With a casual look at it, he verified its identity and presented it at once to Jefferson.

Peale said, "Then solve this mystery, Thomas. How is it that you can appraise me of my fevered guesses as to the reasons for your worrisome condition as I communicated to you in my most recent letter, when . . ." and he paused here for obvious dramatic effect, ". . . here is the very letter I posted to you? And its seal is unbroken and the letter obviously unread!"

"Now you are hitting even closer to the mark, my friend." As Jefferson rose, Peale inched back to give his friend some room.

Peale said, "I had it sealed and sent by special courier because of the secrecy upon which you insisted."

"I know, I know, my friend. I sincerely appreciate your precautions." Jefferson smiled convincingly as he edged toward the interior door that certainly led to his bedroom. "Please wait just one moment, Charles. I have something to show you."

Peale was anxious. He had noted a kind of feverish excitement in his friend just then. Whatever was happening was surely distressing the President's mind. Perhaps he was unwell, Peale thought. Or perhaps the shock of the sorry affair in Richmond was too much for the lonely man, who had now lived without his wife for more than a quarter century.

Jefferson was getting old, Peale had to remind himself, realizing simultaneously that he, too, was no longer a young man. Peale also knew that the years in Washington had been a strain on the President. The division between the parties, Jefferson's Republicans and the Federalists, was widening and Jefferson was being subjected to more political attacks than anyone in public life in the United States had been since the Revolution. Even so, though, it was little more than a year since the country had voted by a landslide to send his friend back to the President's House for a second term.

Peale's faith in democracy was confirmed by the people's faith in Thomas Jefferson.

Just then, Jefferson returned. In one hand he held a single sheet of paper and from the other long arm delicately dangled Jefferson's polygraph. Peale could see it was the device that he had sent to Jefferson about two years ago, back when the President championed the device over the cumbersome copying press he had used previously to keep a record of his letters. Peale wondered why Jefferson had requested a new one, because this one looked intact. The apparatus that connected the two pens over the writing surface looked solid enough. Maybe there was a hitch in it. Unless the mechanism was solidly connected yet flexible enough to account for the slightest movement, then the second pen would not be able to produce so exact a copy of the words written using the first pen.

Peale said, "As you requested, I brought a new polygraph for you. It's here." He pointed to the single bag he had carried into the house.

"Thank you, but not now, Charles. Have a look at this first." Jefferson stepped over to a writing table on which he placed the polygraph. Once he was certain it was firmly on the surface, he returned to Peale and handed him the sheet of paper.

Peale held it at arm's length and examined it. In

sudden alarm he shook the paper vigorously. "Why . . . !
What is this? This . . ." He paused to look at the paper
as if to convince himself. Then he calmed.

He looked mischievously at Jefferson. "A forgery?"

"No," Jefferson said sadly.

"But it must be," Peale insisted. He retrieved the
wax-sealed letter he had moments before identified as
his own and tore it open. With such force did he do this
that small flakes of dried wax burst into the air. He
glanced at the rolled paper and then back at the flat
sheet Jefferson had handed him.

"These are identical," Peale exclaimed. "And this,"
he rattled the sheet Jefferson had retrieved from his
bedroom, "must be the forgery. It cannot possibly be
the original when the original is here in my other
hand."

"Look at it more closely, my friend. What else can
you tell of it?"

"Well," Peale hesitated as he examined the forgery,
"it could perhaps be a polygraph copy of my letter. It
bears the slight indications of that. Here and here," he
pointed to the paper, "where the pen was obviously not
positioned completely against the paper."

"Yes, you are right."

Peale's countenance clouded with confusion, "But
that cannot be either. I did make a polygraph copy of
my letter to you, but first, how could it possibly be in
your possession, and more importantly, this couldn't be
it anyway as this is not the quality of paper I use for my
letters. If anything," Peale shook his head to right his
thoughts, "this is the variety of paper you employ in
your correspondence."

"Precisely so; I knew it was best to call you here."

Peale slumped into his chair. "Well, I don't know,
sir! I must admit this is the most I can hope to divine of
this most entangling mystery."

"And rightly so, Charles. If you could discern any
more than this, then you would be as troubled as I am."

"Oh, dear," Peale said while clutching his forehead,

"my head has not ached like this since I first began my attempts to assemble that mammoth for my museum.

Jefferson said, "Mine troubles me as well, my friend. But observe, you are on the verge of discovering the cause of my distress."

Jefferson reached out casually and took the so-called forgery from Peale's trembling hand. "This is not a forgery. This . . ." Jefferson took a deep breath and forcefully brandished the sheet of paper, "is the copy from my polygraph." Jefferson pointed to the device he had carried into the room. "That polygraph."

Peale almost swooned. His eyelids fluttered and his face flushed. "What?" was all he managed to mutter. Then he composed himself a bit and tried to sit up in the chair. "What can you possibly mean?"

Jefferson absently fingered the polygraph and then jumped when he realized he was touching it. "I mean," he said shakily, "that when I write any sort of correspondence using this polygraph to create a copy of the letter for my records, the second pencil of the polygraph, instead of mimicking my own movements and producing a copy of my own letter, produces the response to my letter instead."

"The response?" Peale said feebly.

"Yes," Jefferson exclaimed with a hint of madness to his voice. "The response. Instead of my words reproduced, I have instead not my words at all, but the words of the person who is responding to my letter."

"But that is impossible."

"Of course it is." Jefferson stumbled back to his chair and sank into it.

Peale was catching the fever of madness as well, and he began to sputter and blather, "It's impossible! How can you have the reply? You've not posted the letter. Days have not passed for it to travel to me in Philadelphia, your daughter in Virginia, or . . . or Meriwether Lewis in St. Lewis!"

Jefferson interjected, "Or George Wythe in Richmond."

But Peale seemed not to hear the President and

forged onward with his tirade. "And then days again for the reply to return. Yet you claim to have it in an instant! I am sorry, my friend, but I must declare you mad."

Jefferson grinned at that. "Then are you also mad? How do you explain my copy of your letter?"

Peale fell silent. The silence persisted for several moments. Jefferson seemed more at ease now that he had revealed his anxiety, though he was still obviously on edge and a great deal of concern was visible in the lines of his freckled face.

Peale, too, was lost in thought. Then he sat forward and rested his hands on his knees. "Show me."

Jefferson smiled again, and some of the creases grooved into his face eased. "I knew I could count on you, Charles. It takes a strong mind, I think, to face this unexplainable thing. And a great curiosity as well. You lack in neither regard, and I know that together we may perhaps resolve this."

Jefferson stood and walked back to the writing table where he had placed the polygraph. "First, I will have you know that I do not care for this particular machine any longer, and that's why I requested you bring a new one for me. I do not know what has been the greater trial for the past several days: remaining sane in the wake of this machine's odd functioning, or working without a polygraph altogether. My old copy press is a poor substitute for such an advance as you and Professor Hawkins made with the polygraph."

"Observe," said Jefferson. He opened the drawer of the writing table and withdrew two sheets of paper. Each was like the "forgery" Peale's response was written upon, and both were clamped down onto the writing base of the polygraph. A complicated sort of pantograph in that it created images identical to the original but in the same size as opposed to larger or smaller, the polygraph in its operational setup resembled a long and wide but short box that had been set on one of its sides and then opened so the top and the bottom folded flush to the surface of the table. This left a squared frame of wood that stood like an arch between the two downturned sections. This frame was the main anchoring for the complicated series of interconnected sticks that laced the now exposed area. At the front, the portion where Jefferson had secured the two sheets of paper, the polygraph consisted largely of a metal strip suspended above the writing surface by sticks that stretched back and up to the squared frame. At each end of the strip was a metal clamp with one end that projected down toward the writing surface and held a pen. The wooden sticks all rotated in such a way that the movement of either pen would result in the identical motion on the other.

Jefferson said, "It happens every time I use the device. Instead of the customary copy of my own letter, I receive, as I have told you and will soon convince you, a copy of the response."

Jefferson readied the pen. "To whom shall I write?"

Peale thought a moment. "Well . . . surely no one in town as what would you address them concerning other than something of political consequence, so perhaps your overseer at Monticello? Or perhaps your daughter Martha?"

"Martha it will be," Jefferson said. "My thoughts are too scattered to communicate anything of import to William Hamilton at Monticello, and Martha, at least, will be forgiving of her old father's blatherings."

Jefferson thought for a moment, and then he began. The writing elicited an immediate gasp from Peale. Beginning to write the evening's date at the head of the paper, Jefferson had already created an anomaly on the copying page. For Jefferson's "1" there was not a "1" on the other sheet, but instead a "2".

"Remarkable," gasped Peale.

Jefferson quickly wrote the next number, "8". By means of the carefully constructed mechanisms of the polygraph, Jefferson's movements were translated precisely to the other pen, but a copy of his "8" did not appear. Instead, the pen scratched out a "3."

"Wait, wait," Peale cried out in alarm and exhilaration.

When Jefferson relaxed his grip on the pen and edged backward a half a step, Peale moved in on the device immediately. He carefully examined the connections among the wooden pieces, but after a moment he was satisfied.

"It seems to be in perfect operational condition," Peale concluded.

"Indeed," Jefferson agreed. "It's not the operation that is in jeopardy but, rather, the result."

Peale requested, "Please continue."

Jefferson leaned back into the simple chore of writing a letter to his daughter. He continued without hesitating or delaying again. His movements were quick and precise, and his penmanship extraordinary. He did not even glance at what the other pen was writing onto the adjacent sheet.

But Peale did. He felt himself disappearing into the event he was perceiving. The first few renewed motions of polygraph startled Peale because they did copy Jefferson's motions when the President wrote "1806," and that set Peale at ease. But then Jefferson wrote "Dear Martha," and only the "Dear" was copied directly— "Father" came afterward. Peale shivered and swooned forward and just managed to catch himself on the edge of the table. Jefferson continued and Peale watched intently as the President's letter, and his daughter's reply dated five days later, were completed at the same time.

"Do you believe me mad now, Charles?"

"Thomas, I believe that we must both be mad."

"Look," Jefferson pointed at portions of the two letters, which were both still clamped to the writing surface, as he read through them. "She responds to the few questions I pose and addresses my concerns."

Jefferson could not stifle a bit of laughter, "Here she even suggests that the tone of my letter is, in her words, 'most abrupt and sketchy,' and she wonders if I am in good health."

"There can be no doubt," Peale agreed, "that this letter is from Martha and is a response to yours. But how is such instantaneous communication possible?"

"Such is the issue that has raged through my own mind," Jefferson said wearily. "I must get away from this nefarious device." At which he returned to his reading chair, stumbling a bit over the piles of books as his feet dragged limply across the floor.

Once he was seated and seemingly more comfortable, Jefferson said, "This is better. A much better position in which to think, though astride a horse serves the purpose as well."

Peale was still standing near the reading table. A thousand questions were burning in his mind.

The first question popped out. "When did this first happen?"

"Just after my return to Washington from Monticello on June 7th. I was also then writing a note to Martha, mainly to let her know I had returned safely and that everything was in order."

"You noticed the oddity right away, then?"

"By no means," Jefferson said. "In fact, I did not detect it until later. I have used the polygraph so often now and am so entirely confident of its proficiency that I rarely look at the copy while my writing is progressing. In this case, I did not look at all and when the letter was nearly completed, I was interrupted by some Congressional business, so I hastily concluded the letter and prepared it for posting. I only noticed the odd 'copy' several hours later. I was confused at first, as my rational mind tried, I suppose, to create an explanation for the letter from Martha. The long meeting I had endured with a handful of Congressmen coupled with my very recent journey, had damaged my sense of time, and this coupled with the authentic nature of the letter caused me to trick myself. This lasted only a matter of moments, though, before I realized that something was amiss. At first, of course, I assumed this was some trick, a jest of my secretary, or perhaps one of my sons-in-law, either John Wayles Eppes or Thomas Mann Randolph."

"Though neither of the two had committed such trickery in the past, I immediately took the issue up with each of them. John was first as he was within the house at the time I sought them. To briefly conclude and bypass a myriad of astonished denials and, I might note, many odd glances when they thought my back turned, no one took credit for the trickery.

"All of this was put aside for a time when I received the unfortunate letter of William Du Val, the neighbor and friend of George Wythe who first communicated the news of the poisoning to me. Not much of import occurred the remainder of that day."

"Understandably," Peale said in a gentle voice.

Jefferson reflected silently for a moment and then said, "Late the next day, the 8th of June, after tending to more Congressional business, I wrote a letter back to Mr. Du Val, and that is the second time the polygraph operated in a similarly inscrutable manner, but it's the first time I realized what was happening."

"Again I didn't notice anything, I was so absorbed in the letter itself because the health and very life of my friend were at issue. Several lines into the letter, though, I gained this very odd sensation. I hesitate to describe it too graphically, or you truly will believe me mad, so I will only say that there was a compelling presence that gave me a chill. It was at this point that I realized with complete certainty what had occurred the day before regarding my letter to Martha, for as I wrote to Du Val, I watched as he wrote back to me."

Peale was astonished. "You mean you believe that Du Val was writing back to you at that very moment and just as your words were mysteriously transmitted to him, his words were delivered through the air to you."

Jefferson shook his head, "I don't have enough information to support any theory, Charles, and certainly not that one."

"There is such a host of questions and even paradoxes to consider!" Peale exclaimed. "Do they receive the letter the instant you write it just as that is when you receive the reply? But then why is Martha's reply of moments ago dated five days after your own letter? What would happen if after you wrote the letter and received the reply you decided not to mail the letter?" He paused in his conjectures just long enough to throw a comment to Jefferson. "No wonder you have been ill at ease."

"Even so, you do not completely fathom it," Jefferson said, but it might as well have been a whisper in a storm, for Peale rallied onward.

"What would happen if you wrote me now? Would I see words that I have not even composed in my head appear via the polygraph? And does this same property function in correspondence across the Atlantic?" Peale hooted. "Just think, Thomas, you could write a letter to Napoleon and receive his answer and act upon it weeks before he ever even received your original letter! Unless, of course, the communication is instantaneous both ways."

Peale fairly well began to shake, so much so that he was forced to grab his head and hold his breath for a moment in order to slow himself down.

"I had not yet considered such ingenious uses for this cursed device." There was a touch of sorrow in Jefferson's voice.

Peale had to laugh at his friend. "Of course not, Thomas. You are not the kind to use such trickery to gain an advantage over another. For that is what this is at heart. Trickery. Trickery of a sort we cannot as yet comprehend, but trickery all the same."

Peale continued, "Imagine if every person in America possessed such a miraculous device. The effect on democracy would be stupendous!"

Jefferson said wearily, "But not everyone in America could afford such an instrument. What, then, of the poor who are left out of your great instant communication revolution? These people will accomplish only in days and weeks what others can do in mere moments. Would not the gulf between those with and without such a polygraph only widen and serve to destabilize the democracy?"

Peale was almost indignant, "Well, then, as President you would have to make certain that everyone was granted such equipment by the government. And then! Why the instantaneous communication of news and correspondence would bind the society together!" Peale was on his feet now, the nobility of his thought taking root all the way through him.

"I must disagree again," Jefferson said. "I may be wrong, of course, but an immediate effect I foresee of such rapid communication is the consequent rapid degeneration of the content of said communication. If words are so easily used, then they will eventually carry no significance, and soon the stream of communication will become a flood of trivialities that will not challenge the brain."

The weight of the President's words pressed Peale back into his chair. "Surely you overstate the case, Thomas."

"I do not think so, Charles. If the time comes when words, too, become malleable to the penchant for efficiency in the human heart, then language itself will become obsolete."

Peale swallowed hard. "This is all beside the point, I think. I am very sorry for the diversion. I am here to help you with a problem, not to lay the destiny of mankind at your feet. In any event, it is only your polygraph that has behaved so peculiarly, and the possibility of another acting thus, and by extension securing one for every American family, is a far-fetched proposition at best.

"So let us return to your troubled state of mind," Peale said. "Why did you refer to the polygraph in so harsh a manner a bit ago?"

"In what way?"

"I believe you characterized it as 'cursed,' " Peale said.

"Oh, yes," Jefferson said. "I didn't believe you heard that. You were carrying on so."

"I apologize."

"No matter, my friend. This is a rather curious affair,

and I completely understand how it might cause one's mind to race a bit."

"Well?"

Jefferson hesitated.

"There's more?" Peale asked incredulously.

Jefferson seemed to deflate, "Yes. The main source of my agitated state is a result of the next letter I wrote. You see, when I wrote the second letter, the one to Du Val, the response I received indicated that George Wythe's condition continued to deteriorate. That news, plus the discovery of this odd property of the polygraph caused me to sink into a melancholy that persisted until the following morning. It was only upon rising, that I realized one way in which I might take advantage of the polygraph. If, as you also have conjectured, the transmission of my own letter was instantaneous, then I could write a final letter to my mentor that he would receive before his untimely death. Additionally, or perhaps I should say at the least, I would receive a final letter from him as well."

Jefferson took a deep breath. "So, I wrote a long letter, the details of which I do not feel comfortable relating, and as I hoped, I received a lengthy reply from George."

"That is wonderful!" A broad and genuine smile surged across Peale's face. "See, perhaps instant communication does have its merits."

Jefferson's face was still long and dark and troubled.

The volume of Peale's voice dropped to a fraction of his earlier outburst, "What is it that troubles you, then?"

Jefferson looked up directly into Peale's eyes. "Even though I was delighted to receive the letter from George, the incident still unnerved me, so I went back to using my old copy press for several days thereafter. Then, upon the 12th of June, I received a another letter by post from Du Val. The letter informed me that the poison had indeed been too much for an old man, and George Wythe had died on the 8th of June."

Peale's voice was still low and consoling, but he was

a little confused as well. "Yes, we have spoken of the hurt the loss of your mentor must have inflicted."

"You do not see it, do you, Charles?"

Peale was silent and shook his head.

Jefferson said, "George Wythe died on the 8th, but I wrote my letter to him and received his reply on the morning of June 9th!"

Peale remained silent and just continued to shake his head.

CREATURE CONGRESS
by Terry Beatty and Wendi Lee

Cartoonist Terry Beatty and his wife, novelist Wendi Lee, have coauthored numerous short stories in a variety of genres. Terry is best known for his comic book collaborations with Max Allan Collins, including *Ms. Tree, Johnny Dynamite,* and *Wild Dog.* His work can also be found in *Mickey Spillane's Mike Danger* and on the covers of *Scary Monsters.* Wendi is the author of *The Good Daughter* and *Missing Eden,* featuring P.I. Angela Matelli. Her Westerns include the "Jefferson Birch" series and *The Overland Trail.* She has published a dozen short stories, and is associate editor of *Mystery Scene.*

The sharp repetitive sounds brought a near silence to the crowded hall as the gavel, seemingly animated by some sort of spirit or spell, called the group to order. Of course, there was a simple explanation for this. The Invisible Man, chair of the Creature Congress, had elected not to wear his gloves today—or anything else, for that matter. Adopting a nudist lifestyle had allowed him to go about unnoticed, at least in warm weather, without having to wrap his face in bandages, wear sunglasses, hat and gloves, all to keep people from shrieking at the sight of a seemingly headless, handless man. Though, frankly, the world had gotten so strange lately he had to wonder if people really would be shocked anymore.

Well, that very subject was the primary reason they had convened here. Hundreds of monsters had come to D.C. to debate the matter. Time to get things started, he supposed. "As duly elected chair of this body, I hereby open this special session of the Creature Congress. As it seems there are no vacant seats in the hall, I move that we dispense with the roll call."

"I second that motion!" said the Thing with Two Heads (well, his left head, anyway).

"Motion seconded, all in favor say aye." The Invisible Man's request was met with a reply of shrieks, grunts, and growls, all translated into one big "aye"—except for, oddly enough, the Giant Eye who shook his all-seeing orb, "nay."

"The ayes have it—motion carried," proclaimed The Invisible Man as he struck the gavel one more time. "On to our reason for calling this special session. As you know, section three, paragraph two of our charter calls for all monsters—living, dead, or undead—to go about their business in utmost secrecy, sharing our existence only with each other, or our intended victims. Now, not all of our members have adhered to these rules." The Invisible Man paused long enough for the monsters to stop hissing and growling, then he continued in an acid tone, "Some of you will recall a certain vampire who gave an extensive interview to a human author a few years ago . . ."

"Phooey on him!" shouted Count Dracula from his seat in the front row. He wrapped his cape tighter around him and sat up straight in his seat.

"The distinguished Count's displeasure is noted for the record. You will recall that the vampire in question was drummed out of our organization for, what was it officially?" The Invisible Man flipped through a few papers he had sitting on the podium. "Ah, here it is—'behavior unbefitting a bloodsucker.' "

Approving howls and grunts filled the room, as The Invisible Man pounded the gavel, calling for order.

"Nevertheless, some of our members believe that it may be time to amend that portion of our charter. I'm

told that one of our founding members has something
to say on that subject, and so the chair officially recognizes the Frankenstein Monster."

Dr. Frankenstein's creation lumbered to the podium to thunderous applause from the other members
of the Congress. No matter how controversial the
subject he was to speak on, this was still one of
the most respected and feared creatures to ever walk
the earth. The applause continued until the immortal
Monster raised his gnarled yellow hand, calling for
silence.

"I am not human," he began in a deep and gut-
tural voice, "but I am made of flesh that once was
human. Sewn together from the limbs and organs of
a dozen men, I have chosen to live apart from
a mankind that has rejected me and called me monster. Yet am I any more monstrous than mankind? Are
any of us? True, there are those in this room who
are predators, who kill to survive—but we kill *only*
to survive. Yes, the vampire drains the blood from
his victims, but he also offers them eternal life among
the Undead. The Zombie may kill and eat portions of his prey, but in doing so, he adds another
member to the great fellowship of Zombiedom.
Humans kill each other, not for food or to add
members to their pack, but for reasons that defy my
understanding. A monster takes care in choosing
a victim—no drive-by shootings or terrorist bomb-
ings with random results—what honor is there
in that? No self-respecting monster would be so
careless in its slaughter—and yet it is we who
must hide in the shadows, while humanity lives in the
sun."

"Who wants to live in the sun anyway?" It was
Dracula, interrupting again. "It gives me such a pain."

The Monster made a pacifying gesture with the
smaller of his mismatched hands. "Merely a figure of
speech, Count. But think of this: For years humanity
has written books about us, made movies, television
shows, toys—they celebrate Halloween every year—

play that blasted 'Monster Mash' song on the radio—
and what do we get out of it? *Nothing.* Nada. Zip.
Zilch. Zowie. Nothin'." The Monster shrugged dramatically. "Oh, sure, Universal Studios and the estates of a
bunch of dead actors collect all sorts of royalty fees on
our names and images, but we don't see a penny. I ask
you, is that fair?" He pounded his fist on the podium,
and the hall erupted with supportive shrieks and
moans.

When the hall had quieted down, the Frankenstein Monster continued. "How can we demand our
fair share when we cannot make our presence known?
The argument has always been that if humans
knew of us, they would hunt us down and destroy us,
that they would fear us because we are so strange.
In the past this was unquestionably true, but I feel
that things have changed. Gangs of young humans
on the streets of this city kill more people every
year than many of us have killed in all our years of
existence. If humanity will tolerate that, then what
problem should they have with a werewolf or a ghoul?"
Frankenstein slipped a hand inside his ill-fitting jacket
and brought out two large pieces of paper. "If it is
our appearance that frightens people, then how do you
explain this?" The Monster held up a poster-sized
photo of an internationally famous "superstar" record-
ing artist. The picture was a close-up of the man's
smiling effeminate face. The entire Congress gasped in
horror.

"This human has had more surgery on his face than
Dr. Frankenstein performed on my *entire body,* and
yet only *some* of his fellow humans regard him as a
monstrosity. And what of *this* woman?" He held up another picture of a female pop star whose thickly
painted face stared out at the audience with a sneer. A
visible shudder ran through the crowd of monsters.
"Not even the Succubus has drained the sexual energy
of as many men as has this horrid harpy." There was
some squawking in the back of the room. The Monster
nodded his understanding as he put the photos aside.

"My apologies to any harpies who may be here this evening. Again, it's just a figure of speech. No offense meant.

"There in the second row sits my friend, Mr. Hyde, considered a monster because of his use of illegal chemical substances to transform himself from his human identity of Dr. Jekyll—but is not the Mayor of this very city a convicted user of illegal drugs? Why is Mr. Hyde a monster and Mr. Mayor a respected citizen? My fellow creatures, I say humanity has caught up with us. We are all monsters, and there is no more reason for us to live in the shadow of Mankind. I say we amend our charter and announce our existence to the world."

The hall erupted with growls and snarls, shrieks and moans—a mixed reaction to the Monster's proposal.

Again the Invisible Man pounded his gavel, and as Frankenstein's creation made his way back to his seat in the hall, the hoots and hollers subsided. "We will now open the subject for debate." Several hands, claws, and pincers were raised in the crowd. "The chair recognizes the Manitou."

The ghostly creature hovered above its seat and spoke in a voice that sounded like the low moaning of the wind. "For centuries my kind lived in harmony with the native peoples of this land, but with the coming of the European settlers, we were forced into hiding. I say that until this land is returned to its rightful owners, I shall remain hidden in the rocks, the trees, and the wind. As the only true native American member of this body, I vote to remain apart from the humans who infest this land."

"Whoa! Hang on a minute there, pal." It was Bigfoot, obviously agitated, and not waiting for official recognition from the chair. He had hoisted his large, shaggy frame out of his seat. Normally, the Invisible Man would have called for order and insisted on procedure, but the eight-foot-tall, fur-covered Bigfoot was known to be a hothead, and it seemed that just letting him speak would be the most sensible thing to do.

"Excuse me for speaking out of order here, but Manny ain't the only true blue American in this crowd. My ancestors have been hiding out in the American backwoods since the days of the wooly mammoth and the saber-toothed tiger, and as far as I'm concerned, it's gettin' old. I mean, they got film footage of my Uncle Leonard anyhow, so our existence ain't exactly been a secret for some time now.

"With civilization chewin' up more and more of the wilderness, it's gettin' harder for us to forage. I'd sure like to be able to just drop into the local Quick-Mart for a Bucket O' Chicken or some Nachos-to-Go, instead of havin' to settle for pickin' through some camper's leftovers."

Bigfoot seemed about to take his seat, but apparently remembered something else. He raised a finger to keep the Congress' attention. "And another thing—my whole family is mighty tired of this 'Bigfoot' moniker. Sounds like some stupid cartoon character or somethin'. We'd like to be called by our proper name, 'The North American Yeti,' and the only way to make that happen, is to come out of the woods and stand up for our rights as American citizens. Guess I'm done. Sorry for interruptin', but I just had to say what I had to say." With that, the furry thing slumped back into his seat.

"Thank you for sharing that with us, Big . . . uh, I mean Yeti." The Invisible Man noted an amphibious claw raised near the back of the hall. "The chair now recognizes the Swamp Creature."

The slimy, scaly Swamp Creature, dripping wet and tangled up with roots and vines, stood to address the hall. "Respected members of the Creature Congress, as the head of the Aquatic Creatures Committee, I'd like to lend my support to the proposal. In the past few decades, the lakes, rivers, oceans, and wetlands that we live in have become increasingly polluted, largely due to human greed and stupidity. We'd like to put an end to that, but how are we supposed to take the offending parties to court and effect any legal change, if we can't even acknowledge our own existence? The Aquatic Creatures Committee wholeheartedly supports the Frankenstein Monster's proposal, the only exception being the Loch Ness Monster. Nessy seems to think that public exposure would *cause* more damage to her environs, what with increased tourism and all, and while we all respect her opinion, we don't agree with it. Let's go public. It's time."

Next up was the Wicked Witch. "Okay, here's my two cents. I'm sick and tired of these so-called 'witches' who have usurped our good name, when they're really just a bunch of New Age trendy Earth Mother worshipers with their crystals and their candles. Foo on 'em! Not a one of 'em could ride a broomstick to save her life, never mind casting a *real* spell. I'd like to see one of them granola-eatin' ninnies just try to conjure up a demon from the pits of Hades—Hell, they couldn't conjure up a swarm of flies! I wanna go public so's we can kick their pretentious fat behinds. Plus, we want some of that Halloween money. I think the Ghosts and Punkinheads agree that we're owed plenty for the use of our images." A Jack O'Lantern behind her nodded so vigorously that the Invisible Man was afraid his head would roll off his bony shoulders.

The Wicked Witch scratched thoughtfully at the wart on her nose before continuing. "And just think—we're doin' so good runnin' our organization, what if we got more involved with human government? If humans only knew that two of their recent presidents were pod people and one was a robot, maybe they'd be more willing to accept us. I can't even *count* how many of the First Ladies have been witches!

"Our bloodsucking vampire members sure would make good IRS employees. How about Zombies in the military? NASA could sure benefit from the cooperation of our Alien Life Forms sub-committee.

I even have this recipe for Eye of Newt that I think . . ."

"Wait just one cotton-picking minute!" Dracula rose from his seat, one hand clutching his cape and drawing it near his body. The other hand was raised as if the Count was waiting to be called on in class. "I have something to say."

"Will the Wicked Witch yield to the distinguished gentleman from Transylvania?" the Invisible Man asked.

"Oh, sure, go ahead," she replied, making a dismissive gesture with her bony, long-nailed hand. "I said my piece anyhow."

"The Chair recognizes Count Dracula, Prince of Darkness."

The Count stood before the gathering of unearthly creatures, deliberately stroking his chin, taking a moment for dramatic effect before speaking. "My fellow monsters, my dear friend Frankenstein makes a persuasive argument, but I am afraid I must oppose his suggestion."

"It is true that humanity has become more and more accepting of the odd and unusual, making heroes of 'shock jock' radio personalities, gasbag political 'humorists,' and so-called 'performance artists,' but the question is not 'are they ready for us?' but rather, 'are we ready for them'? It has always been true that humans have killed each other in numbers that far exceed even our most dastardly efforts. Now they seem to be even more violent than ever before—and more efficient about it." The Count paused for a moment and looked each creature in the eye (well, those creatures who had eyes, anyway), then went on to make his point. "Would the werewolves in attendance truly wish to risk being hunted by humans with handheld semi-automatic machine pistols with clips full of dozens of silver bullets? A humanity that thinks nothing of slaughtering each other over perceived differences of race or religion wouldn't have a second thought about wiping us out. And if they don't perceive us as a threat, then the best we can hope for is to be considered a curiosity. Does the Yeti want to be put on display at the carnival with our former members, the Geeks and Pinheads? They thought they could fit into human society, too."

The Count waggled his finger back and forth. "No, my fellow monsters, our founders were wise to insist we stick to the shadows. We are *immortal*. We are *united*. And the foolish, divisive humans with their tiny lifespans think of new ways every day to make those lives even shorter." Dracula spread his arms in a wide gesture, his cape flaring open like a bat unfurling its wings. "So let them kill each other. Let them poison themselves. Let them rot their brains with their video games and their cable TV. And when they have made themselves so helpless that they can no longer pose a threat to us, *then* we shall make ourselves known—then *we* shall rule the world!" Dracula shook his fist in a defiant gesture and ended his speech in a low, compelling tone of voice. "That day is not yet here, my friends, but it is coming soon, very soon."

The monsters in the hall were on their feet (those that had feet, at least), applauding wildly. Clearly, Dracula's impassioned speech had won them over. Only the Frankenstein Monster remained seated, slumped in his chair, looking dejected.

"All in favor of the Frankenstein proposal, signify by saying aye," the Invisible Man said.

The only "aye" heard in the hall was from Frankenstein himself, spoken halfheartedly, the sound of defeat evident in his voice.

"All opposed say nay."

As one, the rest of the monsters voiced their disapproval, some patting a smiling Dracula on the back and shaking his hand in congratulations. The right side head of the Thing with Two Heads leaned over to Frankenstein and said, "Sorry, Franky, I was gonna vote with you, but Lefty here is hard to live with when I disagree with him."

"The nays have it. The motion is defeated," the Invisible Man said, announcing the obvious. "Now on to other business. The Giant Ant has requested that we make August 23 'Take a Giant Ant to Lunch Day.' All those in favor, say aye."

THE CABINET OF WILLIAM HENRY HARRISON

by Barbara Collins and Max Allan Collins

Barbara and Max Allan Collins are husband and wife; their previous collaborations include the short story "Cat Got your Tongue" in *Cat Crimes III* and their teenage son, Nathan. Barbara is a short-story specialist with appearances in numerous anthologies, including *The Year's 25 Finest Crime and Mystery Stories* and *Celebrity Vampires*. Max is the prolific author of the Shamus-winning Nathan Heller historical thrillers; his other credits include comics scripting, songwriting, and screenwriting. Max is the director, screenwriter, and executive producer of the award-winning telefilm "Mommy" on which Barbara was the unit production manager. They live in Muscatine, Iowa.

From up ahead the voice of the tour guide echoed back to them: ". . . saved by Dolley Madison from the White House fire of 1814 was the portrait of George Washington, painted by Gilbert Stuart in 1805, that hangs over the . . ."

The thirty-something couple at the rear of the little group was paying scant attention to these or other tidbits of White House lore.

The woman, her mousy-brown hair in a short serviceable cut, her gray sweater and slacks casual but not sloppy, wore a look of intense concentration; but the tour guide's words had nothing to do with it.

"I don't know what I'm going to do, Steve," she whispered. Her rather pleasant face—which seemed plain only for its lack of makeup—was contorted with worry.

Her husband, his handsome if horsey face drawn with concern, had wheat-colored hair tied back in a small ponytail, his plaid shirt and chinos making him look more like a college student than a vacationing math professor.

"Darling," he whispered, "we've been over all that. Can't we please just enjoy this? Not everybody gets honored with a VIP tour like this."

But his words made no more impact than the tour guide's. She said, "Can't you see I'm *drowning?* Like a damn bubble sliding toward an open drain . . ."

"Sarah," he said, squeezing her forearm with affection and concern, "you'll be fine . . ."

She didn't feel fine. She felt so tense she thought she was going to explode. Instead, her words exploded in another harsh whisper: "Who would have believed it? Who *ever* would have believed it? My greatest dream has become my worst nightmare!" She swallowed. She was embarrassed to sense her eyes welling up with tears. "It's . . . it's almost unbearable . . ."

And the tour guide droned on: ". . . East Room parquet floor which had to be replaced in 1977 because the twenty-five million visitors who walked on it since the White House has been open to tours, simply wore . . ."

Steve stopped her, turned her toward him. "So you never write another book," he shrugged. "You won a Pulitzer Prize, Sarah. No one can ever take that away, ever."

Sarah was shaking her head. "But what will they say?" A humorless laugh escaped her lips. "What they're saying right *now,* I suppose. She's a one-shot. She got lucky."

Steve's expression was pained. "Honey. It took you five years to write that wonderful novel. They can't expect another in just a *year.*"

"Then I shouldn't have taken that advance, should I? Or signed that damn contract."

Which just yesterday, in New York City, she had

done, at the urging of her agent and her editor and her publisher and, yes, even her husband . . .

Her smirk was as humorless as the laugh. "I have to strike while the iron's hot, they say. When the first book's out in paperback next year, I'll need the 'follow-up.' "

"I suppose timing *is* important," Steve allowed.

"Get another book out before I'm forgotten, they say. Can you imagine? My reputation has a *time* limit. And that advance—so much money. How can I live up to it? What if they're disappointed? What if I can't deliver?"

Perhaps her whispering wasn't a whisper anymore. Was it Sarah's imagination, or was there irritation now, in the tour guide's droning tone: ". . . exquisite cabinet made by local cabinetmaker Edwin Green in 1819 for William Henry Harrison, the ninth President of the United States. Harrison was the first President to die in the White House, just a month into his term. He caught a cold at his inauguration, riding a white stallion down Pennsylvania Avenue in a blizzard, without a hat or coat . . ."

Sarah gripped her husband's arm. "Steve, I want to leave. I feel sick."

"You're just having another anxiety attack," he said, trying to reassure her but sounding patronizing. "Did you bring your medication?"

She put a palm to her forehead and felt herself weaving in place. "I'm so tired . . . so very, very tired. I . . . I have to lie down."

"Just lean on me," he said, and she did. Then suddenly Steve's voice seemed far away, as if in an echo chamber, and fading, fading: ". . . Sarah? Sarah? Sarah! What's wrong? Someone! *Somebody!* Get a doctor! Oh, my God. Oh, my God. No . . . no . . ."

Sarah opened her eyes, waking from a deep sleep, a sleep more restful than any she'd experienced in years. Her body felt loose, like a rubber band. The fainting, she supposed, had relaxed even the muscles in her face.

Washingtoniana

Her eyes tried to focus, as she lay on the floor, staring upward at a large, bright, white object which floated above her.

An angel? The white light at the end of a tunnel? She felt panic rising in her like negative adrenaline. Had she not fainted, but . . . *died?*

The object began to clarify itself, turning into the massive crystal-and-gold candle chandelier of the White House Green Room.

"Just be still," said a gentle baritone voice. "Don't try to move, my dear, because you won't be able to."

He was right. Though she could "feel" her arms and legs, she couldn't budge them. Only her eyes moved. Had she had a stroke, as well?

"You will be fine in a few minutes, you'll see," the male voice said. A face leaned over her. Old, distinguished, yet delicate, with thin eyebrows over deep-set dark eyes, a long slender nose, full lips. Silver, wavy hair cascaded over a high forehead.

He must be a White House attendant, she thought, in his old-fashioned heavy dark wool suit and starched white shirt. Was this nostalgic attire part of the tour? In any case, this was clearly someone who'd been around the White House for a long, long time . . .

She struggled again to sit up, but couldn't. She tried to speak, but wasn't able. Panic, once again, engulfed her, like freezing water, making her instantly alert— and afraid.

"There, there, my dear, do lie still," came a woman's soothing, British-accented voice. "It does take a little while to recover. It certainly did with me."

And then a female face gazed down at Sarah.

This woman was perhaps in her late forties or early fifties. Dark brown curls peeked out from underneath a large white scarf-tied straw hat. Her eyebrows were penciled on over heavily made-up eyes. And on either side of her red bee-stung lips were round pink circles of rouge, which hung on her face like little balloons. The top of the woman's dress (for that's all that Sarah could see) appeared to be made of thin material, like foulard or crepe, with delicate satin ribbons trimming the scooped neck. A strange outfit, she thought, for such a cold autumn day. Why would a grown woman dress up like a Gibson Girl-esque doll?

Sarah could now open her mouth, but she still could not speak.

Then a young boy appeared at Sarah's other side. He wore a navy cap and a brown jacket with knickers and knee socks, and would have been a formal looking little gentleman if the clothing had not been, essentially, rags. The boy knelt down and looked at her curiously from a cherubic, dirt-rouged face, as if studying a bug on the floor.

"She winned her a *prize,* did ya hear it?" the boy said excitedly to the others. "But what's a pula . . . a pula . . . ?"

"A *Pulitzer* Prize," smiled the elderly man. "That's a very distinguished honor—not a stuffed toy from knocking down milk bottles at the fair, lad." He nodded sagely, beaming at Sarah. "We're lucky indeed to have this woman among us."

The young boy's face turned into a pout. "Well, *I* winned a prize once," he said almost defiantly, directing his comment to the elderly man. "At the Century of Progress. It was a . . ."

"We *know,*" a new male voice interrupted. "You've told us a million times, kid!"

A young bearded man with long, stringy brown hair, in a tie-dyed T-shirt and scruffy jeans and scruffier sandals stood next to the kneeling boy, a hand on the little boy's shoulder, and said, "But the Prez is right—the Pulitzer Prize is no toy."

What a strange group of people, Sarah thought. She certainly didn't remember seeing them on the tour. If these were VIPs, then the circus must be in town.

And where was Steve? Had he gone to get help?

Suddenly her body twitched and life coursed through her veins like electricity through a conduit.

She struggled to sit up on the green-and-gold Oriental

rug, and the young boy grabbed her by the arm to help her.

"Where's my husband?" Sarah managed to rasp. She looked around, side to side, too quickly, the opulent, ornately decorated Green Room room only adding to her dizziness. She placed one hand to her temple. "Where's Steve?"

"He's next door in the Blue Room, Sarah," the woman answered. "Am I taking a liberty by calling you Sarah? We're going to be such great friends, after all, and, at any rate, I'm afraid we overheard you and your husband speaking, and . . ."

Sarah smacked her hand against the carpeted floor with such a *whump*, it startled the little group. "What the hell is this about?" she demanded. "Who are you people?"

The Kewpie-doll woman turned her gaze away, as if Sarah had slapped her. "We only brought you in here to . . . recover."

On wobbly legs, Sarah got to her feet, the young boy again assisting her. She thanked him.

Then, firmly, she said, "I must see my husband," and took a few tentative steps toward the closed mahogany door of the Green Room, which led to the Blue Room.

But the woman stepped in front of Sarah, putting her hands on Sarah's shoulders, saying quietly, imploringly, "Please don't, Sarah . . . if I may call you Sarah. I implore you not to open that door. It will only . . . break your heart."

These people were straining her patience, but most of all, fear was creeping back under her skin. "*What* will break my heart?" she asked.

The Kewpie-doll shook her head, and her curls, lifting a gently lecturing finger. "I speak from experience, my dear. There's nothing you can do. Nothing you can say now that your dear husband will hear."

"What do you mean?" Sarah asked, fighting back terror. "Is something the matter with Steve?"

The eyes in the woman's painted face were filled with pity.

"Please, tell me!" Sarah cried.

"I'll tell ya!" the little boy blurted. "There ain't nothin' wrong with your husband, lady. It's you! You're down with a serious case of *dead*—din'cha figure that out yet? Jeez!"

Sarah stared numbly at the boy.

Dead? She wasn't dead. She was anything but dead; she felt fine. As a matter of fact, she couldn't remember ever feeling better. Was the child out of his mind?

The hippie grabbed the little boy's arm. "*Le*-roy," he said, drawing the boy's name out to unintentionally comic effect, "I ought to *clobber* you, man!"

"Yes, Leroy," the painted lady said, in a mildly scolding tone, "that was most *rude* of you. I thought we agreed to bring her over . . . gradually."

"Horsefeathers!" The boy wrenched himself out of the hippie's grasp. "You chowderheads were gonna let her get away!"

"Quiet—*everyone!*" the old man bellowed authoritatively. "Is this any way for my *Cabinet* to behave?"

His *what?* What did furniture have to do with anything? Were they *all* completely out of their minds? Was the queen of hearts waiting in the hallway, to lop off her head?

"Look," Sarah said, smiling, sincerely she hoped, patting the air with her palms, "it's been very nice to meet you . . . all of you, *whoever* you are . . . and I appreciate your help and concern . . . but I really must go now, and find my husband."

She backed away from the strange little group, toward the closed mahogany door.

"We must not try to stop her," the old man instructed.

"But . . . she's gonna *see*," the boy whined.

"We, better than most, know the value of passing along pertinent information."

The little group began to nod at one another.

Oh-kay, Sarah thought, and turned and moved quickly toward the door and opened it. The sooner she got out of this Mad Tea Party, the better.

She moved down the hallway to the room next door,

the oval Blue Room, its door open, revealing para-
medics frantically laboring over a body sprawled on
the gleaming parquet floor.

Her body.

"I can't get a pulse!" one paramedic shouted.

"She's decompensating!" yelled another.

Steve, slumped in a gilded chair nearby, the thinning
patch at the crown in his nest of wheat-colored hair
showing, was weeping into his cupped hands.

Sarah, wide-eyed with shock, backed up into the
Green Room, shutting the door slowly, and leaned up
against it.

Poor Steve. Poor Steve ... So grief stricken. The
sight of him, it . . . it broke her heart.

Sarah's eyes flooded with tears and she, too, wept
uncontrollably into her hands. How could she be dead,
she thought, when she felt so alive, when her tears felt
so wet against her fingers?

After a moment, when she'd composed herself,
Sarah addressed the others who stood half-circled together at the center of the room, a collective look of
sympathy on their faces. "Who *are* you?"

"Leroy," the elderly gentleman instructed the boy,
"let us help Sarah over to the couch. And then let us all
take a seat, shall we?"

The elderly man and the boy, one on each of her
arms, escorted Sarah to the green-and-white candy-
striped couch, and she sat, hands folded almost primly
in her lap. The old man took a place next to her on the
couch. The doll woman perched on the edge of a gilded
straight back chair to the left of Sarah, while the hippie
sat in a matching chair to Sarah's right. The boy
plopped down on the carpet between the couch and a
gleaming Duncan Phyfe coffee table.

And a very happy un-birthday to me, Sarah thought.

The old man patted Sarah's hand. "I know this is
quite a shock to you, my dear. Allow me to try to clear
things up a bit." He paused, then announced, "My
name is Harrison."

Sarah looked at him blankly. The others gathered

around her exchanged little telling expressions—lifted eyebrows, rolling eyes . . .

The old man's mouth twitched with suppressed irritation. "My name is Harrison," he repeated. "William Henry Harrison."

As if he'd said Bond, James Bond.

"I'm sorry . . ." Sarah said with a two-handed shrug.

The old man's face reddened. "William Henry Harrison!" he erupted. The little group around him ducked their heads as if a chunk of flying lava might strike them. *"The ninth President of the United States!"*

Sarah looked at him, astounded. "I don't believe it," she whispered.

He smoothed his coat, returning himself to dignity. "But it's quite true, my dear. I died here, in the White House on April 4, 1841, and have resided within these walls ever since." He gestured to the others. "And this is my Cabinet. I'll allow them to introduce themselves—they earned the privilege."

The painted lady leaned forward in her chair. "My name is Prudence Bentley," she said in her lovely British accent. "My dear late husband and I left England on holiday to visit relatives in the Colonies. This was in 1898, mind you." She paused, then went on. "One day, we took a tour of the White House. We were in the Vermeil Room . . . back then it was used for billiards . . . when, *plop*—I simply dropped dead." She touched her ample bosom. "It was my heart, I do believe. In any instance, the next thing I knew, I was waking up here in the Green Room, and there was President Harrison! At first I was as confused, as disoriented, as you are, my dear . . . but eventually I came to understand what a rare honor had been bestowed upon me. Within hours he had appointed me his Attorney General!" She giggled, touching her Kewpie lips. "Can you imagine, dear Sarah? A Brit like me? But, then, by now I've been here long enough to have become an American citizen."

Sarah's mouth was open, but no words were coming out.

"Me next!" the young boy cried. He thrust a thumb at his tattered chest. "Leroy Jordan's the name. Pleased to meetcha. I used to live in this shantytown and that one, so this pile of white lumber sure is a lot better. Me and my Pop and Ma and the brother, we started out in Chicago, then hopped a freight to D.C., where we heard they had a better class of Hooverville. Don't you believe it! Anyway, one day in . . ." He stopped and looked up at President Harrison. "When was it, again?"

"1933," the President offered.

"Yeah, yeah—1933! I keep forgettin'. Anyway, I was out panhandlin' and it was cold as a witch's . . . well, anyway, it was cold, see? And I seen this line going into the White House, so me not bein' one to stand on ceremony, I cut right in. The coppers seen me and blew their whistles and startin' in chasin' me up to the second floor. I grabbed this vase, to sell later, you know, and run back to the stairs, and the bulls grab me. We scuffle, and I was just gettin' away from 'em, when, whoopsy daisy—over the railin' I go."

"Oh, dear," Sarah said.

"Only when I land, I land *hard,* and I'm still awake, see—only I know I'm a goner because my neck was twisted all funny. I mean, I can see the ceilin', but my stomach's under me. But you know what?" He grinned, snapped his fingers. "I get up anyway! And turn my head back around straight, and I'll be darned if there is President Harrison, gesturin' to me to follow him up the steps past all them people with the long faces, and 'fore you know it, he's askin' me if I'd like to be in his Cabinet . . ." Leroy laughed. "I thought he meant shut up in a wooden box . . . but then he explained it to me, and said I'd be in charge of the Post Office."

Sarah smiled. So Leroy had been in charge of the mail since the thirties; that explained a lot.

"Guess that leaves me," the hippie said, looking at Sarah with intense eyes. "I'm James Kafer . . . maybe you've heard of me."

Sarah shook her head no.

"I was a protester during the Vietnam war," he explained. The eyes above the thatch of beard glittered hopefully. "I'm sure you read about it. Saw it on the tube? The guy who went over the White House wall with a bomb strapped to his chest?"

"Oh, yes," she said slowly, the memory stirring. "I was only a little girl at the time, but I do remember. You . . . blew yourself up."

An odd look came over James' face. "Well . . . it didn't come off exactly like I planned."

"Best laid plans," she said with a sympathetic *tch tch*. Then she asked, "And, so, James—what are you? In the Cabinet, I mean."

He seemed a little embarrassed. "Secretary of War."

She had to laugh.

"I think it's pretty cool," James said, not at all defensive, in fact smiling. "Because you can damn well be sure *I'll* never get us into another Vietnam."

"Does the word Bosnia ring a bell?" Sarah asked.

The room fell silent.

President Harrison turned more toward Sarah on the couch.

"And what about you, my dear?" he asked. "Please tell us of yourself."

"Well," she said slowly, "let's see, now. My name is Sarah Hays. I'm thirty-five. I mean, I *was* thirty-five."

"And always will be, my dear," Mrs. Bentley said.

"Yes. Well, I . . . suppose I will be." Were these the last hallucinations of a brain dying of oxygen deprivation, she wondered? What else could she do, but ride with the delusion? It was the closest thing to reality she had.

"My husband's name is Steve," Sarah said. "A wonderful man. We teach . . . taught . . . together at a small college in Indiana." She paused, fighting back tears.

"Go on, my dear," President Harrison said gently.

Sarah swallowed. "My greatest accomplishment, I guess, was writing a book, a novel, that won a Pulitzer Prize. But you seem to know that."

James nodded. "We overheard you talking."

"I gathered as much," Sarah said.

"What's so special about the book?" Leroy asked.

Sarah looked down at the boy. "It's about growing up on a ranch in Montana, and learning to deal with mental illness in the family." She stared down at her hands in her lap. "It's kind of the story of my life. That's why . . . it was the only story I had to tell. Or ever would tell."

The room fell silent once again. Then James said, with a touch of sadness, "Well, you're one of us now."

She looked at him sharply. "But just *what* exactly are you?" she asked.

" 'We,' " James corrected.

"Fine," she said. "We. So—are we—ghosts? Is this heaven, or hell, or purgatory, or something I ate? I mean, I understand we all died here in the White House . . . beginning with President Harrison, from a cold." Suddenly she'd remembered the tour guide's speech, hoping the President would appreciate that she indeed did know something about him, after all.

But President Harrison slammed one fist on the coffee table, though the heavy silver urn there didn't budge . . . although Sarah jumped like she'd sat on a thorn.

"It wasn't a *cold,* damn it!" the elderly man shouted. "It was pneumonia. Pneu-*monia!* Why do those confounded tour guides keep reinforcing that falsehood?"

He rose from the couch, stalking to the center of the room, hands behind his back, head shaking from side to side, fuming.

"Now you've done it, lady," Leroy whispered up at her.

"When those tour guides show *Jefferson's* portrait," Harrison growled, pacing, "do they say he died of diarrhea? No. That wouldn't be *dig*-nified. But it's perfectly acceptable to make light of William Henry Harrison, who died from a 'cold' after just twenty-eight days in office."

Mrs. Bentley shifted uncomfortably in her chair. "Oh, dear," she murmured, "here we go now."

"Fasten your seat belt, babe," James whispered. "We're goin' on an ego trip."

Harrison raised a hand in the air and pointed to the heavens with one saberlike finger. "Do they mention my illustrious career? My victory at Tippecanoe? My governorship of the Louisiana Territory? No, no—*I'm* just a man who died of a *cold*. And what of my heritage? Do they speak of that? Do they even *know* of it? My father was one of the signers of the Declaration of Independence, and my grandson became the twenty-third President of the United States. But *William Henry* Harrison? He's just a man who died of a cold."

"We know your worth, Mr. President," said James, obviously hoping to placate the older man.

"But what of the world? What of my country?" Harrison asked, spreading both arms wide, palms open. "Don't you see," he said, pleadingly, now looking just at Sarah. "I have accepted that I will never get my due, but I have *not* and will *never* accept not getting my *chance,* not being allowed the time to make my mark on history."

He raised his chin; a tiny smile etched his lips.

"That's why I'm here. Why I'm *still* here. And that's why, making the best of what fate has given me, I've assembled this Cabinet." He gazed at her fondly, his eyes glittering. "And you, Sarah, you will be Secretary of State, and will do a *fine* job, I'm sure."

Sarah felt as though she'd been struck a blow.

Finally, she rose from the couch.

"Mr. President," she said quietly, "with all due respect—and believe me I'm flattered to be asked—I don't want to be Secretary of State. And I don't want to spend my eternity playing this game."

"Game?" the President repeated as if he hadn't heard her correctly. "My dear, perhaps you don't understand. This is no game, no simple pastime for departed souls, like cosmic croquet or celestial chess. I . . ." He looked at the others in the room whose eyes were riveted on him. ". . . *we* have been *running* this country for over one hundred and fifty years!"

Sarah blinked. Then she sat back down on the couch.

"What do you mean, exactly?" she asked, feeling numb again. "Just *how* have you been running the country?"

Mrs. Bentley leaned toward her, whispering conspiratorially. "We talk to them at night, mostly. Or when they daydream. Whenever they are . . . susceptible . . . vulnerable. In their pensive moments."

"Who?" Sarah asked.

"Why, my dear," Harrison said, arching an eyebrow. "Who else. Those *other* Presidents."

Sarah gulped.

"Yeah," added Leroy, "when they're asleep is best, 'cause it don't work as good when they're awake."

James nodded. "And some need a lot more talking to than others, you dig?"

Sarah was amazed. "Are you saying that you have influenced decisions made in the White House by various Presidents?"

Leroy chortled. "You hit the nail smack on the head, lady!"

President Harrison, in the center of the room, hands clasped behind his back, puffed out his chest. *"Directing* would be a more appropriate word, I believe," he said.

"I'm sorry," Sarah said, "but I don't believe it. For the sake of argument, let's say you're real— you're ghosts, and you're really haunting the White House . . ."

"We hardly view it as 'haunting,' " Harrison said, somewhat huffily.

"Fine," Sarah said. "How do you know you're really impacting anything? That anything you're whispering into these ears is registering?"

Mrs. Bentley directed her comment to Harrison. "Mr. President, why not give her an example?"

"Splendid idea," he pronounced. And he returned to the couch and sat next to Sarah.

"During President Cleveland's administration," he began, "there happened to be . . ."

James cleared his throat. "Excuse me for interrupting, man . . . Mr. President. But can I also make a suggestion? Why not use an example from Sarah's own lifetime? I'm not sure she's really into Grover Cleveland's administration."

Harrison nodded. "Another good idea." He winked at Sarah. "You see how wonderfully my Cabinet works together? Now . . ." He settled himself further on the couch. ". . . you were born in . . . ?"

"Nineteen sixty-one," Sarah said.

Harrison pressed his hands together, tenting his fingers, prayerlike. "Kennedy," he said softly. Then, as if gazing into a crystal ball, he began to speak: "October 1962. "Kennedy was up all night, which was a problem, mind you. He frequently worked throughout the night. The man would simply *not* go to bed!"

"Unless there was a good-lookin' lady in it," Leroy smirked.

"Leroy!" Harrison said. "Respect! The men who work within these walls are as human as we once were, as susceptible to human frailties."

"Like pneumonia," Leroy said, nodding.

Harrison studied the boy, looking for sarcasm. Leroy just smiled his smudgy-cheeked cherubic smile.

The President harumphed, and continued: "At any rate, near dawn, Kennedy fell asleep in the chair in the Oval Office and I said to him, 'President Kennedy, Khrushchev is just a man like you, just as scared as you . . . Why don't you simply pick up the phone and *call* him, to avert this impending tragedy?' The next morning, Kennedy had a secret phone line installed directly to Khrushchev at the Kremlin . . . and that began the series of talks which ended the Cuban missile crisis."

"Uh-huh," Sarah said skeptically. "So we have you to thank for that."

Harrison smiled.

"Jack Kennedy couldn't have made that leap without you."

Harrison shook his head, gently, no.

"But you couldn't warn him about Dallas, I suppose."

Harrison frowned. "We cannot foresee the future, my dear."

"What about Nixon, then?" she asked. "You didn't do such a hot job, there. That Watergate burglary, was that your brainstorm, guys?"

"His demise was not our doing," President Harrison said, "but his own. However," he added, "we did hurry his impeachment along a bit."

"How?" Sarah asked.

Mrs. Bentley giggled. "How do you think 'Deep-Throat' got his information?"

"Really," Sarah said, still far from convinced.

James shifted in his chair. "Now, President Ford was a real problem," he said.

"You didn't like him?" asked Sarah.

"The old boy just wouldn't listen," Mrs. Bentley explained. "A more mule-headed man I've never met!"

President Harrison nodded. "He had to go."

"So what did you do?" Sarah asked innocently.

"Let me tell!" Leroy said gleefully. "Let *me* tell!" The boy, seated on the floor in front of Sarah, was waving his hand wildly, like a kid in a classroom surprised he knew the answer.

"Very well, Leroy," President Harrison said. "You may elucidate."

"Well," the boy began, "it was about this time we discovered we could *move* things, see? Not very far, though, and not very fast. Not like in the movie—about that girl who got blood dumped on her on prom night? I watched that on TV with Amy Carter one time."

"*Carrie* you mean?" Sarah said. The film was one of her childhood favorites.

"That's the one, sister," the boy burbled. "We can't throw knives like that . . . sure wish we could. Anyhow, like President Harrison here says, that guy Ford was no good. He didn't want to do *nothin'* we said. Like the time I told him to start watchin' *Star Trek*. But, no, he had to watch boring *golf*. . . ."

"Leroy, dear," Mrs. Bentley interjected, "please get on with the story."

"Okay, okay, I'm gettin' to it," the boy said. He looked at Sarah with big brown cartoon-bunny eyes. "Remember that time Ford had the press conference in the Oval Office? An' everybody but God was there? Me an' James, we moved that bozo's chair out from the desk just as he started to sit down, an' *whump*, right on the floor he went, right smack on his behind!"

The boy howled with glee, and Sarah couldn't help laughing herself.

"And remember the state dinner with Brezhnev?" James asked with a one-sided smile. "It was in all the papers. We got under the table and tied Ford's shoe laces together—it took us an hour, all of us, with all our concentration—and when he stood up, he tripped and grabbed onto the tablecloth—man, what a mess! All that expensive bone china and everything."

Sarah laughed again. "Well, what about the time Ford fell down the steps coming off Air Force one? Surely you weren't responsible for that, were you?"

"No, Sarah," President Harrison said. "As you may have surmised, we cannot leave the grounds of the White House. I believe the man became so unhinged from what happened around here, that he began to do things to himself. Ford began to truly *believe* he was clumsy."

"What about Reagan?" Sarah wondered. "What did you think of him?"

"His first term was adequate," Harrison admitted. "The man didn't always do what we wanted, but I think he listened."

"Anyway, he got them jelly beans like I asked him," Leroy reminded the President. The boy sighed. "Too bad we can't *eat* anything . . ."

"But," Harrison pressed on, "sometime during Reagan's second term, we would talk to him at night, and he would seem to understand, but in the morning he'd have forgotten everything we'd said."

Mrs. Bentley nodded. "That's when we started whispering in *Nancy's* ear."

"It was the same way with Clinton," James added. "But for a different reason, of course. Clinton would go to bed exhausted and sleep so deep it was just *easier* from the start to talk to Hillary."

"That explains a few things," Sarah smiled.

President Harrison took one of Sarah's hands in his, which were surprisingly warm for a dead man. "And now, my dear Sarah, with you in our Cabinet as Secretary of State, I know we'll be able to handle this present administration. You lived as a part of this generation—your insights will be invaluable . . ."

Sarah gently removed her hand. "Mr. President," she said softly, "I'm sorry, but I don't want to be Secretary of State."

Harrison's eyes opened wide; he seemed astonished, stunned—and hurt.

"I'm sorry, sir," she said, "but I don't *want* to stay here. And something tells me . . . I don't have to. Isn't that correct?"

Harrison lowered his gaze and nodded. "Yes, you have a choice, my dear—as we all had a choice—but please consider this: by joining us you would, like the rest us, be acting in the best interests of this country."

"I don't think so," Sarah said, shaking her head. "I just don't agree with you, Mr. President—or with your approach. With all due respect, sir—you are meddling."

Indignation poured out of Harrison, like steam. "I was duly elected President of these United States—"

"Yes, you were—a very long time ago, by people who are as dead . . . deader . . . than you, Mr. President. Now, you're interfering with the decisions of others, the way a mother often interferes with the decisions of a grown child."

"But this country is an *infant!*" Harrison said. "Unable to make the right decisions without us. Come! Where's your sense of adventure, woman?"

Now Sarah took his hand in hers. She looked into his eyes, which were moist. "I'm sorry your Presidency was cut short and you weren't able to show the world what a wonderful leader you would have been."

The eyes of the dignified, very proud President Harrison began filling with tears.

"You have served long—and proudly. Don't you think it's time, finally, to step down?"

A tiny tear trickled down the old man's cheek.

"Don't you see," Sarah continued softly, yet urgently, "that you are becoming increasingly dangerous, trapped in here with only limited information?"

Desperation edged the old man's voice. "But with your contemporary knowledge, my dear . . ."

"Very soon my point of view would become as dated, as irrelevant, as your own. And nobody elected me to be *anything*."

Harrison said nothing.

"All your decisions haven't been correct, have they?" Sarah asked, but it was more like a statement than a question.

Leroy snorted. "Ha! Why don'tcha ask Mrs. Bentley about the teapot dough."

Mrs. Bentley bristled. "The Teapot Dome wasn't all my fault," she huffed. "Maybe I did give President Harding some questionable advice, but I can't be blamed for the entire affair!" She pointed an accusing finger at James. "Maybe *you'd* like to explain your role in the Iran-Contra matter!"

James leaned forward in his chair. "You know I'm against covert activities," he said testily. "But, man— that Ollie North dude would *not* listen! So I just had to do the best that I could."

Silence permeated the room.

"Look," Sarah finally said, "what I'm trying to say is that maybe it's time to move on. To whatever, wherever, that is. Why don't you leave running the country to the living, and seek new office, on some higher plane?"

Harrison lowered his eyes.

Sarah stood. "Come now, Mr. President," she said with a tiny smile, "where's *your* sense of adventure?"

And she walked away from them, across the thick Oriental carpet to the heavy mahogany door. She turned for one last look at the thoughtful little group. "Please consider what I've said," she said.

Her last glimpse of them was a forlorn cluster of fading shadows, Leroy's hand lifted in a sad tiny wave.

She opened the door.

"Oh, my God," she said, amazed as she stepped into the hall to where she could peer in through the open door of the Blue Room, "they're still working on me. They're still *working* on me!"

Sarah turned back to the others, but they were gone, the room now distorting, as if she were looking through someone else's much-too-strong glasses.

An overwhelming tiredness came over her, just as it had before, and she sank to her knees, swallowed up by the floor. . . .

A year and a half later, Sarah and her husband returned for another tour of the White House. An unusual honor, being invited for a second VIP tour; but considering that Sarah's previous tour had been interrupted, the President—a big fan of hers—had insisted the invitation be made.

And she, of course, accepted. This time, her state of mind was calm—she was happily at the midway point of the writing of her second novel (and third book)—and she and Steve walked hand-in-hand, again at the rear of the group, but this time paying close attention to the guide's words.

". . . exquisite cabinet made by local cabinetmaker Edwin Green in 1849 for William Henry Harrison. Harrison was the first President to die in the White House, just a month into his term. He died of viral pneumonia, and his passing was a great loss to the country. There's been a renewed interest in this past year, in William Henry Harrison. The pictorial book displayed on the coffee table, written by Pulitzer prize–winning author Sarah Hays, depicts some little known facts about this fascinating President. Now, next door, in the Green Room . . ."

HILDEKIN AND THE *BIG* DIEHL

by J. N. Williamson

J.N. Williamson's story is his 153rd short fiction sale, and the first time the Indiana author has written about politics. "But where I live," he says, "There are two topics of interest . . . the other one is basketball. I have some passionate beliefs about both politics and hoops, so my greatest use of self-discipline for the year was in keeping this story from becoming an exercise in advocating my convictions." His most recent novel is *Bloodlines* (Longmeadow Press, 1994), with more in the works.

Even though he was buffeted by strong winds and getting drenched by an early spring downpour, Edmund Diehl could not resist turning on the sidewalk to stare, one more time, at the famous building he had just exited.

After all, it was *his* in a way, as an American citizen. And who knew the White House better? Without looking it up, he could tell anyone who asked that an Irish-American architect named James Hoban—*b.* 1762, *d.* 1831—had begun to build it in 1792. That was the same year Tom Paine published Part Two of his *Rights of Man*, the Republican Party was formed, Denmark became the first nation to abolish slave trade, and Mary Wollstonecraft wrote her *Vindication of the Rights of Women*. It was a year for the ages, 1792; after it, every United States President since Thomas Jefferson had had a special home away from home.

Edmund turned to leave but was struck by something odd and glanced back. The slanting sheets of rain washing down on it and on the grounds where it sat with such a reliable attitude of permanence gave to the White House, he realized, an aura of magic that transcended time. This moment might be occurring on any mid-afternoon following a First Lady's luncheon for more than two hundred years. Something about the unchanging character of storms, Diehl supposed, the fact that gusting wind, rainfall, and the grumbling sound in the skies were surely the same dozens, even hundreds, of years ago.

Representative Diehl pictured the current occupants of the storied structure, snapped up his raincoat collar, and thought with passion, *Get out of my house, you clowns—it's my turn now!*

A bolt of lightning touched down nearby, briefly blinding Edmund

Who realized he was stepping into the upraised arms of another man only when they lightly collided! "I'm *very* sorry," he apologized quickly, stepping back to see if he had done harm to the second man. "Are you all right?"

"Oh, I'm fine, thank you," the stranger said, chuckling. He had a faint accent Diehl couldn't immediately place. "You, on the other hand, are in a peck of trouble if you ever hope to stay in that great white whale of a buildin' longer than the occasional lunch!"

Edmund was at a loss of words. He pulled himself to his full height of approximately seventy inches. They gave him a vertical advantage over the stranger. "If you're a constituent, I'm sorry my efforts disappoint you." He took a curbside step around the fellow, suddenly chilled, eager to return to his office.

"Apologizin' for everything is just one of the habits that shall keep you from your rightful office, Edmund." A pause froze Diehl with one foot in a rain puddle. At least it was just drizzling now. "Goin' by such a name as 'Edmund' is another!"

Diehl got back on the pavement. "But it *is* my name," he protested. "Who are you to speak to me that way? What do you want?"

"The first Roosevelt was stuck with 'Theodore,' but he had the sense to go by 'Teddy.' " He had dancing dark eyes, nothing much for a nose, a smiling mouth that seemed to wrap around to the ears, and an illegal number of freckles. "Even the youngest Kennedy brother had that much sense! I'm the lad who's goin' to make you the next President of the United States, and what I *want* is just that!"

Despite himself, Edmund's gray eyes widened. "I haven't announced my candidacy," he hedged. His gaze wandered in the direction of a pretty woman who was approaching and he made a path for her between the homely little man and himself. "If I chose to run, what could you do for me?"

The woman came abreast, started around the small fellow with the plethora of freckles. He said nothing whatever, but Diehl heard him make a peculiar breathing sound, and his gaze trailed after her like a hounddog with its nose near the ground.

She stopped on the sidewalk. It wasn't that she paused. She stopped. Then, waggling an umbrella, she turned around to smile dazzlingly—not at the man who would be president if he could, but at the tiny, homely man. It was very clear to Edmund Diehl that the stranger could have sprinted after the young woman and departed Pennsylvania Avenue with her.

"I'll give you what it takes, Edmund," he said, brows raised, "to do *that*. Do it often enough to multiply the likes of her by numbers enough to coax half the population to the voting booths to pull a lever with *your* name!"

"Surely you mean half the people who bother to *vote*." Edmund found his heart racing and decided to be more polite to this odd fellow. "Not that winning half the votes of those who come out wouldn't do it almost any year."

"I meant precisely what I said." He shrugged. "I could do better with you as a candidate, but there's only so much time ere Election Day, alas."

"I don't absolutely have to be back to the office for

another hour or so," Edmund said, looking around for a cab. "The First Lady was called away for some little emergency, so the luncheon ended early." A taxi was approaching and he took the other man's arm. "I know just the spot for a private chat."

"I thought you might," the freckled stranger grunted, permitting himself to be propelled into the back seat.

He hated waiting.

Sitting on the floor in a corner, he tried to find a better word for this emotion he was obliged to endure—one of the two emotions he was capable of registering—and substituted "loathed," "abhorred," and "detested."

None did his present state of mind justice, though, doubtlessly because they tended to be used synonymously, and Hildekin experimented with words from a few of the other nations in which he'd had to wait: *odiare, miso', feint hoben, mrzeti* and *hassen*. The Yiddish *feint hoben* and Italian *odiare* did come close; they seemed somehow more colorful and, well, more personal.

Yet not a word in all the world's languages would adequately express how Hildekin felt about the requirement to wait, always, between kills.

In the long life of a creature who could know only two feelings, the Wearer of the Hood thought it wasn't unreasonable nor even beyond sympathy to crave a little variety. That was particularly true since Hildekin was not even permitted by his nature to remove the damned Hood before he received an assignment. It was *heavy*, the special thing he had worn throughout most of his existence, it was cumbersome—it got *hot* inside the miserable, magical Hood! Being so enormous his head scantly cleared the ceiling and left him feeling less out of place curled up on the floor like an outsized housecat which didn't keep him from becoming uncomfortable or from perspiring.

Not that he lacked respect for the reasoning that had gone on behind the concept of the Hood, and for the

Wearer. To start with, it was the Hood itself that was the instrument of death, not Hildekin himself; not directly.

The concept was simplicity itself, circular simplicity, darkly lovely in its way. First were the facts that emotionally-limited Hildekin wore it nearly all the way to his immense shoulders—and there were no eye holes through which to see. Being not blind but sighted, not full of compassion for his fellow creatures but as narrow of view as anything rudimentally sentient gets, he often caught glimpses of his own future. The fact did not make him prescient since there was not a lot of range for someone with two feelings.

So all Hildekin ever saw in his future was he, enjoyably fulfilling the single task of the Wearer of the Hood; himself squatting on a floor; and what could loosely be termed "nothingness." This was what he saw most when he was back inside of the Hood, so drained by his return to that state that he hadn't yet resumed his anticipation of the future or even rekindled his *odiare* or *mrzeti* of waiting. Nothingness was so all-encompassing for Hildekin that it kept him numb, stripped him of any sense of independent existence.

Over decades those products of the Wearer's limited awareness were emanations of the ferocity that was his foremost emotion. They had seeped continually into the eyeless Hood—seeped in, oozed around in it like pooling blood, fatally *soaked* it with Hildekin's impatient anger.

So whenever he crammed the Hood over the head of the victim next chosen to don it—temporarily—that individual saw his or her future. Saw it with all the hatred the customary Wearer had invested in it since the prior moment when he was allowed to remove it; saw her or his most terrible possible future and was suffused with such loathing, abhorrence, and detestation of everything about that ongoing life that, one way or the other, the temporary wearer *ended* it.

. . . Strange, that instant when the world of light broke in upon Hildekin's isolated and private world.

Unfailingly, whether he was outside or in a room with artificial lighting, he was blinded for a fraction of a second. But it was a *nice* blinding, it passed swiftly, then he was overpowering his victims, sending them to sure suicide and experiencing a feeling—Hildekin's other one—that was a mixture of sensual thrill, satisfaction from a job done well, and occasionally a queer sensation of companionship. After all, those who were his victims were his real partners. Two or three times he'd wished he might spend a few minutes longer with them before they had to go crazy and murder themselves.

Hildekin suspected some of those on whom he placed the great Hood had lives of more complexity than his own. He realized they probably were not created simply to wear it, and die. He had even dared to think of merely lumbering away at some time when he vanished from the corner and found himself afoot with a shrieking victim-to-be. But then he might have been punished the only way the Wearer of the Hood *could* be punished:

The Authority could have taken away the Hood, permanently. And he did not know how to be anything but Hildekin, who wore it.

Each man had been served what he ordered and neither had done so much as touch his drink.

By the time they had reached Veto, Representative Diehl was wondering what he was doing in a D.C. bar with a man whose name he did not even know. Of course, it had been the little man's boasts and suggestions that compelled a sit-down talk. But Edmund was a person who had always *liked* the fact that he was not flashy, that he was a man of integrity trusted enough by the opposition party to be asked to the White House on occasion. He knew himself to be a graying, unpretentiously dignified, middle-sized gentleman with an enormous amount of practical knowledge at his fingertips—facts and figures, the bedrock of solid politicking.

Yet now, more objective about the homely interloper across the table, the Congressman ached to stand, rise, and leave and simultaneously hoped the stranger had *some* ideas that might magically transform him into a more spellbinding speaker. The hard truth was that he lacked what the TV age demanded of a politician who yearned even to get the vice presidential nomination, let alone the presidential bid.

At this point in my career, Edmund realized, *I don't want to be Vice President. The only place for me on the ticket is* leading *it!*

"Edmund, I'd like to ask a few questions," the enterprising stranger began. He was so intent, even intense. "What is it any person covets when he wants to become President and live in that fine, old house?"

Edmund blinked. "Why, he wishes to serve his country. To point it in the directions of peace and prosperity, for each citizen, which he thinks are best."

The little man shook his head. "The first part of that is crap, forgive the bluntness. Maybe Presidents want what's best for us. What all you hopefuls desire is the most power an American can legally obtain. You passionately want to be *the* leader, the Big Boss." He spread his oversized hands. "You're said to be a realist, Edmund; honest variety. If I'm to be after helpin' you, you need to be honest—with *yourself.*"

Edmund was rankled. He nearly halted this interview he had imagined he would be conducting himself. But he *had* just wished to be the leader, so he nodded, sipped his drink, and thought. "What's that accent? Is it Irish?"

A large hand shot across to him. "Your ear is true, Edmund." He pumped the Representative's hand enthusiastically. "Jimmy Hoban, proud to make your acquaintance!" He released Edmund's hand as rapidly as he had seized it, sat back. "Here's my next question: How did rulers of tribes get power and the knack for squishin' critics like they was bugs—*before* elections came along?"

"I don't know. Proved themselves worthy in battle, I

guess." Edmund brightened. "So someone promoted them!"

"A primitive leader just gave a warrior his own post of leadership?" Jimmy was incredulous. "Edmund, such man seized power. Isn't that correct? And they did so in one of two ways."

Edmund was interested in spite of himself. "Okay, what were they?"

Freckle-faced Jimmy leaned toward him as if passing along a state secret. "Either they challenged the present commander in combat, and beat him. Or, if the other bloke was too powerful, they used *covert means* to win. Now," his brows rose, "what is the reason why you can't just beat the commander in chief?"

Edmund glanced away. "I'm not powerful enough," he said softly.

"Wrong, wrong, wrong!" Jimmy laughed until tears shone. "Power isn't a quality humans are born with, it's something you *get,* for your own purposes!"

"Theoretically, then," Edmund countered, frowning, "why is it I couldn't beat that commander in chief?" It was meant to sound like an intellectual riposte.

"Because we all pretend this is *civilization!*" Jimmy exclaimed, chuckling. "They wouldn't let you keep it even if you challenge him and beat him up, now would they?" He offered his world-devouring smile. "*I* can provide the power you need."

Edmund took a long drag from his drink. "How?" he asked pointedly.

"Well, what was that other way I just mentioned?"

"Covert means," Diehl said. He lowered his voice to keep from being overheard. "Would you go into more detail, please?"

Jimmy beamed. "I will—but that would be *after* I'm hired. For now I'll say you must learn how to surprise your opponent with talents that aren't expected—while presentin' a more effective image than you've projected so far. Believe me, Edmund, a homely lad such as meself knows somethin' about *that!*"

Edmund thought of the pretty girl on the street who

had stopped to smile at Jimmy Hoban. That *had* been impressive. (*His name,* Diehl reflected—*why does it sound so familiar?*) "You were breathing somewhat, well, *differently* when that young lady passed us. Is that part of the secrets you'll share with me?"

Amazing him, Jimmy slammed a palm on the table and his dark eyes danced in their sockets. "I *knew* you were the right one!" he cried. "Lordy, I've quested high and low for another candidate worth my talents and now I've found him!"

"Well, I had a good education." It was an effort at modesty. "Here and abroad."

"Your education is all *internal,* man, you don't *show* it at the right times! Instead of showin' people what you're capable of, you sit back smuglike and wait for the other feller to foul up. Then, you *correct* him. You seem like a smart-ass teacher, don't you see? A President of the United States should be the one with the answers *first* and he don't admit there's even a teeny mistake in 'em, because he can always make 'em *look* all right!"

Diehl considered defending the Presidency, then changed his mind. "I believed my problem was looking like a stuffed-shirt when I speak—sounding like one, also."

"Oh, there's that *too!*" Jimmy Hoban declared. He waved it aside with a sweep of one big hand. "Knowin' how t'breathe will take care of that. Hermes said the human breath either attracts or repulses. A moron would know he can't be talkin' at all if he isn't breathin', too!"

Edmund gazed at him with admiration. "I think that makes sense." He couldn't recall offhand who Hermes was, but he hadn't expected this man to cite any dead Greeks and it basically substantiated his rising opinion of Jimmy. "Do you genuinely think I need just to breathe properly—plus my experience and superior record—to win the nomination?"

"I didn't say that, Edmund." The little man was raising his palm. "There are also the right *gestures* to learn." He grinned conspiratorially and reached into a jacket pocket, withdrew an envelope containing a packet of photographs. "Would you say these are the politicians who stand between you and your dear dream of spendin' a few years in the White House?"

Edmund squirmed around on his seat until he could inspect the photos without the chance of anybody else seeing them. He didn't count but leafed through, isolated three. He nodded toward the others. "Even my gauche personality can defeat one or two of those birds in the big stack. Another three or four would be terrified if the party seriously contemplated trying to install them in the White House. But this *trio*," Diehl tapped the pictures he had put facedown in front of the Irishman, "well, they're why I haven't yet chosen to run,"

One by one, Jimmy turned them over, recognizing them all. The first two, respectively, were an ex Vice President and a current Senator whom most pundits predicted would obtain the nomination Edmund craved.

The third photograph was of the incumbent President of the United States.

"If you make me your consultant," Jimmy said softly, "I promise most of the people in the big pile will pull out of the race—within a *week*." His voice carried authority although he didn't raise it. "The field will be narrowed so fast to only the Vice President, Senator, President, and you that the media will *have* to put you in the spotlight!"

Edmund thrilled to those words, but he had remembered something important, and he actually *was* as honest as politicians got. "Your name," he said, "James Hoban was the Irish-American who built the White House." He swallowed hard. "He's been dead for almost one hundred and seventy-five years."

Jimmy's smirk was very wide. "I don't know me age much, do I?" He chuckled and changed the subject subtly. "Remember, even *your* name has to change. So when we shake hands, you become *Ned* Diehl—and you're not offerin' the people a New or a Fair Deal, you're promisin' them nothin' less than . . . the *Big Diehl!*"

"Not bad," Edmund admitted, but persisted. "What's your real name, Jimmy?"

"I'll wager you there's a 'George Washington' within twenty miles of our beloved District of Columbia," he retorted. "Well, I'm the architect's descendant— philosophically. I'm tryin' to build something wonderful for America, so the name is really symbolic." He extended his arm and hand across the table, emitting a sequence of short, hard breaths reminiscent of when Jimmy had stopped a very pretty woman in her tracks. "What about it—*Ned?* Are you just a man who daydreams about his life's dreams or are you ready to be America's *Big* Diehl?"

Edmund's heart raced with excitement and he had no memory of when it had done that last. "You've made some big boasts, my friend. Let's say we'll meet in half a week and check for progresss. If there's been much, my campaign will be yours to command."

And taking the large hand put out to him, Ned Diehl imagined he felt electricity as their two palms connected.

The contemplation Hildekin had been giving the question of what word best described his impatience at waiting was interrupted by the dim image of *something* replacing his persistent viewing of nothing.

For the fraction of a moment the Wearer of the Hood doubted his judgment. It had been so long. He opened his eyes as widely as he could, even though he knew it was impossible to see through the unique material, trying to bring the expected vision of himself in the act of cramming the Hood over the next victim's head. He also hoped to catch a glimpse of that individual, not because he minded if it was a woman or a frail old person but due to sheer curiosity.

His piercing stare brought into focus the sight of his own broad back and, yes, the Hood was off, ready for action between his massive hands. Hildekin sat up straight against the wall. There was the victim, almost as clearly seen as if they were already together in the same room. He then heard words being whispered into his ears from afar, sooner than he usually received a message. The frightened person was a high personage indeed, yes, he heard; other men would be just outside of the room, eager to protect the victim-to-be; yes, he understood it was imperative he succeed.

The image faded, the scene turned to blackness . . .

But *another* vision was taking form, depicting himself and a *second* victim, older, grayer, but—the whispered data was powerfully conveyed to the Wearer of the Hood—this elimination was "*no less urgent than the first.*" Once more, the victim had "*powerful aides.*" Holding his breath in anticipation as he had with the prior scene, Hildekin waited to see himself clap the Hood down on the elderly gentleman's head. But again the imagery dissipated, disappeared—

And a *third scene,* with a *third selected victim,* unfolded before his mind's eye!

This was the closest Hildekin had come to an emotion of happiness! Awkwardly, banging one tree-branch arm on the wall, he clambered to his feet. He was quite nearly beyond listening for instructions even though part of him ached to be told he might go find the three victims that very moment. "*LOOK at him!*" Hildekin held his ears; it was the first shouted whisper in his experience. He almost believed his personal Authority was somehow with him, near him.

Now he studied the vision, saw it was much as its two predecessors. This man looked no larger, stronger, though he was younger than the one before him; he lay in bed, and he was smiling until he saw the Wearer of the Hood hunched by a closet. "*You will be permitted to show yourself to these three men in one week's time,*" Hildekin was told. Knowing he was alone, he did a clumsy little dance in a circle, his feet gouging chunks from the wall. "*THIS man must be last for he is one of great power. If there is no doubt of his suicide,*" *he will be your* final *victim, and, after him, you shall be free!"*

Hildekin's gaze was fixed on the third man, but he heaved with excitement. He, the Wearer of the Hood, was to be *free?* It sounded wonderful, it was certainly a reward, but who then would he be? Would he have to get an ordinary hood simply to have an identity?

"Wait for me to tell you when to begin," said the voice.

Nothingness replaced somethingness, gathering before his staring eyes like a hell too busy at the moment to get to him.

Hildekin slid back down the wall into a squatting position.

He hated waiting.

The President of the United States kicked back his sheets in fear and sat up, trembling and staring into the deepest darkness he could remember.

The attractive woman who lay where the First Lady belonged, but knew the latter was on a crusade halfway around the world, awoke when she found the bedclothes stripped from her relatively sumptuous naked body. "My God," she said to the President, who ordinarily would have liked her saying that to him, "what's wrong? Someone on the Hotline?"

Too shaken by a dream even to quip 'Well, *you* were," he mopped back the damp hair from his head and breathed deeply. "I'm not sure." He was disinclined to share the dream's details with his house guest as he would have his wife. Laughing uncertainly, he glanced over at the young woman. "Someone walked on my grave."

Marileen was a literalist and had never been good at sayings or anything else old-fashioned. "I didn't think a person *had* a grave unless they were in it." She rolled over on her back without fetching the sheets. "I guess a President can have what he wants—though I don't know what you want with a grave in a scary ol' cemetery."

He stretched out beside her, played with what was handiest. He knew she made a practice of sounding dumb as grave dirt, to get attention and to change subjects. "Just once more," he said, abandoning handiness for a pastime that required more effort, "then you need to leave the White House before morning. I have an early staff meeting."

But it took both the President and his guest considerably more time to achieve their mutual objectives than he had counted on. The President was trying to recapture his nightmare's details. All that came to mind was that someone had come to the White House to kill him and he had been stranger and more frightening than the garden-variety assassin.

Maybe it was Lincoln's ghost, the President thought, then—as Marileen moved a certain way—felt as if he gave up just about everything but his ghost.

A Secret Service man escorted the house guest out a side door a mere hour ahead of the staff meeting, and drove her home. He didn't even have to ask her address.

The individual whose card said he was Jimmy Hoban did his experienced best to clear each of his nostrils.

It was rare, he knew, when anybody breathed equally through both of them and there was good reason why thoughtful nature had made the occurrence infrequent. According to all the magic he understood but especially that of the *hesychasts* monks and certain *sufi*, absolute equal-nostril exhaling left one prey to accidents, illness, and the magic spells of others.

But he had done it long enough to know not only how to restore his good fortune and health but how effectively a shaman could produce effective *curses* so long as the nasal passages were clear and he inhaled with similar precision, with identical pressure released during the exhalation.

All Jimmy's concentration was centered on the fairly high number of photographs of politicians. He'd said he might cause them all to withdraw from the race in a week, but his own candidate had, in essence, given him just half that time.

The success of what Jimmy was accomplishing was not dependent upon complexity or duration, as was almost always the case with most goals of importance. Within ten minutes he had called down upon Diehl's opponents an array of mind-numbing and changing minor ailments, misassessments, and misfortune.

At last he turned on the bath water, sat in and leaned back in his tub, satisfied he had done his best. One or two people pictured would have passing headaches, no more, and would stay in the hunt. At least a couple might die unexpectedly. Most would say things to the wrong people, break bones, chase the wrong man's wife—misfortune and misjudgment of that level. Odds said more than half of them would not, now, be obstructions to Edmund and, once Diehl was impressed by that, a second curse was bound to send the rest scooting.

The trio of extremely tough opponents Diehl had specified demanded a more certain disposal, but Jimmy had already taken the first step toward that goal. Curses had clearly been too haphazard, so he'd alerted the Wearer of the Hood of personal secrets. After Jimmy and Diehl had their second meeting, the killer would be released.

For now it was essential Jimmy care for his own immediate needs, meaning breath restoration and retention. Each was achieved most surely while one was in water; aquatic animals, of all mammals, could hold their breaths longest. The sperm whale could do it a full two hours. Jimmy turned off the faucets and submerged fully. *Embryonic respiration,* he told himself, *that's the ticket.* That meant striving to duplicate the way an infant breathed more or less internally while living, so to speak, in its amniotic fluid. The best ancient minds had learned such life-preserving measures as this, Jimmy knew; what had happened that such basics were considered "arcane thinking" these backward days?

Maybe President Diehl could begin improving the country's educational system, teachin' kids what really *meant* something—after he had fulfilled every one of Jimmy's lifelong desires, of course.

Several minutes later he poked his head above the surface of his bathwater, neither gulping air nor sloshing on the floor. Drying his scrawny body, he wondered if any of the politician's he'd cursed were already having accidents. He padded barefoot to his TV set, turned it on, and sat back to wait.

Representative Diehl gaped at his television screen, amazed.

According to the CNN reporter, a rash of sickness and nasty rumors were "washing away some of the President's ardent critics and possible opponents to his campaign for reelection." Still shots of Edmund's colleagues flashed before his marveling eyes and, though he liked or even admired one or two of the six, all had been in the stack of photographs he set aside for Jimmy Hoban.

"This, just in," said the businesslike and lovely black reporter. "Representative Peter Reichardt and Senator Lewis Adamson, driving together to an annual Congressional softball game, were injured seriously but not critically in a bizarre accident just outside Alexandria, Virginia." She peered directly into the camera. "It seems Adamson, behind the wheel, swerved to avoid striking a landed, apparently stricken spotted owl. The bird is on certain protected lists, and the automobile struck a highway information sign. Adamson and Reichardt were hospitalized but are expected to recover. The owl seems to have flown away."

One full day till I meet Hoban again, Edmund thought excitedly—*I'll bet he gets a couple more by then!*

The need to pee drove him into the rest room adjacent to his office, and as he was unzipping it occurred to him he had no idea in God's green world what he'd meant by Jimmy "getting" a couple more. Yet it was absurd to fret about the details, wasn't it? Jimmy couldn't possibly have caused such incidents!

Diehl rinsed his fingers and glanced up at the mirror on the medicine cabinet. He took in his affably dignified face, lines of character grown prominent due to years of jogging and the best sun lamp he'd been able to buy. *"Ned."* He tried to get the hang of it, sure now that he could. "Ned 'Big' Diehl," he said softly.

At that second he couldn't yet make himself utter the real name change he sought, to President Diehl, Commander in Chief.

Jimmy glowed as if he had been radiated as Diehl ensconced him in the costly, form-fitting chair saved for the Representative's most significant guests.

"You're a wonder worker!" Edmund literally howled with delight. "Everyone but three on our secondary list, canceled out. Aldrich must be scared silly to think he might literally have to be a candidate, so it's really only two left!" He added hastily, "Of course the best thing is that no one actually died."

"I can't necessarily claim *all* those people," Jimmy said modestly. "Those with colds would have had to be near somebody with germs." Leaning back, he propped a foot on the table. "The others *will* drop out, Ned—so if you're ready to shake hands on it for good, I'll start work on the Big Three." His eyes were cold. "Those who stand squarely against your great campaign."

Edmund gazed at his hands, then up at Jimmy. "It's terms like that—'drop out' and 'shake hands for good'—that make me hesitate, Jimmy."

"Why's that, Ned? Or is it 'Edmund' after all?"

Edmund chose his words carefully. Actually, he'd begun choosing them last night. "I don't have to know everything you do. But I need to be sure I'm not—well, not making a compact instead of a business agreement." He shrugged, lost a laugh that wouldn't come out. "A compact with . . . the dark forces."

The Irishman leaned back and laughed so hard he nearly went over backward. "D'ye mean like with the *devil?*" he demanded. His feet slammed down, he giggled and wriggled his fingers like a boogieman. "You're after believin' I'm from hell, is that what you're afraid of, man?"

"Not afraid," he crimsoned. "I'm saying I won't make that sort of deal."

Jimmy exhaled deeply, grew more sober than Edmund had seen him. "I won't deny I have me unorthodox ways. But 'compacts' generally come in two kinds: A voluntary pledge to an angel whose good will may fetch the Almighty's assistance. I'm *no* angel."

"I can believe you," Diehl said with a faint smile.

"Now the *familiar* sort of compact has a fellow who desires t'do terrible things contacting a demon who supplicates *his* boss." Jimmy paused. "You plannin' to do terrible things after you're President, Edmund?"

"Good heavens, no," Edmund said. "Not on purpose, anyway."

"Then this must be a plain business agreement. If you're wonderin', *I* serve *me*. Once you're President Diehl, I'll ask some favors you'll be able to bestow."

Edmund relaxed, let the optimism of the amazing week return a bit at a time. "You're promising me my soul isn't endangered, then?"

Jimmy's head was at a cocky angle. "You *do* aspire to the White House, so how could I be certain of that!" He chuckled wheezingly and Diehl joined in. "Look, I want another handshake and not a drop of your blood on parchment, Ned. When that's done, I'll begin teachin' you what you need t'learn about breathin', makin' the best gestures and the like." He put out his hand.

Diehl took it then and, this time, could have sworn a current of electricity or something very much like it passed between them. Jimmy was even doing the strange, partly-gasping thing he had done before. "When will you begin to deal with our three primary opponents?"

Jimmy hoisted a rakish eyebrow. "Sure and it's underway as we speak."

The Wearer of the Hood was on his feet, unaware of
how he had been transported from the corner of his
damned waiting room but fully aware he was else-
where. The first clue was cooler temperature due to air-
conditioning.

His second clue was the cry of surprise and new
fright from the person whom the Authority had chosen
as the victim.

He worked the Hood up over his head and off, and
the victim—a fine-looking gentleman in his fifties—
shouted in true terror. Hildekin scarcely heard; his
long-blighted vision was becoming accustomed to the
flood of momentarily blinding light, and he was otherwise making sure the victim had no avenues of escape.
He had none, Hildekin saw, except going through a
being whose pate grazed the ceiling. A nameplate identified the victim: SEN. JEB PIERCE WALLIS, it read.

"How did you get in here?" Wallis demanded,
shuffling his feet as if considering a run at the impossible. "Who are you, *what* are you?"

"I am the Wearer of the Hood," Hildekin replied,
voice raspy from disuse. He shot out his arms, hands
gripping the Hood; they were long enough to slam it
down over the Senator's head. Then he dragged the
man across the desk to him and, careful not to squeeze
hard and break bones, embraced him.

Hildekin hadn't known how to answer two of this
"Senator's" questions. Unfortunate; there might be no
other intelligible words coming from the man. In fact,
that instant he began to sob and mutter things beneath
the Hood as it did its job. Clearly, though not suffocat-
ing, the victim was suffering. Hildekin swelled with
the thrill and pleasure at work well done.

Moments later he relaxed his embrace, already reluctant to take the Hood back. Wallis, in a world of his
own tortured thoughts, didn't even appear to see
Hildekin. "I can't—live like—that," he mumbled,

weeping copiously. He fumbled for a paper and pen, scribbled. Hildekin read it over his shoulder: "I'm humbly sorry for all I have done." He signed it just Wallis and the monster stepped back to see how he'd take his life.

As Hildekin raised the Hood over his own big head, he saw the victim get a hand gun from a lower drawer of his desk and touch the barrel to one temple. Hildekin sighed as he donned the Hood—

And the explosive bark of the revolver followed him on his untrackable destiny, lingering even when he was again seated in his corner of the room.

He clung to the memories of what he had seen and done before remembering clearly that he hated nothingness even more than waiting.

"What's that," Jimmy Hoban asked, touching the object in question with the tip of a finger, "and how important is it to you?"

Ned Diehl laughed. "Why, it's my nose. I'd look pretty unusual without it."

Jimmy shook his head sadly. "Mr. President-To-Be, that knob of flesh is where your finest achievement begins!" He held his palm directly under the Representative's nose, and turned his head. "Breathe normally for me."

Diehl did as he was asked regardless of how ridiculous it seemed.

"Just as I thought," Jimmy remarked with a rueful nod. "You breathe mostly through your left nostril." He sighed. "The feminine side, one of daydreamin' and fantasy—also creative, but the amount of belief you put into things is diminished and *real* careful. At least y'don't breathe equally through your nostrils, or your cause might already be lost."

"I just kind of *do* it," Ned said reasonably enough. "Breathe."

The little man jotted down a reminder in his notebook. "We'll get it fixed—without surgery, don't fret! Just cloggin' up the left side to retrain you." He glanced up, hooked an arm over the back of his chair. "Nature allows us to have colds so we occasionally breathe through a different nostril. It's an opportunity, like everythin' in nature is."

"Oh," Diehl said.

"Y'see, the right nostril draws on masculinity, gets you charged-up, helps your nervous system give you energy for your activities. You begin to add real spunk to what you're sayin'."

"I see," Edmund murmured, wondering if he did.

"We'll get around to gestures at the next meeting'," Jimmy pledged. "Let me say a little more about the breathin' part." He stood, laced his fingers at the small of his back, and began to pace. "We breathe different ways at different times. When you're mad, scared, or makin' love—there's three types right there. Think of a dad playin' a game with his boy; then the same daddy when his son has been bad." Jimmy jabbed an index finger toward Diehl. "Each type creates a different *sort* of breath—and that holds for a politician who's dead-sure he's *right* in his views!"

"So," Ned said, understanding, "if he breathes properly through the correct nostril it makes him sound as if he's actually *that sure?*"

The Irishman hugged him. "You've got it, Ned!" he exulted. "Modern folks don't know that every variety of breathin' has one influence or another on people listenin', and that the speaker can learn to influence 'em *exactly like he wants!*"

"I didn't know that," Diehl admitted, closing his left nostril with a fingertip.

"That's why I'm teachin' you." Jimmy smiled and his freckles seemed to dance. "Y'see, every man who's ever been elected President has won because he was plain *lucky* enough to breathe through the left or right nostril at the proper time." He peered straight at his candidate. "You're gonna learn how to do it *on purpose,* fast enough to announce your intention to run within a week from now!"

"Do you really think you can teach me enough that fast?" Diehl asked.

"I shook your hand on it, Ned," Jimmy said soberly. "One more thing for now: It's possible you'll hear some more shockin' news about your opposition in the next week or so. Remember two things, that *I* won't have gone near 'em, and you mustn't question me about them. I might just vanish in a cloud of smoke, and then where would you be?"

Ned, still partly Edmund, considered that. Briefly. "I guess, he said at last, "what I don't know can't hurt me."

Jimmy grinned. "Let's just say it *won't*."

The former Vice President managed to look composed even when he realized the mass of swirling shadows over by his hat rack was acquiring roughly human form. He hadn't been sure at first because he badly needed new glasses, he wanted to make his presidential run, and he was convinced the media would report him entering an optometrist's office. Deteriorating vision would be something else used to prove he was too old to be the President.

But after he was sure a gigantic *something* was moving toward him, the ex Vice President couldn't be sure it didn't vote, so he sought to be pleasant. "How may I be of service to you?" he asked, half-rising, trying not to squint. That was his famous humble saying and it had deflected many an angry constituent's attack.

"You can put this on," the visitor said after removing some odd headgear and extending it to him.

Even with poor vision the former Vice President realized he was gazing up at a face massive enough to have been carved from an oak and so pale it could be bloodless. It also seemed to have no fixed features. Nonetheless, the old campaigner had donned cowboy and Native American hats and bonnets, military helmets, and a hundred other things during a career that spanned nearly six decades.

He helped draw the Hood over his head, then tried to

adjust it to find the eye holes. A sharp picture took shape, followed by others, and he slipped back into his chair. "Interesting," he told Hildekin, smiling. "Private TV, is that it? Like headphones for music? That fellow falling from a window looks like me!"

"Not falling." Hildekin couldn't see the image but guessed. "*Jumping.*"

Having waited the customary length of time, he then lifted off the Hood, inadvertently removing the ex Vice President's spectacles as well.

Hildekin, somewhat confused, was hesitantly slipping the Hood back over his own head when the silver-haired man stood. Searching for his glasses, he turned around, took a step, and fell through a window open to the clean, spring air.

Quickly dropping the bifocals after the politician, Hildekin hoped he had done the right thing. Sighing, he tugged his Hood into place and was gone.

Diehl was watching a CNN panel discussion of the misfortune assailing Congressmen when he realized he was staring at a picture of Senator Jeb Pierce Wallis with two sets of numbers beneath it: His year of birth, and—*this year.*

He turned to ask Jimmy if he knew what had made such a powerful opponent blow scraps of his head in the general direction of the White House. But the Irishman was just hanging up the phone and looked excited. Ned himself looked ludicrous with gauze padding crammed into his left nostril. Every time he'd tried to say anything complex for days, he'd lisped.

"Ned, you're on the King show tomorrow night!" Jimmy said. "To discuss 'the awful things befallin' your fellow Congressmen' or some such hoopdedoo! You'll be expressin' your sorrow but boldly addin' that the chickens of corruption are comin' home to roost—which is why you're announcin' your candidacy for the nation's highest office!"

"You cad be serious!" Ned exploded. "I stad on my reputation—wad *you* propose is sheer opportudism!"

Jimmy's face registered utmost delight. "*Listen to* you! Except for the lisp, you spoke with real *fire*." He tugged the gauze out of the politician's nose. "Let me teach you now about gestures."

"I *do* think I'm breathing through the right nostril now," Ned said, catching the excitement. "I believe I have more piss and vinegar. Do you agree?"

"Let's hope it's enough," Jimmy said. "Now, gesturin' comes from the Latin *gestus;* it was used for actors and speakers. Folks everywhere do it, though. It can mean the whole body—happily, you'll be sitting down on TV—but what you do with your hands really shows up! Think of deaf folks and sign language—or remember Eisenhower holdin' two fingers in a 'V for Victory' sign and Truman pumpin' his arms at his sides. They mightn't have got two terms apiece without their gestures! Remember JFK jabbin' his finger at reporters for them to be next?"

Diehl was enthusiastically practicing right-nose breathing but wanted to show he was listening. "Babies claw their hands and reach up to show they want things." Remotely, he knew he had meant to point something out to Jimmy but he didn't remember what it was.

"And most of what a teeny babe learns is from watchin' its Ma and Da. So it's early magic, and he keeps on gesturin' as he grows 'cause it's the big brother of speakin'. *You*, Ned, don't gesture much at all. You bottle everything up so folks pay attention to only part of what you say. And most of the ways you gesture at all are wrong." A slow, sure nod. "That's the truth, Ned."

"I suppose," Diehl agreed, nodding back.

"See there," Jimmy said, "*I* nodded, so *you* nodded! That's not presidential, agreein' with anything people say! Neither is apologizin', sighin', turnin' red in the face, bein' surprised all the time, or sitting' up straight like a good little boy in a schoolroom!"

Ned bounced to his feet, fists tightening. His breath was fairly dragoning out of his right nostril and, when he spoke, his voice was firmly lower. "I'm tired of how you find fault with all I do! I became a leader in the House of Representatives without your help! Just do what you can by *informing* the man who will be the next President of the United States, not *belittling* him!"

Jimmy, too, bounded up and warmly squeezed Diehl's hand. "That's the posture you need to head straight for the White House—*sir.* Congratulations!"

And all this time, the candidate thought, flushed, *I believed that kind of stuff was showy, juvenile, autocratic, and self-serving.*

The President couldn't remember when he had ever had to send so many condolences and say such warm things about people he couldn't stand, attend so many funerals, or visit so many idiots in hospitals and mental health clinics. It was all for the good politically, of course—not just the human interest media coverage, but the way prospective candidates for his office were falling like flies.

In a few day's time Jeb Wallis had deposited his antagonistic brains on the pavement outside the Senate Office Building and that senile old charmer of a former Vice President had *literally* fallen like a fly! Suddenly the President couldn't remember when life had seemed more promising. The only viable candidate the other party could think of running was that Midwestern Congressman Diehl whose only claim to fame remained the good grades he'd gotten in college! The Chief Executive lay back on his bed, alone and not minding it. If he wasn't formally charged with rubbing out the opposition, the next election would be a guaranteed mandate!

Picking up the men's magazine he'd brought to bed in lieu of Marileen or any of the other women who regularly slipped him notes with their addresses scrawled on them, he opened it to the gatefold and gasped.

It wasn't the photographed beauty that stunned him.

The enormous but amorphous shape huddled by the closest closet had done so. The closest one was *very* close so the President doubted he could even reach his nearby phone to buzz for help before the thing was on him. All he was able to do was freeze, wondering what this being *was*.

Lumbering closer with the Hood outstretched, Hildekin showed the man he had already seen in his vision his face. *If there's no question about this man's suicide,* he had been told, *you will go free.* Despite his concern for whom he then would be, the word itself—"free"—increased his efforts. So did the evocative terror in the important man's face.

This time Hildekin thrust the victim's body up *into* the Hood, then pinioned the man's arms to his sides.

As always, the victim loathed what he was seeing; not only was he twitching in fear, he was mumbling something about trying to convince a woman that even if the evidence showed he had slept with others, "separation" would "ruin" him.

Dropping him to the bed, Hildekin glanced at the magazine the man had been reading. It lay open beside the wide-eyed, mumbling victim who was tearfully trying to decide what to do. Hildekin stared at the picture again. It was hard to replace the Hood on his head without delighting in the victim's life-taking, but he did not doubt it would happen—his task was completed—and if he remained another minute, he might steal the amazing magazine. The Wearer of the Hood was not a common thief!

Again alone in his corner, Hildekin fought against the return of both impatience and nothingness. He dwelled in his thoughts on the vivid images he had seen in the magazine. Yet in spite of a valiant effort, his memory could not, would not, recall the finer details of the gatefold. They slipped away.

Now nothingness was at its worst, so was his hatred of waiting, and a fresh realization crept into his mind for the first time in years.

When the "President" killed himself and Hildekin was freed, he knew what he'd do first. But his *new* hood would definitely have eye holes!

* * *

"How the hell did you make that old man jump from his window?" Diehl demanded when Jimmy entered the room. The Representative was afoot, outraged but puffing away through his aggressive nostril. Jimmy was there to drive with him to the TV studio. "He was a major opponent, yes, but he was one of the decent men left in Washington, D.C.!"

"I promised I wouldn't go near those people," Jimmy said. "I also told you, Ned, you *musn't* question how I work. Want to do this TV interview without me present?"

Diehl whitened. "Okay, okay," he said, turning to switch off the TV and get his suit coat. "So long as you weren't responsible for—" He broke off as he saw the legend "SPECIAL BULLETIN" flash on followed by Bernie Shaw's somber face, then a silent study of the President. Two dates appeared beneath the most famous face on earth as they had with Jeb Wallis. "Oh, no," Diehl whispered, turning up the volume and sitting weak-kneed on a hassock.

"The President is dead, apparently at his own hand." The veteran newsman's eyes were teary. "A reliable report says he took a firearm from a Secret Service bodyguard, and while the White House has issued no clarification, The President is—"

"How's *that* for timin', Ned?" Jimmy cried, smiling. "Tonight you'll reassure the people one political leader remains, ready to serve, untarnished and—"

"Untarnished?" Diehl glanced up, shocked by what it seemed he, himself, had caused. "This was never what I wanted, to become the worst of them—just by turning my head and not *noticing* what was happening. I don't know exactly what you've done, but I can stop it before I'm nominated and you hurt more people." He stood, slipped into his coat. "They'll think I'm mad, but I can tell them what I know, prevent anyone else with ambition from listening to you!"

"Edmund," Jimmy said with soft scorn. His huge mouth was moving, his nostrils twitching, as he breathed his singular way.

"That stop damn isn't going me stuff!" Edmund said quite distinctly. Pausing, he raised a hand beneath his nose. "What hell have the done in me?" Air didn't come entirely from either nostril; they were expelling it *equally*. "Bastard you!" he exclaimed. But he pinched the left nostril shut and, with great effort, shouted, "You are fired—*finished!*"

"Such deals as ours must always be confidential." Jimmy rose, his freckles the deep clefts and crevices of a very old man. "I'm not the one who's finished, for I kept me word. We shook on it." Powerful currents stirred by his right nostril fluttered a newspaper on a coffee table. Two personal notes Diehl had scribbled wafted eerily across the room. "Then, too, I gave me word to—*one other.*"

Edmund strove to answer, could not; he tried to walk through the door, but it slammed shut explosively. His hands—they were rising, clutching his throat! *A speaker can influence folks just the way he wants,* he remembered. His fingertips tightened. *What you do with your hands really shows up.* His were relentlessly closing off his breath, and no air at all entered or left his nostrils.

"Your face and name *will* be in the history books." Jimmy spoke as Edmund slumped to his knees. "*You* are goin' to occupy the White House—as far as anyone but me knows! And the real name, 'Ned,' is . . . Hildekin."

The Representative, gazing up, thought he saw a pale, nearly featureless face instead of Jimmy's; then he neither thought nothing more nor felt a thing.

The instant Ned Diehl's body rose from its knees, the Wearer of the Hood was freed from the darkest corner of its Authority's mind. Just as filled with hatred, a capacity for thrilling at the torment of others, and eagerness to do a thorough job, the usually-concealed and contained half of Hildekin moved into the forefront of the brain propelling a middle-size, gray-haired man as he drove speedily to the nearby television studio.

Everyone said the interview Representative Diehl gave to a saddened and worried nation was the finest of his career. More than a few pundits believed it was outright "presidential."

RELEASE

by Kevin Stein and Robert Weinberg

Kevin T. Stein is author of *Brothers Majere* and the short story "The Hunt" in the Dragonlance series by TSR. Kevin's other works include *The Fall of Magic* (as D.J. Heinrich) from TSR, *Twisted Dragon* (Ace Books), and the *Guide to Larry Niven's Ringworld* (Baen Books). Kevin is a script consultant, and also has had two screenplays optioned by a Hollywood production studio. Robert Weinberg has spent the last thirty-five years ensuring that the thousands of pulp stories published in the first half of the century remain in print today. In his spare time, he writes in all genres of fiction, recently appearing in the anthologies *Dark Love and David Copperfield's Tales of the Impossible*. He lives with his family in Oak Forest, Illinois.

It was late, very late at night and he was alone, walking by himself in the near darkness. Only a flicker of white moonlight illuminated the long hallway. James needed no more. He knew this corridor, had walked it a thousand times. There was no mistaking the inside hall of the President's House.

It was still and quiet. Too quiet. Unnaturally quiet. Only one sound broke the silence. It was a noise James had heard too often during his war years. A man was sobbing. Somewhere in the President's House, a grown man was crying.

With a start, James shook away the last traces of the daydream. Lately, his mind had taken to wandering on strange paths when he closed his eyes for a few moments' rest. Always, it was the same scene. Him walking in the dark hall outside his office, with the only sound that of a man crying. Though not a superstitious man, James found the nightmare troublesome. He had enough worries without being spooked in his sleep.

Face grim, James looked down at the cavalry steel he held in his hands. He had wielded the blade at Middle Creek. The metal of the weapon reminded him of the field. Gunpowder and misery you could smell, sickly winters and sickly summers. He was glad to be rid of it, glad for his country as well.

The steel he preferred was not of the sword but of the spirit. Slavery had been an abomination to the Lord and he was proud to have been part of its destruction. Drawing in a deep breath, he resheathed the sword. The time for daydreams and memories was over. Today, as with all his days, there was a great deal of work to do.

Carefully, James hung the sword back on its wall-peg and returned to his wide desk, taking a moment to adjust the cuffs of his clean, white shirt. He towered over the stack of papers waiting on his blotter, nudging his deep leather chair aside with a hip. Numerous tasks required his immediate attention. He could already feel the pressure building behind his eyes as his first early morning headache stirred in his temples. For his own sake and for his good health, James woke with the dawn before any of his staff. Their incessant clamoring often sent him, stiff-backed but steady, to the washroom in search of a pain remedy.

This morn, there was something new on his desk, something that by its very nature seemed friendly, filled only with warm welcomes and the promise of hands outstretched in greeting and pride. Someone had tried to bury it in the lowest circle of hell, where legal matters and complications rested. His aides wanted to ensure that other, "more pressing," matters, were attended to first. But, he had rescued the letter from the stacks of documents and now it rested on the very top of the pile.

The paper beckoned. It was an invitation to the ten-year reunion of Williams College. James smiled, despite his burgeoning headache. He had no regrets about attending Williams; quite the opposite. His associations there had resulted in his first military command. The rest had been come from his own efforts.

Quickly, James glanced over the invitation for the dozenth time. They wanted him to be the keynote speaker, not a surprise, all things considered. He began composing the answering wire in his head. "... I would of course be honored to speak to my brethren graduates . . ." It made him happy just to think about it.

A knock at the door interrupted his mental telegram, and knowing full well who was about to enter, James dropped the precious letter into an open drawer in his desk and quickly closed it. He assumed the same face that had seen him through a number of Williams College poker nights and more than a few battles with the Confederates.

"James!" The door opened at the same time as the woman's mouth. James gritted his teeth but kept his expression neutral. Still, there was no disguising his true feelings. "Don't use that face with me, James Abram!"

James started to speak, to utter a half-hearted denial, but the woman cut him off with a wave of her hand. She was a foot shorter than James' six feet, but he always felt she touched the ceiling with her presence. Her advanced age and gray, lace clothing only added to the strength of her demeanor.

"And what was that?" she demanded rhetorically, tearing open the drawer he had just closed. The invitation was in her arthritic hands before James thought to protest.

She read it over, thoroughly and quickly, humming and clucking to herself in disapproval.

"You've got better things to do than go to a fool anniversary party, James!"

Her voice, made more shrill by the empty office, was like a vise crushing James' temples.

"It's not a party, it's a reunion," James muttered evenly.

"It's a party, and don't you—"

The opening door interrupted further discussion, for which James was extremely grateful. He knew he would have plenty enough to chew when his staff arrived. Another woman entered, standing somewhere between himself and the first in height. She wore simple, dark clothing for the cooling September air.

"Good morning, James," she said with genuine affection, bustling around the desk and giving him a kiss on his cheek. "Hello, Mother," she said with a nod at the other woman.

"Lucretia," said James' mother sourly. James marveled that the woman could make any word sound like a curse. Somewhere, deep down inside, James felt certain his mother liked Lucretia, his wife of more than twenty years. It was just sometimes so difficult to believe she cared for anyone.

"I'm off to prepare the day's Latin lessons," Lucretia said, reaching to James' chair and handing him his tailored vest. "Do put on a tie," she added.

James sighed loudly as he pulled open his top drawer and picked out a tie from the number that lay there, neatly folded, all of them silk. He quickly fastened it around his neck, Lucretia fussing about as he did so. She glanced sidelong at the paper James' mother held.

"A party?" she asked.

"Class reunion," James declared, sounding defensive. James' mother glared. "It's a party."

"Well, I'm sure you'll enjoy yourself, dear," Lucretia said in the tone that James knew meant that the matter was decided. He felt relieved, the ache in his head easing a trifle. His wife was his greatest weapon in his war with his mother. With a final check of his collar, Lucretia added, "I must hurry, James. Your troopers were only footsteps behind me."

As she turned to leave, Lucretia snared the reunion invitation from the older woman's hands, rolling it up as she made for the door. "I'll keep this safe," she said, turning the doorhandle. "Come along, Mother, leave James to his work."

James' mother let out a short breath of annoyance. She waved for James to bend to her level for a kiss on his other cheek before turning and departing with his wife.

Having spent a good portion of his life in the military, James had learned to estimate time with great accuracy. Such a skill had proven a lifesaver when he had led his cavalry against the Confederates. Old habits died hard, and his mental discipline demanded that he maintain his soldier's edge. He estimated he had three minutes to himself between the time his wife and mother left and the time he heard the first of his staff say, "Good morning, Mr. President."

With a sigh, he shut his eyes, trying to banish his escalating headache. Instantly, his daydream returned.

The President's House was cool and still. The glass was clear, looking into night. James walked forward, never needing to see more than what was ahead. He had no control over his motions. His body felt strange, awkward. Ahead, a man was sobbing. James was getting closer, but he still could not see who was crying. Or why.

Swearing softly, James opened his eyes and gazed around the room. There was no peace for him today, asleep or awake. With a heavy sigh, he picked up the top paper from the stack before him. It was yet another plea from that pest, Guiteau.

"Dear Mr. President . . ." the letter began. "I must insist that you reconsider the post of ambassador to Paris in my favor—"

James tossed the letter into his trash without reading another word. The ambassadorial decisions were already made, and he was not going to rescind or otherwise change his decision. The author of the letter, Charles Jules Guiteau, would never convince him to change, no matter how many trees were felled to provide him paper. Somehow, the politician had found out who was going to represent the United States in Paris.

James didn't doubt that Guiteau's source was one of his many enemies in the Senate. They would do anything to annoy him.

Angrily, he glared at the newspaper resting beside the stack of memos. The lead article blamed his political maneuvering for the country's suffering. In times of trouble, everyone needed a scapegoat. And the President made an easy target.

His three-minute estimate proved to be accurate within seconds. Like a pack of jackals, his staff swarmed into his office. Smiling, he rose to his feet to greet them. If anything, James was always polite.

With a roar of demands, papers and documents were literally shoved into his face. James, caught off guard, swept his arm aside as if he were wielding his saber. His staff fell back as a whole, but they were not daunted by his defense. The pack pressed forward and James quickly retreated behind his desk.

"You've got to do something about Conkling's accusations, Mr. President!" Reisling said, his sharp voice rising above the others. The general clamor of the mob changed, agreeing as a whole with those words. James dropped into his chair and glanced over the papers on his desk, for the moment avoiding any mention of Senator Conkling. Mentally, James corrected himself. Ex-Senator Conkling.

"Blaine can't hold him off forever, Mr. President," Reisling added evenly, pushing his heavy frame to the front of the crowd.

James picked at some imaginary grit beneath his nails and silently cursed the name of Conkling. The man had been the most fervent leader of the street-paving and railroad scandalmongers, and he would just not let up. "I'm innocent of those charges," James heard himself say.

"With enough time and support, anyone can be made to appear guilty, Mr. President," Reisling replied.

A moment passed in silence. Then James shot up from his chair and slammed his fists on his desk. A bolt of pain lanced through his forehead. "This is preposterous! These accusations are slanderous. Listen to me! The President of the United States, pleading innocent like a common criminal!"

"You were the one who appointed Conkling's most ambitious political enemy to the New York Secretary of State—"

"Yes, yes!" James answered with a wave of his hand. "And a Blaine supporter as collector of the port. These facts are nothing new, gentlemen, and they certainly are doing little for my damned headache!"

"Have you made your assignments for ambassadors, Mr. President?" Reisling asked quietly, slowly backing away. The others in the room took his cue and followed suit.

James blinked his eyes, rubbing his hands together, hardly hearing the words. He still had calluses on his palms from when he was young, a reminder of the poverty where he had started. He didn't miss the rough frontier work, but he did find himself yearning for the directness it required.

"I have the President's recommendations," a voice said from the doorway. The crowd turned their attention away from James to the robust man standing in the entrance. "They will be given to you later. Now I must consult with him in private."

Reisling began to protest, but cut himself short. The look in the man's gray eyes made it clear that the President needed no further difficulties from his staff.

With a nod, Reisling and the others backed out of the room. "Thank you, Mr. President," Reisling intoned, pushing his way past the gentleman in the door. A few moments later, the room's quiet was broken only by the sound of the closing door.

"Did your father ever have these troubles, Robert?" James asked, still rubbing his fingers.

"Never," the man replied solemnly, pulling up a chair in front of James' desk. "That's why his beard was dark till the day he died."

James looked up and smiled. "As dark as yours, no doubt."

"Oh, no doubt," Robert replied, pulling on his beard, which had been dark before he first entered politics, but now was iron gray.

"Well, Mr. Lincoln, what have you for me this day?" asked James.

Robert gave him a serious, concerned look. "Only that if you don't get some rest, you're going to die before you're old."

James stretched out his arms and stood up, arching his back. "I'm already old," he groaned. "I have a better chance of surviving a charge on a line of cannon than I do my term in office. But at least I have my Lucretia." ·

"Mr. President," Robert began slowly, standing as well. "Far be it for me to give you advice—"

James interrupted. "Robert, you're my friend and the only one of my staff who doesn't continually have bad news for me. If you have something to say, just say it."

"Very well, then, James. Get some exercise, get some rest, and have a drink," Robert said, hand over his stomach. "Helps the digestion, I'm told."

"Is that all, Mr. Secretary of War?" said James, smiling. The headache continued to pound.

"Get some sleep," said Robert Lincoln, Abraham's son. "It will do you a world of good."

The sobbing grew louder as he swept past the still-standing curtains, pale and cold, though the air was still. The crying was closer, more focused. Somehow, he sensed that very soon he would finally know the reason for the tears.

According to the morning paper, Alexander II of Russia had been assassinated by radical factions of the current political party. A bomb had been placed under his coach, killing, in addition, several of his closest friends and allies, as well as a number of innocent bystanders. James shook his head, saddened. Lincoln had once made mention of Russia's politics. "Where despotism can be taken pure, without the base alloy of hypocrisy." James suspected that the assassination of the Tsar of Russia was going to have far-ranging effects on the military and politics of the United States. He would have to speak with Robert about what must be done, if anything.

Conklin was again at the forefront of the orders of the day. It seemed that the former Senator was gaining favor again among his old constituents, the same Republican party members who had failed to reelect both himself and his senatorial crony, Thomas Platt, when the two resigned in protest of the President's assignments to the New York legislature. It was a problem that never seemed to end.

Still, the one thing that day that remained in James' thoughts was Guiteau's latest letter. "Dear Mr. President. I must again protest in the strongest language the assignment of—"

That letter, like all the previous ones, had found its way into the garbage. But something in the wording, along with the news of the Tsar's assassination, kept the request vivid in James' mind.

In dreams, he walked the corridor in the President's House, moving closer to the weeping. He was much farther in the hall than ever before. There was a room ahead. He looked inside.

White candles filled holders by the score. They flickered, filling the room with a warm glow. There was no scent, no heat. He walked around a forest of candelabras that obscured the source of the weeping. It was a soldier, a solitary soldier, part of an honor guard, sitting, bent, with his back to the door.

James reached out and put a hand gently on the man's shoulder. The fingers of his hand looked strange. They were huge, gnarled digits, ones that he had seen before. It didn't matter. What was important was the other man's suffering.

The soldier did not cease his tears. "Why are you crying?" James finally whispered, as he would whisper to one of his children. The voice was not his. It was a

familiar, high-pitched voice. A voice he had heard
speak many times. "Why are you crying?"

"The President is dead," the honor guard answered
with a shudder. *"The President is dead."*

Three letters from Guiteau, each written with increasing intensity. Insist, demand, command were the
three words that stuck out most in James' thoughts.
Thoughts that were being crushed by that same damned
headache again. No amount of washing with cold water
would ease his pain.

Conkling, of course, was another problem. There
was talk of federal investigations of the President concerning the railroad and paving contracts in Washington. Members of James' own party had now started
demanding that he fight back, and fight back hard.

James rubbed his forehead, letting the water run,
hoping the sound would bring some relief, like the
soothing sound of a waterfall. The date was July first.
Tomorrow he would attend his college reunion and give
the speech he had been working on in his free time. Tomorrow he would finally be able to enjoy himself.
Tomorrow, he would finally find release.

He had his evening meal with Robert in the office
for the tenth night in a row. A sadness crept over
James as he remembered what he had said when first
elected. He had told the press that with his term in office, he knew he would be leaving behind the joys of
previous years, a joyous marriage, time with his
beloved wife and wonderful children, to serve his
country. He could not exactly recount the words, only
the emotion.

"I heard a strange tale of your father," James said,
toying with his wine glass. "It involved the spirit
world."

"Would this be the tale of the floating piano during
the seance?" Robert asked, downing his wine. He
raised his glass and gestured for James to drink the rest
of his own.

Frowning, James took a sip, but the wine tasted bitter to him. He made a face and put the glass down on his desk. Shaking his head, he answered, "I heard your father had a premonition of his own death."

Robert sighed loudly and looked toward the ceiling for a moment before answering. "Father once told his Cabinet that he had a dream of a soldier crying in the President's House. When he asked the soldier why he was crying, the man answered that the President was dead.'

James said nothing. Robert looked at him, his face filled with curiosity. "Have you had similar dreams?"

James remained silent, barely hearing Robert's words. Somewhere in his thoughts, he was walking, walking alone, walking in silence . . .

"James?"

"What?" James looked up with a start.

Robert leaned forward in his chair. Concern was etched on his features. Like most members of the inner circle, he knew that James had been having terrible headaches, problems with his digestion, and a host of other symptoms common to Presidents. But he mentioned none of that. "Have you . . . been having dreams?"

James thought a moment. Finally, he said, "These damnable headaches. They cloud my thoughts, befuddle my reason."

The President sighed, then shook his head. "Your words confirmed my own feelings. Yes, I have been experiencing weird dreams, ominous dreams. But they are not mine. They are your father's.

"In some unexplained fashion, I have been reliving the dreams of Abraham Lincoln, foretelling his assassination." James frowned. "But, why it is happening, I have no idea. It makes no sense. No sense at all."

As James had measured, Charles Jules Guiteau was a small man, angry and frustrated. Guiteau could not understand why the President had not heeded his requests. He was sure that the stronger they became, the more willing the man would have become.

According to Conklin, the President had no intention of changing his appointments to office. Guiteau had, at first, not wanted to believe this, but after sending letters for many weeks now, he was finally inclined to agree.

Guiteau knew he had lost a great deal because of this situation. He was so busy writing letters that he could not, at the moment, remember what these losses were, but he knew they were there, he could feel them. He required no justification for his actions; no man suffering loss did. The two pistols were easy enough to come by.

The invitation to the Williams College ten-year reunion cost him the rest of his fortune. He felt it was well worth the price.

BROKEN 'NEATH THE
WEIGHT OF WRAITHS

by Tom Piccirilli

Tom Piccirilli is the author of *Dark Father, Hexes, Shards,* and *The Dead Past.* He is the assistant editor of *Pirate Writings* magazine, and reviews books for *Mystery Scene* and Mystery News. His short fiction has sold to *Hot Blood 6 & 7, 100 Wicked Little Witches, 365 Scary Stories, Deathrealm, Hardboiled, Terminal Fright,* and others. A collection of five intertwined stories entitled *Pentacle* was recently published by Pirate Writings Press. All of the stories therein have made the Honorable Mention list of Datlow and Windling's *Year's Best Fantasy and Horror.*

B ronze Minerva, situated between lotus column candlesticks on the mantelpiece, watched us as we spoke. Moonlight lashed Ike Hoover's eyes, their paleness intensified in the dim room, his few remaining strands of silver hair nearly glowing. Embers snapped in the fireplace, and fragments of charred papers occasionally wafted about the grill, President Harding's looped script clearly seen from time to time. This choking heat proved unbearable, and I opened one of the bay windows; warm gusts of the magnolia–tinged August breeze washed against my face.

Like the rest of the White House, the Blue Room smelled of ash and illness. Directly above us, in Lincoln's bedroom, the Duchess could be heard throwing books, files, Harding's unfinished love letters to his mistresses into another fire, alternately weeping, giggling, and cursing vilely. The bronze Minerva clock, ordered by Monroe in 1817, kept a baleful gaze turned on a newly-deceased era. Who knew what kind of hell Coolidge had in store for us.

In a harsh whisper, Ike said, "I fear the Duchess has gone insane, Richard."

"Come on, Ike . . ."

"I'm serious."

"Don't overreact," I told him. "Despite being a strong-willed woman and, let's face it, a domineering one as well, Harding was her foundation and glue. The President's death has shaken her to the soul, and these rumors of corruption in the Cabinet have startled everyone."

"Not you," he said, with perhaps a note of accusation.

"Why are we whispering?"

"Shh."

"Look, I knew the Ohio Gang was turning oil and bootleg deals . . ."

"Shh, I say."

" . . . and taking major kickbacks from the disposition of postwar supplies and stocking the Veterans hospitals. So did you. So did everyone except for the President. As for Harding's death—" I glanced out the window to see the shadows of the Washington Monument and Jefferson Memorial carving gouts from the bright moon. Smoke roiled and billowed from the chimneys, "—I liked the man immensely. I respected his naiveté, if you can understand that. Regardless of a life in politics, he refused to believe his oldest friends could be fleecing America right under his nose. He held to his optimism, and that helped kill him. However, after what I've seen in the trenches, I don't think sudden death can shock me anymore, not even when it strikes so vital a man."

He bowed his head a bit. "Sorry for my tone. I've witnessed my share of horrors in my seventy years, but this, Richard . . . believe me when I say I'm not over-reacting. There's some kind of madness here that walks with the Duchess. Florence has become a foul creature. The life's been drained from her the way it was the

President over this past year. One look into her eyes will show you that."

I wanted to tell him that she'd had her moments of madness before, namely when she ordered Bureau Investigator Gaston Means to kidnap Elizabeth Britton, the illegitimate daughter of Warren G. Harding and Nan Britton. Means, who'd committed every unscrupulous act possible on and off the Hill, had stunned me when I'd learned of his refusal.

Ike Hoover had been Chief Usher at the White House for more than forty years, proud to have served ten Presidents in that time. He considered himself a close friend of Mrs. Harding, and I'd seen them chat, laugh, and dance at the grand summer garden parties the Duchess gave. Often a thousand or more invitations were sent out all over the world—to kings of nations, veterans from area hospitals, and the likes of Henry Ford and Thomas Edison, who were Harding's camping trip cronies. As Ike's assistant, I had come to the White House a year ago with fairly wide and star-filled eyes, as well as a number of chips on my shoulder and two Kraut bullets in the left leg, one in the right.

"She offered me my walking papers at the wake, as I paid my final respects," Ike said, his voice hardly more than a whimper.

"After forty years of service? What do you mean she offered them? She fired you?"

He rubbed his eyes wearily and brushed sweat from his bald head. "She pleaded with me to leave, Richard. Begged me, in fact, acting as if, I don't know, like she would be saving my life. She included you in these frantic urgings, as well as the rest of the staff and Secret Service men, too. Something awful is happening. What have you heard from your . . . associates?"

The "Ohio Gang" had taken a shine to me for two reasons: I was their token veteran and thereby a good conscience salver, as if they thought that through me they were somehow linked with "the people," and also because I had already gained a tad of infamy in Baltimore as a card sharp. President Harding had been a compulsive card player, and his cabinet—friends from his youth in Marion, Ohio, and not one of whom belonged in a seat of national power—allowed me to sit in on their exclusive and notorious poker games from time to time. Considering all the money they'd stolen in office—especially Charlie Forbes, the head of the Veterans Bureau—I think they took a perverse pleasure whenever I walked away from the table with a few hundred of their dollars in earnings. Only President Harding never deliberately threw a hand my way, and I respected him the more for it.

"Nothing," I said. "I'm not friends with them, not like you and me, and now that the administration has gone belly-up, you'll see them turn on one another to avoid prison. Some of them, if not all, are bound to rot. I doubt that any of them have offered personal condolences to Mrs. Harding."

Murmuring filled the corridor. "Shh . . . here she comes to toss more of his papers into the fire."

"Stop shushing me, Ike."

Like some beaten animal Florence Kling Harding, the Duchess, entered the Blue Room, stopped with a box of papers in her arms and the firelight glinting off her spectacles. Her breathing was rapid, wet, and shallow, sounding like men who'd died beside me, the way someone in mortal terror breathes. Ike hadn't been exaggerating her condition: I'd seen Mrs. Harding only briefly over the last half year as her perennial kidney ailments kept her secluded in her private rooms when she was in attendance at the White House. She'd spent the past two months on the President's cross-country "Voyage of Discovery." They had traveled the Midwest in a repeat of his famous Front Porch Campaign that had elected him to the presidency, taking them up and down the Alaskan Coast, only to end in San Francisco where Harding suddenly fell ill and died.

Now her face was drawn, eyes tired and shadowed, and when she threw the box aside and reached out to welcome us, I noticed her thin arms were pale and fragile as glass, though her unusually large fists remained strong as she clutched my hand. Her Spanish shawl and flowered dress hung loosely on her frame.

She glanced up and said, "Ike, my dear, you are a fool for coming here this day."

"Mrs. President, please don't," he moaned. He struggled with words and came up with nothing, always the gentleman, and after a moment finally managed to eke out, "I am always at your service."

The Duchess smiled at me, her lips crawling like colonies of insects, and I swallowed thickly. She took my hand again and, gazing directly into my eyes, giving me a type of stare I'd never been given before, not even by the Krauts—one that brought me rearing to my full height—said gently, "This is a house of the damned, Richard. Don't go any farther or ever enter again. Ike is already doomed, and so are you in your own fashion. But you can still escape for a brief while. I suggest you take the chance. Leave us to the dead." And then, as if in kindly afterthought, she added, "The wretched Third Division resides with us, and they want your heart. Your wife and child are here, and they, too, hate you so very much."

A sickly grunt escaped me and my knees wobbled.

My stomach tugged sideways, and I reached for the upholstered bergere armchair to steady myself as all the intolerable memories came flooding back; at the thought of my men screaming, and Marisa and Jon *blazing* again, fire pouring over all of them. Fist clenched at my side I yearned to strike the Duchess. If she was insane, she needed help, and if she wasn't, she needed even more. Ike's Adam's apple bobbed wildly, and he made a plaintive sound in the back of his throat.

She must have had Gaston Means investigate me as well. I smiled weakly and drew back a step. "Well, what can I say to that?"

"Say nothing," Mrs. Harding told me. "Simply leave and never come back. Until you must. When we all must gather again."

"All right, Mrs. President," I said, and spun to go before I shattered her jaw.

His hand on my shoulder, Ike's grip was more powerful than I'd expected from a seventy-year-old man. "Please, Florence," he implored, his chin weaving back and forth between both of us. "We're here to help you through this time of trouble."

"I know, my friend, my poor fool. And so you are lost as well. The dead are here, Ike. All the dead in the entire world, throughout history. What aid can you give beneath such a tide?"

I was beginning to feel diseased and desperately foolish, but Ike seemed more horrified than earlier and gave me a grimace and slight nod, as if afraid to leave this woman alone, or to be left alone with her.

I asked, "The dead reside here, Mrs. President? In the White House?"

"Yes."

"How did that come to be?"

Her plump face contorted as if pinched in many places. She stared into the fire as if taunting me, knowing I could not look into flames after what had occurred in my life. I saw evil loosed in her and thought it quite possible she had murdered Harding herself.

"Because of Mr. Edison," the Duchess said. "And his machines. In recent years Thomas has become rather bored with his former achievements and advancements of technology. Whatever genius inspired him to create electric light and the voting machine and other great works no longer holds any sway over him. Now he seeks to communicate with the dead, and has played with his machines here like a boy with toy trains."

"I've seen him," Ike said.

"As always, he has unlocked truths no one else has been able to master, yet has done so in a hideously awry manner." She broke into an ecstatic grin that never reached her eyes; my Christ, I thought, Ike was right, she'd gone completely out of her mind. "I see them, and they are jealous and they despise those who are not dead yet."

"Where are they, these spirits? Right now, I mean."

"Here, of course, doing all they can do." She leaned

in and crooked her finger at me to do the same. "They are laying traps." She sighed and cocked her head, listening. "They are waiting."

Ike looked close to tears. Serving ten presidents had not prepared him for this. He spoke softly and touched the Duchess on the shoulder, and I wondered if they had been lovers while Harding frittered away with his many other ladies. "What will it take to convince you, Florence, that the White House is not actually . . . ?"

"Purgatory." Mrs. Harding shivered, her lips making their profane motions again. "Far more than it shall take to convince you, sadly. Since you will not listen and flee, we must see this condemnation through to the end." She wheeled on me and rushed forward until our noses nearly touched. Her shawl draped about her like furled leather wings. My reflection in her spectacles seemed shuddery and grotesque, and my gorge rose until I had to clear my throat. "Your friends from the Third Division damn you for leaving them in the trenches, blind and drowning in the Marne. Your wife and son, they . . ."

"Shut up, Mrs. President," I growled.

I'd been wounded twice during the war: first while helping the French hold the Germans at Chateu-Thierry, and again after being transferred to the Third Division, serving directly under Marshal Foch at Reims during the second battle of the River Marne. From there we pressed the Germans back for forty-seven days straight during the Meuse-Arconne offensive. We managed to battle them thirty miles across their farthest advance line of the Western Front. It cost 120,000 American casualties.

Mrs. Harding tittered.

"God damn you," I said, and Ike gasped.

"Yes, He has, Richard," she said. "He has practiced long and hard at that very sport. Just ask them. Ask any of them."

"I'm leaving."

Getting the hell out of the Blue Room, I walked down the corridor, thinking of a ditch on the side of a dirt road outside Baltimore where I'd lain drunk and broken for hours while my wife and son gagged blood and charred before my eyes . . . of what Marisa would have thought of the noble portraits of our nation's leaders displayed on the walls, rococo-revival punchbowls and American Empire sofas, Jon riding his trike over the great floors of the East Room, where history was made and magnificent balls given. Shadows bulged, swollen against the walls.

If anything, I had only assured myself that the Duchess should have entered the hospital for a longer stay, and focused on her mental health as much as on her kidney ailments. It appeared that Ike was of two minds: protecting Mrs. Harding's interests and protecting her feelings. I heard him sniffling behind me.

There was a soft skittering noise of something moving in the halls.

"Is that you?" Ike asked, suddenly standing directly beside me.

"No." I concentrated, and heard nothing more. "You'd better get her to Doc Sawyer as quickly as possible, and tell him to scurry her away to a sanitarium. If I get my hands on her, I think I'll snap her neck."

"You can be shot for talking like that."

The acrid smell of the smoke set me off on a sneezing fit. "Where are the Secret Service men?"

"I don't know." He sounded so forlorn I nearly choked.

Mrs. Harding, her heels pounding out frantic rhythms resounding through the White House, perhaps danced along the corridors as she called out several names, rushing from room to room in the distance. Her inflection held more than I believed a human voice could carry. It was filled with too many emotions at once. She sounded broken, defeated, enraged, and apologetic at the same time. She screamed Elizabeth Britton's name.

"Edison's done something to her," Ike said. "His electric machines have brought demons to possess her."

"She's insane all right. Delusional, and you're buying into it. You're making her worse."

He shook his head, sweat pouring off his brow. His hands were trembling badly. "You never met Mr. Edison. He's a true genius unto himself, like no man who's ever lived. If anyone could create a device to contact the dead, it would be him."

My own rage rose; he *wanted* to believe her. I faced echoes here and there, the cloying heat stifling. "My God, it's hot. What's she doing?"

The moon shone smeared across the windowpanes. Ike had been completely unnerved, uncertain now of where to go or what to do, whether he should put in a call to Coolidge or simply leave this place once and for all. Mrs. Harding was a perfect reflection of him as she appeared on the stairwell. She glided up to Ike, and they stood huddled close together like the lovers I thought they might be. She barked a single chilling laugh. Ike regarded the ceiling, but I could tell his eyes were filling with tears.

"He's here, my friend," Mrs. Harding said as he made an effort to hug her, pressing himself near without actually managing to touch her. "Right behind us. What do you want to say to my husband?"

"Shh," he told her.

"How much you love me, eh?"

"Richard is right," he whispered. "I wanted to believe you, Florence, but I see now your own guilty conscience has driven you to this. I understand why you burned all his missives, and the letters from his mistresses. They remind you of our own infidelities." He glanced at me, too much insanity held so tightly in his arms.

"We never reach the fire," Mrs. Harding chuckled. "Or anything else. That is the essence of damnation."

And then I smelled the stench.

A brief odor at first, of magnolias I thought. Quickly growing stronger, and then a billowing of . . . my eyes watered. I covered my mouth and nose with my hands. "Ike, the House. It's burning. She's set it on fire."

"What?" He watched me gag. "There's nothing, Richard."

Agony skewered my thighs as the stink of burning flesh enveloped me. I looked down to see if my legs were broken and bleeding, bullet holes leaking my blood across the corridor floor. They were, and I swallowed my screams as I found myself in the trenches again, and in that ditch once more, here in the hallway. Mortar exploded in the walls and my men screeched in agony as the hills blazed, rushing for the Marne. My son Jon reached for me, his hands blistering against the windshield, and Marisa behind him, splinters of glass in her throat, fading in flames. I tasted illegal whiskey. Shards of bone blew out my thighs.

Ike said, "Richard? What is it? What's happening?"

"Damn her," I told him, wavering, ready to fall, the mud in my mouth. "She's set the House aflame, Ike, can't you smell it?"

Ike spun as if stung, and gaped. "Mrs. President, why are you . . . ?"

The halls suddenly filled with an unimaginable pressure and we both cried out. Ike fell beyond my reach as if hauled by an undertow, reeling away, sprawling and rolling down the shadow-soaked corridor until I couldn't see him anymore. My Christ. I tried to rise and could barely get my chin off the floor. Faces drew close as Mrs. Harding's heels and jingling jewelry continued to clap as if tolling for us. I drew back as I mumbled prayers, and faces and figures marched and whirled and pirouetted before me. Oh, God, how many of my men were here . . . all the dead? . . . each one of them blaming me for the chaos at Reims, and the darkness behind them twisting into bodies, so much like the Presidents. Grant's snobbish leer and Lincoln's towering frame, Jefferson's angled in chin tilted back in a howl as he pranced forward, all of them grinning and baring their teeth.

Despair set adrift in the stale air, the same in every room as I lumbered to my feet and ran. Stuffed to splitting with the remnants of all we've ever been, souls stuck in purgatory like clumsy animals. Struggling, biting, holding on—their jealousy, I could feel it like an ocean boiling around me—ancient and lost men and women rose into view and fell to dust, and the skeletons racked with rage beneath the dirt trampled by their progeny. The Third Division came for me, smashed gas masks on, coughing up their mustard-gas-poisoned lungs. They swelled beside me, empty of substance but not of spirit, and their weight grew more substantial. Swirling motes of the damned spired to the ceiling, brushed the window glass and toppled like the Washington Monument.

I shrieked until blood filled my mouth. Marisa, my life, and Jon, my life, now standing before me on the South Portico. My wife and son—as they looked before, during, and after I nearly drove into the Chesapeake, drunk after a night of playing poker with the Ohio Gang, four hundred dollars of Harding's money in my vest pocket; spinning the wheel and going over the ridge where the lock on the passenger door clacked and squealed and the windows shattered, tree branches grabbing me like my wife's hands, only stronger, plucking me from the car. Marisa's face now, still so lovely, smiles always reaching her eyes, stood grinning and grimacing and without a face. Blackened masks of fury called to me.

Dadee. Dadee!

"Baby," I whispered without breath, slinking backward down the hall to see Ike struggling with President Warden G. Harding crawling on top of him, wailing into his face, and Jon and Marisa were wrapped around my ankles and neck, the jealous and bitter dead keeping us for their own. My child's tongue and fingers in my eyes.

Careening, I kept running through the White House, clutching at doorknobs, calling the Duchess as if she might help. It took only another minute before I stumbled back and fell over her feet. She stared with that haunted, hideous smile and said, "I have died but will not lay down for another year."

Ike, now dead on the floor near me with his gritted teeth broken and lips bleeding before the wraith of a dead President—both looking the same, like any two old men as their wasted souls now stood side by side—stood up beside Harding and both moved out to stop me.

"Ike, no . . ."

I rushed to the front door with all of them tumbling and giggling, George Washington plucking at my chin as worms squirmed in his rotted wood teeth. I looked outside at the freedom awaiting me in this great and democratic land, moon a bloated white toad crouching in the sky, and, grinning myself now, understood that there was no point, no escape possible. With amputated arms, my men mocked me with salutes. We all belonged here and would gather eventually. Closing the door, I let the dead fall upon me, Lincoln carrying his own skull fragments and his beard full of gore, even Harding moving in to bleed against my flesh, hatred of my wife and son hissing so malevolently in my ear, and wondered how much I, too, would loathe the living world in another instant.

A WORSE PLACE THAN HELL
by Peter Crowther

Since the World and British Fantasy Award–nominated *Narrow Houses* (1992), Peter Crowther has edited or coedited eight further anthologies, continued to produce reviews and interviews for a variety of publications on both sides of the Atlantic, sold some fifty of his own short stories, and completed *Escardy Gap*, a collaborative novel with James Lovegrove due out in September 1996 from Tor Books. A solo novel, a short story collection, more anthologies, and *Escardy Gap II* are all currently underway.

> "If there is a worse place than Hell, then I am in it."
> —attributed to Abraham Lincoln
> following the Fredericksburg collapse, 1862

Prologue
1:30 A.M. 15 APRIL 1865, WASHINGTON, D.C.: The tuft of hair is removed almost lovingly by Corporal John Lansing, its thick strands—matted by blood and tissue—carefully removed from the wound by means of a folding-knife that the soldier had bought from a one-eyed trail scout in Abilene the previous year. John Lansing, a Church-going Baptist, is not a thief and the "taking" is one born out of respect, admiration, and profound loss.

At this time the patient is still alive, lying diagonally across a walnut bed in a room measuring fifteen by nine feet, but he is unconscious, lower exremities cold to the touch, pulse feeble. As Corporal Lansing steps back from the table, he places the swatch of hair in the fold of a theater handbill and, his hands now clasped across his stomach, he stealthily refolds the handbill before dropping it into his tunic pocket.

One of the two medical men present—name of Leale—proceeds to cover the body with mustard plasters. Lansing looks away, his eyes traveling the topmost circumference of the room, and he immediately feels a telltale tear roll down his left cheek. After almost thirty minutes, the other doctor—Barnes—straightens up and drops the shiny instruments onto the small folding table by his side. He cannot locate the bullet, a small lead ball less than one half-inch in diameter, which is embedded amidst shards of pulverized bone fragments in the anterior lobe of the left hemisphere of the brain.

When Doctor Barnes speaks to the people in the room, his voice is tired and without hope: further explorations will be of no use, he tells them.

Soon, he will be free, the doctor says. *We must simply wait.*

The present: A bizarre mixture of smells floated across the dark, early morning street, the gentle wind blowing the disparate elements into one single aroma: a cloying, olfactory amalgam of smoke, sweat. It was a smell that was familiar to him.

The sixteenth President of the United States of America had been alternating running with brisk walking for several hours now, feeding off a heady adrenaline cocktail of wonder and fear. He stepped out of the shadows onto the pockmarked sidewalk and once again breathed deeply the myriad aromas of New York City.

It was almost five hours since his escape and with each passing minute the smells floating on the wind had strengthened, grown bolder. He had made good speed, at first moving without clear knowledge of where he was going save to put distance between himself and the doctors but then weaving his way across the city and then heading down toward Greenwich Village.

For the past few hours he had been lying on a bench in Washington Square, reputed—according to his map—to be a park, but which in truth amounted to the barest scattering of trees, several concrete pillars (the function of which he could not fathom) and what appeared to be a huge fountain though it contained no water.

The entire area had been littered with homeless people who drank boldly from brown-bagged bottles an elixir which, while it did not provide any answers, at least fogged some of the questions. He had picked a piece of wall against which he sat and watched. And though he tried with all his might, he could not get out of his head another image—Devil's Run, when the Union forces had been overrun by a Confederate charge on the second day at Gettysburg—of men equally bereft of hope and stamina, propped against mounds of soil piled up into gullies by a constant barrage of cannon fire.

But now he was back on the street, a little replenished.

A plaque set into the concrete wall across from him reflected the orange glare from the intermittent sodium lamps:

THE BOWERY

it said.

Half-crouched, so as to avoid or at least delay discovery of his current position, he looked back along the way he had come. Could this dark and dismal street truly be the same Bowery that he had passed along, albeit briefly, on his last visit to New York City? Of course, it must be: after all, could there be *two* such famed thoroughfares? Presumably not. But the broken and occasionally boarded-up windows and the graffiti-festooned building fronts were indeed a far cry from the gay and picturesque entertainment center he remembered . . . for his memory did not accord with the actual passage of time which had taken place.

This street stretched far away to his right, a generous pathway more than wide enough for four sets of coach-and-horses to ride abreast. A distant humming noise sounded and lights bathed the street. Lincoln stepped back into the shadows and watched in fascination as another of the infernal mechanical carriages bounced out of the street across from him and disappeared up the street to his right.

Could it be looking for him? It seemed unlikely. Not that people would *not* be looking for him, but rather the apparent lack of any urgency on the part of the vehicle suggested an altogether different and more leisurely motive behind its appearance. Though what could bring any respectable person out into the streets at this time of night—or rather *morning*—was quite beyond him.

He looked again at the sign and then removed the folded paper from his coat pocket, scanning down its key of landmarks until he reached the one he wanted. He then referred to the map and noted the position of his destination. He had been right: The Bowery led into it. He refolded the paper and returned it to his pocket, checking the gloomy buildings opposite for any sign of someone watching him but everything seemed deserted.

Along the other way, toward the City's heart, it was the same, though there the pathway seemed to curve gently to the left. As he stared into the shimmering, orange-hued gloom, something moved from the protection of the left-hand wall. It moved slowly, apparently cautious at first, and then it stopped and seemed to settle in the middle of the road. He knew it was watching him. He squinted and rubbed his eyes. Was it a cat? A dog, perhaps? *It's a rat,* a secret inner voice whispered to him, though such a suggestion was surely ridiculous. The thing was ten—nay, *twenty*—times bigger than a simple vermin, even bigger than the battle-bloated carnivores that inhabited the areas outside the circles of protective light on the fields at Fredericksburg and Antietam Creek, where the dead and dying lay on the bare ground and the blasted and torn limbs were stacked as high as piles of pumpkins in the fall. He shook his head, breaking up the quickly-forming mental picture into a series of half-remembered shards.

But the smell remained: the smell was here, now.

He straightened up and stood his ground, removing the white gloves—now somewhat stained, he noted disapprovingly—and slowly inserting them into his coat pocket. The fact that there were other gloves in there seemed somehow reassuring. Lincoln lifted his head, jutted out his chin, and, rubbing his hands down the sides of his legs, stared, concentrating all of his attention on the creature on the path as though it were the only thing in this Godless place.

The thing's eyes seemed to wink and it shrank lower upon itself . . . either trying to hide or preparing to attack. Lincoln straightened his hat and stepped forward.

Quick as a flash, the creature turned and darted along the street a little way and then off at a right angle into the shadows surrounding a series of metal containers, leaving behind it an insidious echoing patter of tiny clawed feet.

Interlude (1)

8:10 p.m. 26 June 1892, by the Colorado River, Northern Arizona: Prentiss Ingraham, noted dime novelist, holds the young man tight, the roar of the river blustering over to the right. The man's collarbone protrudes from his shoulder, a thin slice of bluish-white bone, while the jumble of intestines that has partially spilled from the gash in his belly now lies quivering on the folds of his ripped shirt. His partially severed left foot sits limply on the rocky slab beside his hip, the leg above it twisted and broken like a piece of driftwood. The man's lips are the deepest blue that Prentiss has ever seen. He will use that fact in a story the following year.

Yore not gonna make it, boy, Prentiss tells the man—whose name is Jedediah Lansing, only surviving son of Captain James Lansing, late of the Union Army—over the sound of the water.

In the background, sounding like excited children at play, muffled calls ring out as Cody and the others wade into the shallows as far as they dare in order to retrieve the waterlogged provisions from the smashed raft. Jedediah shifts awkwardly and cries out in pain, momentarily losing consciousness, but he manages to remove the leather pouch from his pants pocket and presses it into the writer's hand. Responding to Lansing's nods, Ingraham leans forward so that the dying man might speak into his ear.

As he listens, his eyes open wider and he glances down at the pouch.

The present: Lincoln relaxed and lifted his head, listening.

It was not silence that he heard, he suddenly realized, but rather a faint humming, like some kind of electrical generator. He looked around at the darkened street and saw only dereliction and waste. This was not a hospitable place. In that respect, it was not dissimilar to other places of confrontation. For that was what this was, a battlefield of sorts though the combatants were not visible. Rather, this war was one waged from a distance. And the hum he heard was the hum of the city itself, breathing with a life of its own.

Suddenly it seemed as if there were three possible sides to this conflict: the forces of law, the forces of chaos, and some intermediary power, a sentient being imbued in the bricks and mortar and coldly glowing streetlights.

Staying within the comforting shadows, the President edged his way along the sidewalk. Somewhere in the distance, a howl rang out, rising and falling in pitch. He stopped and waited. To his other side, again far away, a second cry sounded, its mournful wail echoing the first and seeming to build in intensity until, quite suddenly, both faded away.

And only the hum of the city remained.

Interlude (2)

4:30 p.m. 11 May 1895, a funeral parlor in Guthrie, Oklahoma: Having removed all of the clothing from the bullet-riddled bodies of the two men—whose names, his sheet of paper tells him are Charlie Pierce and Bitter Creek Newcomb—Doc Hinkel, a medical man of some questionable repute as well as a philanderer and unsuccessful gambler, proceeds to remove their boots. In the lobby outside the room, two Deputy US Marshals go through the details of the ambush again for the benefit of a newspaper man up from Oklahoma City.

The newspaperman—whose name is Dan Remington—plans to headline the piece:

DESPERADOES EARN THEIR FREEDOM!

In Pierce's left boot the doctor discovers a wad of papers. He unfolds them as he listens to the reenactment in the hallway. The first paper is a likeness of a man and a woman. The creases make any formal identification impossible. The second paper, a folded fifty-dollar bill, the doctor slips into his waistcoat pocket. After careful examination of the third and final paper—a crumpled theater handbill advertising a play entitled *Our American Cousin*, containing a lock of hair which still bears traces of skin and dried blood—and the scribbled writing on its reverse, Doctor Hinkel places this also in his pocket. Then he washes the excess blood from the bodies and clasps the two pairs of hands neatly on their respective stomachs.

As he calls for the newspaperman to come and take

the photograph, the doctor thinks excitedly of the potential betting power of his new prize. Tonight, he will be lucky, he tells himself: tonight, he has himself a fine stake with which to play.

The present: Crossing 4th Street, Abraham Lincoln went over the events of the past few hours.

The last thing he remembered was sitting in a private box at Ford's Theater watching a play of some kind. He could not remember the name of the presentation itself, although the name Tom Taylor seemed familiar. Could that be the title of the play? He did not think so. Perhaps it was the name of the writer.

He remembered that it revolved around a Yankee lighting his cigar with an old Will and Testament, thereby sending up in smoke his chances of inheriting some $400,000. It was not a bad play, but then it was not a good one either.

A sound to his right caused him to pause.

A stooped man carrying a small paper bag of some kind stumbled out from beneath the awning of a store, the nature of whose merchandise—boldly displayed in the two large windows—the President could not discern. The man, clearly the worse for the effects of alcohol, held his ground, body tilted to an extreme side-angle while his feet remained stationary ... as though they were in fact attached in some way to the sidewalk. With his free hand, the man was attempting to pull up his fly. The front of his trousers was wet and, behind him, in the doorway, a widening pool could be seen snaking its way toward the sidewalk.

Lincoln considered trotting off the street and into the shadows but, even as he weighed up the likelihood that he could do it without being seen, the man looked up, gave a loud rasping belch and saw the President. Almost immediately, he started laughing.

Interlude (3)

1:30 p.m. 16 May 1920, District School #94, near

Pecatonica, Ill.: It is the first year of teaching for Miss Erna Meyer. She is in the middle of conducting a crayoning project for the first grade. Charles Buntjier, privileged earlier that morning by being assigned the task of holding the flag to which the rest of the class pledged their allegiance, is talking to his friend, Leland Meiers. Unaware that the teacher is watching him, Charles hands over the fieldmouse to Leland and accepts in return a small leather pouch and a large beetle through which a string has been pulled and knotted.

Charles, Miss Meyer calls out, *Leland.* The class, as one, stops what they are doing and all eyes turn to the two boys.

Yes, miss? their eyes say, though their voices remain silent.

Please come to the front of the class, Miss Meyer says. *And bring with you whatever it is that you are playing with.*

While the other children wait and watch, Miss Erna Meyer studies the objects set before her on her desk. Leland and Charles stand at the other side of the desk, their hands clasped behind their backs.

The teacher drops the unfortunate beetle into the waste basket by her side.

She calls for Keith Fisher to take the fieldmouse outside and set it free.

Opening the small leather pouch, Miss Meyer asks, *And what is this?*

Part of President Lincoln's head, Miss, says Leland Meiers.

The present: Still laughing, the man staggered forward and then back again. He lifted his free arm and pointed at the President . . . or, more accurately, at his hat. "Shum kinda fancy dress, huh?" the man said.

"My attire may not be entirely to your liking, sir," Lincoln responded, "but neither is your attitude acceptable to me. I suspect it would be equally distasteful to

any right-minded folk. I suggest you be on your way."
And, with that, he turned on his heel, removed his
white gloves from his pocket, and strode onto the sidewalk. His destination was just another two or three
blocks ahead, he remembered. Time was wasting.

Interlude (4)

8:45 a.m., 6 January 1946, a residential house on Hous-
ton's Gold Coast, River Oaks: Ex-Governor William P.
Elkins hands the contents of a small metal box to his
wife, Oveta. He says, *You must guard this with your
life,* though the cancer has affected his vocal cords and
his voice is too soft for her to hear above the sound of
her own grief.

He settles back onto his bed, the pillow momentarily
engulfing the sides of his head, and he breathes out a
final breath slowly. It is a deep breath, a luxurious and
well-earned last breath, and it carries with it the insepa-
rable dual scent of jasmine and goodness. He can die
happy now, he thinks, content in the knowledge that his
wife will preserve his treasure for posterity.

Oveta Culp Elkins recognizes her husband's release
from life, sees the unseen veil lift from his pain-
stricken face, and she cries out in desperate sadness. As
she rises from the bedside chair to throw her arms
around her dead husband, the small metal box drops
from her lap and rolls under the bed.

The present: He recalled the upholstered rocking
chair in which he had been sitting. There had been two
other people in the room: his wife and a guard. The
guard was fully armed and had, for the most part, remained at the rear of the box. However, now that he
thought about it, the President clearly recalled the man
moving down closer to the stage and taking a seat to
his right.

Had that been a part of some elaborate plan to take
his life?

Then there had been a slight chink of light, as the door behind him opened. He remembered paying no heed to it, suspecting that it was merely John Parker checking that all was indeed well inside the box. Then . . .

Lincoln shook his head and staggered as though momentarily faint, stretching out his left hand to the wall for support.

Then there had been the noise and a flash as bright as that produced by Mathew Brady's exploding gunpowder contraption, and a searing, profound pain in his head.

The next thing he remembered was coming to in a brightly-lit room. He was lying on a table, surrounded by people—each wearing a white half-face mask—and a profusion of gleaming equipment which appeared to be of a surgical nature but the like of which he had never before encountered.

Where am I? he had asked, in a sleepy voice. *Has the play finished? Did I pass out?*

The two people leaning over him had smiled then— he had recognized their smiles even through the masks—and had looked at each other triumphantly.

Where is my wife? he had asked. *Where is Mary?*

That is when they had told him a story more fantastic than the most far-fetched dime novel, stranger even than the strangest dream.

One of the men—there were six men and two women present—explained that he was in New York City, but in addition to his having to endure a physical displacement of several hundred miles, he was no longer even in his own time.

Abraham Lincoln looked up at the towering buildings that lined the street, gray-bricked and mirror-windowed monoliths that stretched way, way up into the early morning sky, and he marveled at the advancements that had made such constructions possible.

New York City but a handful of years short of the turn of the millennium . . . and a New York that was more than a century older than the one he had visited so recently. This was indeed some rare kind of magic.

As though to emphasize the sense of wonder, a Yellow Cab turned out of 6th Street and headed up to Cooper Square.

Interlude (5)

10:10 p.m., 23 October 1989, Wells, Maine: Having changed hands sixteen times in nine states over 125 years, the lock of hair once belonging to Abraham Lincoln is discovered in a collection of virtually mint comic books, *Big Little Books, Classics Illustrated,* animation cells, and cinema lobby posters cautiously valued in the upper single millions.

The collection belongs to the widow of the recently deceased Jonathan Morrill, whose lifetime of collecting has amassed some 14,000 items and has caused the couple to spend almost $100,000 on customizing their home to accommodate the vast bulk.

In addition to the "Tuft of Lincoln," as it has become known, the collection also includes a small selection of similar personal effects removed from equally auspicious bygone notables, primarily those involved in the art of writing. A twine headed hammer, for example, allegedly used by Henry David Thoreau to construct his one-room hut by Walden Pond; the pencil and notebook used by Laura Ingells Wilder; and assorted other items of interest.

The comic books and cinematic collectibles have been sold at auction over a three-day period at a special convention in Atlanta's Hilton Towers Hotel.

Generally considered to be of little financial value, the non-comic-book-related ephemera has been sold as a single lot to William H. Goddard, a wealthy New York-based garment manufacturer whose grandmother was one of the survivors of the tragic conflagration of the Triangle Shirtwaist Company in 1911.

On the train returning home to New York, the new

owner now considers his purchase and discovers Lincoln's hair. As it turns out, it is one of two almost identical artifacts ... but the unquestionable connection between them goes beyond mere physical similarities.

The present: They had talked to him of a special process known as cloning, the art of extrapolating the DNA of a living creature from part of its skin ... or, as in his own case, from the follicles attached to hair roots which were still alive when removed.

Could you bring back my Willie? the President had asked, in something of a daze, not quite catching the snigger from one of the men at the rear of the room. *He died only—*

He had been going to say that his eleven-year-old son, William Wallace Lincoln, had died only three years ago but, of course, it was much, much longer now.

And ... and Mary, my wife?

The man had shaken his head.

A woman had stepped forward and said, *She died in 1882, Mister President.*

"Oh, Mary, Mary," he said now to the cold buildings and the unblinking lights.

There was no response, only more grief.

Interlude (6)

10:10 p.m., 12 December 1993, The Beekman Tower Restaurant, New York City: William H. Goddard hands over a case to a man he knows only as Dolman. Quite how the man came to know that he had the artifacts he does not know. He will never know. He knows only that the man—and presumably the woman with him—are in the employ of the government.

More than this does not seem to matter. Even *this* does not seem to matter.

Goddard is in need of the funds this transaction will bring him. It has not been a good year in the garment business, and a pending divorce settlement looks set to take most of his remaining capital.

The case is handed across a plate-festooned table overlooking the lights of First Avenue. Dolman, a fat man who perspires a lot, accepts the case. A few minutes later, he hands a small envelope to Goddard who smiles and places the item carefully in his waiting billfold. The billfold is then returned to Goddard's inside jacket pocket.

The woman with Dolman—Goddard does not know her name—considers the contents of the leather pouches passed to her by her colleague. She matches Goddard's smile: she knows they would have paid twice as much if they had been pushed. Goddard's smile grows even broader as their eyes meet: he knows he would have accepted half the amount he has now pocketed.

Below them, the sirens continue their litany of amusement.

The present: He rubbed his hands down his legs. Everything felt and seemed the way it had always done and yet this was not his body . . . as the people had explained. They had explained, but he had not understood . . . artificial, they had called it: a mixture of plastic, rubber and silicone, only one element of which he was familiar with.

But what did it matter what he was constructed from. Without Mary, it did not seem important.

All that was important was that he was here. And, even more important, that he did not want to be. Now, all he wanted to do was rest.

They had left him alone in the room at his request, telling him that there was someone they wanted him to meet, but while they were gone, he had slipped out of another door, walked along the brightly lit corridor and down a seemingly interminable series of stairs until he reached the street. Then it was simply a matter of running straight ahead, away from the river, and occasionally turning left when a street appeared suitably deserted. Then it was right again for a way, then left again and so on until he reached the park which was not a park . . . and all the veterans of the war of life. It was there, checking his bearings after his rest, that he stopped a young man and asked where he was.

The young man seemed reluctant to speak to him at first but then, with an expansive sweep of his arm, announced *Enn Why You.* It was an enigmatic response which the President decided not to pursue further. Instead, he inquired how he might reach the Cooper Union Building and the man had given him a small handbill and a map of the city . . . some of the street names which he recognized and remembered. He had decided to walk the route.

The President had passed by several small restaurants and what seemed to be drinking establishments, from which loud and raucous music bellowed, despite the lateness of the hour. Clearly, the Prohibition movement which started in Maine in 1851 and spread to New York State in 1855, had been repealed.

He had passed by grocers' stores, whose wares were stacked resplendent on large trestle tables which extended way out onto the sidewalk.

And he had passed by a series of young ladies clad in the most minuscule of clothing who offered amusement, wry smiles, and even an occasional expression of sympathy. He had, however, been unable to contain his amazement when two of these "women" had turned out, on closer investigation, to be men. Lincoln immediately recalled Jefferson Davis' capture near Irwinville, Georgia, dressed as a woman so as to evade atonement for his crimes against humanity. The President wondered what it was that these individuals sought to escape.

All the way along his route, Abraham Lincoln had watched the jumble of people and faces, noting the mixture of color and realizing that the state of "insurrection" he had declared on April 15th just four short years ago had not been in vain. For here, all had a place and, or so it seemed, all were equal.

When at last he reached the Cooper Union Building, he felt more at ease though he was tired, his energy sapped by the need for stealth and an almost over-whelming grief and profound loneliness.

Interlude (7)

12:45 a.m., the present, New York University Medical Center, 1st and 30th: The latest search party returns . . . again unsuccessful. Meredith P. Sansome, Head of Bio-engineering and the doctor in charge of the cloning project, slumps into a chair and closes his eyes.

Dwight Jablonski, right-hand man to the Joint Chiefs of Staff and now specially appointed temporary Direc-tor of the Center's security, steps out of the washroom and runs his hands through his hair. He looks tired. When he opens his eyes, he looks around the room, studying each face in turn. *Great,* he says, *just great. From the team that brought you Nagasaki, Agent Orange, and AIDS . . . a resurrected former President left to wander around modern-day New York.* He shakes his head. He has no idea as to how the elaborate secu-rity arrangements were so easily broached, though his mind has reflected on similar embarrassments over the years, Kennedy, Oswald, Kennedy, and Reagan to name only four. He knows that questions will be asked and answers will need to be found. *If anyone here has any balls to spare, just leave them on the table,* he an-nounces to the hushed room. *We'll need a hell of a lot of them to satisfy the media. Any that we have left will make up a nice pie for the President.*

It's not the end of the world, Sansome says. He doesn't sound totally convinced.

No, but I'm sure we'll get around to that next week.

On the table is a large file of other "possibles"—including a rock and roll singer from Memphis, a draftsman-turned-dictator from Austria, and a much-loved architect from Wisconsin—all of whom were considered either inappropriate ("no Spielberg factor," was how Jablonski put it) or, by virtue of the source materials available for their respective "reawakenings" (the alleged piece of John Kennedy's brain being an obvious example), deemed unlikely to succeed. Because of the enormous costs involved in the complex process, the first one not only had to be right . . . it also had to be popular.

In the cloning of one of the country's most revered statesmen and one of its favorite literary figures—each of whom, being contemporaries, had spoken highly of the other (though they had never actually met) and both of whose reputations had survived the intervening years entirely intact—had seemed to provide all the necessary elements to win the nation's support. But now, all bets were off. When—if—they managed to track down the President, the entire project would have to be shelved. Jablonski had already explained this situation—and its implications—to Sansome.

Where the hell has he gone? Jablonski asks nobody in particular.

Maybe the muggers have got him, somebody says.

Don't even joke about it, Sansome says. *How about the poet?*

One of the men says, *Marilyn is down there with him now. Seems they've been having a few difficulties.*

Difficulties? Sansome leans forward in his chair.

The door bursts open and a woman rushes into the room. *He's on,* she says. *We had a few problems with the fact that the hair was clipped and so there were no complete follicles present.* She walks across the room, lifts the Mister Coffee pot and pours into a cup.

Sansome stands up. *But he's up and running?*

The woman nods as she takes a drink. *Mmm, that is so good,* she says. *He's a little groggy, but he is up and running. We had to sedate him, though.*

Sedate him! Jablonski slaps his forehead dramatically. *Jesus Chri—*

Keep calm, the woman interjects, *keep calm. We had to give him a little something to keep him loose while we explained the situation.*

Sansome says, *And how did you do that?*

The woman smiles awkwardly. *We told him he was in Heaven,* she says. *We told him that we had created a magical futuristic version of New York City and that Abraham Lincoln had gone missing. 'Where would he go, Mr Whitman?' we asked him.*

Did he know? Jablonski says, hardly daring to wait for the answer.

The woman nods, smiling. *The Cooper Union Buildings,* she says. *He saw him there in 1861.*

The present: Walt Whitman sat in the car between two unsmiling angels in gray suits and marveled at the scenery they passed by.

"I am so delighted at this opportunity, gentlemen," he said. "It is here—where we are now going—that I first saw the President."

Meredith Sansome, turned around in the front passenger seat, nodded and smiled beatifically. This was how he thought an angel would smile.

"He was—and, I presume, still is—a man of unusual and almost uncouth height and, on this occasion, he was dressed entirely in black with a similarly dark complexion and an insolent composure." Whitman smiled and stuck his neck forward, running his hands through his hair. "A bushy head of hair—equally black—and a disproportionately long neck." He laughed and shuffled excitedly in his seat. "What a man!"

Huge buildings scraped the night sky of this dream world, its darkness now softening on the horizon, and everywhere was lit by bright lights and colorful displays. Perhaps this was indeed Heaven, he mused silently, watching his own thoughtful expression reflected in the window of the car.

The last thing he could recall was lying in his room, a gentle rain falling outside, and saying to Horace Traubel—dear Horace!—that he should take something with which to remember him. He had reached out then and, with a pair of nail clippers, had removed a sizable chunk from his beard. This thatch he had presented to Horace with a sad gleam in his eye.

Whitman saw that gleam again now, reflected in the glass before him.

The silent carriage in which they traveled pulled out to overtake a colossal vehicle which sprayed water over the gutter and sidewalk, following with a mechanical brush that swept it clean. Whitman stared at it as they went by and turned to watch it through the back window. It seemed for all the world like some gigantic creature, lumbering through this wondrous kingdom of Heaven doomed to a single purpose: to clean. He presumed that everything here would be similarly employed.

The man in the driving seat periodically checked the rearview mirror, shaking his head each time he saw the shaggy-bearded man whose eyes blazed with each new revelation.

They had tried the Lincoln Center.

They had tried City Hall, where the President's body had lain in state while 120,000 grief-stricken New Yorkers had filed past to pay their last respects.

They had even tried the Lincoln statue in the park, combing the grassland and paths surrounding it for hundreds of yards.

But it had all been to no avail.

Then the poet, when he came round and could respond to questions, told them the Cooper Union Foundation Building was where the President would go. It was the only place that would be familiar to him, Whitman had explained. The only place where he would feel even a little comfortable.

Minutes later, they were there.

The car screeched around the corner into Astor Place and pulled up in front of the red-brick building on the left. As the driver turned off the engine, Sansome pointed toward the shadows by the reception entrance.

There, his stovepipe hat in his hand and his head bowed, President Abraham Lincoln stood looking up at the early morning sky.

"Let's go," Sansome snapped.

They got out.

"Mr. President," Sansome called as soon as he was out of the car. "That was quite a chase you led us on."

The President turned to face the small group that walked across the road toward him. If he was surprised or fearful, Sansome thought, then he certainly didn't show it.

"We have brought someone to see you, Mr. President," he called, and he flicked the protective seal off the hypodermic nestled in his jacket pocket.

Lincoln frowned at the portly man with the bushy mane of beard hanging from his chin.

"Mr. President," Walt Whitman said softly, "I am indeed honored to meet you."

His face a mask of smiles, Sansome walked calmly by the poet and around behind the President.

Whitman, his attention momentarily attracted to the angel who had brought him here, watched as Sansome plunged a weapon of some kind into Abraham Lincoln's back.

The President gasped and, dropping his hat, reached out for support. But the chemical now coursing through his artificial veins was swift and powerful. The darkness rushed up to greet him, to soothe him and to take away the pain of remembering and loss . . . to restore the freedom he had earned, the freedom he had fought for all of his life.

"Mr. . . . Whitman?" he said.

Then he crumpled to the ground.

Sansome knelt by the body and felt the President's neck. He looked up and smiled sadly. "He's gone," he said. "Again."

Walt Whitman stared in disbelief. He looked at the other angels he had traveled with, saw one of them remove a shiny object from his jacket pocket. Shaking his head, he watched as the man—a normal man, not an angel at all—stepped forward and jabbed the hypodermic into his arm.

Somewhere, way in the distance, a siren wailed its shame.

Epilogue

The future, The Foggy Bottom Cafe, 25th Street, Washington, D.C., close to the Kennedy Center: The man called Jablonski walks across to pay the bill.

The man called Dolman makes a final entry in his notepad. Both men are relieved at the way the entire Tuft of Lincoln matter has been resolved, particularly in that they have retained their positions and that the project has been given a second chance so soon.

While his colleague pays the bill, Dolman glances at his pad. There are two lists of names. The first is a column of pairs, couples, all of whom have been thoroughly checked and rechecked for their suitability. All are "good" people, people whose deaths would be felt by the entire nation ... people whose subsequent rebirths in the event of their deaths would be greeted with unanimous acclaim. Two of these pairs of names—one married couple noted for their philanthropic work and a two-man songwriting partnership—have been ringed in red ink.

The second list, a column of six names only one of which has been ringed, comprises operatives who would, if asked, be prepared to effect the sanction even knowing that to do so would result in their own deaths. These people would be told that they would themselves be brought back at a later date and with a new identity. Although his colleague has not said as much, Dolman knows that such a potentially disastrous loose end could not be permitted.

He closes the pad and smiles up at Jablonski, happy in his work.

In blowing airs from the fields back again give me my
    darlings,
give me my immortal heroes,
Exhale me them centuries hence, breathe me their breath,

let not an atom be lost,
O years and graves! O air and soil! O my dead, an aroma
   sweet!
Exhale them perennial sweet death, years, centuries hence.
                    from *Pensive on Her Dead Gazing,*
                              by Walt Whitman (1865)

(For Dr. Keith D. Sorsby)

JACK BE QUICK

by Graham Masterton

Graham Masterton is the author of more than fifty best-selling horror novels and thrillers, as well as dozens of short stories. His first book, *The Manitou,* was made into a movie starring Tony Curtis, Burgess Meredith, and Stella Stevens, and a later novel, *Walkers* is currently in production in Los Angeles. He has won a Special Edgar from the Mystery Writers of America and two Silver Medals from the West Coast Review of Books. He lives with his wife Wiescka near the famous Derby racecourse at Epsom, Surrey, England.

She called him on his private number at 3:17 in the morning, and she was hysterical. "It's Jack! I can't wake him up!"

"Hey, ssh, calm down, will you? What do you mean, you can't wake him up?"

"He's just lying there . . . I shook him and I shook him but nothing happened."

"Listen, calm down. Is he still breathing?"

"I don't know. I couldn't wake him, that's all."

"How about a pulse? Is his heart still beating?"

"I don't know. I didn't try."

"Well, go try. I'll wait while you do it. And for Christ's sake, get a grip on yourself."

There was a lengthy silence. Next to him, Ethel turned over and said drowsily, "Who is it? Couldn't they wait till the morning?"

He reached out and squeezed her hand. "It's okay. Something came up, that's all."

After more than a minute she came back to the

phone. "He's not breathing, and I can't find a pulse. I lifted up his eyelid and his eye was all stary."

"Okay, then. Where are you?"

"The Madison, the Presidential Suite."

"What security do you have?"

"Two men in the hall outside. Bobby—what am I going to *do?*" Her voice rose almost to a squeal.

"Don't do anything. Don't touch him anymore. Get your clothes on and leave as quick as you can. Don't say anything to the agents, nothing at all. Just smile and try to act normal."

"But what about a doctor?"

"Leave the doctor to me. Just get dressed and get out of there."

Ethel turned over again. "Bobby? What's all this about a doctor?"

"Henry Kissinger," he said. He put down the phone, and switched on his bedside lamp. "Listen, honey, I have to go out for a while. I'll give you a call later."

"Is it really so urgent?"

Bobby was already unbuttoning his pale yellow pajamas. He gave her a quick, ambiguous nod, which was all that he could manage. Urgent wasn't the word for it. This was the end of the world as everybody knew it. He went into the dressing room and found a pair of gray pants, a shirt, and a blue golfing sweater. When he was dressed, he leaned across the bed and gave Ethel a quick kiss. She said, "Look at you. You look so pale. Are you sure that you're feeling all right?"

"I'm fine. I'm really fine." And that was when he realized that he had told her three lies already.

From his car, he called just three people: Jack's private doctor, Toussaint Christophe; Harold Easterlake, from the State Department; and his own closest confidant from the Attorney General's office, George Macready. He didn't tell them what had happened, but he asked them all to meet him at the Madison as soon as they could. "And for Christ's sake, be discreet."

He thought of calling Ted Sorensen, Jack's closest

counsel, but he decided against it, just for now. If Jack were really dead, he wanted his own people around him, not Jack's. And he didn't want to be out-maneuvered by LBJ.

He went up in the elevator directly to the penthouse floor. His reflection in the elevator mirror looked un-shaven and strained, and his hair stuck out at the back. He tried to smooth it down, but it kept springing up again. Outside the Presidential Suite the two Secret Service agents were sitting on folding chairs. One was staring at the ceiling and the other was reading *To Kill A Mockingbird*. They jumped to their feet as soon as they saw him coming.

"Good morning, Mr. Kennedy. Something we can help you with?"

"I have to see the President right now," he said.

"He specially asked not to be disturbed, sir."

"That's all right. Just let me in and I'll wake him my-self. Has his—uh, friend left already?"

The agent's eyes scarcely flickered. "About fifteen minutes ago, sir."

He unlocked the doors and let Bobby into the suite. The large sitting room was lit with a single lamp. A room-service trolley was still parked in one corner, with the remains of two lobsters on it, and an empty bottle of Perrier Jouët rosé. A damp white bathrobe lay on the couch as if somebody had shed it like a pelt.

Bobby walked quickly across to the bedroom and opened the door. The ceiling light was on, which made the scene look even more sordid than it really was, a badly-lit B-picture. The sheets of the king-size bed were twisted, and on the far side lay Jack, facedown, one arm crooked behind him and the other arm dangling. There were bright red smudges on the sheets which Bobby thought were blood; but as he came closer he could see that they were lipstick.

Jack. My brother. Oh, God.

Bobby went around the bed, knelt down, and laid his hand on his brother's tanned, freckled back. He was still warm, but his muscles felt oddly flaccid. "Jack? It's Bobby! Jack, what's wrong?"

Jack's eyelids slowly opened and for a wonderful terrible instant Bobby thought that he was still alive. But Jack wasn't looking at him at all. He was staring at his bedside alarm-clock with an expression of total disinterest, and Bobby didn't need to feel his pulse to know that he was dead. Jesus. He stood up, his knees quaking, and took deep, slow breaths to steady himself. He felt as if his larynx were crammed with broken glass, and his eyes filled up with tears. He had always believed that they would live forever, he and Jack, as gilded and youthful as they always were.

He let out a howl of anguish that sounded barely human, frightening himself; and he had to wedge his hand between his teeth to stop himself from doing it again.

After the first surge of grief, however, came overwhelming panic. What the hell were they going to do now? How were they going to explain what the President was doing in the Madison Hotel? And how long was it going to take before some bellboy leaked the information that he hadn't gone there alone? Even more catastrophic than that, they were supposed to be confronting the Soviet Foreign Minister Andrei Gromyko tomorrow morning, for further talks on Cuba. They were facing the tensest test of their entire administration, and now Jack was lying dead in a lipstick-stained bed.

Harold Easterlake arrived first, quickly followed by Dr. Christophe. "Have you touched anything?" asked Dr. Christophe, trying to be matter-of-fact, although he was clearly very shaken. Harold Easterlake, pale and puffy-eyed, stood in the far corner and smoked furiously and silently cried.

Dr. Christophe gave Jack a quick examination. He was neat-bearded, lean and dark and handsome, in a French-Caribbean way, with liquid black eyes and a long curved nose. Jack had brought him to Washington seven months ago to help to deal with his 25-year-old back pain. "If the regular doctors can't help me, I don't mind trying somebody irregular." And Dr. Christophe *was* highly irregular. He had founded the Saturday Clinic in Sausalito, California, which promoted "spiritual solutions for every ill," including his controversial trance therapy, an out-of-body rest cure, and whole-skeleton manipulation that was supposed to disperse all of the bad spirits that clung to your joints and gradually paralyzed you.

It was the whole-skeleton manipulation that had particularly appealed to Jack; and Dr Christophe had kept him active and free from pain, even when he was highly stressed. He hadn't found it necessary to wear his back brace for almost three months.

"Any idea what he died of?" asked Harold. "I mean, shit, he's only forty-five."

Dr. Christophe picked up a small brown-glass bottle on the nightstand. "Did the President have heart problems?"

"You're his doctor. You should know that."

"Mr. Kennedy, sir, I was the doctor only for his soul, not his body."

"Well, he didn't have any heart problems. None that he told me about. Apart from his back, he was the fittest man I ever knew. The first thing he did when he moved into the White House was tell his staff to lose five pounds apiece."

Dr. Christophe handed him the bottle. "Mr. Kennedy, sir, this is amyl nitrite. It is a vasodilator, usually used in the treatment of angina pectoris."

"But Jack didn't have angina. I'm sure of it. You don't think that—"

"No, Mr. Kennedy, sir. I don't think that his companion had angina either. Apart from the treatment of heart disease, amyl nitrate is commonly used as a sexual stimulant. It dilates the *corpus spongiosum,* the spongy tissues of the penis, so that it can accommodate more blood, and thence become stiffer and larger. Unfortunately, there are associated risks, one of which is heart seizure."

Bobby pressed his hand over his mouth. He simply

couldn't speak. Harold lifted his hand in resignation. "Oh, fuck," he said. "Oh, fuck." He repeated himself over eleven times before Bobby turned and stared at him, and he stopped.

At that moment George Macready arrived, looking as haggard as the rest of them. He was big and paunchy with a shock of white hair and a face that looked like a prizewinning Idaho potato. They didn't need to tell him what had happened. He took one look at Jack's body lying on the bed, and he turned to Bobby with such pain in his eyes that it was hard for Bobby not to start crying again.

"We'll have to get him out of here," said Harold, lighting another Winston. "We'll have to put him in a laundry basket or something and get him back to the White House."

"I guess that Jackie doesn't know about this," said George.

Bobby shook his head. "As far as she's aware, he's working late on the Cuba crisis, and he's sleeping alone so that he doesn't disturb her."

"Maybe we can prop him up between us and make it look like he's walking," Harold suggested. "I saw that in a movie once."

"Are you crazy?" George hissed at him. "This is the President of the United States, and he's dead and naked in a hotel suite where he's not supposed to be, after having sexual congress with somebody he wasn't supposed to be having sexual congress with." He turned to Bobby. "Was it—?"

Bobby said nothing. He didn't really need to. "God almighty," said George. "Look on my works, ye mighty, and despair."

"What the hell are we going to do?" said Harold. "If Jack isn't there tomorrow, Khruschev will wipe the floor with us. This is eyeball-to-eyeball."

"Maybe it'll save the situation," George suggested. "If we announce that Jack's dead, the Russkies can hardly keep up all this aggression, can they? It'll make them look like A-1 shits."

But Bobby shook his head. "If we announce that Jack's dead, then Lyndon will have to be sworn in as President, and he's going to go after Khruschev like a beagle with a firecracker up its ass. Jack was playing this cool and calm. Lyndon could screw it up completely." He looked down at the bottle of amyl nitrite. "Jesus. Talk about a heartbeat away."

"Well, then," said George, "what are the options?"

Bobby had another try at patting down his hair. "Either we try to get his body back to the White House and announce his death in the morning; or else we leave him here and cover up the evidence that anybody else was here—which will still leave us with the awkward question of why he came over to the Madison to sleep, when he has a whole selection of perfectly good beds in the White House."

"We could play for time," said Harold. "We could say that he's gone down with the grippe or something."

"Yes, but then his regular doctors will want to see him."

They all stared at each other. There didn't seem to be any alternative but to bite the bullet and call for the coroner, and announce that the President had died of heart failure. Maybe, with luck, they could keep his companion out of the news.

"There is one more alternative," said Dr. Christophe quietly. "It is a desperate measure, but then perhaps this is what you might call a desperate situation."

"Well, what? Anything."

"Apart from developing my trance therapy and my out-of-body experiences, I worked for many years with the drugs that they use in Haiti for bringing the dead back to life."

George said, "Am I hearing this right? Are you talking about zombies?"

"You can call them what you like," said Dr. Christophe. "But there is nothing supernatural about what they are or how they are resurrected. In many cases, people are deliberately given the drug tetrodotoxin, which comes from the puffer fish.

Tetrodotoxin has an anesthetic effect 160,000 times stronger than cocaine, so somebody who has ingested some may appear to be dead. In Japan they call the puffer fish the *fugu* and eat it as a delicacy, and there have been many reported cases of tetrodotoxin victims being certified as dead, and then reviving after three or four days—in one case in 1880, a gambler came back to life after more than a week in the mortuary."

"But Jack's dead already," said Harold, through a cloud of cigarette smoke.

"That is where my research may be of benefit. Apart from investigating the ways in which people were made into zombies, I researched the ways in which they were revived. The voodoo doctors use a drug derived from the *Bufo marinus,* which is a species of toad. It excites the heart rate, it promotes synaptic activity in the brain. It is the chemical equivalent of electro-convulsive therapy. If it can bring people back from tetrodotoxin poisoning, perhaps it can also bring people back from death."

"You really think you could revive him?" asked Bobby. He tried not to look at Jack's dully-staring eyes.

"I could only try. The *Bufo marinus* drug is capable of investing the human body with enormous strength. That is why you hear stories of zombies having to be restrained by six or seven people."

"Where can we get hold of this drug?" asked George.

"I have some myself. If you send somebody to my house, they can collect it."

Bobby looked at Harold and George, racked with indecision. Dr. Christophe's suggestion seemed like the only chance they had. But what if it didn't work, and a post-mortem showed that the Attorney General of the United States had tried to revive the dead President with a drug made from toads? The most sophisticated nation on Earth, turning to voodoo? The administration would collapse overnight.

But George said, "Why don't you go ahead, Dr.

Christophe? We can't make it any worse than it is already."

"Very well," said Dr. Christophe. "All I ask is that you give me immunity from prosecution, in case this fails to work."

"You got it," Bobby nodded. Harold picked up the phone and said, "I need a dispatch rider, right now. That's right. Put him on the phone. No, this isn't urgent. This is red-hot screaming critical. You got me?"

At 5:03 a.m., Dr. Christophe tipped three spoonfuls of milky liquid between the President's lips—500 mg of the *Bufo marinus* powder in suspension. They had turned him over onto his back and covered him with a bedspread. Harold had already removed the lipstick-stained photo and directed one of the two agents to wheel away the room-service cart and make sure that it was returned to the kitchens and its contents comprehensively disposed of. "I don't want one shred of lobster with the President's teethmarks on it, you got that?"

Bobby kept checking his watch. They were supposed to be having a working breakfast with State Department advisors and the Joint Chiefs of Staff at 6:30 a.m. "How long do you think this will take?" he wanted to know.

Dr. Christophe sat at the President's bedside. "If it happens at all, it will be a miracle."

Harold sat slumped in front of the dressing table, his head in his hands, staring hopelessly at his frowzy face. George stood with his arms folded, tense but unmoving. It wouldn't be long before people would be asking where the President was—if they weren't asking already.

The sky lightened, and Harold opened the dark brown drapes. Outside, it was a gray, overcast October day. Traffic along M Street was beginning to grow busier, and the buildings echoed with the impatient tooting of taxis.

At a quarter of six, George switched on the television

in the sitting room and grimly watched the early-morning news. *"The President has called Soviet Foreign Minister Gromyko back to the White House today to give him a strong warning about the placement of ICBM missile sites on Cuban soil . . .*

At 6:11 a.m., Bobby called Ted Sorensen to say that he and Jack had talked all night and that the breakfast should be put back an hour. When Ted wanted to talk to Jack personally, Bobby told him that he was "in the shower."

He went back into the bedroom, feeling exhausted. Jack was still lying there, and his face was even grayer than it was before. Dr. Christophe was leaning over him as if he were willing him to come alive, but it seemed as if willpower alone wasn't going to be enough. After a while, he turned to Bobby and said, "I'm going to try one last thing. If this doesn't work, I'm afraid it's the finish."

He reached into his leather satchel and took out a long pointed bone and a rattle decorated with hair and chicken feathers.

"Oh, come on," said Harold. "If your drug hasn't worked, you don't think bones are going to do the trick?"

"All medicine is a combination of drugs and ritual," Dr. Christophe replied. "Even in America, you have your 'bedside manner,' yes?"

"Jesus, this is nothing but mumbo-jumbo."

But George said, "Let him try." And Bobby, completely dispirited said, "Sure. Why not?"

Dr. Christophe pointed the bone so that it was touching the President's forehead. He drew a cross with it, and murmured, "Il renonce de nouveau à Dieu, aussi au Chresme . . . il adore le Baron qui apparait ici, tantost en forme d'un grand homme noir, tantost en forme de bouc . . . il rende conte de ses actions à lui . . ." At the same time, he violently shook the rattle, so that they could scarcely hear what he was saying.

After a while he stopped murmuring and began to make an extraordinary whining sound, interspersed with hollow clicks of his tongue against his palate. He shook the rattle in a slow, steady, rhythm, knocking it against the bone. Sweat broke out on his forehead, and he clenched his teeth. Gradually his lips drew back, and his eyes rolled up, and his face turned into a grotesque, beastlike mask.

Bobby glanced at George in horror, but George reached out and held his arm. "I've seen this before. It's the way they conjure up spirits."

Dr. Christophe's voice grew higher and higher, until he sounded almost like a woman crying out in pain. He lifted his rattle and his bone over his head and beat them faster and faster. The back of his shirt was soaked with perspiration, and his whole body was clenched with muscular tension. "Je vous prie!" he cried out. "Je vous prie!" Then he fell back as abruptly as if somebody had punched him, and lay shivering and twitching on the floor.

"This is it," said Harold. "I've had enough."

But at that moment, Jack opened his eyes.

Bobby felt a thrill of excitement and fright. Jack hadn't just opened his eyes, he was looking at him, and his eyes were focused, and moving. Then his mouth opened, and he tried to say something.

"He's done it," said George, in awe. "Son of a bitch, he's actually done it."

"Harold—help the doctor up, will you?" said Bobby. He went around the bed and sat next to Jack and took hold of his hand. Jack stared at him without saying anything, and then tried to raise his head from the pillow.

"Take it easy," Bobby told him. "You're fine. Everything's going to be fine."

Jack spoke in a slow, slurry voice, his chest rising and falling with effort. "What's happened? What are you doing here? Where's Renata?"

"You had a heart attack. We thought we'd lost you."

"George," said Jack, trying to smile. "And Harold, how are you? And you, Dr. Christophe."

"It was Dr. Christophe who saved you."

"Well done, Dr. Christophe. You'll have to increase your fees."

Dr. Christophe was patting the sweat from his face with a bath towel. "You take it really easy, Mr. President. You've just made medical history."

Jack tried to sit up, but Bobby gently pushed him back down again. "It's okay . . . the best thing you can do is rest."

He went through to the sitting room, where Dr. Christophe was packing his bag and putting on his coat. "It's a miracle," he said. "I don't know what to say."

"You don't have to say anything, Mr. Kennedy. I didn't think it was going to work either. That's why I tried the invocation." He paused, and then he added, "I never tried the invocation before. I never dared. I don't know what the consequences are going to be."

"He's alive. He's talking. You'd hardly think that he ever had a heart attack."

"Yes, but I called on Baron Samedi; and I'm not at all sure that was wise. The President doesn't just owe his life to a drug, Mr. Kennedy. He owes his life to the king of death."

Bobby laid a hand on his shoulder, and grinned widely. "He faced up to Nikita Khruschev. I'm sure he can face up to Baron Samedi."

"Well, we'll see," said Dr. Christophe. "In the meantime, keep a very close eye on him. Make sure that he keeps on exercising . . . the worst thing for heart recovery is too much sitting around. No more amyl nitrite, ever. And watch for any sign of depression, or moodiness, or violent temper. Also . . . watch out for any behavior that you can't understand."

"You got it," said Bobby. "And, Doctor . . . thanks for everything."

Bobby was astonished by the speed of Jack's recovery. He was able to dress and return to the White House by mid-morning; and that afternoon he confronted Andrei Gromyko and gave him one of the sternest dressings-down that Bobby had ever heard. He appeared confident, energetic, quick-witted. In fact he seemed to have more energy than ever. He almost *shone*.

"You should call it a day," he said, after Gromyko had left.

"What the hell for?" Jack asked him. "I never felt better."

"Jack, you had a heart attack."

"A minor seizure, that was all. Things got out of hand. Lobster, champagne . . . too much excitement. That Renata reminds me so much of Marilyn."

"It wasn't a minor seizure, Jack. You were technically dead for more than three hours. I'm amazed you don't have brain damage."

"Listen," said Jack, jabbing his finger at him. "I'm fine."

The Russians shipped their missiles back to the Soviet Union. Afterward, Moscow agreed to the President's scheme to connect the Kremlin and the White House with "hot line" teletypewriters, so that he and Khruschev could communicate instantly in times of danger. Jack was ebullient, full of new ideas. He broke a Cold War precedent and allowed the Russians to buy American wheat.

In mid-July, Bobby came up to Hyannisport to spend a few days sailing and relaxing. Ethel and the kids were there already, and although Ethel was distracted and fraught and kept complaining about Rose, the kids were tanned and happy and having a good time. The first day, Bobby and Jack went for a walk on the beach. There was a strong southwest wind blowing, and the grass whistled in the dunes.

Jack said, "I've been having these strange dreams."

"Oh, yeah? What about? The Civil Rights movement?"

"No, nothing like that. Not political dreams. I've been having these dreams about blood, about killing things."

The sand was very deep and soft here, and Bobby's bare feet plunged into it with every step, right up the ankles. "I guess it's the responsibility, you know. The whole responsibility for life and death, having your finger on the button."

Jack shook his head. "It's more personal than that. It's like I want to kill something, and kill it for a reason. An animal, a child. I can almost feel myself doing it. I can feel the knife in my hand. I can smell the blood."

"You're tired, that's all."

"Tired? I never felt better. I hardly need any sleep; my appetite's terrific. I feel like sex about every five minutes of the day."

"So what do you think these dreams are all about? Why do you want to kill things?"

Jack stopped, and looked around. The wind was fresh and salty, and the sea sparkled like hammered glass. He was tanned and fit. His eyes were clear, and he had never looked so strong and charismatic.

"I don't know," he said. "I just feel the need to make a sacrifice. You remember that time at the Madison Hotel, when I had that heart attack? I feel like somebody gave me my life; and I owe him a life in return."

"Listen, I shouldn't worry about it. What do you say we take the dinghy out?"

"No," said Jack. "I've got too much to think about. Too much to do."

Bobby was about to say something, but couldn't. They started to stroll back to the compound together, their bare feet kicking the sand, their hands in their pockets. An amateur photographer took a picture of them which later appeared on the cover of *Life,* and they couldn't have looked more carefree, two brothers with their hair blowing in the wind.

"Do you still see Dr. Christophe?" asked Bobby, as they reached the house. John-John was sitting on the porch swing wearing a white sun hat and determinedly stroking a white kitten that didn't want to be stroked.

The swing went *sqqueeaakkk-squikkk, sqqauccakk-squikk,* over and over.

"Christophe? That quack?"

"He saved your life."

"I recovered, that's all. I was naturally fit. There wasn't any mystery about it."

"But you want to make a sacrifice to somebody that saved you, even if it wasn't him?"

Jack hooked his arm around Bobby's neck, almost throttling him. "Hey . . . these are dreams, that's all. Don't get upset."

But later that night, unable to sleep, Bobby put on a toweling robe, left the house, and walked down to the beach. The moon had concealed itself behind a cloud, but the night was still bright, and the sky was the color of laundry-ink. The sea glittered and sparkled, but its waves wearily washed against the shore, as if they were tired of washing, as if they had really had enough washing for one millennium.

He walked westward for a while, but then he began to grow chilly and he decided to turn back. Suddenly the idea of a hot, restless night next to Ethel seemed much more attractive, stringy sheets and all. As he started to trudge back, however, he saw an orange flame flickering not far away, among the dunes. It was almost like a flag waving. He hesitated, and then he started to walk toward it. Some students, most likely, camping on the beach.

He climbed the long, soft side of the dune, and then he reached the top. At first he couldn't understand what he was looking at: his brain couldn't work it out. But then he gradually made sense of it; and it was the worst carnage that he had ever seen in his life.

On the far side of the hollow, a driftwood fire was crackling and spitting. In the middle of the hollow, there were three bodies, all cut wide open, their entrails and their stomachs dragged out of them, and all piled together.

Standing over this grisly array was Jack, his white

short-sleeved shirt spattered with blood. He was sifting ashes onto the bodies, and chanting, in the same distinctive voice with which he had said, *"Ask not what your country can do for you, but what you can do for your country."* But the words he was saying tonight were not the words of a political speechwriter. They were the words of a religious supplicant. "I offer you these bodies, Baron. I offer you their lives and their agony. You gave me life. You gave me strength. Take these lives in return, as my homage."

Bobby stood staring for almost half a minute, numb with shock and terrible fascination. He watched Jack chanting and sifting ash, prowling around the bodies like a satisfied predator. His sacrificial victims were three sheep, but it was no less horrifying because of that. The shadows from the fire danced across the hollow, and made the scene look even more lurid.

He retreated down the sand dune before Jack could see him. He walked stiffly to the ocean's edge, his stomach churning. He stood in the surf and vomited, and the warm thick vomit was washed around his ankles.

He called Dr. Christophe in Washington; and discovered that he had left his house in Georgetown more than three months ago and returned to Sausalito. It took two and a half hours before he found him at a supper party in Mill Valley. The line was crackly, and there was a hubbub of guests in the background.

"It's Jack. He killed three sheep today, cut them right open."

"They were a sacrifice, Mr. Kennedy. Nobody gets anything for nothing. The President has to repay his debt to Baron Samedi—not just once, or twice, but a thousand times over. Baron Samedi is a very demanding creditor, particularly when it comes to human life."

"Why the hell didn't you warn me?"

"I beg your pardon, Mr. Kennedy. I did warn you. But you wanted the President back to life at any cost."

"Shit," said Bobby. "If anybody finds out about this—"

"That is the least of your worries," said Dr. Christophe. "Now you must watch for even greater sacrifices. Not just sheep, but children, and women . . . Baron Samedi always wants more and more, and it is very hard to say no. If you don't make the sacrifice, you lose whatever he gave you. In your brother's case, his very life."

"But most of the time he seems so normal. In fact, he's very much *better* than normal."

"That was Baron Samedi's gift, Mr. Kennedy. But one never gets anything for nothing; and a gift can always be taken away."

"So what do I do?"

"You have to make a decision, Mr. Kennedy. That is what you have to do. I thought that was what politicians were especially good at."

"What decision? What in God's name are you talking about?"

"You have to decide whether to continue to protect your brother, or whether you might have to take steps to protect those who might innocently cross your brother's path."

Bobby said nothing for a long time. Then he hung up.

During the fall, Jack made a number of trips around the country. Next year was election year and he wanted to rouse up as much support as he could. He visited Pennsylvania, Minnesota, and Nevada; then Wisconsin, North Dakota, Montana, California, Oregon, and Washington.

He seemed to have endless reserves of energy, and his back trouble had left him completely. He was always smiling and handshaking and he was full of optimism for 1964—even in Washington, which hadn't supported him in 1960.

Bobby flew out to Seattle to join him. It was late October, and it was raining hard when he stepped off the plane. He had brought Harold with him and a new junior assistant, a pretty young Harvard law graduate, Janie Schweizer. Jack and his entourage were staying with a wealthy Seattle Democrat, Willard Bryce, at his huge Gothic–style townhouse overlooking Washington Park.

Willard appeared in the porch as Bobby's limousine came curving up the driveway. He was portly and affable, like W.C. Fields without the vitriol. "Welcome to the Emerald City. Or should I say the Soaking City. Don't worry. The forecast says it should clear by May."

They went inside, and found Jack in the drawing room, holding an informal conference with twenty or thirty local Democrats. He was leaning back in a rocking chair, dressed in his shirtsleeves, and he looked unexpectedly tired and strained. All the same, he made the introductions and cracked a joke about Seattle voters. "They never get it right. I came here asking for a landslide and they gave me a downpour."

When he saw Janie Schweizer, however, his smile completely changed, and he lifted his head back in that way that Bobby had so often seen before. Janie was a tall girl, with blonde hair bobbed in the style that Jackie had made almost obligatory, and a strong, Nordic–looking face. She was wearing a dark, discreet business suit, with a knee-length skirt, but it didn't conceal the fact that she had a very well-proportioned figure.

"This is Janie," said Bobby. "Just joined us from law school. I thought the experience would do her good."

Janie flushed. This was the first time that she had met the President. "Honored to meet you, Mr. President."

"How come you get all the lookers, Bobby? Most of my staff look like the Wicked Witch of the West."

And all through the morning's discussions, in the gloom of Willard's drawing room, with the rain trickling down the windows and the cigarette smoke fiddling to the ceiling, Jack hardly ever took his eyes away from Janie Schweizer, like a man caught in a daydream.

* * *

That night, Willard held a formal fund-raising dinner for one hundred supporters. It was a glittering white-tie affair with a string quintet, and the cutlery glittered like shoals of fish. Jack gave a speech about the future of world democracy, and his hopes for an end to the arms race. They didn't manage to get to bed until three a.m., and there was still laughter and talking in the house until well past four.

Bobby found that he couldn't sleep. He lay on his bed staring at the elaborately-plastered ceiling, listening to the rain as it trickled along the gutters. He hadn't liked the way that Jack had been looking at Janie today; although he guessed that he couldn't blame him. She was young and pretty, and she had a law degree. He would have been interested in her himself if the timing had been different.

An hour passed and still he couldn't sleep. He switched on the bedside lamp and tried to read another chapter of *Specimen Days in America,* by Walt Whitman. "I had a sort of dream-trance the other day, in which I saw my favorite trees step out and promenade up, down and around, very curiously, with a whisper from one, *We do all this on the present occasion, exceptionally, just for you.*"

Eventually, he climbed out of bed, put on his warm maroon bathrobe, and went outside into the corridor. Jack had the largest bedroom, on the other side of the galleried landing. A Secret Service agent sat outside, reading a magazine. Bobby went round to Jack's door and pointed at it. "Is the President asleep yet?"

"I shouldn't think so, Mr. Kennedy, sir."

Bobby paused. There was something in the agent's tone of voice that aroused his suspicion. "Are you trying to tell me that the President isn't alone?"

"Well, sir, it isn't for me to—"

"Who's he got in there?"

"Sir, I couldn't—"

Bobby came right up to him and seized hold of his necktie. *"Who—has—he—got—in—there?"*

He burst open the double doors and stepped into the bedroom. Behind him, the agent said, "Jesus Christ."

The far side of the room was dominated by a huge, four-poster bed, more like a ceremonial barge than a place to sleep. All its blankets had been stripped off and heaped onto the floor. On the bed itself, naked, hunched up like a wolf, Jack was kneeling next to the sliced-open body of Janie Schweizer. He had cut her apart from the breastbone downward.

Quivering, he slowly turned around and stared at Bobby with suspicious, animal eyes.

Bobby didn't say anything. He was too shocked to think of anything to say. He backed away, one step at a time, and then he closed the doors behind him.

"He's killed her, for Christ's sake," gasped the Secret Service agent. His face was the color of wet newspaper. "He's cut her to pieces."

"Don't do anything," said Bobby. "Just stay by the door and make sure that nobody else goes in there."

"What if he comes out? What if he tries to do the same to me?"

"What do you think? Run like hell."

"I don't see any other way," said George, tiredly. "We've been over it time and time again, and it's the only way out."

"What if he misses?" asked Harold.

"He won't miss, not at that range."

"What if he gets caught?"

"He won't be. We'll have three other guys there to help him get clear."

"How about this Oswald character?" Bobby wanted to know.

"*He'll* get caught, don't you worry about that."

"And there is absolutely no way that Oswald can be connected with us?"

"Absolutely none. He thinks he's being paid by something called the Communist Freedom League, and that they're going to give him political asylum in Russia."

"Supposing *he* manages to hit the target, too?"

"Pretty unlikely. But if he does—well, the more the merrier, if you know what I mean." After Bobby had left, George said, "When it's all over, there'll be one or two loose ends that need to be tied up. You know, such as that Secret Service agent, and Dr. Christophe. Especially Dr. Christophe. We don't want him bringing the President back to life a second time, do we?"

Harold lit a Winston, and nodded wryly through the smoke.

On November 22, 1963, the Kennedy motorcade approached the triple underpass leading to Stemmons Freeway in Dallas, Texas. The sun was shining, and crowds were cheering on both sides of the street.

Under the shade of a tree, shielded by three other men, ex-Marine sharpshooter Martin D. Bowman took a high-powered rifle out of a camouflaged fabric case, lifted it, and aimed it. As the Presidential limousine passed the grassy knoll on which he was standing, he fired three shots in quick succession.

It appeared to five or six of the eyewitnesses that "the President's head seemed to explode." But there was more than a spray of blood and brains in the air. For a fleeting second, a dark shadow flickered over the limousine—a shadow which one eyewitness described as "nothing but a cloud of smoke," but which another said was "more like a cloak, blowing in the wind, or maybe some dark kind of creature."

A third witness was even more graphic. "It came twisting up out of the car dark as a torn-off sheet of tarpaper blowing in the wind except that I could swear it had a face like a face all stretched out in agony with hollow eyes. I thought to myself, I'm seeing a man's soul leaving his body. But if it was his soul, it was a black, black soul, and more frightening than anything I ever saw."

The shadow appears on two frames of amateur movie stock that was shot at the time, but it was dismissed by photographic experts as a fault caused by hurried development. But 2,000 miles away, in Sausalito, California, a feathered rattle that was hanging on a study wall began to shake, all on its own. Dr. Christophe raised his eyes from the book he was reading, and took off his spectacles.

"You're back then, master?" he said. "They took away your host?"

He stood up. He knew, with regret, that it was time for him to pack up and leave. They would be coming for him soon. "They want everything, don't they, Baron, even life itself; but they're never prepared to pay the price."

He went to the window and looked out over the garden. He wondered what Brazil would be like, this time of year.

Science Fiction Anthologies

☐ **FUTURE NET**   UE2723—$5.99
  Martin H. Greenberg & Larry Segriff, editors

From a chat room romance gone awry . . . to an alien monitoring the Net as an
advance scout for interstellar invasion . . . to a grief-stricken man given the
chance to access life after death . . . here are sixteen original tales that you
must read before you venture online again, stories from such top visionaries as
Gregory Benford, Josepha Sherman, Mickey Zucker Reichert, Daniel Ransom,
Jody Lynn Nye, and Jane Lindskold.

☐ **FUTURE EARTHS: UNDER SOUTH AMERICAN SKIES**
  Mike Resnick & Gardner Dozois, editors   UE2581—$4.99

From a plane crash that lands its passengers in a survival situation completely
alien to anything they've ever experienced, to a close encounter of the insect
kind, to a woman who has journeyed unimaginably far from home—here are
stories from the rich culture of South America, with its mysteriously vanished
ancient civilizations and magnificent artifacts, its modern-day contrasts between
sophisticated city dwellers and impoverished villagers.

☐ **MICROCOSMIC TALES**   UE2532—$4.99
  Isaac Asimov, Martin H. Greenberg, & Joseph D. Olander, eds.

Here are 100 wondrous science fiction short-short stories, including contributions
by such acclaimed writers as Arthur C. Clarke, Robert Silverberg, Isaac Asimov,
and Larry Niven. Discover a superman who lives in a *real* world of nuclear threat
. . . an android who dreams of electric love . . . and a host of other tales that
will take you instantly out of this world.

☐ **SHERLOCK HOLMES IN ORBIT**   UE2636—$5.50
  Mike Resnick & Martin H. Greenberg, editors
  Authorized by Dame Jean Conan Doyle

Not even time can defeat the master sleuth in this intriguing anthology about
the most famous detective in the annals of literature. From confrontations with
Fu Manchu and Moriarty, to a commission Holmes undertakes for a vampire,
here are 26 new stories all of which remain true to the spirit and personality of
Sir Arthur Conan Doyle's most enduring creation.

Buy them at your local bookstore or use this convenient coupon for ordering.

PENGUIN USA   P.O. Box 999—Dep. #17109, Bergenfield, New Jersey 07621

Please send me the DAW BOOKS I have checked above, for which I am enclosing
$_____ (please add $2.00 to cover postage and handling). Send check or money
order (no cash or C.O.D.'s) or charge by Mastercard or VISA (with a $15.00 minimum). Prices and
numbers are subject to change without notice.

Card #_____ Exp. Date _____
Signature_____
Name_____
Address_____
City _____ State _____ Zip Code _____

For faster service when ordering by credit card call **1-800-253-6476**

Allow a minimum of 4-6 weeks for delivery. This offer is subject to change without notice.

Elizabeth Forrest

☐ **PHOENIX FIRE** UE2515—$4.99
As the legendary Phoenix awoke, so too did an ancient Chinese demon—and Los Angeles was destined to become the final battleground in their millenia-old war.

☐ **DARK TIDE** UE2560—$4.99
The survivor of an accident at an amusement pier is forced to return to the town where it happened. And slowly, long buried memories start to resurface, and all his nightmares begin to come true . . .

☐ **DEATH WATCH** UE2648—$5.99
McKenzie Smith has been targeted by a mastermind of evil who can make virtual reality into the ultimate tool of destructive power. Stalked in both the real and virtual worlds, can McKenzie defeat an assassin who can strike out anywhere, at any time?

☐ **KILLJOY** UE2695—$5.99
Given experimental VR treatments, Brand must fight a constant battle against the persona of a serial killer now implanted in his brain. But Brand would soon learn that there were even worse things in the world—like the unstoppable force of evil and destruction called KillJoy.